Robert is un

Following a mself distraught, desperate, ar

When his literary hero, Mark Twain begins to communicate with him, Robert initially takes solace in Twain's innate wisdom. Quite quickly though warning bells start to sound, and it becomes clear that Mark's whispered, often cryptic advice, could prove dangerous.

As Robert's mental health continues to deteriorate, he embarks on a quest around London using Twain's words as his guide and inspiration.

Will listening to his hero lead to solace and recovery, or is it an undertaking that can only end in tragedy?

H.B. O'Neill

First published 2024 by Fahrenheit Press

ISBN: 978-1-914475-63-4

10 9 8 7 6 5 4 3 2 1

www.Fahrenheit–Press.com

F 4 E

Cover Design & Manuscript Typesetting by www.SkullStarStudio.com

According To Mark

By

H.B. O'Neill

Fahrenheit Press

For Carmel

(Who never doubted)

"I am the King of the Buffoons.
I am a dangerous person."

\- Mark Twain

Prologue – December 2012

I'm closing my eyes now.

And I'm standing on a blue painted number 3 on platform 3 at Chadwell Heath Station. The blue painted 3 is one of two painted 3s that signal where the two doors of carriage 3 will open. When the train arrives, I enter carriage 3 and find a seat. It's at the far end. In the corner. Ideal.

There's a discarded copy of the *Daily Mail* at my feet. Its front page has a picture of Kate Middleton attending a royal engagement. The caption mentions her 'daring hemline' and a previous passenger has taken the trouble to biro an arrow toward her head and scribe the word *Golddigger*. *Ha!* Thinks I. *I know you!* An angry, jealous and bitter person. Someone sad and despairing.

Someone lost.

I allow myself a sigh as the train gathers pace and another journey begins. One which Mark Twain and I have determined will be my last.

Chapter 1

I'm closing my eyes now.

And immediately I'm back there. And I'm not joking (I don't joke much anymore) this is exactly how it happened. I was wearing a yellow security jacket but for the next 60 minutes was officially off–duty as I was spending my lunch break sat on a bench upon Hampstead Heath.

And I recall I was only halfway through sandwich two and most probably musing along typically trivial cheese and tomato lines when I heard the commotion. Splash! A big one. A right royal reverie breaker. A sharp yelp had accompanied the splash and the two had precipitated an immediate intense hissing. I looked around. Nothing and no one to be seen. But the commotion continued. The drama was obviously unfolding out of sight.

Like so much drama does.

I re–Tupperware'd the remnants of my sandwich, placed it on the seat and stood up. I stepped forward – cautiously moving toward the steep grassed slope – whereupon I precariously peered above the reeds and down to the water's edge and all was instantly revealed.

He was engaged in a desperate battle with a swarm of swans – two angered whites and a plethora of feisty browns – big cygnets coming of age by way of stretching their necks and asserting their beaks. The dog was in trouble and splashing up a storm. He'd get one paw up on land, then two paws up on land, then with a surge of effort half his torso would emerge up out of the murky water onto land, but then gravity would strike and the whole of his belly wouldn't quite make it and with a pitiful yelp he'd slip back. Splash! Back in. Back amongst it. Back amongst them. Hiss hiss. Flap flap. Peck peck. Nip nip. Then he'd try again. One paw. Two paws, Bit of belly. Desperate stretch. Urgent kicking of the back legs. Little splash – little splash... almost there... hope building... salvation in sight... then no – BIG SPLASH! Defeat. Panic. Try again immediately. This time a little weaker. A little wider–eyed. A little more anxious.

I moved along the bank toward the chaos. Stepping up my pace as I saw his tortured face. All the while scanning left to right and back again in search of the stricken canine's owner. There was still no one to be seen. It would be up to me. It was my moment. I broke into a jog. Then a sprint.

Now, looking back with an honest if heavy heart, I'm not sure if you could truly describe it as a "plaintive welcoming wail" (other than to embellish the tale). In truth it was more of a sheepish whimper when he saw me. A kind of *Whoopsy me* type plea. A desperate, exhausted and yet still politely humble appeal. At least that's how I interpreted it. And that's what made it irresistible – I could fully empathise with an embarrassing self–propelled predicament – I often did stupid things too. And so now I simply had to intervene. Even though I wasn't overly confident that I could help. I've been called many things in my life but "sure–footed mountain goat" was never an accusation prominent on the list. I knew I would be risking my own dignity by attempting to re–establish his.

But I still did it. And it turned out it was the very best thing I ever did do.

I stumbled down the slope to the river–bank shouting "Shoo" to the swans even though I was vaguely concerned that wasn't the correct colloquial. Surely "Shoo" was something you said to geese? Or was it to the stray cat about to squat near your hollyhocks? No, it wasn't shoo to a goose it was boo to a goose. Or not. We wouldn't or couldn't or shouldn't or something like that. No matter. I could have probably shouted anything as it would have made no difference – they ignored me and continued to hiss horrendously and flap ferociously whilst joyously jabbing their serrated beaks in the direction of the flailing flanks of the floundering dog.

I'll spare you the details of the next few minutes. They weren't my finest. They were fraught and a little frightening. I'll fast forward to the moment when I finally emerged from the depths with a soaked and bedraggled dog under one arm, a painfully throbbing peck–marked other arm, a large wet patch on my backside and ankle to knee pond–weed staining on both legs of my uniform trousers.

"Thank you so much, are you okay?" The dog's owner, who had finally appeared, asked as she held out a hand (which I very gratefully grasped) and with a firm tug helped me clamber ashore.

"I'm fine thanks." I breathlessly answered. And it was true, I was. Relatively speaking. And already beginning to feel suitably self–proud.

"Gosh! I was so frightened. Thank you. Thank you so much. Oh, you silly silly thing!" That last sentence was directed at her pet and the dog did a remarkable thing then – it apologised to her. It genuinely did. It noticeably squirmed under my armpit and then produced a low, softly–barked, unmistakably remorseful cough. I was impressed.

"Oh. Are you Security?" The owner now added. That question directed at me as I passed the shivering dog into her outstretched arms. I made sure I was firmly stood with both feet on solid ground before I looked up to answer. And then I did. And I saw her properly for the very first time – a no longer in distress damsel nuzzling a very relieved dog – a radiant vision hugging a much–loved friend – a luminescent lady with a bulging black plastic bag dangling prominently from her wrist. And for a moment I was speechless. I honestly was. But then I recovered. And I responded in a manner of which I am still quite proud.

"Yes, I am Security. Can I see what's in your bag please?"

She seemed a tad confused. She frowned at first but then eventually looked down at her wrist's unsavoury accessory.

"Pardon? That? Oh, it's nothing, it's just...that's what I was doing...that's where I was... I was cleaning up after...you know..."

"I need to take a look Madam."

"Sorry?"

"Immediately. I need to ask you to open your bag."

"What? This bag?"

"Yes. That bag."

"Oh..."

She placed the dog back in my arms and seemed about to acquiesce. I leaned in (not too close) and pretended to prepare to peer. There was a pause for a moment. Both of us staring intently at the suspicious item. And then we moved our eyes away from the bag and looked directly at each other. And smiled. At the exact same next moment. And then, perhaps sensing a moment, the dog barked and stretched to try and lick its owner's face. And then he twisted his head and tried to lick mine. And now we were both laughing.

"There's a scooped poop repository over by the gate."

"Right. Good. Thank you. Oh gosh! You're bleeding!"

"Eh?"

And then I looked and I was too. The pecks had obviously hit home. And almost bone.

"Oh..."

"Your arm! I'm so sorry."

I laughed again then. She was apologizing on behalf of the swans. It was nice. In a generous, kind and extremely polite kind of way. And then she produced a tissue and told me we could get some more napkins at the café near the bandstand.

Rebecca

Robert and I didn't meet in a conventional way and looking back now that feels appropriate. If he hadn't had been around on that day on the Heath and if Monty hadn't been silly enough to wander off and upset the swans then I'm sure we would never have met – it wasn't as if we mixed in the same circles. Robert was completely unlike anyone I'd ever met before – I could tell that almost immediately. But he'd just saved my dog and somehow, I just sensed that he could be trusted. I wouldn't usually chat to strangers and yet I felt at ease in his company straight away. I still view that day as one of the best in my life. Even now. Even after everything.

Chapter 2

I'm closing my eyes now…

…and I'm instantly back to that day on the Heath. And now the dog is leashed and walking alongside us. And I note that in truth it's more of a waddle than a walk. Encompassing an occasional stagger. But it's a noble gait nonetheless. A positive one. Proud. I realise I genuinely like this dog. And when we arrive at the scooped poop repository (it's enroute to the café), its owner ceremoniously deposits. Whilst I watch intently.

"Quite an offering."

"Yes."

"He must eat a lot."

"She does."

And now we both smile down at the rescued adventurer and her grateful owner begins to explain. The dog was a neither nor – neither a miniature nor a giant. It was a midi. An aged midi black poodle with a touch of arthritis and a hint of halitosis. And he was a she not a he as I'd assumed. I was surprised at first but then guessed females could do ridiculous and reckless things too. She was called Monty and was very friendly. An incessant licker which was fortunate as it meant I could now impress in the role of licker–allower. We were allies from the start.

And now Monty looks up at us looking down at her and she wags her tail and then vigorously shakes herself dry. Mostly on me. It's disrespectful in a way or perhaps just mischievous. It hardly seems a thank you but you never know. And it's not as if I'm not already wet. I don't take offence. I laugh. I like her style. I truly do.

I listen intently then, nodding sagely, as her owner crouches down to stroke and explain to Monty that she isn't as young as she used to be. And that she shouldn't wander off and then slip and get into swan–annoying dramas when her guardian is busily engaged cleaning up after her. And that she most certainly shouldn't then shake herself off on the hero who'd just saved her. Monty wags her tail in a way that suggests she knows the scolding is coming from the good part of heart and that she is already fully forgiven. I sense that too and offer a discreet thumbs up to the misfortunate dog.

Her owner then stands again, smiles again and asks again about my security jacket. She says I "Don't seem typical". I earnestly explain how I've been diligently officiating at the annual Octogenarian Arm Wrestling Championship in Belsize Park. We then discuss the dangers of brittle bones, osteoporosis and splintering. How sport can have negative as well as positive outcomes. We're smiling a lot now but all is not quite perfect.

"You're still bleeding. Let's get those napkins."

I'd completely forgotten but she's right, I am. And that's okay, inspirational even. For then, on a wondrously inexplicable impulse, I take a risk. It feels daring but imperative and is completely out of character. I've never acted like this before but today I do. I do a chivalrous. And I can see that it's ridiculous – I'm an early 21st century bedraggled pond-bloke about to offer my arm to a lady.

Offering my arm to a lady. Like a young knight of medieval old. Showing respect and honour toward someone of grand importance. I'm suddenly one of King Arthur's finest, ready to protect, defend and if necessary give of my life in her service. And I'll admit I've always been a bit prone to impulse and have sometimes edged toward whimsy but I'd never previously acted in such a recklessly romantic manner. And yet remarkably, I don't feel foolish. Just suddenly extremely nervous. Like something very precious might be at stake.

I theatrically offer my non–swollen un–pecked and non–bloodied arm. And then, after only a fully–understandable moment of hesitation, she accepts my offer and offers her trust. She links my arm. She honestly does. And we head toward the café near the bandstand. United.

And of course, there isn't really an Octogenarian Arm–Wrestling Championship held annually in Belsize Park, at least not one that I'm aware of. In truth I'd been moonlighting at Budgens, a few hours extra weekend work to supplement my measly monthly office–monkey remuneration. But that's not relevant; not all details have significance. It's more about life's unique collisions.

And their aftermath.

I was wearing a yellow security jacket but I was off–duty and I had been taking lunch upon Hampstead Heath and I had never for one moment expected. And now I would be late returning back from my break but the supermarket would survive without my protection; Belsize Park is not a crime hot spot.

After a cappuccino, more chat and a shared KitKat we headed back to the gate where we shook hands rather formally and I suddenly realised.

"I don't know your name."

"It's Rebecca."

"Well Rebecca, it was a pleasure to meet you, my name i…"

"No wait! Let me guess… is it Vidal? It must be – Vidal Sassoon."

"No, it's Robert…"

She smiled then, handed me a business card, turned her back and walked away.

And I probably frowned a bit but then it clicked. Yes, very clever, *très drôle* in fact. It was a windy day and I was obviously suffering a bit of a blusterfringe. "*Vidal…*" I grinned and carefully deposited the card in my wallet. I maintained that smile as I squelched all the way back to Budgens. I like to imagine Rebecca was smiling too.

And that's honestly how it happened. That's exactly how it occurred. That was our beginning. That was Robert and Rebecca. That was fate. That was kismet. That was destiny. That was it. That was us.

That was then.

Rebecca

Amantes sunt amentes is Latin for 'Lovers are Lunatics.' Robert wrote that in a card he sent me for my 29th birthday. We'd been dating for about 6 months and I'd been expressing concerns about his eccentricity (I wasn't really concerned – I loved it. He was the fabled 'breath of fresh air'). It's a phrase that comes to mind now though as I've been tasked with something that feels appropriate to such sentiment. I don't honestly believe any life is reducible to the dry pronouncements of psychology and equally, perhaps, art merely provides question and not answer. Maybe the 'essence' lies somewhere in between? Or perhaps the elusive 'truth' is always ephemeral? I've no idea. I'm not sure of anything anymore and I doubt that this will help, but I've promised to try, so here goes.

24th January 2013

Dear…

Dear who? Dear Me? This feels ridiculous.

Dear Rebecca,

I am writing to you even though you are actually me. This is ridiculous. This is the kind of thing Robert would have loved to have teased me about. Or have enjoyed doing himself. I don't think it worked out with him and the Life Coach. That wasn't one of my best ideas maybe but I thought it would help him realise things. I thought it would help him organise himself, take control of his life, change, I guess. I remember the way he looked at me when I told him I was treating him to a session with Sebastian. "A Life Coach." he said. "You mean like a lifeguard?" He went off on a tangent then, talked about how ridiculous words were. How they intermingled to produce gibberish and jargon – nonsense that we happily accepted. Could you really coach a life? I didn't know but I more or less begged him to try. He was getting weirder by the week. Or not weirder, sadder perhaps, and as this is 'A Truth Letter', I should probably admit that his sadness was partly my fault.

I'd given him an ultimatum.

Chapter 3

That was then.
And now is not.
Now is not then.
So much has happened.

Monty is no longer at my side.

Rebecca is not linking my arm.

And now Mark Twain is whispering in my ear.

And he's reminding me of what he's told me numerous times before, what he's been telling me almost every day since the day that Rebecca told me that she… with him…

And Mark Twain's argument is powerful, convincing and insistent tonight.

> "Suicide is the only sane thing the young or old ever do in this life."

Rebecca

I honestly didn't mind, that's what I told him, in the early days, and it was true; we used to stand by his kitchen sink and watch the sunset over the derelict car park and graffiti'd warehouse that once housed Dagenham's B&Q. I didn't mind. I told him it was fine, nice even. But it wasn't Muswell Hill and it certainly wasn't Hampstead.

Christ. It sounds so crass reading that back – shallow and inconsequential. Well, anyway, there I've admitted it. Mary would be proud. Mary is the one who suggested I do this. She's my psychotherapist. "Why don't you try writing yourself a letter?" (That's the advice £80 an hour gets you these days.) Robert would laugh at that too no doubt, if he knew. If he were still sitting next to me grinning and bursting to comment. Apparently "Writing about experiences can help us to come to terms with them." I guess we'll see. At the moment it's just making me remember lots of the little details – the threads in our tapestry perhaps? Gosh, that sounds rather florid – maybe this exercise will turn me toward poetry too.

I'm finding it's hard to remember and write at the same time. Or maybe it's just hard to remember. I'm struggling with the chronology but the little moments pop back into my head without much beckoning. Maybe I should just write them as they come. Robert was a headcase. (The memories are often preceded with that thought.) He once made me a lingerie set out of empty hula hoop packets; they were all salt and vinegar flavour (my favourite) and he'd trimmed then sellotaped them to make a matching bra and knicker set. He wrapped them up in pink tissue paper and awarded them to me on Valentines Day.

No boyfriend had ever done that for me before.

Chapter 4

When I closed my eyes last night Mark Twain was clear in my ear. And he was insisting that it was now time for me to revisit the British Museum. To do as we'd discussed. And of course, that made perfect sense. And so I promised him I would.

And so today I am.

And it's been a surprisingly uneventful journey. Inconspicuous. No fanfare. No horde of black–shrouded mourners. Chadwell Heath station to Stratford International. Change there for the Central Line to Tottenham Court Road. Take Exit 2 and turn right on Great Russell Street. Then the British Museum is approximately a 5–minute walk.

Quicker if you quick–step. Faster if you joy–jog. Under 4 if you scamper not meander.

A surprise upon arrival. Surprise then no surprise really. We used to walk freely in and out of the museum but can do so no longer. Today there's no carefree jaunt up the imposing stairs. No sauntering hop, skip and slip between the Parthenon styled pillars. No unfettered entry to the ancients. Not today. Things have changed.

So much has changed.

Today requires patience and determination. Today involves a diversion then a queue then an abundance of curt questions before a continuation is allowed.

All delight has departed.

Today all must turn left once through the gates instead of merrily marching forward. Each would–be visitor must join the zig–zagged herd snaking through the maze–like barriers. Today all must shuffle and inch toward the newly erected plastic marquee that houses the gatekeepers.

All trust has gone.

Fear has replaced faith.

My backpack has three compartments. I have helpfully pre–emptively unzipped and opened one and now the gloved man in uniform asks me to open another. He shines his torch, has a peer, performs a perfunctory poke. He generates a somewhat confused frown, conducts a moment's hesitation but then offers no comment. Instead he nods and pushes my pack back. I'm free to enter. And, arguably due to the vagaries and leniencies of chance (or perhaps the celestial intervention of a trusted friend) my third compartment remains unzipped and un–rummaged. My most controversial contents remain undiscovered.

And now I was in. And I was in control. It was our (Mark Twain and mine's) museum plan in manifest. And I felt surprisingly calm. Under the circumstances. I was a man with a mission. A perp with a purpose. A Dude with direction. I hurried past the Rosetta Stone – *Meh, seen you before, bought the fridge magnet* – and into Gallery 23.

Where I pulled up short. Because there she was. Part of the Royal Collection lent by Her Majesty Queen Elizabeth II. 'Venus the Goddess of Love.' A stride–stopper. A thought–inducer. Hmm, had she been placed on a plinth or a pedestal? 'Crouching Naked Aphrodite'. Words and their meanings. Suggestions and acts. *The Goddess of Love* – white marbled and naked. Smooth contours. Brazen. Breasts and buttocks on show. *To all.* The sight of her reminded me instantly of Rebecca. I felt my scrotum shrivel – felt its contents grind together and contract. The sight of her reminded me instantly of Rebecca and then in the next instant my mission, my full intent. The reason Mark Twain and I had agreed that this was where I should come. That this was where it would all end. It was surely time.

I'd just quickly pop to the Gents first.

Rebecca

"Why don't you write yourself a letter, just let your thoughts flow, don't edit it after, just begin to write and see what comes out." *Yeah thanks Mary.* It's not as easy as it sounds and rather ironic really – me seeing the psychotherapist and all the time Robert was… well…

Actually, he wasn't. It's not fair and too simplistic to think that. I never worried about that, not really. At least... I don't know, this is difficult. Robert's Dad used to refer to him always "Acting the goat." I liked that expression and it made sense. It always came to mind when Robert was messing about – doing things like the cup of tea dance or trying to convince me there was a Dagenham tradition that all visitors must perform a speed striptease the moment they heard the Archers theme tune on Radio 4.

Chapter 5

I'd descended to the Gents in the bowels of the British Museum and had chosen cubicle **3**. I found I was doing that much more often lately, counting things in threes, grouping them as trios. Seeing three where there'd only ever been two. Thinking three instead of two. Two plus one. Two, and then another. Two, and then that one. That dreadful one.

Robert–Rebecca–Damien   Robert– Rebecca–Damien

Robert–Rebecca–Damien!

I had counted then chosen and entered cubicle **3** and then had locked the door and dropped my trousers and the increasingly ubiquitous midnight–blue underpants. I had decided to sit for both nostalgic and practical reason – if it was to be my last then I might as well be comfortable and, in any case, I needed my hands free to check the contents of my backpack.

As I sat, I thought back. Then forward then back again. And it still made sense. Of course it did. We'd discussed it in detail. I was at the right place. Where better to end my mammoth malaise than amidst the magnificent marbles? They had a beautifully relevant history and a significance and symbolism that I surely couldn't better. It was Rebecca who'd revealed most about them and all that she'd told me only fuelled my certainty.

The Elgin Marbles were controversial. I had always kinda known that. Not that I had a great interest in politics. I'd been through the process; long since hooped the loop of believer to sceptic to cynic. And so I could have been wrong but I was reasonably certain–sure–enough that we naughty Brits had sneakily taken the marbles from the ever–so–nice but far–too–trusting Greeks. And that was that. A historical footnote of little to no note. Rebecca however was always far sharper and passionately engaged when it came to analysing bigger pictures. Especially where an artefact or two were involved. She had been shocked when I admitted my sketchy grasp of the details and had promptly proceeded to tell me the full unexpurgated.

Rebecca was always sincere, thorough and detailed when revealing things.

Apparently, a bloke called Bruce, who was also the Earl of Elgin, obtained a dodgy permit whilst he was ambassador to the Ottoman Empire. He and his team then started quickly dismantling chunks of the Parthenon and other Acropolis accoutrements and shipping the classical Greek sculptures home to Blighty. And were rewarded with immediate accusations of looting.

And I recall that I listened intently as she explained and then I proceeded to provoke Rebecca with a playful bit of Devil's advocacy – asking along the lines of whether she should perhaps consider the counter–arguments: that if we (the ghastly greedy) didn't plunder them then someone else might have; and that at least we were looking after them properly – treating them well – at least we weren't leaving them out in the sun all day. That sort of thing, that sort of spin. At which point, Rebecca rolled her eyes and pinched my waist in order to let me know that she knew I was being an arse. And I grinned an apology because I knew it too and urged her to tell me more.

But today that bit doesn't interest me, not the details of the crime nor the excuses offered; it's the story that has resonance. THE DEED. I could relate. *I could now.* I'd had something precious cruelly stolen from me.

That was Link Number 1. And Link Number 2 has already had a half–mention; the marbles have not travelled well. They are not fully intact. All have bits missing; men without hands, women without heads, horses without feet, warriors without genitals. They are men bereft and women fallen. Rebecca had brought me here (on Date Adventure 9) because she thought they were beautiful. And I could kind of see what she meant but that didn't stop me from telling her they seemed reminiscent of the aftermath of the Hainault Sunday Morning Car Boot Sale; when all the unsold china was simply dumped – piles of cracked crockery and discarded knick–knacks left littering the grass. And I recall wondering out loud if, when the boxes had arrived from Athens, were they opened only to find bits and pieces of snapped off appendages in the bottom of the boxes. As had happened to me when I bought a Winston Churchill bust from eBay and found his cigar languishing in three separate pieces. That's what we would often do – Rebecca would introduce me to London's artistic treasures and I would gently mock them. She would laugh a little and I would learn a little. That's how it worked. And it did work.

It had worked.

But now I was here for the irony, that's what I and Mark Twain had decided. Here was the perfect place for poignant demise, here amidst the men bereft and the women fallen.

Rebecca had brought me here when we were whole.

Rebecca

"Take your pen and paper and then spend some moments engaged with your soothing rhythm breathing…" I really don't know about this – it still feels ridiculous – I'm writing a letter to myself about a man who is... who was... I don't know what to write – what to tell myself, what to acknowledge. *The truth, Rebecca.* Well the truth is I loved him and I knew I was lucky. There – it's said or written or told to myself or admitted to the universe in a compassionate manner or whatever the idea is. I loved him and he could always make me laugh and so I would always forgive him (even at his most infuriating). That was the thing I suppose – I could never stay cross with him for long. Not in those early days, not in the first years. In truth I guess not ever until I forced myself to, until I foolishly convinced myself that was for the best.

He would have truly adored the idea of me having to write a letter to myself. I just googled 'therapist Hampstead' (where I'd hoped we'd one day live) and I got 353,000 results. Then, in honour of Robert, I googled 'therapist Dagenham' (where he seemed more than happy to stay) and I got a mere 118,000 results (mostly beauty and massage). I'm sure he would have enjoyed that, he would have wittered on about the middle–class malaise, the bourgeois blight – time and money for self–indulgence but little knowledge of what truly mattered. *Like nails and waxing.* He'd have made it sound funnier but it would be something like that – heads being shrunk in Hampstead whilst pluckings and paintings reigned in Becontree Heath. We would have laughed about it.

We always did laugh.

Chapter 6

As it turned out, my last sitting wasn't in any way ceremonious. I squeezed intently but to little avail. I hadn't really needed to be there. Especially as the contents of my backpack were all intact, as so they should, and were always going to be. They'd been checked more than a hundred times – this was not going to prove an amateurish performance. I counted them all out and in again anyway, ran through the familiar deed–enabling checklist:

- One Double–Edged Blade 19cm Stainless Steel Grapefruit Segmenting Knife. *Check.*
- One dog–eared dog collar, identity tag and leash. *Check.*
- One (slightly unfocused) photograph taken of a happy couple on Hungerford Bridge. *Check.*
- One jar of Duchy Originals (Royal Purveyors) Organic Lemon Curd. *Check.*
- One t shirt with the slogan 'Fall in Love Don't Fall in Line.' *Check.*
- One packet of Salt n Vinegar flavour Hula Hoops. *Check.*
- One *Financial Times* title page declaring 'Disrupters Bring Destruction'. *Check.*
- One slightly faded much fingered business card. *Check.*
- One stale packet of mid–priced mince pies. *Check.*
- One 'Cours camarade, le vieux monde est derriere toi.' pin badge. *Check.*
- One pair of Heavy–Duty Ratchet Action Pruning Secateurs. *Check.*

All present and correct.

Right then. Well then. Time then. Time to hitch and zip and get on with it. I exited cubicle 3 then washed my hands. Habit I supposed; what relevance were germs now? I washed and I rinsed and then I turned, just as I had in a hundred public toilets a thousand times before. I washed and I rinsed and then I turned and then I stopped. And I stared. Because I'd just noticed there was someone else in the Gents partaking of the facilities. Someone familiar. Someone famous. Someone we all know – The Count of Monte Cristo!

So I assumed at least. Not that I could pick out the Count of Monte Cristo in a line–up that also included a few musketeers, the Pimpernel and a couple of Draculas. But his was the first name that shot to mind. He was of that ilk. You know the type – long black jacket, lacy white shirt, black trousers, shiny boots. But no cape, now that I come to think of it; no cape and his hat may have been of the black beanie variety – it possibly wasn't felt nor feathered. But still, the overall impression was of Count or Pirate, Musketeer or Cossack; the overall initial was man of importance, a romantic hero or some such. He seemed very much out of place. And yet completely at home. Very comfortable in his surroundings. At ease with himself. A leader, an example–setter, a man of action. Oh, and tall, he was impressively tall. Which made sense, logistically speaking, once all things were considered. I don't recall his face, and frankly, I'm not surprised – that wasn't where my eyes were drawn. I had turned and now suddenly there he was. I had turned and then suddenly I saw him – The Count of Monte Cristo.

Drying his penis in the Dyson Airblade machine.

I hadn't been expecting that.

He was stood there with his hands on his hips and his head thrown back and for a moment I thought 'Titanic.' But that was a weak link really – the wind wasn't in his hair. At least not in quite the same thatch. It's strange how the mind works. Shock maybe. First impressions. Last conclusions. The Dyson Airblade; 'the fastest most hygienic hand dryer.' And the first to invite artistic interpretation? The machine had the look of a large single slice bread toaster and the expected technique was to point your fingers vertically down and insert them in the narrow whistling gap. The cleverly designed wind tunnel would then gust away all germs and disperse any lingering drips. And it was a sight I'd seen many perform numerous times before. But never quite like this. There he stood, completely at ease. And I wondered was the Count confused or simply non–conformist. But whatever the case, he made me laugh and he made me wonder.

And that made an unexpected dent in my full intent.

I gave him a round of applause and a clap on the back. Which in retrospect may have been dangerous – health and safety and who knows what not – but he didn't seem to mind. He rocked forward a little, staggered slightly, possibly touched the sides, but then steadied heroically and gave me a smile and a nod in return.

The Count of Monte Cristo had perfect white teeth.

Of course he did.

Anyway, I guess the point is if I hadn't gone to empty my bladder in the bowels of the British Museum I wouldn't have seen Dick Van Dyson. And I thought I'd seen everything. Or at least a version of. I was certainly convinced I'd seen everything I wanted to see. Everything and more. Too much. But now I was suddenly conflicted, a little less sure. Perhaps… well… perhaps just maybe… perhaps I hadn't…

And one thing I had definitely discovered is you can't top yourself if you've just had a good chuckle. You lose focus. You can't top yourself if you've just had a good chuckle even if that's what you and Mark Twain have consistently and earnestly been discussing. Even if that's what the literary legend has been hinting makes most sense. Even if it's what he's been encouraging you to do. Even if it's something you've plotted, planned and agreed together.

I smiled once more, gave the Count the thumbs up, re–zipped my backpack then exited the Gents. Then exited the British Museum. Then got back on the tube. And headed home. I felt kind of okay.

But that was yesterday.
And only a moment fleeting.

Rebecca

Robert's dad was lovely – a quiet and gentle man, and they were very close. His death hit Robert hard and I don't think he could ever really accept it. We never really spoke about it, I tried but it was almost as if Robert couldn't as if that would make it too 'real.' (If that makes any sense.) There's so much I still don't fully understand. It's sad and it's frustrating.

But maybe that was Robert in a nutshell – infuriating. Yesterday I made a list of his positive attributes – I didn't want the anger. (It was my idea not Mary's so I've no excuse.) It read:

Eccentric, Unorthodox, Hilarious, Intelligent, Fun, Kind, Sensitive, Imaginative, Loyal, Romantic and Sexy (most of the time).

And it was all true. But then I tainted the list by scrawling in marker pen across it a one–word summation

– *INFURIATING*

And that was just as true too.

Chapter 7

A lot has happened in a short time – a cliché but nonetheless true. Life flipped and tossed. Battered. And now that I'm determined to beckon them the recalls are coming fast. Rapids. They remind me that so much has changed. That there's so much that will never be the same. I'm closing my eyes now…

…and it's not as if any further attrition is required but it arrives anyway – through the medium of text.

A sad day. Still vivid. U did so well. Hope you're doing OK? Call me if u need 2 talk x

It's from Sis and it spurs me to consider the date, it forces me to face another fact, it's exactly the day, it's exactly one year to the day. One year since we buried our father.

And I remember that day only too well. It floods back and washes over me.

Rebecca was by my side.

And we'd had a conversation. *The type she liked.* The ones she increasingly seemed to crave. The honest and open types of conversation. The ones without spin. The transparent ones. The ones without wit to dilute or joke to deflect. The ones not laced with clever nuance or subtle ambiguity. The ones without a diversionary twist of sly.

"You can't read that out, Robert. You just can't. You cannot read that out in the church!"

"People read poems at funerals."

"Not like that. I'm concerned about you, Robert, and I'm not going to let you read that out."

"But... it's my duty to provide a eulogy."

"You can say a few words but do not read that poem."

"But my dad..."

"I know. But you can't..."

And in the end I didn't. In the end I did know Rebecca was right. But only after I'd insisted on reading the poem out to her. Three times. And only after she had begun to cry. I only knew after she had begged and made me promise and asked me to consider how Sis might feel and it was only after she had implored me to understand that it wasn't just about what I wanted and that I needed to realise there were times when following convention was essential. And it was only when she had screamed through her tears, when she had finally screamed and shouted,

"STOP BEING SO FUCKING SELFISH! SO FUCKING SELF–INDULGENT! YOU'RE NOT BEING DIFFERENT! YOU'RE JUST BEING A TWAT!"

That I had known.

And later, ten minutes or so later, when we had both stopped crying, she had helped me write an alternative eulogy. And she had held my hand throughout the service. And she had smiled encouragingly and squeezed my hand when it was time for me to stand up and walk to the altar and then turn to face the mourners. And when I looked down she had nodded and smiled again and I had somehow managed to focus and I had reached into my pocket and I had pulled out two pieces of paper and I had looked at Sis who had her head lowered and who had her husband's arm around her and whose shoulders were shaking under his embrace and then I had looked at Rebecca once more. And she had smiled a third time. And then I took a deep breath and I read out the jointly written Eulogy B and not the tear–sodden and crumpled solo effort Eulogy A. And then the congregation had applauded and I had walked back to the pew and I had sat back down and Rebecca had squeezed my arm and then held my hand again until it was time for me to get up once more and help carry my father's coffin from the church whilst a soloist sang a haunting rendition of *Abide With Me* and all around was awash with jaw–clenched men in dark suits and eye–dabbing women signing the cross.

And afterwards, when beer and sandwiches and tea and cake were being served, people came to shake my hand and they told me they were sorry for my troubles and they praised the perfect ceremony and my bravery and lovely speech. And they told me how my father would have been proud. And now that I come to think of it, I probably owed Rebecca a lot. And yet I don't think I ever properly thanked her – I never praised her for talking me out of reading out the 'Dad is Dead' poem.

And maybe I would thank her now. If things were the same. But they're not. Things are different. Rebecca is not by my side. And that's OK. I don't need Rebecca because I have Mark Twain to advise and guide me now.

I have him to thank.

Rebecca

"As you write your letter Rebecca, try to allow yourself to understand and accept your distress."

Understand and accept…Wow… Okay, well I guess I need to start to write about *him* then. Damien and I grew up together; I suppose that was just fate and if Robert were here we'd probably now discuss such a glibly accepted phrase as "just fate" – is anything ever *just fate*? He'd probably scold me then and state that there was only one true fate – Robert and Rebecca together forever fate. Something pseudo–adolescent (but very convincing) like that. He never once showed any sign of doubting that. Nor did I for a long time. Well fate or otherwise it was determined that Damien's mother and mine would share a ward at Whittington Hospital and that Damien would be born exactly 1 hour and 32 minutes before I was. I would estimate that during the course of our lives Damien has reminded me of this fact more than ten dozen times which perhaps gives an inkling into how original and amusing Damien is.

Chapter 8

Memory can prove incongruous, bereft of logic, order irrelevant. I'm struggling with the correct chronology but perhaps it's okay to piece it until the whole forms. I'm finding it's the details that take precedent. You can mislay whole chapters of your life but never forget particular lines. Certain things sting. They cement. They're an easy recall. I can remember the workplace. I can remember the day. I can remember the words...

"I enjoy seeing my wife in just her bra, how about you?"

I have an office job. I work in payroll, which is a strange expression. I don't actually 'work in payroll' I work in an office where we (mostly I) produce the payroll. I'm thinking about that job now and I realise the reason I am being pedantic is partly because I can often be pedantic but mostly it's because I do not enjoy working in payroll, or working in an office where we produce the payroll. Not any longer; I have a new boss. A new and loquacious boss.

"I enjoy seeing my wife in just her bra, how about you?"

His name is George. And he's been trying to destroy me. He's been grinding me down. Systematically chipping away. Inexorably crushing. Today is his cruellest assault yet. *And cleverest.* Today he hits me with that devastating over–share.

George has effusive facial hair, and not only that, George has taken exams in payroll. I did not know payroll exams even existed before George arrived but apparently they do and that may explain his salary and the fact he has been awarded a company car. Not only did I not know that payroll exams existed but had I known payroll exams existed I would have been unable to imagine the type of person who might wish to sit payroll exams. I do not have to imagine any longer.

George has just returned from "the washroom" (that's how he refers to the toilet) and obviously assumes it's acceptable for him to confide.

"I enjoy seeing my wife in just her bra, how about you?"

Just like that. No warning, no preamble, no pretext, nothing. I notice his hands are still dripping.

"I… I've never met your wife."

"Hey! Steady on. Cheeky. No, I meant your girlfriend."

He wipes his paws on the front of his rigidly pleated grey trousers. I notice there are curled hairs around his knuckles.

"You… you want to discuss… my... *girlfriend...*"

"No, well, yeah – you know. I just meant you know, do you like…"

"She's a vegetarian."

"Pardon?"

"And she collects antique china."

"Oh. Right. No, I meant do you like to see her…"

"She searches the charity shops for curios."

His wet hands have left damp prints on his thighs. I'm appalled and unwittingly reminded that for some inexplicable reason he refers to his trousers as "slacks". And that there is no excuse to mention your trousers in the office. At all. Ever. I want him to stop talking but he doesn't.

"OK, but how do you prefer…"

"And she likes books."

He's still standing. Slack stained and proud.

"Yes, but…"

"Difficult ones."

"I was asking about what you…"

I wish he'd sit down. I wish he'd shut up. He doesn't do either so I have to keep talking. I have to deflect.

"She rates Jane Austen above E. L. James."

"Yes, but…"

"And she has her refuse collected on a Wednesday."

"But do you like to see her…"
"Recycling is on Thursdays."
"Do you have a favourite thing she…"
"Green waste once a month."
I'm desperate for him to sit down. I'm suppressing a screech.
"I was just asking about you know…"
"For bulkier items you have to ring the council."
"I was just wondering if…"
"AND I'M JUST NOT TELLING YOU!"
"Oh. I was just curious…her name's Rebecca isn't it?"
"BE QUIET! Please! For the love of Marigold, please…"
"Hey now, don't talk to me like tha… remember I'm your superior."
"Supe..? Oh Christ, you actually believe you're my…"
"Well, I am the Payroll Director."
"You're… yes… yes you… you are… you honestly truly are…"
He does sit down. *Finally.*
I left then. I exited. I had no other choice. My turn to visit the washroom.
When I got there, I chose cubicle 3 and sat with my head in my hands. And I don't know how long I'd been there but eventually I was not alone. I sensed Mark Twain's jocular presence a mere moment before I received his gentle taunting. His teasing whisper in my ear,

> "There is no sadder sight than a young pessimist, except an old optimist."

Fair enough – I must have looked a sorry state; midnight–blue underpants round my ankles and goosepimples on my thighs – it was a poor venue for a prolonged melancholic slumping. I asked Mark Twain what the answer was. (I thought it was worth a try.) He answered immediately; he didn't avoid the question or even ask for clarification of what exactly the question was. I liked that. He just gave it to me straight,

"It is an odious world, a horrible world – it is Hell; the true one, not the lying invention of the superstitious; and we have come to it from elsewhere to expiate our sins."

And even though his answer arguably wasn't *the* answer, it was *an* answer, and an answer that gave me explanation rather than comfort. But that was semi–soothing too. I liked his honesty. Of course I did, I very much liked him. And at least he'd been listening. I liked that too. And I liked the word 'expiate'. I'd forgotten what it meant but I would look it up when I went back to my desk. I felt better; Mark Twain knew how to put things in perspective. How to state the truth and not be bowed. He gave me strength. I thanked him and hitched my trousers.

When I exited the cubicle Liam from accounts turned from his point position at the urinal. He gave me the sly–curious look.

"Who were you talking to in there?"

"Me? No one, what are you on about? All those numbers must be crunching your mind."

Mark Twain's whispers cannot be heard by others. He has chosen only me and consequently I am proud, I am grateful and I am protective. And I was not about to explain. I have no desire to share. Liam wears brogues and knows little about me but by nature he is cautious and prudent. I am aware of his type and so I gave him the Dagenham stare. He immediately quietened, turned his head and refocused on his aim.

Rebecca

Memories are flooding back now – all the little but special things. We'd only been going out a few months when we discovered Robert couldn't wink at all with his right eye and the left eye's efforts, though better, in all honesty produced something more akin to a pained squint than a seductive wink. We discovered it in the bedroom; or rather I somewhat gleefully pointed it out. He had been confusing himself with Don Juan or Russell Crowe or someone, walking in from the bathroom sporting only a hand towel and that brazen smile that I'd loved from the very beginning. He had turned his gaze toward me, dropped the towel and grimaced. When I asked if he had indigestion the realisation slowly began to dawn. It turned out he had been in denial for years or rather he'd been in ignorant bliss – no–one had ever pointed out his limitations before. I made him practice in front of the mirror whilst I stroked his back to show my support. He gurned desperately and we laughed until it hurt. Then he made me solemnly swear never to tell anyone he was wink deficient. That was what it was like. When it was good. (Which it almost always was.) I can still see that smile – it was always wide and uncompromised – warm, complete and honest.

Chapter 9

On the way back to the Payroll Department (deciding to take the long route past Marketing and PR) part of me wondered was I overreacting – was I perhaps being unfair? Was I being too quick to judge and despise? Part of me recognised I had been curt with Liam and part of me was part–ways prepared to doubt my righteousness re. George. I even gave it some thought – *here you go, have some, it's yours* – as I re–directed and took the very long route back (two circles of the quadrant lapping Accounts and HR as well as Marketing and PR) before finally bracing up and re–entering Payroll. Room 313.

I'd considered how some men find it hard to bond with other men and admittedly ours was a strange blurring of power situation. I had been carrying George for most of the 6 months since his arrival and we both knew it. He had struggled with the quirks of our particular payroll system and I had been very patient whilst picking up his slack. Perhaps he recognised this and was trying too hard to be friendly or some such? Making clumsy efforts to engage? Gruesome attempts at gratitude? Maybe he was just an awkward type and I should be more tolerant? But "I enjoy seeing my wife in just her bra, how about you?" How do you answer such an enquiry without losing self–respect? Or self–control?

Especially today.

Anyway, when I returned, I was kind of almost ready to appease but as I sat down opposite George, he looked toward the clock and raised an eyebrow. He honestly did. And that did it. I'm ashamed to say my reaction was immediate. I picked up the red metal Winston Armitage Long Arm Full Reach 20 Sheet Capacity Stapler and raised my own eyebrow.

We shared a moment. Then finally George spoke.
"Our recycling's collected on a Monday..."
And immediately Mark Twain asked,

> "Who is that overgrown pirate with the whiskers and the discordant voice?"

"George." I whispered to Mark. And now I stared Dagenham at George. But, unlike Liam, George didn't give it up. Perhaps he's never been to Dagenham. Whatever the case he only hesitated for only a few moments then was off again.

"They did want to only collect fortnightly but I organised a petition."

That triggered Mark Twain to chip in once more – he offered George some sage advice,

> "It is better to keep your mouth shut and appear stupid than to open it and remove all doubt."

George didn't react but I laughed loudly. George looked nonplussed. For a moment I had forgotten he couldn't hear Mark Twain. My laughter was effective though – George finally stopped his inane drivel. We stared at each other for a while longer and his eyes were the first to drop.

We kept our heads down and worked in silence for the rest of the day. And my anger simmered. You see it's not difficult; it should be easy; the rules are simple, there's no excuse to get it wrong. Neutral football or popular TV. Not wives and *girlfriends!* Especially not today. If he had come in on a Monday morning and said "How lucky were Arsenal on Sunday?" Or "Hey, did you watch the new Doctor Who?" Anything along those lines and we'd have been off and running and that's how seam–free a transition it could have been: boss to colleague, colleague to mate, stress to calm. But no, he hadn't. He'd thoroughly irritated me from Day One and now he'd just topped the icing on the cringe cake. On today of all days. What impeccable timing. "I enjoy seeing my wife in just her bra, how about you?" Dear oh dear oh dear…

And I was aware that now, under these new circumstances, even looking toward the man was unhealthy. I knew I had to block certain thoughts and I had to avoid all that could be avoided. And I had no idea why I had even come in to work today – was it just habit? Forgetfulness? Masochism? Idiocy? Why had I got out of my bed and on to the train? Why when I hadn't slept a wink? Maybe because I hadn't slept a wink? I didn't know. But I did know George should not be mentioning wives and girlfriends. And certainly not their bras or his peculiar penchants. There was no excuse. Particularly not today. Even though I know George is unaware that Rebecca and I have split up. *And what a perfect description that is. Split–up – sliced apart – cruelly carved like the slabs of meat decomposing behind the deli counter.* George is unaware that Rebecca and I have split up but that doesn't absolve him.

"I enjoy seeing my wife in just her bra."

Why on earth did he have to tell me that? I couldn't get over it. The intrusion. It was not forgivable. (And I did try.) The trouble was I could now imagine it. *I had no choice but to imagine it.* He'd planted the image in my mind. He had violated me. The image was there. The seed had grown. Anchored. I'd never met her nor seen a photo but I could picture her clearly and the sight was shocking. And I knew it was warped but that didn't help. I realised I was procuring a picture of a person's partner purely from my passionately subjective point of view but that didn't help either. I had no choice. I could only imagine her courtesy of my cursed view of him. I knew that it was wrong, unfair, disquieting, damaging and bizarre. But I had no choice. It was unavoidable. There it was – *another unwanted image* – firmly planted and deeply rooted.

Now every time I looked up from my desk and toward the man sat opposite (and believe me I tried not to), every time I looked up from my desk and toward the man sat opposite, I saw her image. The woman whose torment I could only imagine.

The Sherry Wife of George.

That was how I viewed her. That was my image of the person I had never met but now knew so intimately. That was the coping strategy I had granted her. A bottle of sherry. A sad–eyed woman, bare below the breast, clutching a bottle of Christmas sherry. I didn't want the image but it was embedded. And it was no less real for being unreliable. And it was no less vivid. I had constructed a spectre based upon biased suspecting. I hadn't wanted to but I had no choice. And I was on her side. I was completely on her side. And her pain was excruciating. And I felt that pain. I recognised it. I understood it. I empathised completely.

She was married to George.

And I hated George for what he had done to her and for what he was doing to me. *George the Destroyer.* And I did not want to see his half–naked other half in my already half–hampered mind. BUT I HAD NO CHOICE. There she was, larger than life–sized – her hair dishevelled and her nail varnish chipped – he had done this to her. He had done this to me. And do you know what was the worst thing? Her smile. It was pained to the point of… I don't know. I didn't have the words. I didn't have the words I just had the image. And the pain. She was looking at him and all he stood for. I felt for her. Unequivocally. I saw the tragedy and the blight and the bitterness of never–to–be–realised dreams. I saw the acceptance and the regret and the shame and the disappointment and the humiliation. I saw all that it meant to be married to George. I saw it all as she stood there, regretful, vulnerable and inebriated under his greedy beady–eyed gaze.

In just her bra.

And I wish Mark Twain would talk to me more, but he doesn't. He's choosy with his timings. And, when he doesn't talk to me, I become agitated and I fear that Samuel Langhorne Clemens is ambivalent; I fear that in reality he giveth not one iota of a flying flipfuck whether I live or die. And then I feel bad because I try unfashionably hard not to swear. But that's not the real tragedy; the real tragedy is the doubt, the lack of faith. And I feel guilty for thinking of him as Samuel Langhorne Clemens, for although that is his 'real' name, the one he was awarded at birth, he chose to be known as 'Mark Twain' and that's one of the reasons I admire him. I like to be known as 'Robert' and not 'Horatio' even though that was my own birth award. It's just one of the many things we have in common.

And then because of my guilt and lack of faith I chastise myself; I chastise myself for letting him down. I chastise myself for not following through at the British Museum. And then I curse the Count of Monte Cristo but I know that it was ultimately my decision. And no doubt Mark Twain now thinks I'm a time waster. He is no doubt angered that I failed him and he is punishing me – giving me the intermittent treatment. And I desperately want to expiate (which means atone for – I did look it up) but I don't know how.

And tonight it's worse than ever because the Sherry Wife is there; she's stubbornly on the periphery. She has left the office and boarded the train with me. She clings to me tenaciously. And even though on the journey home I sit on my hands and tap my feet and keep my eyes closed tight and hum the national anthem incessantly, it doesn't work. It doesn't work on the tube to Stratford or the train to Chadwell Heath. Their images are still there but Mark's soothing voice is absent. Rebecca and Damien and George and now the Sherry Wife are all there (in full HD 3D CCTV) but there's no Mark Twain to help me cope.

And when I arrive home, I pour myself a bath and even though the water is not hot I get into the bath and I close my eyes and this time I am determined to wait. For as long as it takes. I am going to lie here and expiate as best I can. And I do. And my patience is eventually rewarded – eventually Mark Twain is in the bath with me. His words once more are in my ear. And he confirms again what I now know to be quintessentially true. His whisper is clear, calm, concise. It's reassuring and it's warm. It's contrast to the icy waters. It's a reminder.

> "Suicide is the only sane thing the young or old ever do in this life."

And with huge relief I realise that he does still care whether I live or die. He is not ambivalent. Of course he is not. He has reiterated his advice. And now I can open my eyes and I can get out of the bath.

Now I can finally reach for the towel.

Rebecca

Damien and I grew up together but when I say that I don't mean it in the usual sense – we grew up together purely because our mothers were best friends and incessant visitors. They drank coffee (or possibly gin) whilst we played Lego on the carpet, that sort of thing. I don't mean there was anything particularly special about it – it was just circumstantial. I had no choice and neither did he. I'm not suggesting it was ever a particularly pleasurable experience and well, I'm not sure what I am actually saying. Just perhaps that as adults surely we determine our own fate? I can't just blame circumstance or a ridiculous fake nostalgia. Which just makes all that happened all the more...

But I can't write about that. Not yet. So I'll stick to wondering about fate for now. Damien and I spent time together simply because our mothers bonded at that maternity hospital. I guess they had shared an experience, been through a similar trauma, maybe they felt an affinity, like war veterans perhaps. They had also discovered they lived only two roads apart. Was that just fate or something more? I wish Robert were here and we could discuss coincidence versus fate and maybe whether free will and choice were ultimately influenced by circumstance. Was there ever an excuse or was integrity all that truly mattered? Actually, maybe I should be careful what I wish for – that might not prove a conversation laced with our usual friendly tease and laughter. I do wish he were here though. So very much.

Chapter 10

It's remarkable really – I remember them all. Dates. Going on a date. A strange expression really – 'I'm just off on a September 23rd'. Our language is very limited. I honestly do remember them though – all of them – but most vividly the early ones. We didn't call them 'dates' of course, I insisted they must be known as 'Adventures.' I liked that – planning then enjoying an 'Adventure.' It made our meetings extra special, gave them gravitas – set us apart. Not that they were always without their cringe moments, especially early on when I was still finding my feet – still coming to terms with all that I'd found. All and everything. Consider Date Adventure 3 for example:

I had laughed when I realised what she was reading, it was a kid's book. I had laughed gleefully and jumped at the opportunity – I went straight into tease mode. I was good at that. Easily as good as she and today Rebecca was offering easy pickings, offering me a wide–open goal.

But I miss–kicked.

Rebecca didn't laugh along. Instead, she assured me it most certainly was not just a story for kid's and that no, she was not a member of the Primrose Hill Primary School Year 4 Book Club. I could tell immediately that she wasn't particularly amused, in fact she appeared more confused than anything. Disappointed even. I panicked a bit then, felt a full fluster fall upon me. I had to respond quickly and so I slipped on my sincere face and asked her to explain what it was about. She didn't say anything initially but I could tell by the way she looked at me that she was surprised that I didn't know. That embarrassed me a bit too. She acted as if she wasn't dismayed though – she just stared at me for that moment – seemed to weigh up my worthiness, then perhaps rejected any inclination toward scorn and began to reveal.

"Well, before I tell you what *it's about*, did you know that Ernest Hemingway stated all modern American literature comes from *Huckleberry Finn*?"

"Urm, no..."

"Yes. He argued that there was nothing as good before and that there has been nothing as good since. "

"Right... so he obviously thought it was alright then?"

I was careful not to mention that I wasn't overly familiar with Ernest Hemingway either, I had no desire to be labelled a buffoon.

"You're funny. Yes, he did think it was *alright.* And so did millions of others. So *do* many millions of others. And quite rightly so. I think you would too, I think you'd like it. In fact I'm sure you would."

"Right... so go on then, tell me what it's all about."

"*The Adventures of Huckleberry Finn* is a book about freedom and integrity."

"Oh..."

I hadn't been expecting that. Rebecca had suddenly gone a bit earnest herself.

"Yes, it's about being true to yourself, your real self, it's about clinging to inner truth – what you know is right and it's about avoiding the curbs imposed upon personality by an imperfect society."

"Right..."

She was leaning forward now, kind of in my face. But in a nice way. I looked into her eyes.

"Mark Twain was a magnificent writer. He's a literary legend."

"He wasn't just writing for kids?"

"No. No, he most certainly was not."

"I spent my formative years in bed with Enid Blyton."

That threw her, for the merest matter of moments. But it succeeded, it gave me a reprieve, it gave me time to compose myself. Early dates are a minefield, a battle where you have to establish the rules of engagement, where you have to learn your roles. Where you do your best to project an image. *That's what they're usually like.* I wanted to be Charming Witty Boy. She stared at me again, for a longer moment, a somewhat disconcerting one. Was she assuming Shallow Half–Wit Boy?

Then she appeared to give me the benefit of the doubt.

"Mark Twain is not Enid Blyton. Although I'll admit she was a bit of a character too, did you know she played naked tennis?"

I'd discover that Rebecca could often do that, chuck in a casual titbit and throw me completely. I liked it. It proved she wasn't into role playing; she was herself, first, foremost and always. She wasn't interested in projecting images. Or playing games. She was happy just being Rebecca. And others were free to take that or leave it. She would say what she decided to say and if that wasn't what you anticipated then so be it. I was surprised – I couldn't really imagine Enid Blyton at the net, but I immediately got a strong image of a sporty Rebecca. I could see her playing tennis. In whites and without. I could see the two of us playing. Volley and serve, backhand and forehand, rally and return.

"Shall I read you a bit?"

"Enid Blyton? Well, yes, that would be nice, I always enjoyed The Famous Five. And Malory Towers. Maybe that torrid tale of Aunt Fanny and Uncle Quentin? Or the one about a mischievous good egg playing marvellous tricks on the French Mistress? Or poor Timmy stuck down the well?"

"No. But again, points for being mildly amusing. How about I read you some Mark Twain? A bit of *Huckleberry Finn*? It's far better in my opinion."

"Okay..."

And she did. She read me a chunk. And by the end of it I'd forgotten Enid Blyton. And even all thoughts of risqué tennis. I'd nudged up a notch. I'd engaged. I'd been bettered. She read me a passage – part of which went like this:

> *"Then I set down in a chair by the window and tried to think of something cheerful, but it warn't no use. I felt so lonesome I most wished I was dead. The stars was shining, and the leaves rustled in the woods ever so mournful; and I heard an owl, away off, who–whooing about somebody that was dead… and a dog crying about*

somebody that was going to die... I got so down–hearted and scared, I did wish I had some company."

And when she finished, I realised I had been holding my breath. She had read it beautifully, expounded with a softly pronounced passion that had slithered through my earlobes and sank deep down within. And I was suddenly profoundly aware that no–one had read to me for years. Not since I was a child. Not since Mum. And the words had been haunting and evocative. And I was surprised and I was moved. And for a while I didn't say anything. Neither of us said anything. And then eventually Rebecca said

"I thought you might like that."

And then I did say something, I said, "Can I get you another drink?"

And she requested Pinot Noir and I headed to the bar.

And when I got back Rebecca smiled and thanked me and we chinked glasses and we said "Cheers." And then she began to tell me more about this wonderful writer man, the man I was already beginning to strongly admire too. She told me Mark Twain was America's first real literary celebrity and she told me that diners in restaurants rose and applauded whenever he entered and she told me that the paparazzi of the day followed him everywhere. And she told me that this was in large part because he was very much considered a 'humourist.'

"A funny guy?"

"Indeed. Very much so. Mark Twain was the archetypal funny guy. And so much more besides."

And then she warmed further to her theme – she told me more about that book, she told me more about *Huckleberry Finn*, she told me it was about many things and one of those things was the battle between conscience and expectation. She said it was about instinctive goodness versus corrupt values. And she gave another example – she informed me *Huckleberry Finn* made the reader question man's deepest motivations – it made them consider the choice between moral or material values. And then she said she wouldn't tell me too much because the book was mine once she had finished it and that as she only had 3 pages to go if I shut up for five minutes then I could sooner discover its genius for myself. I did shut up. I sat and smiled while she completely un self–consciously returned to her reading. I was amused that she would do that. And proud. I knew from the very earliest days that she was unlike any other I'd known.

And exactly what I wanted.

In the end it took her more than 5 minutes but eventually she sighed and closed the book. "All yours." She said and pushed it toward me. I asked was she sure and she replied that yes, that was the third time she'd read it and maybe that was enough. She then elaborated – saying that in any case it would be selfish to keep it as it was very much a book that should be passed on. Especially if it were to someone special.

We both smiled then. Rather shyly.

Rebecca

Robert spilt wine on my wrist on our first date ('Adventure Date the First' as he referred to it). He had ordered a bottle and was chivalrously pouring when it occurred; I noticed his body tense in horror. I liked that so I pretended it hadn't happened. I didn't react, Instead I allowed him to get away with it (or rather I allowed him to think he had gotten away with it). I let him convince himself it hadn't happened then I reminded him of it months later when it was safe. When it was okay for us both to laugh at his misfortune. When there wasn't an outcome to be determined and no decision in the balance. Looking back, I suspect it might not have mattered though anyway. Robert was always able to laugh at himself. I guess it was mostly me – I didn't want to risk something that I could already sense was precious.

Chapter 11

<A link to book will appear here at 12pm (Midday)>

I was internet–connected, poised and ready. £300 for a one night stay in a one–bedroom ship–shaped hotel overlooking the Thames. An art installation calling itself living–architecture or some such? *Ridiculous.* That was my first thought. My initial inclination. But it had ensnared Rebecca's heart. 'Imaginative use of time and space and location... truly unique… re–invigoration of an established London landscape...' That sort of jargon, that style of spiel – you get the idea. Rebecca could articulate it better than me, but you get the picture – she was enchanted, mesmerised by the thought of spending a night there. And her enthusiasm was infectious and even though I pretended otherwise I soon became hooked on the idea too. I'd started to fully imagine it too. The Art Boat, that's how we referred to it when we stood hand in hand on the Southbank and gazed up till giddy, The Art Boat.

Arseboat.

Rebecca explained that it was all to do with Conrad's *Heart of Darkness* – that it was based on his novel and the boat he had called the *Rois des Belges.* That was another tome I was unfamiliar with but I didn't mind, it didn't lessen the idea. Especially once Rebecca revealed that lots of writers would be invited to stay there – I was caught with that thought – men and women like

Mark Twain held aloft alongside another great river whilst scribbling away in order to entertain, educate and amuse.

Mostly though I recognised its romance – I imagined it being like the ark washed atop Mount Ararat (but without the noise and mess of two of every species). I imagined just me and Rebecca. Just us. Just the two of us. And the beast of the River Thames. And Big Ben chiming. And traffic funnelling on Waterloo Bridge. And all the tiny ants scurrying below, completely unaware of our stare. Horatio Robert Foxley and Rebecca Susan Morley – The Omnipotents.

It would cost £300 for the night. But I didn't care. It was something Rebecca desired. And I would give her anything I could. £300 for one night. Nothing. Not really. Not when all was considered. In no time I'd imagined it all. I'd imagined myself and herself and a candlelit crow's nest dinner. I'd imagined myself and herself clasped in an embrace whilst looking out over the skyline. I'd imagined myself and herself gaily copulating on an elevated stage in the middle of London. I'd even imagined her special–for–the–occasion lingerie, my mind's eye had provided all the essential detail. It would be more than well worth the outrageous price. It would be an Adventure, an 'experience', a memory and a triumph. I'd probably even write a poem about it.

Rebecca had first come to know of the curious accommodation after having read a review in the Art section of the *Sunday Times.* She breathlessly explained how it was to be called the *Room for London* and that it was a houseboat that would never know water. Instead, it would be 'moored' courtesy of a crane and clever engineering to sit atop the Queen Elizabeth Hall. Rebecca enthusiastically explained how it would have a shower room behind burgundy leather curtains and many other splendid accoutre–wonderments.

Four minutes…

I'd clicked at exactly midday and immediately the 'great minds think alike, you are in a queue' electronic message had appeared and the web's worldwide cogs had started their whirring. I had my credit card poised, ready and waiting. I had our names, birth dates, email addresses and phone numbers already typed out ready to satisfy all potential security requirements; I'd done my homework and my preparation. Rebecca would be impressed. Very. And delighted. She would cry the happy tears.

Then came THE message,

`<Unlucky! LOSER!>`

Words to that effect. Being in the queue had obviously been no guarantee, all nights were now sold, there were no other options, no other availability, no second chance. Sorry you were unsuccessful. *A failure.* It was 12:04.

Four minutes...

And that was that; that was one of the cracks that let in the trickle. If we'd had that treat to look forward to maybe things would have been different, maybe she wouldn't have...

But we didn't have that Ultimate Adventure Date to look forward to, I'd failed her. I'd raised her hopes only to let her down once more. If I'd achieved my promised intent then maybe the rekindling would have worked. She might have believed in me anew. Perhaps she'd have been more patient.

And maybe Damian wouldn't have seemed so diametrically desirous.

Four minutes…

Heart of Darkness…

Rebecca

Robert did become pseudo–obsessed with Mark Twain but I never thought of it as a problem. I accepted it as just another quirk and it was quite flattering that he'd gone to all that trouble to research the author after I'd introduced him to *Huckleberry Finn.* Robert would say things like

"Did you know Gertrude of Nivelles was the patron saint of cats? I bet Mark Twain knew that, he loved cats you know."

Bizarre in a way, but rather endearing, it never worried me. I accused him once of being in love with Mark Twain, told him I could easily become jealous, but again I was just teasing (or 'slandermongering' as Robert would refer to it) in the way we always did. I never actually thought...

I was truly shocked when his sister told me to what extent it had grown.

Chapter 12

The months passed, the Date Adventures rolled on majestically, and I read and researched Mark Twain fervently. I discovered that he had been great pals with an archetypal 'mad scientist' – the pigeon–loving genius Nikola Tesla, and that Mark would sometimes help him conduct exotic electricity experiments.

I'd also earned that Mark Twain had not had the easiest of lives and that he'd suffered both physically and mentally – from bouts of depression and years of constipation. I was concerned by this news and then very relieved when I later found out that one day Tesla had invited Mark Twain to stand on his 'Healing Machine' and then quite literally sent a shock up him. Mark swore this cured his constipation.

When I dug deeper, I discovered that actually this was the very least Tesla could do for his friend – indeed it was a classic case of quid pro quo as Mark Twain had once saved Tesla's life. The great scientist had been physically ailing and given up any faith or hope in his doctors saving him. Then,

> *"One day I was handed a few volumes of new literature unlike anything I had ever read before and so captivating as to make me utterly forget my hopeless state. They were the earlier works of Mark Twain and to them might have been due the miraculous recovery which followed. Twenty–five years later, when I met Mr. Clemens and we formed a friendship between us, I told him of the experience and was amazed to see that great man of laughter burst into tears."*

I was not amazed. That was what I had very quickly realised and so many seemed to have missed; Mark Twain was not just a 'humorist' (as our American friends are keen to spell it), he was also an incredibly sensitive soul who would, could and wanted to do all in his power to alleviate the suffering of others. He was a friend to all. He knew us and he understood our pain. He spoke to each and every one of his readers and all he ever wanted was for us to be happy. If he could help anyone in any way then he always would.

I also learned that Thomas Edison turned out to be another chum and that he had made a video of Mark Twain in 1909. I found it on YouTube and watched it incessantly. And although it was silent it was still brilliant. In it Mark wears his white suit and he doesn't do a lot – he stands for a bit, smokes for a bit, walks for a bit and then sits down for tea with daughters Clara and Jean for a bit. But it's perfect.

In the short film Mark is talking to the camera but you can't actually hear him. Which at first is a bit weird. Then after further research I discovered there are no voice recordings of Mark Twain in existence and although I was initially disappointed it didn't matter because I could always imagine what his voice sounded like.

I just could.

I continued my immersion, I read every one of Mark Twain's books and was always royally rewarded; *A Tramp Abroad* described how he and his chum (the Reverend Joseph Twitchell) took a month–long tramp together (a 'tramp' turned out to be a trek). It was a book about a walking tour through the Alps in which they went out of their way to avoid actually walking any part of it. Mark Twain stated it was a book "written by one loafer for a brother loafer to read." That was his genius too; he made you feel like a brother, a part of his family, he spoke to you directly. He understood you completely. He told you what you already knew but hadn't known you knew. And he didn't patronise or preach he just made you recognise and realise.

He understood.

And it wasn't just his books that revealed, I was getting to know the whole man and not just the writer. I had to. I was compelled. I wasn't satisfied merely knowing his literary life, I needed to know it all. I was gripped from the start. And I was surprised to discover that his genius didn't infect all of his life – for example he wasn't the brightest of businessmen – he had lost a huge amount of money through the demise of his publishing business and then took another hit when the Paige Compositor (an early type–writer–type invention that he'd invested heavily in) proved pretty much useless. (He'd kinda bet Betamax when he should have voted VHS.) I discovered such entrepreneurship broke him but didn't break him. In fact, it was his ability to scribble and spout like no other that soon put him back on his feet – he did an "Around the World" tour in 1895–1896 that comfortably cleared his debts. His priceless humour always worth twice whatever the price.

I explained all this to Rebecca (it turned out she knew some of it but had never delved into the detail). "Why would I?" She asked a trifle wearily when I interrogated her. I smiled and told her that it was forgivable to be only partially informed and that I would happily fill her in. And I did – I told her about Mark Twain's triumphant turns in London – the packed concert halls and the press adoration. I told her about the satire and wit and social commentary that had left them rolling in the aisles. I told her how I'd have loved to have seen it. And how I could so very easily imagine it.

Mark Twain in my home town…

I continued to delve and discover (and to share my research with a mildly bemused Rebecca). And the more I knew the more I wanted to know. I wanted to be a know–it–all. A complete and utter. And of course, there are things that lots of people know about Mark Twain – the fact he predicted his own death being one of the most common ones. It's true, he predicted his demise stating,

> "I came in with Halley's Comet in 1835. It is coming again next year, and I expect to go out with it. It will be the greatest disappointment of my life if I don't go with Halley's Comet. The Almighty has said,

> no doubt: Now here are these two unfathomable freaks; they came in together, they must go out together."

I now know a lot of people know that and quite a few more know about his persistent wearing of a white suit and also the "greatly exaggerated" death quote; those things were fairly commonly known but there was so much more. There was a great depth of goodness. I discovered that Rudyard Kipling had stated

"To my mind Mark Twain was beyond question the largest man of his time, both in the direct outcome of his work and more important still, if possible, in his indirect influence as a protesting force in an age of iron philistinism."

And Mr Kipling wasn't the only one, there were many others heavy with their praise – a multitude – a vast array of complimenteers – and all they stated were his facts – humourist – satirist – genius – thoroughly good egg – Twain was all of these; the more I discovered the more all the platitudes rang true. He was much and more to all men.

I learned other things too – I found out that the steamboats Mark Twain piloted were precariously flammable and this meant you had to drive in the dark as no lamps were allowed. For this reason, a steamboat pilot needed an in–depth knowledge of the ever–changing river. I discovered Mark Twain had to study 2,000 miles of the Mississippi for more than two years before he received his steamboat pilot license in 1859.

Then I found out something else and it shocked me significantly. I discovered that Mark encouraged his brother, Henry, to follow his lead and gain employment on a steamboat too. Henry did. And then died. On June 21, 1858 to be precise. When the steamboat Mark had advised him to work on exploded. Can you imagine that? I tried to. The heartbreak – the remorse – the torment – the regret.

The guilt.

I spent a long time trying to imagine. And I researched more and I learned that Mark Twain continued as a riverboat pilot (with all the demons that may have been onboard) journeying up and down the Mississippi ala Huck and Jim until the American Civil War broke out in 1861.

And I realised from my research that despite the mourning of his brother this was largely a time of freedom and happiness for Mark Twain. I was able to imagine that too. A great man at the wheel of a mighty vessel. Just as I could imagine Huck and Jim equally happy on a rickety raft. I could picture all three of their smiles: genuine, wide and honest.

I also discovered (this time without the merest flicker of surprise) that Mark Twain was a very popular Steamboat pilot and that he drew eager crowds and entertained throngs wherever he anchored. Of course he did. That was what he was like.

Mark Twain.

Bringer of joy.

Rebecca

That meeting with Robert's sister was hard. I dreaded it but knew it was right so I agreed. I thought she would hate me. Blame me for Robert's upset and the state he'd gotten himself into. She wasn't angry though just thoroughly saddened and that was ten times worse. She didn't mention Damien but I'm sure she knew. She didn't outright accuse me or slap me or anything that I might have expected. Maybe she recognised I couldn't feel any worse or any more guilty. We just hugged and I tried not to cry.

Later she made us tea and (avoiding the wanton elephant in the room) we talked about the better days – Robert and how funny he had always been. His sister told me about the time Robert was sent home from school because he'd written a love poem from the head mistress and placed it in the pocket of the caretaker's donkey jacket. Apparently, there'd been quite a commotion when the caretaker's wife, the local lollipop lady, stormed into assembly demanding an explanation. I told his sister about the time Robert wanted me to send a jar of posh lemon curd and a packet of Brussels sprouts to the head of BBC commissioning with an elaborate cover letter explaining his proposal for a new show called 'Feastsenders.'

We smiled a little then and wondered if perhaps it was just the two of us who had found him amusing.

Chapter 13

This one's easy, it's one of those vivid memories that stay locked. The ones you step into regularly and without warning – slip–whoops–BANG! One of an increasing collection which I've come to know as The Excruciators.

Our sex life had been deteriorating when it could have been improving. When it *would* have been improving if Rebecca had been prepared to put as much effort into adapting it as I was. And I was surprised because she was supposed to be the arty one. She was always the sexier one. I had hope–assumed the experiment would be right up her street. I'd generally guessed right in the past.

I tried to explain it all to her: how work was increasingly intolerable; how although George had only been my boss for 1 month 3 weeks and 4 days it was patently obvious that he was from the planet Tedia–Mundanium – that he was unarguably an alien irritant sent to insensitively suck my soul and mercilessly mash my marrow. I tried to explain to Rebecca how it was imperative that I respond if I was going to survive. How I had to strengthen in order to be able to retaliate. How, if I was going to cope, I had no option but to completely re–think my sex life.

Our sex life.

I explained that things would have to be different. I'd read an article.

"Tantra doesn't advocate hedonistic indulgence that depletes the life force."

Rebecca had nodded slowly after I afforded her that revelation, as if she might be slightly dubious. Then she said, "What?"

And then, before I could elaborate, she'd followed up with,

"Actually, whatever, let's give it a go if it makes you happy."

And it did make me happy; I firmly believed it would help. But after only a few sessions I could sense Rebecca was less sure – she had begun to be irked. And one day, sat cross–legged and directly opposite me whilst completely naked and supposedly focused on sharing my breath, she said, "Apologies if I appear to be repeating myself but, all this… it's just… *what?*"

(It was around this time that I began to notice she was using a lot of italic words during our conversations.)

I tried harder to explain.

"Sexual energy is an important reservoir that should be used wisely to boost the spiritual process rather than block it through orgasmic release."

"And that's why we're not allowed to touch?"

"I need to practice ejaculatory retention."

"That sounds like an ailment."

"Rebecca, please. It will help me cope with work, with George."

"My aunt Gwendoline retained water on the knee. It didn't improve her mood any."

"I think that's different. I need to retain because then stimulation will build and push upward into my higher Chakric centres which will make me more spiritually powerful. George won't be able to annoy me then."

"Oh right. I understand completely now. Exactly. *What?*"

"We can't be too tactile as one mishap could ruin everything. If I physically release my energy now then tomorrow I'll be akin to a drowsy antelope – helpless and vulnerable. Prey to the beast."

So instead, I insisted we sat close and naked and yet notably apart. I tried to teach Rebecca what to do; explained it was supposed to be goose for the gander too. I wasn't meaning to be wholly selfish.

"Clench your PC muscle on the inhale and on the exhale release"

"I beg your pardon?"

"You know… your… what you use to… never mind, just

push your hands up in the air – leave your heart open to the sky."

At his point, I reached under the sofa for my brand–new Chakra Tuned Tibetan Singing Bowl (which had arrived the day before from an eBay shop located in Kowloon). I raised it high between us and let the light of the enlightened centuries pour unto it. (And on one level yes, I knew that it was really the light of an energy saver bulb from Morrisons, but that wasn't what mattered, it was about getting all metaphysical.) And so, after bowing to the elaborately decorated pot three times (which again, may or may not have been necessary) I gave it a resounding tap with my singing stick. Then tried to match my vocals to the sound of the singing metal.

"Ooooooooooooooooooooooooooooooooooooo."

Rebecca just stared at me. Stared hard. Which was somewhat off–putting. But I continued.

Then, after my chant finished, I rested my forehead on the bowl and felt the need to explain.

"I'm going to try and see through the Third Eye."

"Pervert."

"It's located between the eyebrows. Touching the vibrating rim of the bowl will stimulate my ajna."

"That's nice. But listening to you wail like a lunatic certainly isn't stirring my *ajna.*"

"I… I've read about it."

"It doesn't sound like Mark Twain."

"No. No it doesn't. No, it's not him actually… but it's just something that I hope will help.

I've googled it, you are obviously suffering…"

"I certainly am."

"You are obviously suffering from the expectations burdened upon you by the mainstream media – sex and how a woman should respond – it's not always going to work."

"It always *used* to work."

"Our waves of energy need to be engaged and able to flow – feel the sacredness within me."

"I think I'd prefer to feel something within *me.*"

She had her arms folded at this stage and that was never a good sign. It certainly wasn't going to help her relax. She did look incredibly beautiful though and it's almost too hard for me to explain; it physically hurts to recall. *It's the details that do the most damage.* Maybe if you can just imagine a cross–legged naked angel? With a frown. There was never a moment when I didn't realise I was lucky.

But I decided to ignore the danger and continue.

"Energy from my head will reach your yoni…"

"Chance would be a fine thing."

"Rebecca! You don't seem to be taking this seriously. You're spoiling it."

"I'm spoiling it? Me? You haven't touched my *Yogi* in a month!"

And with that she got up and started to dress. And she turned away from me as she did so. And that had never happened before. And I tried not to worry about that but to stay in the moment and so I tried to circular breathe but I couldn't really remember how because I hadn't written down the instructions and now my leg was cramping and Rebecca was putting her shoes on and I was kind of starting to panic a little.

"Rebecca? Where? Don't… It's not all about union of the sceptre and the lotus!"

Now Rebecca was buttoning her coat. And I was properly panicking. I tried to undo myself but I've never been very supple (it had taken a while to assume my cross–legged position and now I was somewhat locked in–situ).

I bum–shuffled toward her.

"Rebecca?"

"What Robert? What! Can you actually see yourself?"

And then she was leaving and her toe was colliding with my brand new, Chakra Tuned Tibetan Singing Bowl and sending it spinning across the floor.

And that was that as far as Rebecca, Tantra and I were concerned. There was worse to follow. Not that I knew that at the time. There was the ban to come. Then the worse thing.

Then everything.

Could I see myself?

She certainly could not see what I saw, she didn't have to see what I had to see (for 8 hours a day) – George in all his gory. Rebecca was blessed with choice. She did not have to spend five days a week staring into the infinite craw of over–spiel. She did not have to endure the full gamut of his fur–rimmed tunnel of torrent. She wasn't faced every morn with a pair of healthy pink metronome gums and an over–generous set of incessantly mobile and meticulously flossed enamels. All framed by that ridiculous forest of foliage. (George even has a special brush specifically for "beard sustentation." He honestly does. He actually showed me. He uses it in the office.) I googled (I felt impelled) and concluded – George is a full–on pogonophile.

Rebecca didn't understand. Rebecca worked amidst objects of exquisite art not opposite a hirsute life–blotting arse. She wasn't seeing what I saw and hence she didn't get the urgency of my need. The healing ceremonies I'd been encouraging were not for the purpose of sexual gratification but rather to expand my potential – to help me reach new heights of fulfilment on a mental and emotional level. To help counter–act the crucifying. But Rebecca didn't appreciate their importance. Didn't accept my need.

The next time I tried to discuss it she just told me that I was the most frustrating man she had ever met. And that I should decide what I wanted from life. And if work was really so challenging and George wasn't my cup of tea then why didn't I show some initiative and do something about it? Why didn't I just leave? And then she told me that to "*help me*" (and that's how she said it – unambiguous italics) to get a new job she'd provide me with "*an incentive.*" She said there'd be no more sex – tantric, exotic, mainstream, Maori, Moroccan, Mauritian, Mancunian or otherwise, until my CV had been updated and half a dozen employment agencies approached. No sex at all. In effect she had decreed that now everyone would suffer.

Everyone except George.

And perhaps on some level I realised the frustration she spoke of had been building, that it was something she'd been feeling for a while, that maybe it wasn't just having to listen to me whinge about George, that perhaps she might have had other concerns, things I maybe avoided talking about, conversations I would always try to divert. Perhaps on some level I was aware but I was never truly concerned. I knew that I loved Rebecca Susan Morley and I knew that she Loved Horatio Robert Foxley and so surely all the rest was mere detail? Things would always work out. I never worried about our relationship. I knew nothing could threaten it. I never had any doubt that we were destined. That it was meant to be.

Not from that very first day...

I ended up telling his sister lots of things – just little things; I told her of our frequent kitchen debates – how Robert had made me promise not to use the crusts of a loaf till last – how this would ensure the rest of the bread remained restrained, fresh and feisty. How it would "maintain order within the ranks and avoid riots within the wrapper". She agreed that yes, he could be vocal and persistent on curious things. I told her how I'd retaliated by telling him that not only was it barbaric to add milk to a teabag whilst waiting for the kettle to boil but had also patiently explained the idiocy in such action – that any time saved was then lost due to the subsequent brewing process now taking considerably longer. I told her how one or other of us would roll our eyes at Monty during these debates and how she would happily wag her tail to offer support. His sister laughed and said it sounded as if we were as bad as each other and wondered how the dog had put up with the pair of us.

I was half–tempted to tell her about this letter. Writing it does seem to help a little.

But it can't in anyway explain.

Chapter 14

I'm changing at Stratford; I'm going underground. Alight here for the Central Line. I head for the end of the platform. When heading west rear is best.

The train emerges from its tunnel – up and into the daylight (a gloom–ish grey). Its head rattles toward me then past me then its carriages follow and finally there's a halt in front of me. The Central Line has buttons on its doors but they are dysfunctional – a green square for open and a red square for close – but they are redundant. Without any prompting each door opens at every stop. Each door closes without encouragement too. These buttons are no longer pushed. They are useless. They've had their time and are no longer required. The doors open without bidding and I step straight on. I've positioned my standing exactly – experience ensuring inch perfect alignment. I step straight on and immediately turn left making bee–line for my usual – the end seat – the corner – the very last edge of the train. It provides solid steel against my shoulder. Comfort of a kind.

I sit then look. Look around. The inner surroundings. The familiar furnishings. The red clutch–me poles are in need of a lick. They appear aged. Their colour has ebbed, their shine diminished, they bear the scars of apathy. Chipped veneer and a dark rusting underbelly. Disquieting when revealed. The seat cushioning is suggestive too – a slackened patriotism – an almost union – red white and blue mostly greyed. Thrones for London's millions. Tatty arse–rests wearied by the weight of responsibility, jaded of the honour. One has been savaged. Split open. Scarred. A two–inch horizontal. Frayed droopings either side. The fractured face of Fu Manchu?

I don't have to look around. I can look forward. I can look up. Face the messages. Allow the ads to speak. They will anyway. *I can't stop them.* Not anymore.

I AM HAIR LOSS? I AM IT NEEDN'T BE THE END OF THE LINE. I AM FEMFRESH. I AM WOO HOO FOR MY FROO FROO.

I can look down. stare at the detritus. Listen to their trauma.

I AM CRUMPLED COFFEE CUP. I AM STAINED MAGAZINE. I CAN CLOSE MY EYES.

And now the doors close and the train moves and we're heading off. I'm on my way to work.

George will be waiting. Clammily clasping the Late Book.

Rebecca said I shouldn't let him stress me out.

All too not quite soon enough we reach Oxford Circus. I can exit. Out the door and up the escalator. Clasp tight to the rail.

I AM 'STAND ON THE RIGHT'. I AM 'NO SMOKING'. I AM 'PENALTY FOR IMPROPER USE'. I AM "DON'T PUSH!" I AM "CAREFUL!" I AM ILL–PREPARED. I AM OVERWHELMED. I AM HYPERVEN... I AM…

Up – through the barrier – out into the light – breathing.

My old boss, Christine (who taught me all the payroll I needed to know) left to indulge her passion for iguana breeding. She was the type to follow her dreams and she did actually; she left to set up a specialized pet shop called 'The Reptile Renaissance.' I had liked Christine. We got on. We were comfortable around each other. *She* never embarrassed me by confiding bizarre details of her marital sex life. *She* never made me squirm. When she sat opposite, I worked diligently to ensure there were no errors on the payroll, as much for Christine as for myself. And I was pleased for her when she resigned as I could tell she was excited about the future. It would have been wrong to be resentful. I bought her the Jurassic Park Box Set as a leaving present.

Because I produce the payroll (having learnt on the job), I have a fair idea of everyone's salary. Actually, that's not true; I do not have a 'fair idea' of everyone's salary. I have *exact* knowledge of everyone's salary. Consequently, I know that George's salary is exactly 2.847 times that of mine. I'm also very much aware that I do not have a company car (as George does). But he has ponderously explained to me (with no apparent awareness irony) that I can apply for a low–interest loan to purchase a train season ticket.

Now I've arrived in the office and there are no more ads to distract. My options have narrowed. I'm left looking up at the cheap white plastic that truly taunts.

I AM TICK. I AM TOCK.

I know its face like no other.

It's a face that sits above his face.

Hard to look at one, hard to look away from the other.

I never watched the clock when Christine sat opposite. We worked calmly until we were feeling the need and then one of us would suggest "Chocolate?" and head for the vending machine. Meanwhile the other would head for the coffee dispenser and procure two. Then we'd re–convene, put on the answer phone and chat about interesting stuff for a full fifteen minutes.

Christine had a nice husband called David. He used to pick her up from the office sometimes and every time he'd smile a welcome and shake my hand. He once pretend–whisper told me that Christine wanted him to dress up as a lizard on Valentine's Day. She of course overheard and friendly scowled him. I could tell they were happy.

I never imagined I'd be remembering Christine's conversations and comparing them with George's. When the fifteen minutes 'Coff n Choc' break was up, the phones would go back on and we'd return to our tasks without the merest slither of resentment. George has never bought me so much as a mini Mars Bar and I don't bring him a beverage. I don't do much at all now. Today, for example, I have only produced one thing of any neo–worth – a poem.

The Tragedy of the Workplace

It's the trivial that breaks us,
The small irritations that chip away and ultimately destroy,
George promised to buy some new self–seal envelopes,
He has forgotten,
I'm having to lick old–school traditional gummed efforts,
They are cheaper,
George may have forgotten deliberately.

It's perhaps not Percy but it is helping get me through the day.

Then I will be able to leave this box.

Trade it for another.

Go underground.

But be it Shelley or Shirley, Byron or Bean it can only ever help a tiny bit because it hasn't taken long and there are 8 torturous hours in every torturous day and each one now lasts far longer than the last. Time is stumbling, ticking through treacle. The clock is tormenting me with its care–not crawly face and George is asking me increasingly inane questions. Questions I don't want to answer because I know that to do so will lessen me. I don't want to speak unless I have something interesting or entertaining to say. If I speak merely for the sake of it I will become something other, something amiss. I don't want to add my half–hearted mutter to his relentless spew and hence I desperately wish he wouldn't speak. *At all.*

Rebecca said I shouldn't let George stress me out.

I mostly wish George wouldn't tell me things; for example, I don't care if, "The milk in the staff kitchenette has a use by date of only tomorrow."

And I don't necessarily agree that, "Whoever buys it should check to ensure they get the freshest."

I don't necessarily agree and I don't care and I don't want to add my comment to this pointless pile. I could tell him that all the milk will be drunk today anyway. Or I could inform him that it's Sarah 2, the early receptionist that buys it on her way in and I can well imagine that she has neither the time nor the inclination to rummage around inspecting every pint in the Sainsbury's Local wardrobe–sized refrigerators. That could be my comment. But I don't add it because it's not interesting, worthy or amusing. Not interesting, worthy or amusing enough. So instead, I just give a half grunt which in my mind translates as *Please please please just shut the Fellaini up!* But in his mind no doubt translates as *Hmm, yes, a sage and perceptive point, well done George, tireless inspirer and leader toward greatness – you truly are the champion!*

Rebecca said I shouldn't let George stress me out.

There was a month between Christine's departure and George's start. He had to work his notice or some such. During that interim I ran the Payroll Department on my own and there were no errors reported. At the end of the four weeks the Personnel Director thanked me and shook my hand but my salary was not increased and I received no bonus. As far as I'm aware I had not been considered for Christine's job. And I had certainly not approached management to ask if I might be considered for Christine's job. Even though Rebecca had urged that course of action.

Last week there were 6 errors and this triggered some angry calls to the payroll department. When they arrived, I asked if the callers would like to speak to 'The Payroll Director' (that's not George's official job title but it is how he has asked me to refer to him). George was unable to answer their queries and on each occasion the phone call was transferred back to me.

Rebecca said I shouldn't let George stress me out.

Initially I was open–minded about having a new boss. I hadn't been a–feared; Christine had been involved in the recruitment process and she had assured me that they'd only offer the job to someone I'd get on with. I had absolutely no reason to distrust Christine but I have since learnt that good intentions don't always result in fine deeds. There weren't too many candidates as far as I could gather but Christine was involved in the interview process and beaming when she informed me that one chap had impressive qualifications *and* liked football. I perked up and asked which team he supported. She told me Oldham Athletic. I said, "Oh."

Rebecca said I shouldn't let George stress me out…

Rebecca

Robert's sister told me how pleased his Dad had been when we'd gotten together. She'd agreed with him that I would be a good influence. (His sister didn't seem to be sarcastic when she told me this – I guess they're all nice in that family.) She said they were both just pleased to see him happy and that they knew he could be difficult sometimes. Her praise made me feel worse. We talked for hours that day and now speak regularly on the phone. I've told her more than I ever imagined I would. Much more. Not quite everything though.

Maybe that's because it still doesn't feel real. It's still so difficult to accept. To imagine even. Or am I not being *truthful* enough? Maybe I need to consider *him* more – *Little Dick Damien.* Maybe focused reflection on that might provide the realism that threatens to escape me?

I don't think the growing up together thing bothered him half as much as it did me; it possibly didn't bother him at all. He was an only child; I was an only child and our mothers had become bosom buddies hence we were destined to spend much of our childhood together. Then be somewhat socially–tied as adults – obligated to be friends. I don't believe it was fate. Just coincidence that ultimately had consequence. Horrific consequence.

Chapter 15

I suppose there was an inkling even in those early days, not that I had it, not really. I chose not to have it I guess. You don't have to have an inkling you see, indeed I would argue it's often best not to. It's healthier not too. *There's an inkling here if you choose to accept it, sir?* No thank you. *No thank you very much indeed.* What would I want with an inkling? What could I have done with the inkling they were offering? What use would it have been? It was their questions more than anything – their subtle nip chip nip chip chippings.

"So… You met our daughter in Hampstead? But you don't sound... typical. Where do you live, Horatio?"

"You can call me Robert. I prefer it. I live in a beautiful Grade 2 listed cottage in Dagenham."

"Really?"

"No. It's a two–bed flat. Top floor."

"Oh."

"Yes. It has very nice views. Of the derelict B & Q warehouse and car park."

"Oh. And where did you study?"

"Warren Comprehensive."

"Oh. And university?"

"No, it's just a comp."

That was the sort of thing, you could never truly relax. Christmas dinner was the worst, the one that I got invited to (the first and only one). It wasn't just "Pass the sprouts – pull the crackers – more cranberry darling?" Not in that house. It was the undercurrent. *The undertow.* The trailing statements that weren't questions yet asked so much.

"We've always encouraged Rebecca to be ambitious... her cousin married a vet... children can be very expensive... Damien's bought a lovely new car..."

It was OK though, I could deal with it, I enjoyed the challenge in truth. Kind of. Bait is only bait if it gets a bite. I employed diversionary tactics. Tried to at least.

"Pigs in Blankets eh? I wonder who came up with that? Why don't we say Sows in Sweaters? Oh, and did you know King Wencelas has pizza for Christmas dinner? He rings up and asks for deep pan crisp and even. No? Okay, never mind, old joke… but it usually gets a half a smile… if just out of politeness… oh well, anyone for charades?"

Rebecca seemed uncomfortable, agitated, angry even. But I wasn't sure who with. Then things got worse when Damien popped in for mulled wine. He received a hero's welcome and produced biscuits from Fortnum and Mason. Well and truly trumping my Tesco Finest mince pies. Then he sat down at the piano and tickled out some yuletide tunes. Even though no one had asked him to. And he kept calling Rebecca's mum Elizabeth. And I suddenly regretted calling her "Mrs Rebecca's Mum." Especially as she seemed completely enthralled with the chino–wearing champion. I could tell she was making comparisons. Which was rather uncharitable. Quite rude in fact. Especially considering the season.

He wasn't finished there either, not old Damey. As soon as he had finished his tinklings he was straight on to revealing the size of his bonus. I fair spluttered my eggnog. (More at the cliché than the audacity.) Next up, and without any of us having asked for advice, Damien told us he had to be careful about giving advice what with insider info and what–not. He then tapped his nose, winked and proceeded to advise us to buy Unilever for a safe long–term bet, Hamra for a reliable dividend yield, to be wary of over–fancying the emergent economies and of course to always ensure we had a risk–balanced diversified portfolio. He summed up by declaring that, in his game, the secret of success and satisfaction was to "find the value of something and then pay less."

Everyone seemed fascinated.

Most everyone.

When he finally got up to leave Damien got an affectionate hug followed by a hearty clap on the back from Rebecca's dad, Norman. Damien grinned and slipped an expensive–looking cigar into Norman's shirt pocket. He then got a double cheek peck and an enthusiastic squeeze from 'Elizabeth' and even Rebecca granted him an air kiss. By way of deliberate afterthought, he finally turned toward me. We swapped the merest of cursory nods.

The next morning, when I made my own excuses, I had to settle for a very firm handshake from Norman. One allied with a silent yet steely–eyed warning. Mother Dear followed up that jab with one air peck, no squeeze and a question – "Do you want to take your mince pies with you?"

I remember feeling quite nauseous.

But then Rebecca slipped her hand in mine and informed her parents that she was taking me for "a fun drive to Highgate" and we walked together out of the door and into the air and instantly everything was excellent again.

And hence I ignored the inkling, I didn't allow it, I chose not to accept it. I didn't have an inkling because I most definitely did not want one.

Rebecca

Our mothers had far more in common than Damian and I did. They both attended St Joseph's religiously; they were regulars at 10 am every Sunday and tried to fit in at least one or two weekday masses. They were stalwarts I suppose you might say, pillars even, they would always eagerly volunteer to present the offertory and both signed up for the cleaning rota. Which was comical really seeing as they both employed the same home help, her name was Miu. Damien's mother and mine were competitive in a sort of polite middle–class friendly–yet–not–unimportant way. They would always Bring and Buy at the annual sale and they always baked their cakes with the finest ingredients. It was strange to think of them on their knees in the pews, each trying to outdo the other to appear most conscientious, most feverish with their generosity. I sometimes wondered what Miu would have thought if she knew. And I never told Robert as I was sure he'd be unable to resist a wry comment. I knew I couldn't tell Robert as I could guess the look he'd give me.

Actually, who am I kidding? I did tell him. Of course I did. In the end I always told him everything. I told him and he did give me that very look I'd imagined. And of course, I blushed but later we laughed and he said something like "irony is the only reality" then promised if I kept mum about his winking impairment, he'd keep mum about my ridiculously rivalrous mum.

Chapter 16

Mark Twain *is* a funny guy. Even when he's not joking (which he never truly is.) He's never just making light when he's making light, I understood that from the start. I got it. Mark Twain is a funny guy whose humour veils essence. Expiate... a word with resonance – I was in his debt. Expiate – to atone for; make amends or reparation for: to *expiate* one's crimes…

Atonement.

Maybe that's what's going on here? I don't know though. In truth I haven't a clue. It turns out it's Wednesday morning and it transpires I'm in a meeting. One I've apparently been warned about but had fully forgotten about. One I probably should have prepared for. But of course, I hadn't planned to be here. In any capacity. And I no doubt wouldn't be if I hadn't encountered the Count and he hadn't made me chuckle with his unorthodox Dyson interpretation. Hah! Maybe that was his message – *Don't die son*. Ha! Or do? *Do die son.*

Maybe Mark sent him to remind me but I misinterpreted and now it's too late to rewind. Now I'm back here. Unexpectedly. And it's only down to insomnia and a certain homage to irony that I came in today. Actually, there were practical considerations too – I thought I'd spend some quality time in Cubicle 3 plotting my next steps and the company Wi–Fi would help me double–check some important facts.

But that was obviously going to have to wait as right now I was being distracted by this curiosity; there are three of us present in this arranged yet unexpected meeting and it has a very formal feel. There is no fruit in a bowl nor filtered coffee being offered. It's one of those. And 'atonement' doesn't seem the right word somehow – it's too upbeat. 'Punishment' comes more to mind. Or 'Retribution.' No one looks particularly delighted. And I feel a bit sorry for Margot – she probably doesn't overly want to be here either. But I don't feel that sorry for her as I know whose side of the bread she'll ultimately be buttering. She's one of those hierarchical types, and if this is what I'm beginning to expect it is then out of the company's four Human Resource Officers, George has chosen well. I've nodded to Margot in the corridor on more than several occasions but received barely a begrudged nose twitch in return. I've always imagined she's 'professionally aloof' (but only as "rude" would be a very uncharitable presumption).

Our little gathering doesn't have an official title as far as I'm aware but if it did it might be classified as the 'The Friday pm Sleep Disciplinary'. Or some such. (There could well be other misdemeanours under consideration.) It's intriguing to an extent; I'm feeling quite relaxed, expectant. I hadn't anticipated this cosy little rendezvous.

No one is talking. I guess we haven't officially started; the three of us are sat at one end of the large table in the Board Room. I take a moment to consider how 3 should be the more fearful number. It's far worse than 13. Margot has her head down and is reading through notes and I don't know what George is doing because I can't bring myself to look his way. It's OK though, it means I've time to take in my environment; I've time to consider my current situation and to recall situations past. I've been in this room once before. It was during Jo's leaving do, I shared a glass or two of champagne at the gathering in reception then, upon finding the door unlocked, wandered in here, used the monogrammed phone to call my friend Oz in Australia and on the way out dropped a crabstick into the whisky decanter. I feel a bit guilty about that. I glance over, but of course it's not there now.

I turn my attention to Margot and her furrowed brow. I notice her sharp edged briefcase and her plainly cased Smartphone. I think about deficits of imagination, the prevalence of clichés and then the hierarchical thing again – how so much action is pre–

determined – how so little is separate from the game. I then think chains of command. And then just chains. And then I fixate on Margot's brooch. It's purple. A purple crow. I realise I am doomed.

And then the meeting appears to start and so I go with the flow, nodding encouragingly even though I'm not really focused. I'm peripherally aware that someone's being praised for lacking a daisical hence I'm still nodding enthusiastically when I realise Margot is waiting for a verbal response. And so I give her one.

"Release your chains Margot."

"Pardon?"

"Unbuckle your defaults."

"I beg your pardon? Are you being rude?"

George interjects, saying something along the lines of this is what he has to put up with all the time. I let them talk amongst themselves whilst I stare out of the window. A cherry blossom tree sways chaotically in the breeze. It is completely bare. Undressed. It's blossom now departed.

I'm not allowed long in reverie.

"How much did you drink, Robert?"

"Are you referring to Friday?"

"Of course."

"Friday lunchtime?"

"Yes."

"Three bottles of Peroni."

"Three bottles?"

"It's Italian."

"Three bottles in a 45–minute lunch break?"

"Brewed by virgin peasant girls in the Sicilian hills." (I embellished that bit.)

"Three bottles. And did you eat anything?"

"Two vodka jellies." (I made that bit up as well.) "And I may have chewed the beermat, I do that sometimes." (This was true.)

"George is very concerned about your performance."

"He needn't buy a ticket."

It's at this point that I notice Margot's hair. Really notice it I mean. It's bouffant, it's *very* bouffant. Much more so than is usual in HR. I immediately sympathise. Surely she's been teased? Then I panic slightly when I realise there's a theme – she reminds me of another – the Sherry Wife flashes in front of me and I baulk – lurch back in my chair. Imagined sorrow can be shocking. Then just as quickly I regain myself – perhaps acknowledging the suffering of others helps you cope with your own? And then I surmise it's possible that Margot's hair might not be a fashion decision – I think genetics and then the quirks of curl. Perhaps I'm too quick to make assumptions? And in fairness I've never properly studied Margot's hair before. I do now. Intently. I focus and become fascinated. Margot stares back at me. I begin to feel uncomfortable. I'm relieved when she speaks.

"George told me you fell asleep at your desk."

"My sister uses a product called Frizz–Gorn, swears by it."

"George also told me you are not always co–operative."

"George told me he likes to see his wife in just her..."

"Are you being deliberately obstreperous?"

That throws me a little, obstreperous, what does it mean? And now I'm thinking hierarchies again and I'm realising that command of the jargon means command of the jungle. And I'm aware that bullying exists and that not all bullying involves Chinese burns.

"If you wish to waterboard me then just hurry up and get it over with please."

"I don't find that *or you* amusing."

"Oh. I'm disappointed. And somewhat surprised – last year I raised a grand total of £4.73 for Comic Relief." (Another fib I'm ashamed to say.)

"Let's just cut to the chase. This is an official verbal warning. Do you understand that, Robert?"

That throws me too. I wonder about that phrase, 'cut to the chase', it immediately conjures an idea, I suddenly have the images in my head, it's a TV show based around fox hunting. I think it could be a winner – I can picture it – an inner London contemporary version of a long–held upper class tradition. This one would be all inclusive and called 'Urban Hunt' – a panel of highbrows would be sat discussing the ethical arguments for and against when suddenly an Oliver Twist type bursts in and shouts

"Sod this! Let's just cut to the chase!"

And so we do. Suddenly we go live. We hook up to CCTV cameras and watch kids on BMX bikes chase mangy foxes round the back of *Dixy Chicken* then down the alleyways and through the back gardens of East Ham. It could be a winner. I know it has potential. I realise they could regionalise it too, sell the franchise – the scouse version could be called *Scally–Ho*.

Margot interrupts my reverie and the idea instantly dies.

"Robert? Are you listening? This is an official verbal warning. Do you understand, Robert?"

"Oh yes, Margot. Verbal. Then written. Then termination. George has mentioned the triumvirate. Often. Very regularly in fact. Approximately fourteen times. He seems obsessed."

"Right. Good. I'm glad he's made things clear. Well, I'm sorry it's come to this but you still have time to redeem yourself, Robert."

"Expiate."

"Pardon?"

"Atone."

"Yes."

"Redemption..."

"Yes... You still have an opportunity to buck–up your ideas, Robert. To knuckle down."

"Knuckle down and be a buck up…"

"Do you have anything to add, Mr Ainsworth?"

Margot's using full names now, even though it's company policy to be informal. She's being professional. She's using the correct protocol. She'll have attended a course. George T. Ainsworth.

Terrence.

"Thank you, Margot. I would just like to reiterate your thoughts, it's a great shame that it has come to this, Robert. I know you are capable of better and I hope we can move on now and be a lot more professional in future."

"Thank you, Mr Ainsworth. And you, Mr Foxley? Is there anything you'd like to say?"

"I would like to perform a reading from the Holy Rascal according to Quaint Mark."

"I beg your pardon?"

"Nothing. Did you know the Japanese word for cherry blossom trees is Sakura?"

"Excuse me?"

"It roughly translates as Japanese flowering cherry. A lady once told me that…"

"Mr Foxley?"

A *lady*…

"Robert?"

"May I use 'the washroom', please?"

Rebecca

The family dynamic affects us all I suppose. When I introduced Robert to my parents, he wasn't exactly an immediate hit. I had never met anyone like Robert and I guess it's safe to say neither had they. Christmas was a disaster.

That Christmas Day sticks in my memory, the one he spent with me and my parents, *the only one*. (Dad in particular was not keen on a repeat invite.) Robert wasn't really a drinker but had accepted all offers – the single malt scotch on arrival, the wines at the table, the champagne toast, the port with the cheese, the brandy instead of the coffee. He was being quite entertaining, he was clinging to the good side of the cusp, crap jokes about King Wencelas and he'd even gotten away with a risqué Santa poem. It probably would have been alright; it could have been a good day – mum and dad seemed to be defrosting a little. But then Damien arrived and almost immediately Robert faltered – he spontaneously performed his Ostrich dance and then called Damien a "Flummery Fib Face" when he overheard him tell my mother that her vol–au–vents were the greatest he'd ever tasted. The day was steadily downhill after that.

Chapter 17

I suppose they were the happy days. Actually, I don't *suppose*, they *were* the happy days. The happiest of days. But you never realise at the time, you don't clap yourself on the back and say 'hats off mate', you're just happy, you don't think about it. You don't ponder it or analyse it or consider it. But I do now, Christine and Rebecca, two women on my side, it was a good time. It was a time before George was ever imagined, and a time before Damien's devilry was even remotely conceivable.

I think about it now and I remember. I remember all sorts I would otherwise have forgotten.

"It would be a kindness..."

That's what the vet says when he really means, "That poor creature is ready to go. Let me kill him. Destroy him. End his life. Send him to sleep. Put him out of his misery."

It's what "Call me Tom" the Vet said when we took Monty.

"It would be a kindness..."

He said it solemnly. Rebecca cried all the way home. But she realised Tom the vet was right; it had been a kindness. That's what love is about. She loved Monty so she let her go. She stopped the pain. It was a kindness. Love is a kindness. And sex. Sex too. Sex should be associated with cleverness and kindness. Love, sex, cleverness and kindness – you can't hope for more...

"I love you" was the hardest thing I ever said to Rebecca because it was the most important. It was hardest thing I ever said to Rebecca because it was the most risk–laden. It was the hardest thing I ever said to Rebecca because I knew what it meant. How much it meant. And how difficult a non–reciprocation would be. So, for a time I resisted – I didn't say it

– I bit my tongue – fought the urge. But eventually I was brave. And later when I had overcome the obstacles of reticence and fear and I had said the words and they'd been very well received and repeated eagerly in return, then suddenly all was peace. A perfect peace. And we became ourselves – our complete and perfect selves – not our previous worried–about–fully–being–ourselves selves.

And in bed lying face to face we'd smile and silently celebrate. And Rebecca might ask how my winking practice was going. And I might gurn. And then I might complain that there was nothing I could do that she couldn't. And she would at first agree but then she might admit she couldn't do proper press–ups and would position herself on her elbows and then proceed to demonstrate. And I might at first sympathise and then quickly position myself behind to provide focused encouragement and help. Those were the types of things we might do. Just little fun things...

Perfect things.

Kind things.

Sexy things sometimes too – things like Rebecca might say, "I think I've got a bit of a girl–crush on that actress in the new Bond movie."

Then we would spend a–time telling the story – we'd adlib a narrative about me and a tuxedo and a shaken not stirred and a "Whoops! Rebecca what are you and the leading lady doing in my Parisian penthouse? And where are your clothes and no, I have no objections if you and your friend wish to undress me too and lead me to the Jacuzzi. My name is Foxley. Robert Foxley."

Kind, friendly, fun, nonsensical little things.

We never created narratives involving Rebecca shagging the evil transparent villain.

And in truth I'm not sure how long I've held my head here. Or why. My chin is perched at 90 degrees on the middle shelf alongside the punnet of tomatoes. Tomatoes which I don't recall buying and which I now notice have acquired a white furry fringe making them look rather festive. I'm not 100 (or even 12) percent sure why my head is held here. But I am somewhat aware that 'held' is not a wholly accurate word – 'rested' maybe? Or 'wedged'?

I imagine the idea may have been to cool off a little. It's been another trying day – I spent a long time in the washroom and when I returned to room 313 George looked at me strangely and suggested I go home early, in fact why didn't I have a couple of days off, come back after the weekend, he would authorise it and it would mean I could spend time at home doing some serious thinking. I wondered did he practice being so cruel.

But I left anyway and I must have found my way here and I realise I do feel calm. Calm and ready. And that's possibly why when I speak, Mark Twain answers me immediately. The conversation goes like this.

"Do you think maybe I'm stressing about the little stuff too much? Rebecca, Damien, George... Is it all just trivia I mean? Should I be able to see above? See beyond? Paint a bigger canvas or some such? I mean, basically, am I just being a bit of a buffoon?"

> "An autobiography that leaves out the little things and enumerates only the big ones is no proper picture of the man's life at all; his life consists of his feelings and his interests, with here and there an incident apparently big or little to hang the feelings on."

"Right... Er, thanks... So I'm right to be uptight? It's nothing to do with the size of the trivia, it's how deep a chord the trivia strikes?"

> "You can't reason with your heart; it has its own laws, and thumps about things which the intellect scorns."

"Yeah... yeah, that makes sense... you can't reason with your heart... You can't dissect analytically everything that we feel. Gosh, it's a minefield isn't it, Sir? True wisdom can be very elusive don't you think?"

I don't know why I'm calling him Sir; it just seems appropriate, right, respectful. I'm tempted to call him 'Your Highness', I'm well aware how fortunate I am to have his ear.

> "Of the demonstrably wise there are but two: those who commit suicide, and those who keep their reasoning faculties atrophied with drink."

"Yes, sorry… I didn't mean to let you down… so suicide's still the solution eh?"

No answer from the great man. No need? His message was a clear reminder? Straightforward enough? He must be exasperated. He was losing patience but still kind enough to reiterate. It's obvious. He's not a man to keep repeating himself… But… arguably he's being just a little cryptic? He mentioned drink too. But no, who am I kidding – he knows I'm not really one for alcohol abuse – he knows the Peroni and vodka claim was mostly spurious – he knows the real reason I was slumped at my desk. So of course he's still of the same opinion. There's no doubt his advice is unchanged. He must still be urging me to…

"Can you just clarify it completely please Mark? You know, once and for all like…"

No answer. I hold my head steady for another 43 minutes but he doesn't speak again.

Why would he.

Rebecca

I was reading *Huckleberry Finn* when I met Robert on our third date. Our third 'real date' or 'Adventure' as he insisted we call them (we'd agreed not to count the poop inspection, KitKat and coffee one; we referred to that as 'our intro').

As soon as he arrived, he grabbed the paperback, laughed and asked me why I was reading a kid's book. I snatched it back and explained to him that it was not a children's book and that TV adaptations had a lot to answer for. I also informed him that '*The Adventures of Huckleberry Finn*' was regarded by many as the greatest American novel ever written. I told him that Hemingway was a big fan and so were many others. Robert seemed dubious but half interested and so I persevered; I gave him the benefit of the doubt and once we were both cosily settled with drinks I read him a bit.

Robert seemed to like it and I told him that in some ways he reminded me of Mark Twain, that they were both humourists. I explained that Mark Twain was in effect an internationally famous stand–up comedian and how that the lecture halls where he spoke were always packed fit to burst.

Robert seemed to like that comparison, men like a bit of flattery I guess, and although Robert was different he wasn't that different, he wasn't immune. Maybe I shouldn't have mentioned it though, maybe I shouldn't have suggested they were in any way similar and maybe I shouldn't have read to him either because the next day he went online and bought a copy of every single book that Mark Twain had written.

Chapter 18

I said I would and it wasn't a lie. I vowed to endeavour, and endeavour I did. I bought his books and I uncovered his tales. I searched his name and pieced his game. I discovered snippets and nuggets, ingenious gems and lesser known facts. I filled notepads with notes and an album with photos. Then shared my findings with she who'd set me on his trail.

"Did you know Mark Twain used to stay in bed writing every day till noon and that he went prospecting for silver and mining for gold in a place called Jackass Hill?"

"No, I didn't know that Robert."

I drenched myself in his shorts and sundries. I recounted and memorised, retold and regaled. I discovered that it was his 'Jumping Frog' story that first catapulted his career and led to people clamouring for his penning. I loved that – a fictitious frog had gotten the world–a–leap. And the more I read and the more I discovered the more I was there. I was there on the Mississippi steamboat piloted by Twain and I was on the raft he created for Huck and Jim and I was in Calaveras County cheering his feisty frog. That was his genius – his words worked – they made you imagine and they made you believe. And I knew why, instantly I knew why – it was because there was profound truth behind the humour, that's what made you believe – made you *truly* believe – made you *genuinely* believe – made you *fully* believe. His words were alive and honest and too insightful to leave any doubt.

And that one in particular became a constant – that one beautiful book – the gifted one – the Rebecca gifted one – the one called *Adventures of Huckleberry Finn* – the one that had been read so beautifully to me and had triggered my Twain journey and which had now become essential – the one that now bulged my pocket and formed the apex of my exit the flat pyramid checklist: Keys–Wallet–Phone–Paperback.

One man. One book. One whole new world of knowledge. And all thanks to Rebecca.

And I didn't analyse it – I just drifted along enjoying the adventure. I didn't analyse it but if I had I would have realised life at that point was perfect. I had Rebecca Susan Morley and when she wasn't available to entertain me I had Samuel Langhorne Clemens (though of course I mostly used his pen–name – I sensed he would prefer to be addressed as he was best known and loved, Dearest 'Mark Twain'). And it worked perfectly because in the hours when Rebecca wasn't available for Adventure I immersed myself in the words of Mark Twain and researched ever more enthusiastically the life and times of the genius from Missouri. And the more I found out about him the more I felt I knew him – I could picture Mark at home with his one perfect love Olivia, relaxed and happy. Confident. Content. Calm. Composed. I could picture him in his white suit playing billiards with his mates. I could picture him on the veranda smoking his pipe. Confident. Content. Calm. Composed. I could see him stroking a much–loved cat. I could picture him onstage in his iconic white suit entertaining huge crowds. I could see their faces all turned toward him. Admiration and gratitude. Lives enhanced.

"God Bless and Thank you Mr Twain!"

I could see him waving after his encore. I could picture him walking off stage in that legendary and outrageous suit. I could hear the applause of all those lucky enough to have seen him in the flesh. I could fully understand their adoration. Confident. Content. Calm. Composed... Four Big C's. Four difficults to attain. Four trickys to maintain.

I was shocked when I delved deeper and discovered the interweaving of up and down in Mark's career and life – the huge ascents and the horrific descents. I was dismayed by the devils in Twain's details. I felt for him. And admired him all the more – he was a man who understood life because he had experienced pain. I realised the Four Big C's were not an everyday accoutrement, there were scratches beneath such veneer. *Scarring.* Mark Twain knew mankind because Mark Twain had suffered. The Four Big C's were public image. A projection. A cloak atop the suit. I realised that, I sensed that, I was getting to know the real Mark Twain. I was gaining knowledge of the whole man. A man who understood because he'd been hurt.

And I read on and I read more and I read everything Mark Twain had written. And if I wasn't with Rebecca then I would be with Mark. I spent time in bed with both. I spent time in pubs with both. I spent time sipping coffee with both. I took the train and the bus always with one or the other or both. I was getting to know them both. Completely and intimately. And I relished discovering all I could about both because I knew everything I discovered brought me closer. Each new nugget or snippet was another window opened, a further depth seen.

I discovered all sorts, I discovered that Rebecca had always enjoyed art and that the museum curator job had been a dream come true. I teased her a little at first when she admitted that.

"I bet! Rocking with the relics eh? Arseing around with the artefacts. Partying with the portraits n paintings..."

But she wasn't amused, she gave me that slightly disappointed look, the one I dreaded and which would cut me short immediately. She told me she had studied then worked hard to secure her position and she said it was important to know what you wanted from life. To have a goal. And that not everything in life should be treated as a joke. I immediately apologised for being an eejit and told her I was glad and proud that she'd found employ she enjoyed. *I was too. Secretly envious even.* Then she immediately smiled and apologised for over–reacting and then we poked each other in the ribs and all was well again. And I told her more of what I'd learned of Mark Twain.

"Did you know that all of Mark Twain's major nineteenth–century titles were sold by salesmen door–to–door rather than as trade publications in bookstores?"

It was true and discovering that meant I went on to discover more too; I discovered that the subscription publication industry had blossomed in post–Civil War America and that tens of thousands of sales agents, many of them veterans and war widows, canvassed small towns and rural areas armed with sample pages and illustrations and multiple binding options to fit every wallet or purse.

I loved that idea. This was a wonderful discovery – Mark's books being brought to the people by the people. The ordinary people. The everyday people. No big city bookshop needed, no Amazon required. I discovered that Samuel L. Clemens sold more Mark Twain books and attained a broader audience in this way than he would have reached with regular trade publications but he had to contend with the lower status that subscription authors were accorded. His books were bought by the masses – "who never knew what good literature they were." I loved that because it tickled more of my boxes – it proved he truly *was* a hero – he entertained those most deserving. He was a man of and for the people – *all* the people – the 'me' and the 'you' and the 'him' and the 'her' and not just the 'them'. I knew what it meant – he was known by everyone and liked by all – the hype was true – the slogan earned. The man in the street or the man on the throne – no hierarchy, no prejudice, no pandering, no patronising.

And above all I loved the irony – the best literature written and yet snooty noses were twitching to rise; "Oh… you're a *subscription* author…" It was one of his many victories – another championing of equality – the right people were being rewarded – wordy wise paupers were being elevated – the literary playing field was being levelled. He was offering access for all.

And when I relayed all this to Rebecca she would smile and listen intently and I could tell she was impressed and pleased and didn't really think of me as too much of an eejit. Mark was helping me even then.

I finished a second reading of *Huckleberry Finn* and then I read *The Innocents Abroad* from cover to cover in one day and one half of a night. It was another joy and provided much to remind me of Rebecca because it seemed to be mostly about adventures and fun and understanding what truly mattered in life. And on one page Mark Twain had wrote, "She kept up her compliments, and I kept up my determination to deserve them or die."

It was one sentence in a detailed anecdote about being convinced by a flattery–powered shop girl to buy a pair of too small buckskin gloves. But that wasn't really what it was about – it was a sentence designed to be lifted out of context – I knew instantly exactly what that phrase really meant. How much it meant. How true it was. It could have been written solely for me. For me to describe us – Rebecca would shower me with verbal niceties and I would do anything to earn them. I copied that sentence out – wrote it into a hand–made steamboat strewn greetings card then presented it to Rebecca on our 'First Date–Adventure 5 Months and 2 Days Anniversary Day'.

I'd been doing the by then traditional Saturday night stop–over at hers and presented it to her in bed. I brought it in on a Picasso print tray that also held two mugs of tea, four slices of generously–buttered toast and one bowl of glossy green seedless grapes. She opened it, read it, squeezed my hand and called me "Loon". Then she kissed me and I kissed her back and Monty barked as she sometimes did when we embraced. And when we ignored her she jumped onto the bed and tried to lick us and the tray toppled and the tea spilt and Rebecca shrieked and I swore and we both laughed. Then we un–embraced and fully rescued the situation – I made more tea – Rebecca changed the bedsheets – Monty picked the card up with her teeth and wagged her tail apologetically.

We were a perfect team.

We truly were.

Rebecca

It was sweet really, cute and eccentric. I laughed at the time but it got a bit tedious when he started up with what he called his MTDYK's (Mark Twain Did You Knows). I'd obviously unleashed a monster. He read all the novels and short stories then he started reading Mark Twain's speeches and his letters and anything else he could discover. Shopping lists probably if he managed to find any. Then every time we met he'd give me three quotes, a few facts and desperately want to read me a passage. I had to pinch his arm hard on numerous occasions and explain I was impressed but how about we discuss something else for a change. He'd grin then and apologise and we would talk about other things, he was always entertaining.

He did make me laugh.

Chapter 19

Rebecca said I shouldn't let George stress me out. But his energy is frightening, he never relents. He provides a commentary on everything I do.

"Oh! Robert's putting his coat on! He must be going somewhere for lunch."

I ignore him but it doesn't help. It doesn't stop the torrent of drivel.

"Oh! He's picked up his mug! It must be time for a cup of tea."

I'm clenching my crockery tight. This shouldn't be happening…

"Oh! He's got a copy of the Metro! I wonder what the headline is today?"

I don't give him anything. No response. No recognition. Not a word. I don't encourage him in any way. But he doesn't give up. He doesn't let it lie.

"Oh, Robert's looking at the clock a lot today. He's probably meeting his girlfriend!"

My silence after that one doesn't help. It just sends shards of pain splintering around my body. A spot between my shoulder blades bears the brunt; it aches and begins to bend me. I'm wearied. Chip chip chipped. My silence means I'm bottling it up but what else can I do. What is the option?

Rebecca said I shouldn't

let George

stress me out.

But George reads out his work as he does it. He thinks aloud.

It's a sign of the not very bright. The casual staff worksheets recital has become as familiar a weekly spouting as that of the National Lottery. "Jason Devonshire… 52 hours ... he's had a busy week... Kevin Brooking... 47... interesting, he only did 41 last week... Raymond Parkes… just the bare 35… no overtime payment for him…"

Rebecca said I shouldn't

let George

stress me out.

But so much of his performance makes my cringe crawl. It's worst when I have to listen to his unique brand of jargon infused patronisation when he takes a call, "Which form are you referring to? We are familiar with all… well, there's P45 P46 P6 P9 P38 P43…"

I have to listen to him enunciate every syllable clearly. I hear his side of the proceedings and I imagine the confusion and frustration of whichever employee is receiving the dull dulcets on the other end. It must be agony for them. And it's peripheral pain for me. He's crucifying us both.

"BACS stands for Banks Automated Clearing System. I firmly believe it is the ideal system for making regulated automated payments."

I try and think of how to describe it and the best I can manage is 'Inane gibberjarg.' These anxious salary related queries are the worst. They allow him full rein. They're truly terrifying.

"Let me explain. To calculate Income Tax, the employer determines the cumulative tax free allowance in a specific week or month and deducts this allowance from the cumulative gross wage or salary that employee is due at that tax week including both current wages or salary and all previous income earned during the current tax year including any earnings from other employers. Having established the taxable pay that amount is then applied to the percentage of Income Tax to be paid under the current tax rules for that financial year."

Rebecca said I shouldn't
let George
stress me out.

"As the BACS process is electronic, it removes the need to write cheques, which can be a costly process... I'm merely explaining to you... Individual electronic payments are subject to human error. We try to avoid them... Well, yes you can talk to Robert but I'm confident he'll only tell you the same thing..."

He then reddens at something that is said and puts the call through to me.

"Alright mate, what's up?"

And when I conclude with a… "No problem, glad we got that sorted, take care. Cheers."

George doesn't enquire, George doesn't say thanks, George just states, "We mustn't forget year end on–line filing of P14s and P35s."

Draining. That's what he is. Diminishing of those around him, *Me.* I think about it a lot. *Too much.* Maybe it's an art form or a skill or some such – the know when to shut up talent. Maybe it's a gene. An intuition? A link he is missing. He has recently added MIPPM after his name. It stands for Member of the Institute of Payroll and Pensions Management. He has it added on the end of his emails and it's prominent on the gold embossed Toblerone shaped name tag plaque thing that he's acquired from who on earth knows where and which now sits proud and prominent upon his desk. He likes telling people what it stands for. He hopes they'll ask. He's chuffed when they do. And if they don't, he tells them anyway. Brian from the post room was wide–eyed with wonder when George enlightened him.

"Oh. That's interesting. I thought maybe you just had one of those long names – George Terence Ainsworth Mippem. I was gonna let everyone know. Tell them to update their lists in case you got pigeonholed incorrectly."

If George is not in the office (on those rare, beautiful occasions) and we have a visitor who enquires re the caption abbreviation curiosity, then I happily offer explanation.

"Oh that? Yes, isn't it nice? M.I.P.P.M. it stands for More Interesting Person Post Mortem."

It's a pleasure to clarify – to eradicate any confusion – it's one of the few tasks I've enjoyed lately. One of the few I've been able to engage with. I find myself hoping the inquisitive will enquire every bit as much as he does.

But it's not enough.

It doesn't alleviate.

It doesn't counteract.

It doesn't redress the imbalance.

It's fleeting flicker.

It's scant consolation.

There's too much else to contend with.

George reads his emails aloud. And when he hasn't any more to read he hums. And now even his mouse clicks infuriate me. And the sound of his breathing causes my own to falter.

Rebecca
said
I
shouldn't
let
George
stress
me
out.

But Rebecca has never worked opposite George in a cramped office that feels more like a cupboard every day. And her advice about avoiding stress was rendered devastatingly ironic when, shortly after these seemingly sincere warnings, Rebecca confessed to me (her devoted boyfriend of five and one quarter years) that she'd been unfaithful.

With Damien!

Rebecca

The Mark Twain thing was strange though, looking back, it probably was an obsession. One that seemed to increase after his dad died. That was a sad time, a sad and very difficult time. Robert had started reading to his dad in the hospital during the last weeks; everyone was getting a dose of *Huckleberry Finn* it seemed. Robert was devastated when the inevitable happened and never really able to talk properly about it. He wanted to read a poem at the funeral, he was insistent. I managed to talk him out of it but only just. Robert just didn't get it sometimes, he wanted things to be as they couldn't be. The poem was one he'd written himself and I had no doubt it was sincere but I couldn't let him read it – not in front of his sister and a mourning congregation. I remember it well, he read it to me incessantly; he couldn't see that it wasn't appropriate. He couldn't accept it.

Dad is dead.
Dad is dead.
No longer sat
At table's head.
No.
Dad is dead.
Dad is dead.

That was the first verse, the first of two, I couldn't see his sister liking it, I could only envisage her being upset.

Chapter 20

"Robert."

"Sis."

"Just thought I'd give you a call. How are you doing?"

"I've been hearing things."

"Hearing things? What do you mean?"

"Cars, buses, lorries, all sorts of things."

"Right. Well that's okay. That's normal isn't it. That's just London, it's a noisy place."

"Yes, but..."

"Are you okay in yourself?"

"Yes, it doesn't really bother me."

"What doesn't?"

"Hearing things. The trains, the tube, the people, none of it..."

"No, well like I said, it's just normal city life and you do live on a busy main road."

"Busy... a strange word don't you think? Bus and y, bus–y, why not bizzy? You know B I Z Z Y ?"

"Well yes, I suppose, I've never really thought about it. Are you sure you're okay Robert?"

"Yes. I don't always listen. I can often block it out."

"Block it out?"

"Yes."

"What?"

"The hearing things."

"Oh... Right... Good... I... are you sure... I... I don't suppose you've heard from Rebecca?"

"She's changed her name."

"Really?"

"Apparently so."

"Okay... what's she called now?"

"Rhoda Newman."
"Robert?"
"Sorry Sis, I have to go now."
"Robert? Are you…"
"I've a commute to endure."
"Yes, okay, how is work?"
"Heavenly. Ciao."

Announcements. That was the most accurate way to describe them. It didn't bother me but it might have bothered her. It was probably best that I didn't explain. And it would have been difficult in truth. Complex. I walked toward Chadwell Heath High Street and I listened out. Without choice. I couldn't help it. They spoke when they passed me. Or when I passed them.

> I AM PEUGEOT. I AM CITROEN. I AM FORD. I AM NIKE. I AM STATIONARY. I AM SPEEDING. I AM BLACK. I AM BLUE. I AM WORN. I AM SHINY. I AM SOILED. I AM THE PINNACLE.

It takes 23 minutes to reach the station via the High Street route and the hearings were with me all the way. The windows were at it as well as the roads.

> I AM BRITANNIA FISH BAR. I AM PEKING AND CANTONESE. I AM HAPPY HOUSE. I AM ONE LOVE RESTAURANT. I AM BRITANNIA PHARMACY. I AM AT THE HEART OF YOUR HEALTH. I AM CRIMINAL DEFENCE SOLICITORS. I AM FREE 24 HOUR POLICE STATION REPRESENTATION. I AM IN TROUBLE? I AM BENEFIT FRAUD? I AM BURGLARY? I AM DRUGS? I AM ROBBERY? I AM ASSAULTS? I AM MURDER? I AM WELCOME MASSAGE. I AM COUPLES £75.

It was OK, what the hell, if it's good to talk then surely it's fine to listen?

I AM VETS 4 PETS. I AM NEUTERING. I AM THE BARKING & DAGENHAM YOUTH PARADE.

And I didn't always have to. Just now. And then. Just sometimes. Just sometimes frequently.

I AM SCRUFFY CAT AND DOG GROOMING. I AM NO CAGES. I AM SIAM MASSAGE. I AM ROMFORD DELIGHTS.

The trains are every ten minutes from Chadwell Heath to Liverpool Street. And there's a fair chance of getting a seat. When they run on time. And you're prepared to ask to be excused.

"Excuse me...excuse me please...excuse me..."

I weave down inside and get one toward the back of carriage 3 but it's not quite the corner seat and as soon as I sit I remember I have not picked up a copy of the *Metro*. I have failed. I have nothing to read and little option now but to sit and to stare and to hear.

I AM PASSENGER. I AM ANDROID. I AM JOURNEY. I AM IPHONE. I AM COMMUTER. I AM PAINED.

And in truth it's not always unpleasant; it can help the time to pass.

I AM KINDLE. I AM IPAD. I AM BEVERAGE IN CARDBOARD. I AM HANDKERCHIEF TO NOSE.

It takes approximately 19 minutes to pick up passengers at and pass through Goodmayes Station, Seven Kings Station, Ilford Station, Manor Park Station, Forest Gate Station, Maryland Station and arrive at Stratford Station. And from there it's a cross–platform interchange on to the westbound central line. And although it's a brief interchange it's a chaotic one. Especially if you like to head for the end of the platform rather than straight across. If this is your choice then you are soon engulfed. You are in the tide. You are mingled with the Stratford Station exiteers and the DLR desirers and the Jubilee Line headers. You are wrapped inside. Part of the swarm.

> I AM FRAGMENT. I AM SNIPPET. I AM MOMENTARY. I AM GLIMPSE. I AM PASSING. I AM HERE. I AM GONE. I AM WORD. I AM EXPLETIVE. I AM SNEEZE. I AM COUGH. I AM TRIVIA. I AM WIND. I AM DUST.

The Central Line trains are full. I let three come and go and all are full. Even standing at the end of the platform does not give me an advantage. Not today. The end carriage is just as stuffed as its front and its middle. I board the fourth train. Which is full too. No corner seat availability. No edge. No comfort. No reprieve.

> I AM SARDINE. I AM SARDINE. I AM SARDINE. I AM SARDINE. I AM SARDINE. I AM PRAWN.

And to get from Stratford Station to Oxford Circus Station you pass through and pick up MORE at Mile End Station, Bethnal Green Station, Liverpool Street Station, Bank Station, St. Paul's Station, Chancery Lane Station, Holborn Station and Tottenham Court Road Station.

> I AM SARDINE. I AM SARDINE. I AM SARDINE. I AM SARDINE. I AM SARDINE. I AM PRAWN.

And it's not just the hearings – there are voices too – these are dulcet zones.

"Move down! Come on man! There's room down the end, move down! Come on man! Fuck's sake! Move down man!

There's load of space! Come on Bruv! Come on man!"

It's a relief really. In many ways. It's a distraction. When I'm focused on listening then I'm not truly thinking. And I'm not questioning. When I'm focused on listening I'm not reminiscing. When I'm focussed on listening I'm not recalling. And sometimes hearing can be heartening.

"... he said to me you're getting a hard time for a reason … I'm bleeding money at the moment… getting cabs to the station…. getting in at quarter past just to please him …. he's riding me so hard… he said it's for your own good … he's a cunt…. I'm irrelevant… I'm getting nailed to the cross…"

Perhaps Sis is right, it's just noise. It's just noisy. It's just London.

The second verse was similar and equally as concerning.

Dad is dead.
Dad is dead.
That's the truth
When all is said
Dad is dead.
Dad is dead.

Chapter 21

'Then I set down in a chair by the window and tried to think of something cheerful, but it warn't no use. I felt so lonesome I most wished I was dead. The stars was shining, and the leaves rustled in the woods ever so mournful; and I hear an owl, away off, who–whooing about somebody that was dead… and a dog crying about somebody that was going to die… I got so down–hearted and scared, I did wish I had some company.'

It still seemed like only yesterday. Or the day before. Or Sunday which was the day before the day before yesterday and it could have been either. And all of that is drivel too. *It seems like only yesterday.* Nothing seems like yesterday. What's done is gone, it can never seem the same. You can never seam the same. You can't recreate the weave. You can't stitch up a stitch–up.

"He seamed alright – we just patched him up and sent him back out there."

'Then I set down in a chair by the window and tried to think of something cheerful, but it warn't no use. I felt so lonesome I most wished I was dead. The stars was shining, and the leaves rustled in the woods ever so mournful; and I hear an owl, away off, who–whooing about somebody that was dead… and a dog crying about somebody that was going to die… I got so down–hearted and scared, I did wish I had some company.'

It's becoming another long night. I've been reading that paragraph at least once an hour every hour. I need to. I feel the need. I need to hear it – *The Huckleberry Din.* And it is need. It's need not intention. Need. Needed. Knead. Kneaded. *He needed her. She kneaded him!*

But I've put the book down now. I've been distracted. I'm

clutching a precious piece of cloth.

ZARA
BASIC T-SHIRT
MADE IN PORTUGAL

I found it at the end of the bed.

90% POLYAMIDE
10% ELASTANE

I've been clutching the t–shirt and reading its labels and remembering the feel and recalling the moments. And now I have placed it over my head as I lie. But I have not been rewarded. Her odour does not linger. Rebecca's scent has left the Bedroom. Or Perhaps it can't compete because of the strength of the competition – my sniffing has led to a realisation – it has been some considerable time since I changed the bed sheets.

The t–shirt is white and sleeveless and I can remember how it ended up under the covers at the end of the bed. I can imagine it at least. I recognise it you see, it's part of a combination, a shorts and t combo, it's the equivalent of a pyjama top. Rebecca did not sleep naked. She did not come to bed unshed. Things would happen, things would progress, things like I would be sat with my back against the headboard and Rebecca would be sat astride me and she would put her hands up toward the ceiling as if she were the bank clerk and I was the robber. She would put her hands up toward the ceiling so that I could peel her t shirt up over her head, and once I succeeded it would be immediately discarded, tossed asunder as her breasts stole my attention.

I can still imagine it.

I can still imagine it even though it actually happened. I can imagine the unimagined. I can imagine the unimagined but it's the unimaginable that I struggle with. It's the unimaginable thought of Damien's grubby paws peeling Rebecca's t shirt. It's the unimaginable thought of his little piggy eyes lighting up as her flesh is revealed. It's the unimaginable thought of his gruesome slobbering tongue. It's the unimaginable thought that she allowed that to happen.

She allowed that to happen.

I look around and take stock of my situation. I can't envisage a solution. Rebecca used to help me change the duvet cover, she had a knack, she didn't get frustrated by the endeavour, she didn't find it excruciating, she had a practical attitude. She would turn it outside in then grab three ends and pull a corner through. Or some such voodoo. She made it seem simple, she made life seem simple. She had a practical attitude, a pragmatic approach toward the mundane necessities. One I could never emulate. One I could never understand. But one I appreciated. One I admired immensely.

I need to stop my sniffing.

And I can do that. I can stop the sniffing. I can fold the t shirt carefully and place it in my underpants drawer. I can do that. I can do that easily. I can do that but I can't stop the imagining. I can't neatly tuck the imagined away.

I do it anyway. I do the first bit, the easy bit; I fold the t shirt carefully and place it in the underpants drawer. Where it looks incongruous. And lonely. The drawer is otherwise empty, I realise I do not have a drawer of underpants, not any more, I have a floor of pile. And that's OK. I only need one pair.

And in any case I know it's not about laundry. This is not about laundry.

This is more than that.

Rebecca

I felt for Robert, his mum had died when he was 6. I couldn't imagine what that must have been like, and now his dad was gone too and it was just him and his sister, who had recently moved to Norwich. Him and his sister and me. I knew I had to be there for him and so I had to stop him reading that poem. I had to try and stop grief getting the better of him. I couldn't let him just get up, read those two verses and promptly sit down again which is what he wanted to do. I had to explain to him that eulogies were meant to celebrate the life just passed; they couldn't be a self–indulgence on the part of those left behind.

Maybe the poem was partly my fault. Like the Twain obsession. The thing was Robert was naturally skilled with words and I told him he had talent. It was me who encouraged his poetry (they weren't all like the *Dad is Dead* one) just as it was me who encouraged him to read great books by inspiring authors. Maybe I shouldn't have interfered but I couldn't help it. I felt Robert was underachieving, underestimating himself and missing out. In so many ways. I wanted him to dream, I wanted him to realise that he could achieve more than he had. I wanted him to be him but the best him he could be. That sounds like such a cliché when I write it now. Maybe I should have just left well alone. He wasn't unhappy when I met him. In fact, he seemed completely content. He wasn't asking me to re–educate him. Perhaps literary ignorance is as blissful as any other. My efforts to enlighten him certainly don't seem to have done him any favours now.

Chapter 22

And I also realise that rushing home from work has provided no solace, far from it, a frying–pan–to–fire scenario if ever there were one. Goodbye George…Hello Ghosts. Farewell Cloying Office…Greetings Haunted Homestead. Hurrah – I'm away from George and Margot and meetings that make no sense! Boo – now I'm alone in my flat.

Completely alone.

And every room has its memories and its triggers and its taunts. Every room and every accessory. The washing up sink is one of the worst, I can still see her standing there, black lace boy–shorts and that vest top. I can still hear me telling her to leave the dishes, that I would do them sooner or later. I can still remember her saying that she didn't mind and that it wouldn't take long. I can remember insisting we changed places and now she was behind me and she had wrapped her arms around me and my dressing gown and I had then clasped my hands together behind her back and now we were locked tight. And I remember saying I had nothing to offer her but panoramic views of a gritty urban landscape. And I remember us staring out the window at the broken fences and the colourful graffiti and the damaged garage doors and the boarded up B & Q and the disused now overgrown car park and the lone magpie pecking at a pair of greyed and wayward Y fronts.

And I can remember us not being depressed.

And then I can remember her asking if I'd ever had a chin massage and I can still feel the way she then jabbed and pressed her chin between my shoulder blades and how she asked if I had any pain there and how I told her I hadn't had up till now. And I remember how she had then gently nipped my neck and how I tightened my grip and how we stayed twined like that for an age.

And how we didn't need any words.

And it doesn't help if I try to forget because although I do want to forget I don't want to forget. Not really, not if I'm honest. And I am honest and that's one of the reasons Rebecca likes me. *Liked me.* She said she admired my honesty and that was why she felt she had to be honest too. She had to be honest and confess. She admired my honesty and that was why she had to tell me the truth. And she did tell me the truth, she did confess, she told me she had recently had sex with Damien.

She honestly and truly and admirably did.

Rebecca

George just sounded a bit weird to me. I didn't consider him a real problem, George was just George, just peripheral. But I guess it's often about timing, timing and circumstance. It was unlike Robert to whinge and it's not an attractive trait in anyone. When he began to constantly whinge about George it was terrible timing – my patience was wearing, my sympathy was already stretched. Part of me could actually imagine sitting down with his new boss and consoling him, *yes George, I know, Robert can be bloody infuriating!*

I feel hideous thinking about that now, surely my job was to be loyal to Robert? Come what may…

If I'm honest I thought George's arrival and Robert's almost immediate disdain for him might have been a good thing. I suppose I selfishly hoped it might make him do something to change his work situation. Robert had been in that same job for more than a decade; apparently he'd arrived as a security temp to cover sickness for 2 days, had gotten into a stairwell conversation about whether a captive chameleons appearance could be dictated by a determined fashionista and in no time Christine was revealing her need for a new assistant and was insisting payroll wasn't rocket science and she could easily train him up. And that was that. (Robert used to tell the story better.)

I suppose it suited him perfectly. I guess when he was happy Robert simply liked to drift, he enjoyed it. It made perfect sense to him so that's what he did. If he was satisfied with something he saw no need to alter it. He obviously didn't buy into the whole 5–year plan never stand still always pushing on expectation that I was used to. That all the other men I'd known seemed so focussed on.

Chapter 23

"Robert."

"Sis."

"How are you doing?"

"Strange expression."

"Pardon?"

"How are you doing? What does it mea..."

"Listen, no time for that, what are you doing tonight?"

"Trimming my toenails. I saw a chap on TV. He was married to a Spice Girl. She said he bit his toenails. I thought I might try it. I'm not very supple though..."

"Well, fun though that might be I have a better option, you're coming to a party."

"A party..."

"Yes, do you remember Caroline? Who I used to work with at Johnson's, well you probably don't but that's fine, she won't mind. She's having a get together and I'm getting the train down and you can meet me there."

"London is a noisy place."

"Yes, so you keep telling me but I'm sure I'll be fine, I did use to live there remember?"

"It's changed."

"I think you just need cheering up Robert, that's why you're coming to the party."

"I..."

The phone call continued and was a long one. It culminated with Sis insisting I jot down an address and saying she would be sad if I didn't come. I realised I would be sad if I did and I would be sad if didn't. And when she said "What else are you going to do tonight?" I could have been honest and said, "Aimless circuits of the lounge in a pair of very worn grey moccasin slippers. Which Rebecca nagged me to get rid of, and which now I know I never will."

But I wasn't honest. Not this time. I'd learned a lesson.

And now we (my shabby shoes and I) have recklessly wandered into the bedroom. And that is a worse thing to do than to wander into the kitchen. The bedroom is treacherous. Of course the bedroom is treacherous. The bedroom taunts me the most. It taunts me viciously and relentlessly. It's not only a minefield where you might find an ex–other–half's under–things it's also a relentless fine–times flashback–sparker. The bedroom torments me, reminds me, ensures the games are still fresh, still vivid, still real. It ensures the bedroom dialogue is too.

"I think there's something about the size of your forearm – it means it's the same size as your foot, from your elbow to the wrist is the same as from your heel to your toe."

And I don't remember why or how such dialogue would begin because such magic just occurred.

"No, you're thinking of arm span matching height – if I stretch my arms wide then that's exactly how tall I am. If I measured the two, they'd be the same."

"That's impossible. How can you measure your height when your arms are spread wide?"

"You'll have to help."

And so she did. I lay with arms outstretched and Rebecca lay across my arms. And we knew it wasn't scientific because I was taller than she was but it still worked because the fingers of my right hand could now tickle her toe and the fingers of my left hand could pinch her nose. And it also worked because her delicious derrière was now just beyond my chin and if I craned my neck…

And there weren't just the frivolous games there were the learning games too. Rebecca had suggested we listen to the shipping forecast on Radio 4 after I had that little problem in the early days – the one she kindly referred to as "The Quickness." She made me focus on the shipping forecast each evening whilst we "made love" (my terminology) or "had a shagaloo" (hers). It meant the same thing. She encouraged me to relax and concentrate on the curious words and not so much, not so intently (flattering though it was) on the glory – on her glory. On our glory. I would close my eyes to block the visual triggers and try and do as she advised.

I'm closing my eyes now.

And Trash Sang Dollop! It's as real now as it was then. It's as in the moment as it was at any moment. But even though I've clambered in and rolled around, the duvet does not wrap me in the same way her arms once did. It cannot do the same job. It doesn't clasp and it doesn't caress. It is not possible. I can't have what we had. Rebecca is no longer in my bed. But I still have the memories. I can't escape them. I still remember the words. Hauntings. The curious phrases. Tauntings. I recall them now. No option. Remembrance recital. Out loud. Masochistically proud.

"Good morning here is the shipping forecast. Dogger Fisher variable occasionally veering south. Fitzroy becoming cyclonic for a time. Hebrides Bailey. Increasing 6 or 7 for a time. Stornoway rising. Occasionally 6 in the North Channel. Crosby rising slowly. Expect Viking. Boomer rising more slowly. Including Orkney. Dogger. Fisher. Expected Humber 989. Portland Plymouth Biscay. Good occasionally poor. Faroes South East Iceland. 9 8 7 Rising. Occasionally 6 or 7 in the east. Rising more slowly."

The forecast would finish at 1:00 am and that was the end of Radio 4 broadcasting for the night. It was followed immediately by the National Anthem. At the end of which I would be formally permitted to veer my own Cyclonic Boomer. It was a fun game, with successes and failures but always with smiles. My eyes would be open again at the end. They'd be locked with

Rebecca's. We'd grin and salute her majesty. But really, we were saluting ourselves.

And that was then.

And this is not.

Now the kitchen sink is piled high and the bed is not a playground.

God Save the Queen...

Rebecca

I was happy at the beginning, happier than I'd ever been. Though it did take a bit of adjustment. Robert lived in a top floor flat on a main road in Dagenham. On the morning after the first night I stayed the traffic noise woke me early and so I decided to surprise him with breakfast in bed. I did the washing up whilst I waited for the kettle to boil and this meant I was able to peer out of the kitchen window and notice the activity. In the time it took to wash two plates, one bowl, a couple of glasses and a handful of cutleries I had seen the police retrieve a vast array of vehicle parts from behind the garages at the end of the ten–foot square communal back garden.

I asked him about it later and he explained that some of the garages were rented and no doubt there was a carjacking, murder, kidnap and ransom cell operating in the area. I must have looked horrified because then he grinned and said "Or it might just be nothing. Probably just a run of the mill cut and shut operation."

Chapter 24

"Robert!"

"Sis…"

"Where are you?"

"Hel… home."

"You're supposed to be here! The party I told you about! I'm coming to get you. Get in the shower I'm getting in a cab. Twenty minutes!"

"Sis? Sis…"

Shower…

<u>Rebecca</u>

On our second date ('Adventure 2' as he would insist I refer to it) Robert had told me he lived in a Grade 2 listed building. On the morning after the first night I'd stayed at his flat I queried him on the accuracy of such claim whilst we sipped tea and crunched toast in bed. He smiled and claimed I must have misheard him and that he had actually been stating a warning; he was adamant he had described his abode and certain of his neighbours honestly – his block was "a greyed, too–quick–fisted building." Robert and his wit and word play. I admired that talent from the start – he was always so quick to manoeuvre words, could twist them into shapes few others would imagine.

Maybe there was always too much going on inside his head.

Chapter 25

Upon arrival at Caroline's party Sis steers me toward a girl with a bejewelled pierced eyebrow. The girl transpires to be called Emma and is drinking a beverage she refers to as "Blue Shit." She immediately insists I must try one. I'm not sure about that but she's already heading off to the kitchen to procure on my behalf. Sis maybe senses my disquiet as she squeezes my arm and tells me to relax. She informs me "They're all nice people here" and then tells me "You should let yourself enjoy yourself." *I should let myself enjoy myself.* It's a curious expression. And I'm still pondering it when Emma returns with prosecco for Sis and a turquoise tipple for me. "There weren't much food colouring left" she explains "But don't worry there's still plenty of alcohol in there." Then she raises her own glass and declares "Cheers!"

Shortly after we chink Sis catches the eye of another and waves. "Sorry, I need to mingle" she informs us and heads off through the throng. I'm left thinking about what she's just said.

"Do you think that's a curious word?"

"What?"

"Mingle."

"Yeah, does sound a bit rude doesn't it?"

"Does it?"

I ask Emma to explain and she asks me if I'm trying to be saucy. And it doesn't really sound like an accusation but it still disconcerts me. Then she tells me it's fine if I am because she quite likes blokes who are a bit cheeky and goes on to smile and say "I don't mind you trying to chat me up." I assure her that I most certainly am not trying to chat her up. And it's true. At least I'm fairly sure it's true. I'm certainly not meaning to try to chat her up. She laughs then and is still smiling when she tells me I'm lucky that she's not easily offended and then asks why I don't tell her a joke or something. She says my sister is always saying how funny I can be.

And for a moment I was kind of stuck for words and that can be embarrassing and so now I've slipped into reverse. And I've started regurgitating. I'm regurgitating tales from long ago. Old words. Ancient vocabulary. I'm regurgitating tales previously spun in pubs. I instinctively imagine Emma might enjoy the pub. I'm regurgitating tales I didn't even know I once knew. And I can remember them with a clarity that surprises me. I remind her of olde sayings and ask her ancient questions. I reel them off easily.

"Ever wondered why seagulls fly over the sea? Well, it's because if they flew over the bay they'd be bagels."

Her brow creases for a moment after that one, she's concentrating, the workings are whirring, then the penny drops, I actually hear it. And I get a vision of it – shiny spinning copper on a wood laminate surface. It lands heads up. Emma's head comes up too – the creases unravel and she laughs shrilly. Then delightedly declares "Knob–end!" and punches my arm. I feign severe injury and continue.

"*Ouch!* What's the ultimate definition of noise?"

"Me singing in the shower!"

"No. A Skeleton masturbating in a biscuit tin."

"Haha! Knob–end!"

I have a moment then – a crashback – I recall telling Rebecca that joke and she looking at me mock–confused and stating something about skeletons not having genitals. I had to explain that she couldn't be both pedantic and also enjoying of my vast array of glib humour. She had smiled and argued perhaps I just needed to work harder. And be more selective.

Emma jabs me in the ribs.

"Helloo? Where'd you go? I liked that. Tell us another one."

I'm pleased that she liked it and decide I will tell her another one. It's a longer one and used to be popular. At least I think so.

I don't fully recall. I decide it probably doesn't matter. Not when all is considered.

"Okay. There's this lady in a pub, she's sat at the bar looking all mournful and miserable when a bloke comes in and sits beside her and asks what's up?"

"The price of gin?"

"No, shush, don't interrupt. I need to concentrate for this one."

Emma tilts her head to the side and pokes her tongue out. I notice that's pierced too. And I consider offering an apology but she doesn't appear too offended by my scolding and so instead I continue.

"So anyway, he asks her what's up – why is she so sad looking? And she says it's my husband, I hate him, he makes my life a misery. And the bloke says I can kill him for you if you like, that's what I do, I'm a contract killer. And she says thanks I'd love that but I'm skint, I couldn't afford it."

I realise at this point that it's been a long time since I've had a long and detailed conversation like this – I analyse it – it feels slightly incongruous but in truth not overly excruciating. Emma jabs me again.

"Oi! Concentrate! I'm still here you know, what happens next?"

"Right, yes, sorry. So anyway, the contract killer thinks about it for a while and then says OK, I tell you what, I can see you're really miserable, your husband is obviously ruining your life and I don't like to see that, I'll do it for a pound. The lady can't believe her luck; she'll be rid for a quid – excellent! Of course she agrees and now she asks the bloke his name, the contract killer says just call me Arti and now tell me what your husband looks like and where I can find him. So the lady explains he's bald–headed, 5'10" and finishes work at the local supermarket at 6. Arti says fine I'll do the job tomorrow. The two shake hands and the lady smiles properly for the first time in months."

"Bit of a long one this, hurry up, I need to pee."

"Shush. I'll speed up – so anyway the next night Arti hides in the supermarket car park and sees the husband coming out and when he passes him he jumps out, strangles him and throws him in a dumpster. A couple of hours later he goes down the pub and there's the wife at the bar but she still looks miserable as sin. Arti whispers in her ear – I've strangled your husband and chucked him in a dumpster you should be happy. And the lady says what are you talking about? He's at home – alive and nagging – worse than ever, you've let me down. Another false promise. You men are all the same. Arti is shocked and rather put out, he says show me a photo of him and so the wife does and Arti realises he has strangled the wrong man. He's very embarrassed and apologetic and says give me the photo and I'll make sure I do the job properly tomorrow night. And he reassures the wife he won't charge any extra – he'll honour the initial £1 deal. And he's a man of his word – he lies in wait the next night and he sees the husband come out and he checks the photo and it's definitely the right man this time and so he jumps out and strangles him and chucks him in the dumpster too. He then decides to head straight down the pub and break the good news. The trouble is the police are staking out the supermarket – their suspicion having been raised following the murder the night before. They arrest Arti and take him to the police station. They also tip off the local press. What's the headline in the newspaper the next day?"

"Dunno."

"Arti chokes two for a pound at Tesco."

There's a pause. Then Emma laughs. Then she aims another playful punch and tells me this is the best chat up she's had in ages. Then she totters off in search of the toilet. I'm somewhat disconcerted by her claim and wonder if in fact I am chatting her up. I think if I was Sis might be pleased, she keeps appearing in the doorway and giving me a thumbs–up. It's hard to fathom but something seems to be occurring.

I then recall that upon our arrival, after the standard hugged greeting of two good friends and then the introduction of me, Emma had informed Sis (after Sis had said "wow") that she loved an excuse to dress up and was wearing what was known as a "Wench's outfit." It seems to involve a lot of lace, exceedingly tall shoes, a short skirt that means her stocking tops are prominently evident, a string tied blouse that appears a size or two too small and a cloudburst of glitter upon her escaping bosom. I think about it now while I wait for her to return. And I'm not expecting Mark Twain to put his oar in but suddenly there it is – a paddle poke in the guts via the left ear drum.

> "I would have loved to live in the time of Shakespeare and Queen Elizabeth, the best dressed period of the world. You know I like color and flummery and all such things--I was born red-headed--maybe that accounts for my passion for the gorgeous and ornamental."

Right... I assume this unexpected interjection means something; the man is nothing if not profound. He doesn't appear in my ear without reason. And now there's Sis again, all thumbs up and smiley again. Maybe they're in cahoots, which is an intriguing and rather disconcerting thought. Mark's message is initially a trifle confusing but as Mr Twain is my friend, guide and mentor I am of course profoundly grateful for any hint. And now I think I know what he wants me to do. When Emma returns, I take her hand and declare, "You are gorgeous and ornamental."

She punches me again and calls me a Knob–end again but I think she may be pleased. Our conversation continues.

"Your sister reckons you need a good night out."

"Does she? Oh... Well, I suppose I have been staying in a lot lately."

"Oh yeah? Who with?"

"With my friend, Mark..."

"Right. Well that's OK, don't get me wrong I like a party but I also enjoy a night in with the girls. What do you do? Watch the footy and drink beer together?"

"No… Actually I've never actually seen Mark. He just talks to me..."

"Haha! You are proper funny! An imaginary friend! Love it! Let's get drunk and make unwise choices. Vodka and ginger beer – try it! Like it! Get on it!"

Before I can explain she thrusts a large glass toward my lips. She's obviously restocked on her way back from the bathroom. And I'm distracted now anyway – I'm thinking about her expression *get on it – on it get – get it on.* I think I can hear the Rolling Stones in the background, but I can't be sure. After a moment or two I realise Emma is asking me a question. "I know you've said you don't, but if you *did* want a girlfriend what *type* of girlfriend would you like?"

"One with reliable knicker elastic."

She doesn't laugh at that line. I don't blame her – it's unfunny, cryptic, ambiguous and bitter. Now is not the time and I know it's not her fault. I shut up and get on it. Her concoctions are impressive. I've theatrically drained my turquoise and now Emma has laughed, drained her own glass and is racing toward the kitchen for "reinforcements." I'm left alone and able to concentrate – to become better aware of the music playing. It may be ABBA. '*Having some time on your wife…*' I conduct an experimental toe–tap. I seem to be out of rhythm. Perhaps it's not ABBA, not anymore. Maybe it's the Bee–Gees. '*Ooh–ooh–ooh–ooh – flaying alive…*'

I stop my tapping.

Mark whispers again, and I'm relieved when it becomes obvious that he's still thinking of Emma and not the other thing – the thing I've vowed to do but not yet done thing. Emma seems to have put him in a good mood. He's being complimentary again, perhaps he sees her as a kindred spirit.

> "Light-colored clothing is more pleasing to the eye and enlivens the spirit. Now, of course, I cannot compel everyone to wear such clothing just for my especial benefit, so I do the next best thing and wear it myself."

"Yes, I know, I know all about your famous white suit."

> "I talked in a snow-white full-dress,

swallow-tail and all, and dined in the same. It's a delightful impudence. I decided to call it my dontcareadam suit. In the case of the private dinner I would always ask permission to wear it first saying: 'Dear Madam, may I come in my dontcareadams?"

He sounds chuffed with himself, very much in the party mood. Emma has obviously had an effect on him. She returns now with a glintsome eye and two half pint pots full of refill. "Good health!" She says with no inkling of irony as she hands one over.

"Thank you, Dear Madam, a fine cocktail indeed. By the way, did you hear about Mr Whippy the ice–cream man? The police found him dead, he was covered in strawberry sauce and chocolate sprinkles, they suspect he may have topped himself."

I'm surprised in a way, surprised at the flow and the gleeful reception they receive. Perhaps there's value in the trite and the trivial. Less difficulty. No challenge. I drink some more. I maybe even smile.

"Oh, and a piece of advice – never crawl under a cow. You might get a pat on the head."

Even the truly poor ones are well received and we have a kind of a conversation too. Emma has lots of enquiries but they tend to be OK. I can handle the interrogation. I'm still able to steer.

"Do you reckon you were maybe destined to meet me tonight?"

"Interesting question, I wonder why you ask, I assume you've been studying Chaos Theory?"

Another punch then she asks me if I know any sexy stories and I tell her that a sparrow's testes are usually the size of a pinhead but swell to the size of a baked bean during the mating season.

Emma then tells me a story, it's an autobiographical one, a true one, I tense a little as those are often the worse. This one turns out to be OK though, she tells me that she was recently being seen in hospital for a somewhat intimate biopsy and the surgeon had asked if she minded if some students take a peek at the procedure. No of course not, that was fine; it was all part of their training after all. However, she was rather perturbed when a huge troupe suddenly marched in whilst she was wide and resplendent in stirrups. She tells me how that, unusually for her, she was suddenly hit with a large dose of self–consciousness, especially as all that was going on was being displayed on a very large monitor. She tells me how she urgently started informing all present that, "It doesn't usually look like that...It's not really that big...the camera magnifies it...magnifies it a lot!"

We both laugh and I assure her, "I'm sure you're perfectly proportioned."

She squeezes my groin and says, "Maybe you'll find out."

Then, perhaps sensitive to my shock (I had dropped my glass), Emma grins and tells me to relax. She then scoops the shards and declares she's off to fill us up once more. I watch her colourful exit then look down at my own attire, threads carelessly pulled from the top of the pile. I'm no chirpy peacock. No sartorial giant. No Mark Twain. I have a moment's reverie.

And I must have mused aloud as he is quick to answer me. I'd been thinking about his suit.

"So, it kind of gives you strength, confidence, hope? Maybe I should buy one?"

And he'd instantly replied.

> "This suit, I may say, is the uniform of the Ancient and Honorable Order of Purity and Perfection, of which organization I am president, secretary, treasurer and sole member. I may add that I don't know of anyone else who is eligible."

I take that as a no.

And I don't have time to think of alternative uniform as now Sis wants my attention. She has approached in the manner of Cheshire Cat and asks if I'm having fun. I'm not sure. I hadn't considered that possibility but I tell her that I am as I sense that's what she wants to hear. I then tell her a story too.

"I was sitting in a bar last night and in came a bloke with a black top, black shorts, a yellow and a red card in his pocket and a whistle in his mouth. I thought to myself oh no – this geezer's gonna kick off in a minute..."

She rolls her eyes but smiles. She reminds me that I haven't told her a joke in ages. Emma returns and I think Sis winks at her, but it's all getting a bit hazy now. Emma thrusts a new glass into my hand.

"Race you!"

Shortly after, we have retrieved our coats and are kissing Sis goodbye. She says its kind that I've offered to walk Emma home and asks if I'll be OK. I reply in the affirmative and I leave her with another old fave.

"What's the world's most important invention?"

She doesn't know.

"Venetian blinds. Otherwise it'd be curtains for the lot of us."

Emma laughs loudly. Sis rolls her eyes again and pushes us out the door.

The air hits. I like that expression. Or rather I appreciate it for the first time – *it is like an assault.* Suddenly I'm swaying and slightly nauseous and aware that I'm drunk – and aware that such awareness is not such a good thing.

Turquoise cocktails then copious vodka and ginger beer…

And I'm aware that Emma is clinging to my arm and tottering somewhat and I'm aware that I'm suddenly very weary. And I'm aware that I know this is a bad idea even though I'm not fully aware of what the idea is. And I'm aware that Emma's leading me home and I'm aware that it's time to go home. But I'm not completely aware which home I should be going to. *Aint you got a home to go to?*

I'm aware that that expression has taken on new meaning too.

Aint you got a home to go to?

Yes. Yes, I have. But what is there for me at home? *Home.* I think about it now. A four–letter word. H.O.M.E. *Home.* I'd never realised it was such a complex word. And I'm aware that there is also a word called 'maudlin' and I'm aware I'm heading toward it and I don't like all this awareness. And so I try to blot the awareness and drift but I'm unsuccessful as I can't quite conjure a raft amidst the succession of images that are now erratically scrolling. And now I'm upsettingly aware again – I'm aware that prime among them is a man in a pair of saggy blue underpants being introduced to a gorilla holding dumbbells.

"Hello Horatio, this is your Aunty Maudlin."

Rebecca

The thing was Robert seemed happy enough there, living in a deprived suburb in a top floor flat on a noisy main road where the windows rattled when the traffic drove by. He didn't appear concerned or dissatisfied in the slightest. Maybe I shouldn't have interfered. Maybe I was just being a snob. I always felt calm there too if I'm honest. I don't know why but looking back I guess he always made me feel safe. Ridiculous really but that's what it was like, that's what it was like at first. I enjoyed his outlook – he liked people and they liked him. He gave everyone the benefit of the doubt and his confidence in others was contagious. He made me believe there really was a best to be seen in everyone. And he very much made me believe in *us*.

Chapter 26

We keep stagger–walking and the air keeps hitting.

It continues to provide imagery and also now a flashback. I suppose there's a link – the chat I was providing Emma, the words that have led me into predicament, they were words I had heard before. Regurgitations. I remember how I was truly saddened when the internet started sharing jokes. How previously it used to be a public house art form, a Friday night *Prince of Wales* art form. And how you were judged and rightly granted kudos commensurate with the quality of the grin inducements you shed. How it was very much a meritocracy.

The flashback is more complex than that though – it's not just old jokes old news. It's about how I explained all this to Rebecca on Date Adventure Number 5 (The Charles Dickens Museum followed by a walking tour of Soho culminating in a small glass – they didn't serve pints – of lager in *The French House* olde–style–historic pub).

I explained it all during *The French House* bit. I explained my joke–sharing–sadness–thing after Rebecca had explained a few things to me; for example, she explained that Brendan Behan had written in this very ale house and not only him – apparently Dylan Thomas once left his *Under Milk Wood* manuscript under a chair. Perhaps the very one I was now sat on. We both looked down at that point, then under, then up again disappointedly. Then smiled.

It was an unorthodox pub – mobile phones were banned and there were no fruit machines, music or TV – the idea being you were forced to converse and that was arguably why it had remained popular with artists, writers and such sorts. It was ironic really – there were no communication problems between Rebecca and I in those days.

And they're the days I remember best. Rebecca wore a purple lace top on Date Adventure Number 5. I complimented her on her décolletage. It's one of the few French words I know and I felt it was perfect considering the environment. Rebecca blushed a little and rearranged herself slightly but I think she was pleased underneath. She was quite shy in some ways.

I liked that.

Rebecca had bought me a postcard at the Charles Dickens museum – I think she had seen me studying it; it depicted the author sat at his desk with all his thoughts and creations whirling around his head. He seemed stoic, calm amongst the chaos, like he was in control, like he could handle it. It stayed wedged into the corner of the bathroom mirror for months but there would come a time when I could no longer relate, when I realised he wasn't convincing me, when I had stopped believing in the suggestion. Charles Dickens seemed far too assured, unruffled by the ragings. I didn't believe him.

He was not Mark Twain.

The postcard eventually went on the pyre along with the Hula Hoop lingerie. But that would happen later, much later, that would only happen after every Date, every Adventure, every*thing* we'd had was sullied. On Date Adventure 5 such a possibility was an implausibility. On Date Adventure 5 Rebecca was telling me about Dylan Thomas and *The French House* and how Charles Dickens had wandered London and witnessed 'wild visions of wickedness'. And I was telling her how I was upset that nowadays any half–wit could pass himself off as a comedian. I was explaining how Friday nights down the pub were no longer a riotous assembly, how the talented amateurs would no longer hold court, that they refused to be sullied or drawn into a competition against a previous witflop who now had a smart phone.

Rebecca had nodded patiently and let me vent my spleen.

So I did. I went on to tell her that Kev T and Bully used to be the best; how they used to have at least three quality new gags every week but now not a single offering. Kev had just stopped one week, he had shook his head and shrugged his shoulders. He had retired gracefully. And that was a disgrace. I explained to Rebecca that now people don't perform in the pub anymore, that the art of genuine storytelling was very much ailing, how an oral tradition had been savaged, how nights in pubs across the UK had been blighted by the curse. How a modern–day Mark Twain was very unlikely to stand up and make himself known in the *Horse and Crown.* How it was no wonder pubs were closing at an alarming rate. Rebecca listened intently then she smiled and patted my forearm; she said maybe I was worrying about it too much. I grinned and agreed that she might be right.

Rebecca was kind of good at putting things in perspective.

But come on Rebecca, this letter is about revealing and remembering truth and to be honest after a time it did begin to bother me that he lived there. I used to tell friends that he lived in Chadwell Heath even though that delineation was a clear 400 yards from his block of flats. They'd usually not heard of Chadwell Heath and it sounded as if it might be, well it just sounded better than Dagenham.

I was being ridiculous. I recognise that now. I guess you could say dating Robert has taught me a lot that I didn't fully appreciate at the time.

Chapter 27

AND THEN I FEEL THE PAIN.

"Ouch!"

Emma is twisting my left nipple. She has her hand inside the crumpled Christian Lacroix (must have been top of the pile) shirt that Rebecca found for me in a charity shop near Penzance. (She had referred to it as booty.)

Emma twists again.

"Earth to knob–end!"

"Ouch!"

"So? You coming in or what?"

"I don't know... maybe I shou... "

"Be good and you will be lonesome."

"Hey! You're still here?"

"What? I've been here all the time Knob–end. Let's get inside before you stop being funny."

"No, I didn't mean you, I meant Mar… I mean no–one. Nothing…"

I'm aware she can't hear what I can hear. I'm aware she can't hear *who* I can hear. I'm also aware that his appearance is a surprise and a complication. *That irksome flood of awareness again.* I hadn't summoned him. This time I hadn't pleaded. I hadn't beseeched him and yet here he was. Back again. A somewhat ironic arrival and with a message that needed some thought.

Be good and you will be lonesome…

A cryptic message but clear nonetheless. I let Emma steer me over her threshold.

The phrase 'alien territory' now pops into my head but I don't want it there. I try to clear it. I try to blank all phrases, all 'awareness'. I certainly don't want to wonder about 'heightened awareness.' I don't want the image of dozens of question marks turning into light bulbs as they clamber up a ladder. I don't want to see them reaching the top then stepping off and plunging down. I don't want to hear them scream.

"Tea, coffee or blow–job?"

"Er, I don't mind… Do you have decaf?"

Emma is laughing again, I feel calmer. She tells me I'm a strange one but a funny one and reaches for my fly.

Rebecca

Now I'm thinking about the Norfolk Broads. I don't know if that's how the mind works or the writing process or just memory but that holiday remembrance has just hit me from nowhere, hit me hard. We'd been together for close to a year and we'd been joking about couples and how they only got to truly know each other after a certain time, how their true selves and individual habits were only gradually revealed or noticed. We were doing it in that slightly smug our–relationship–is–perfect–so–we–can–smile–about–this–stuff kind of way, safe in the knowledge we were strong and this was right and all would always be well. The next week Robert declared he would be testing our compatibility further as we would be spending a whole week adventuring together, he'd booked us a holiday and I had to guess where. I didn't manage to but perhaps I should have known, he'd inevitably gone for something with a (albeit tenuous) Mark Twain theme – he'd booked us a week on a barge.

It was October. I remember us stood in the cold and rain wrapped in kagouls but grinning stupidly next to a boat called *First Freedom* whilst the owner patiently talked us through the basics of river mooring, steering and safety. He seemed a little dubious of how us city folk would get on but Robert reassured him (and embarrassed me) by declaring "Fear not! All will be well, Rebecca is from a long line of saucy sea dogs."

Once we'd managed a stuttering start and a bit of a float and gone hardly any distance Robert decided enough was enough and adventure was about the details not the distance so we steered to the side, tied the boat up and opened a bottle of wine. After we'd toasted each other and our great fortune to live in a country of guaranteed inclemency he produced and unwrapped a package he'd carried in his backpack. It was a small, stretched art canvass on which he'd painted the silhouette of a couple stood by a river and underneath he'd added some of the poignant words of Huckleberry Finn,

"What you want, above all things, on a raft is for everybody to be satisfied, and feel right and kind toward others."

He propped it above the microwave and then he kissed me. It set the tone for the week, we hardly ventured anywhere, just stayed in bed reading and chatting, enjoying the gentle shift of the river and listening to the steady beat of the rain. I don't think I was ever more content.

Chapter 28

And now things have developed.

I'm *fully aware* that things have developed. They have evolved. And I don't know what to call it, it's a strange one – intersexual discourse perhaps? Sexual interdiscourse? Sexual internaldiscourse? Basically we're having a three–way. Or rather I'm having a couple of twosomes – there's me and Emma and there's me and Mark and we're all in it together. Except we're not, not really – they're both in it with me but not with each other. But he is definitely there just as clear as she is there even though she is unaware that he is there. He's experiencing it with me. I'm experiencing it with him. I conclude we're both in–it–together–with–an–unsuspecting–Emma.

And I'm finding that tonight Mark Twain's presence is more of a hindrance than a help. He's been very vocal ever since my first fumbling entry and his interjections are doing nothing for my concentration. His mischievous nature is not amusing me nearly so much tonight.

Perhaps that's the point.

Perhaps that's his intention.

Perhaps he's punishing me for my excess.

Or for my previous failing when given direction.

It had started out OK. there were no initial problems, I was receiving positive feedback.

"Ooh yes! You *are* a bad boy! That's very nice! Wait till I tell your sister!"

I'm sure it might have all concluded satisfactorily but Mark almost immediately threw me off my stride. I'd been aware that Emma's verbal responses were positive ones; at least I'd thought that was what my awareness was telling me. Her words were surely pleasured ones? I'd had no reason to doubt their authenticity, to suspect my awareness, but then just as her delighted (so I assumed) decibels appeared to be increasing to a neighbour annoying level, Mr Mark Twain suddenly piped up and all awareness and assumption was tipped asunder.

> "Noise proves nothing. Often a hen who has merely laid an egg, cackles as if she had laid an asteroid."

In a matter of moments I was flaccid.

And mortified.

"I can turn over if you like. How's this?"

It's Emma that has spoken this time, not Mark. She's looking back over her shoulder, raising an eyebrow but otherwise appearing unfazed.

Mark seems more taken with her derrière than her patience. Though again his comment is cryptic.

> "Everyone is a moon and has a dark side which he never shows to anybody."

"Er, yes. Yes, I suppose they are. Thank you for sharing your moon with us Emma."

"Do what?"

"Oh. Er, nothing…"

"What d'ya mean *us*? I can't see myself. But we can move in front of the mirror if you like?"

"Er."

"I don't mind. I quite like the kinky stuff."

"Urm."

"There's two mirrors in the bedroom actually – you can watch in both. You can imagine you're shagging two of me at the same time."

"Right..."

I'm panicked – surely that would only add to the confusion? I don't know what to say. I don't know what to do. But I feel she wants me to make a decision, she wants me to use my imagination. I guess I could do that. But my imagination feels overloaded, under pressure.

"Well?"

"Sorry, I've forgotten the question."

"Forget it. Just put it back in. Oh… you can't…"

Now Mark pipes up again now. (He interrupts if I'm honest.)

> "The mind exercises a powerful influence over the body."

For once I kind of wish he'd wait to be asked. It's nice to have his support but with all the interjections and observations I'm increasingly unable to focus. And of course, now we're all staring at my genitals. At least Emma and I are. I hope Mark Twain isn't but I'm not completely confident. In fact, I'm peeved for a moment; I consider this malfunction situation is largely his fault – him and his interjections. Then the next moment I'm racked with guilt. I'm being churlish – Mark is my friend, of course he's on my side. He's here to lend an ear, to provide a shoulder. Thankfully Emma does not appear unduly concerned by the situation, she's an impressively confident lady.

"Don't worry, I'll soon sort him out."

For a moment I'm truly taken aback – I think she's about to scold Mark Twain. But then she reaches for my wilted. This time my penny drops.

She's surprisingly tender.

And very patient.

Sensitive even.

Kind.

She's carefully holding it and gently stroking it and kind of compassionately staring at it and she's starting to get a reaction from it and I begin to assemble an appropriate word, 'Hypnotherapenis'. And after only a short while there are definite signs of progress. But Mark refuses to let nature take its course. He's talking to Emma now, attempting to at least, he's trying to give her his wisdom, not that she can hear it. He's talking as if to Emma but running his words through me, and frankly he's being rather insensitive. And pessimistic. Or perhaps he's taking the rise. He's advising that her efforts may be futile.

> "You can straighten a worm, but the crook is in him and only waiting."

He's definitely taking the rise – I have an almost immediate relapse. *Thanks mate.* Emma's face remains friendly whilst I wilt once more but I'm fairly aware I detected a sigh. She's obviously not the type to give up easily however. She continues to hold me gently and asks, "Do you want me to talk naughty? Would that help? How about I describe my recent visit to the Beauty Salon? There was a cute new girl working there who seemed incredibly keen to give me a waxing…"

I let her continue. The story is a lurid one and quite shocking, it's also undeniably entertaining. I'm *kind of aware* that I'm enjoying it – on a sort of some level – though I can't help but feel a little dubious – would that sort of thing really happen? It sounds very unprofessional and a tad unhygienic. I wonder is Emma embellishing and I'm not expecting Mark to jump in and defend her tale but he does.

> "Eloquence is the essential thing in a speech, not information."

He definitely seems to like her.

"I think he's ready to go back in now, don't you?"

It's Emma speaking this time. I shrug uncertainly – I have no idea which 'he' she is referring to. I'm completely exhausted. Emma is staring at my face intently and it's rather disconcerting.

I try hard to smile. Perhaps a message passes.

"I don't know..."

She continues to study my face. Then finally she smiles and I guess she's decided to give me the benefit of the doubt. I realise she is genuinely sensitive and kind. Not quick to anger. Non–judgemental. I feel a tear well. I honestly do.

"Right… your sister did say... So, the mirrors in the bedroom or more salon stories on the sofa? Or we could just have that coffee? There's no pressure, maybe just toast and TV?"

She truly is a saint.

"Alternatively, if you're feeling really adventurous and up for fifty shades of whatever tickles our fancy, then I do have some equipment in a box above the wardrobe."

"Oh…"

Another decision required. Another choice to make. Another quandary. Life no longer runs fluid. And I'm not expecting Mark to again make my mind up for me but it's turning out to be that sort of night.

> "Twenty years from now, you will be more disappointed by the things that you didn't do than by the ones you did do. So throw off the bowlines. Sail away from the safe harbor. Catch the trade winds in your sails. Explore. Dream. Discover."

Fair enough. Point taken. I'm dubious but manage a half smile and mutter "OK Pandora, let's open it up." I don't sound convincing and Emma doesn't seem to get the link. She looks at me and mine quizzically. Mark is obviously frustrated too.

> "Whatever you say, say it with conviction."

It's another fair point. I help Emma to her feet then take and kiss her hand theatrically.

"Lead me to the wardrobe!"

Robert ceremoniously awarded me with the canvas when we got back to Liverpool Street station and he was about to head East and I North. He insisted it was mine to keep and to remember. It was hard to part after 7 days together, it had been a success in every sense. The canvas was prominent in my bedroom until recently. I took it down when instead of making me smile it made me want to cry.

"What you want, above all things, on a raft is for everybody to be satisfied, and feel right and kind toward others."

It seems unreal now. Such a simple message but one that proved impossible to maintain.

Damien is the polar opposite of Robert, the antithesis, and maybe that complete contrast had an effect on me. An influence. Maybe it was a relief. Damien and his predictability. Damien and his obviousness. Damien and his ordinariness. Damien who I'd never had to second guess. Damien who was straightforward and uncomplicated. *Boring but comfortingly so.* Maybe that's what I needed, what I needed at that time, what I thought I needed. Not that I'd really thought about it, not that I'd really considered ever…

IT WAS NOT WHAT I NEEDED!

Chapter 29

All the time I kept searching and trawling and re–reading always wanting to discover another of Mark Twain's sage snippets, another of his fine facts, another of his humorous hintings. Soon I could tell Rebecca far more than she could tell me about the mighty man; facts such as the fact that in 1903, Harper and Brothers made Mark Twain the best paid writer in the United States. Its president, George Harvey, gave him a contract that paid 30 cents a word for everything he wrote, regardless of whether it was printed or thrown away.

"Imagine that!"

I said. I could and it made me feel proud. *Ridiculous as that might sound.* I genuinely felt proud of Mark Twain. And I continued to delve and ferret and I discovered that though he became more of a pessimist as he aged, he still continued to voice strong opinions against cruelty and social injustice. That was what he was like. He didn't give up on others.

He was not a selfish man.

I discovered all the dates and details too. I discovered Samuel L. Clemens aka Thomas Jefferson Snodgrass aka Mark Twain died on April 21st 1910 at 6.22 pm. (in an ornately carved bed that he and Olivia had bought in Venice in 1878).

> "The most comfortable bedstead that ever was, with space enough in it for a family, and carved angels enough to bring peace to the sleepers, and pleasant dreams."

I discovered he was buried on the 23rd. and in between the death and the burial thousands of mourners walked past an open coffin and a familiar white suit. I could imagine that too. I did imagine that – a procession paying homage – a long winding snake trooping past and shedding tears – he was the best known, best loved and most recognisable person in America at the moment of his death – I could imagine their despair – a nation bereft.

I discovered that his death had triggered front page headlines in all the newspapers and brought eulogies from far and wide. I read every one I could find and decided that William Dean Howells summed it up best when he stated,

> *"Emerson, Longfellow, Lowell, Holmes—I knew them all and all the rest of our sages, poets, seers, critics, humorists; they were like one another and like other literary men; but Clemens was sole, incomparable, the Lincoln of our literature."*

And now he was all that and so much more to me too: friend, confidante, advisor. My best mate.

Rebecca

For a long time it had been perfect with Robert and I; there was no awkwardness, no weirdness or worry. No agenda I suppose. We'd spend hours under the duvet just reading; whole weekends sometimes. His bed was the nicest thing about his flat – king size and very comfy – an iron frame at both the head and foot which meant we could sit opposite each other and smile or footsy between the paragraphs. I bought him nice pillow cases, sheets and covers; I guess it was a little like I was building a nest within his nest, leaving my mark. That bed was a happy place – breakfast, lunch, books and innumerable cups of tea. We would sometimes write collaborative saucy stories – email each other using our smart phones – he'd write one paragraph I'd write the next. We'd create little scenarios – the Gun Slinger and the Saloon Girl – bourbon and petticoats – that sort of thing. Uncomplicated. An unorthodox type of foreplay and fun; another little Robert and Rebecca thing.

We never wrote the narrative of an unfaithful girlfriend.

Chapter 30

Best mate and Inconsistent Whisperer.

I won't reveal exactly what happened next at Emma's (where I recklessly went the way of the wardrobe) but it's adequate to say Mark became conspicuous by his absence.

He totally abandoned me.

Emma kissed me after. Then she said she would call me a cab. She said she had to be up early and not all girls needed cuddles all of the time. She pecked my cheek on the doorstep, gently squeezed my arm and said "See you soon."

And it was only ten minutes later, travelling in the back of the cab, with the grim–eyed driver eyeing me suspiciously in the rear view and wittering on about how he carries a baseball bat in the boot and has zero tolerance for passengers attempting to "do a runner." It was only then, as my melancholy steadily crept and my genitals registered a morose tenderness, it was only then as the early skies turned grey and the rain began to fall, it was only then, *only then,* that Mark Twain deigned to speak to me again.

> "A self-complacent ass, ready to be flattered out of your senses by every petticoat that chooses to take the trouble to do it!"

I was somewhat put out by that – it sounded like he was having a pop – surely he had encouraged me in the endeavour? Wasn't it being a bit hypocritical to criticise me now? That said, if I'm honest, he didn't sound too reproachful. If anything he sounded kind of mournful, disappointed more than angry. But still…

It was probably because I was so colossally weary that I

sharply snapped back.

"It's not like you were always perfect!"

I wasn't going to mention the Isabel Von Kleek Lyon 'other woman' rumours as I knew that would be churlish and I didn't believe them anyway – *vibrating sex toy* – I hardly think so. That bit of my research I had filed under 'Spurious and Exceedingly Unlikely.' But I'd learned enough to know Mark Twain had made his mistakes too. For example he was certainly no investment wizard.

He wasn't a Damien.

Of course I immediately regretted my snap at my friend and I was about to apologise but didn't get the chance. Mark Twain's own riposte was instant and surprising. It came with a discernible melancholic undertone and was missing the least hint of joviality.

> "Delicacy - a sad, sad false delicacy - robs literature of the two best things among its belongings: Family-circle narratives & obscene stories."

Maybe I'd hit a raw nerve or something; I certainly hadn't meant to upset him. I didn't want to bring him down. I didn't want him to suddenly reminisce on any personal regret. What did or didn't occur after his wife's death was his own business and what he may or may not have omitted to write about was of no consequence – he'd blessed us with more than enough. I'd been out of order to even hint at any flaw. Remorse flooded in with a huge side order of self–disgust and I guessed he'd quite rightly be gone now. But no, not this time, he almost immediately continued.

> "We are all inconsistent. We are offended and resent it when people do not respect us; and yet in his private heart no man much respects himself."

And he was obviously on a roll for he followed that incisive gem with

> "Such is the human race. Often it does seem such a pity that Noah and his party did not miss the boat."

I was relieved after that one – he was OK, he wasn't fully furious with me, he was being humorous again. I had to smile at that one too, Mark Twain was right alright, he always is. How could I ever be cross with him? I allowed myself a long wry chuckle. The driver's head immediately jerked up; he twisted his face to behold mine.

"I'm serious. I've told you. No–one takes the piss out of me!"

"Missed the boat but got a cab, hahaha."

"Mess with me and I'll proper fuck you up!"

"Yes, well, that's very comforting to know. You can drop me here please. May I pay in Drachmas?"

In the end I paid him in pounds, shillings and sterling, he didn't share Emma's faith in my funniness.

Rebecca

I hadn't considered cheating, not ever, certainly not consciously, not then, though I do consider it now. I spend time every day wondering why. Perhaps unconsciously I wanted to punish Robert? Or perhaps I just had a need, a desire for some ordinary, reassuring, uncomplicated, straightforward, no-nonsense, no-fuss, recognizable sex. A bit of traditional British if you will. A bit of lights out before pyjamas off, grunt and gasp and that was quite satisfactory and thank you.

No, I didn't need nor want it. Whether I thought I did or not. I did not want it.

Chapter 31

And of course, it wasn't Emma I thought of once I was in through the door and over the newspapers and past the over–brimmed bin and around the mammoth clothes pile and into the unchanged bed. It wasn't Emma I thought of as I wrapped the duvet around me, rolling from side to side until I was completely cocooned. It wasn't Emma's face I saw as I stared up into the contours of the cobweb on the corner of the ceiling. It wasn't Emma I was thinking of as I started to caw in the manner of jackdaw.

It wasn't Emma…

Rebecca

Robert and I had not had sex for four months, not proper sex at least, not since shortly after Robert was faced with a new boss at work. The transition from Christine to George had been hard for Robert to adjust to; the change in him was pretty much immediate and became increasingly noticeable. George did sound a bit of a pain and I was sympathetic at first, up to a degree. I even went along with the tantra initially but my patience didn't last.

Chapter 32

Of course, the education you receive from a lover is only appreciated at the time. Once things shatter and fall apart you realise that all you thought she knew was nonsense. Her perspective was skewed not yours. Yours is clear and clever, obvious and unambiguous, you were right all along.

Rebecca lives a world apart.

It's the Sabbath hence we meet at Alexandra Palace Park. It's a path much travelled, we've been doing such like for years. You're probably familiar with the scenario – you know the kind of thing – boy meets girl – rockets in the sky – drinks on a Friday – something arty on a Saturday – a stroll on a Sunday. I probably don't need to explain.

Today there is a crowd at the perimeter fence – young families pointing at the deer that have deigned to put in an appearance. We've seen them before and hence we walk on by. Next up is a herd of teenagers with helmets and knee pads riding on big wheeled motorized lecterns. They pass by unsteadily; thrilled but self–conscious, chuffed yet cautious.

"Whatever next?" we simultaneously ask. It's one of our things; we pretend to be old–fashioned and quaint.

We walk on and discover there is a 'Compost Giveaway' going on in the Paddock car park and the event is proving popular. Posters have advised the green–leaning keen to bring their own bags and shovels, consequently an array of tools are in evidence. Earnest types are digging deep into the black mound then loading their cars with the good stuff. Whilst the less industrious are winning homemade cupcakes by answering correctly in an eco–quiz.

The questions are unchallenging and hence I nibble at my pink icing and jelly bean garnished prize as we wander on. Then wonder too late if it may have been resplendent with a layer of compost dust. Rebecca did not engage with the quiz, claiming she was not in the mood for cake. I'm reminded that she is the wise one.

Next on the unwritten oft–repeated itinerary is a walk through the Farmers Market. This is usually our favourite part although Rebecca seems less enthused today. I however have full appetite and partake of every sample offered. Would I like to try an 85 percent meat sausage? A prize–winning cider? Would I like a taste of antioxidant stuffed black garlic? Pear crumble? A spice infused fruit juice? Some homemade chutney? Some fruit bread? A cheese bomb?

"Tonight sir, some of that with a glass of red and Antiques Road Show, heaven!"

Would I like to try? *Yes I would!* I eat, I sip, I chat cheerily to vendors, chuckle and walk on.

"Swordfish pattie? Shiatsu massage? Organic five–seed sourdough? Free range quail eggs? Stuffed vine leaves? Locally sourced walnuts? Goose breast shreddings?"

"Yes please. No thank you. Yes please. Yes please. Yes please. Yes please. Yes please"

All too soon it's over. It has to be. Rebecca has oft reminded me that it's bad form to double–back and repeat the process.

But today's Adventure is not yet done. We walk on.

There are numerous, indeed a plethora of coffee shops to choose from in Crouch End. In the end we opt for cappuccino and a shared plain croissant in *Spiazzo.* They win because there we can sit outside and we yearn to sit outside because it's a bright sunny day. Our table is a good one, we are very lucky. That's always been one of our things too – things work out in our favour – the Gods like us. Rebecca however seems a little agitated today and says she is, "Just going to the loo."

Whilst she has gone a pirate walks past. He's been to the supermarket. It's 12.30 pm and he is a fully–grown man. He has a braided beard, he has a cutlass, he has a hat, he has seaworthy knee length boots, he has a big buckled belt, he has full piratical drapery and two Waitrose carrier bags. He honestly does. And yet no–one is hurling unkind expletive–laden abuse or even batting the proverbial eyelid.

I'm reminded how much I like Rebecca's world.

Rebecca returns. We usually dip the shared croissant in the cappuccino. Today she doesn't want to. I'm allowed to have it all. We don't speak much but instead watch a very determined yet meticulously refined squabble develop over the adjacent table and chairs.

"I believe I was here first."

"No. My daughter was instructed to secure a seat for me."

We share an eye and smile our special amused smile. Then we sip up and we pay. We cross the road and visit the Cancer Relief shop (£5:50 for a pre–unloved by the look of it, t–shirt from Topman? No, I think not), then into the House of Books for a browse.

"This one sir? *Tales from Shakespeare* by Charles & Mary Lamb, it's on offer, £2?"

"Yes, why not. He's not as good as Mark Twain though you know."

"Yes sir. If you say so sir."

"Thank you, sir. I most certainly do say so sir."

Then it's time for the walk back and although Rebecca is quiet, I assume that she like me believes it has been a pleasant enough Sunday morning Date Adventure. And hence I fully assume the familiar stroll back up the hill to Muswell and her two bed with front and back garden, cherry blossom tree, flavoured tea bags and middle–class toilet seat (it lowers itself calmly rather than dropping with a slam) will be a joyous if uneventful one. The tried, tested, trusted routine will again unfold. But today turns out to be different. Today Rebecca pauses at the Bounds Green tube station entrance and she takes my hand and turns me toward her and she drops the bombshell. She says

"Sorry to drop this bombshell but…"

And for a moment, just a small split moment, I wonder about

that expression – bombshell – the shell of a bomb? The outer casing? Would that explode? Cause damage? Should the expression merely be 'drop this bomb'? But it's only for a moment; I'm intrigued to hear more and I'm suddenly very nervous. Icily so. And when she continues, when she reveals, when she completes the offload, I know for certain, absolutely unequivocally, the expression should undoubtedly be 'BOMB!'.

"I… I've been unfaithful…"

Boy meets girl – rockets in the sky – drinks on a Friday – something arty on a Saturday – devastation on a Sunday – I wish somebody could explain.

Immediately after Rebecca dropped the BOMB, she began to cry.

And I slipped into Dagenham default. An immediate chest out – an instant jaw thrust forward. Bravado unbridled.

"What! Who with?"

"D... Damien..."

"That fu... Right. Well… I'll be off then."

"No, wait… we should talk…"

"Bit late for that."

"Please. I didn't mean it to... it just... we were... he took me to the art boat... the Room for Lon.."

And that point I snorted, turned, marched and did a double quick down the escalator.

Rebecca

Robert had his own unique theory on most things and I guess I indulged him a bit. He was an entertaining storyteller and often likely to intersperse a ridiculous dance or a bit of poetry during his explanations. He was always keen to share his philosophies and I guess I was always keen to listen. The one that most sticks in my mind was his 'Summation–of–Verbal–Professions–of–Affection' theorem, (I wrote that one down – they tended toward long titles.) Robert called them 'attention grabbing teasers' which I told him made them sound rather like high maintenance girlfriends. If I remember correctly, and nowadays I find I strive incredibly hard to remember every detail, he gave that particular theorem a subtitle – he called it 'The Love–Witter–Power–Fear–Gamble Expose.' (I wrote that down too.)

He explained it to me on a day that I will always recall.

Chapter 33

On the train home I started to notice things. I noticed that when people exited their seats they left a very individual indentation. And I also noticed that when the doors opened at each new station air would be sucked in and that would slightly raise the outer coverings of the seats not sat in. This meant they kind of undulated. I also noticed that no two seats were exactly the same. The patterns were similar but each one was slightly out of kilter with the next. I was on the Piccadilly Line hence they were predominantly blue but with orangey red squares and lighter blue blotches. Some looked newer than others, some looked bright and hopeful and their padding was perky. Most however looked worn, weary, crushed into submission, bereft of any hopeful expectation. The arm rests were red and plastic and uniform. Many were scratched and gouged. Casually brutalised.

And during my journey one part of me is now urging me to take the gift – to be thankful – here's your truth – plain and simple – irony *is* the only reality – you knew this right? When you least suspect it's time to expect. *Damien of all deviants.* You've often mused that life spun its webs this way. When you can never believe then comes the deceive. So rejoice! You were right! You clever clever man!

But most of me just wants to grip the armrests and scream.

Especially when another part of me whispers that perhaps Rebecca deserves a man with prospects who can always provide a perfect prosecco. And instantly I inherently know this to be true. It's justice. Inescapable. Caustic Karma will inevitably capture the Fate Fleeing Few. So I laugh. Long and out loud. Rebecca and Damien and Robert – finally we've all got what we were always meant to receive. Celestial balance is restored. The Cosmos rests sated.

And now I do scream.

And then I stop screaming and decide that instead I need to thank her. Suddenly it's imperative. I will thank her via text. Thank her for providing me with insight and reassurance. Tell her how I shall now happily sit down with a packet of cherry bakewells and a nice pot of tea and write an insidiously thoughtful poem about destiny and justice.

I would start now but I can't compose it immediately because I find I can't hold my phone steady. Then later, when I am back at my flat, back in *my* world with no cherry blossom tree and a toilet seat that slams, I can't compose it immediately either. For as soon as I'm inside the front door I start to undress and I do not even think of putting the kettle on or getting pen and paper out. I can't compose it immediately as I am naked now and lying face down in the hall with my head on the bristly doormat that advises 'Muck Off!' and my hands are otherwise engaged – uselessly cupping my icy cold and hideously shrunken genitalia.

And I don't think that I can move.

Rebecca

I had arrived late for a "Drinks Adventure Date" – sweaty and stressed after a signal failure on the District Line. I'd almost cancelled. I wanted to go home and shower rather than meet Robert feeling sticky and covered in an unattractive perspiratory sheen. I didn't want him to go off me. I was unusually nervous and cursing the 30 minutes 'Robert Time' London Underground had denied me. I hated the thought of keeping him waiting and the fact my hair would now be lank.

I needn't have worried. He didn't seem to notice my bedraggled appearance nor care about the time. He was stood on the corner underneath the sign heralding the *Ye Olde Cheshire Cheese, Rebuilt 1667*. It was becoming our regular. He was stood under that sign and smiling his own wide smile and when I arrived, he quickly grabbed me before I could apologise. Placing a widespread palm on each side of my rib cage he squeezed and said, "I love you."

I laughed. Initially I laughed – this was obviously his way of making me feel bad about my timekeeping. But then I realised he wasn't laughing and that his eyes were unusually intense and he seemed to be holding his breath. Then I knew he was serious. That he felt the same. I said, "I love you too" and then I just wanted to cry. I'd honestly never felt happier.

Chapter 34

I continued my Mark Twain research even when I was aware Rebecca might be tiring of listening to my constant relaying of knowledge. It was soon obvious I had become an even more enthusiastic fan than she. I was taken with the details of the man and his life as much as his writing and wanted to discover all. One day I found out that after his death Albert Bigelow Paine, Mark's biographer to be and literary executor, said that for the last year at least Mr. Clemens had been "weary of life".

Weary of life…

I then discovered that some of his works were never published during his lifetime for fear of a marketable reputation being ruined. He'd wanted to tell it like it was but had been dissuaded. I smiled wryly and inwardly applauded – the unpalatable is rarely popular.

But some truths should be told?

I recognised the fact that he'd written such texts were all the more proof of his bravery, his pursuit of depth and his unremitting integrity.

Mark Twain was a man like no other.

Robert explained his Love–Witter–Power–Fear–Gamble theory that very same evening, over dinner at mine. I'd asked him if he minded foregoing his pint of Taddy's lager and instead would consider escorting me home and helping me to shower. He had been happy enough with that suggestion (probably pleased to get me off the street – I truly looked a mess). His face had lit up when I said, "I love you too" and then had morphed instantly to concern when I did indeed begin to cry. We'd later refer to them as "smile tears". They'd get me unexpectedly; usually when he'd do ridiculous things like wave manically, whoop loudly and break into a sprint as soon as he saw me. Even if we were in a crowded shopping centre.

Nutter.

Chapter 35

Rebecca was unique too.

"At least she was honest."

That's what Sis said when I finally admitted that *yes*, it *was* over.

"At least she was honest."

It wasn't all she said as you can probably imagine (it was a long phone call) but it was the thing she said that is now the most resonant thing. The thing that is now forging a jagged tear from the tip of my tongue through to the back of my throat.

At least she was honest.

By saying that of course Sis meant *at least she told you the truth* – Rebecca did not tell a lie. I didn't think about it at the time – it was the least of the rawness. But I dissect every detail now, I want to know even though I can't understand. And I find I'm confused. Are integrity and honesty not the same? It was Mark Twain who led me to this particular ponder. I'd finished four packets of Jaffa Cakes, the last of the food in the Treats–to–share–with–Rebecca–at–Christmas–Cupboard (I genuinely had one) before Sis finally hung up. And then I had been left thinking that maybe she was right; Rebecca was to be admired for her bravery or some such. But then, once we were alone once more, Mark chipped in with his opinion.

> "Courteous lying is a sweet and loving art and should be cultivated."

Yes! Why did she tell me? What was her incentive? Why drop the bomb? Surely it was masochistic? Why punish us both?

> "What I bemoan is the growing prevalence of the brutal truth."

I knew what he meant. I knew *now*. Who was she hoping to impress? What purpose did her confession serve? Who benefitted from it? Mark allowed me a little time to ponder it all for myself but he hadn't finished offering his opinion.

> "An injurious truth has no merit over an injurious lie. Neither should ever be uttered."

Another good point. What was her intention? Was it purely to salve her conscience? Did she really feel *she owed it to me?* Or was it purely to make herself feel better? Was she selfishly self–flagellating – be angry Robert, be upset Robert, be destroyed Robert – just so that I may legitimately feel terrible? Some kind of conscience curing? Was that all it was? *Pass me the salve pass me the salve* – I'll get the weight off *my* chest by twisting the serrated dagger of truth deep into *his*?

> "The man who speaks an injurious truth lest his soul be not saved if he do otherwise, should reflect that that sort of a soul is not strictly worth saving."

When Mark says 'man' he means 'man' or 'woman' that's just how they spoke back then. I know that and I recognise that yet again he has spouted a perfect summation – *Souls worth saving.* Maybe that was it – a pre–emptive Pearly Gates apology – Bless my soul! Save my soul! *Rest his soul.* Souled out… souled down the river… souled to the highest bidder… *The soul recipient... The soul benefactor... Hurt and sole…*

In truth, I could do with Mark quietening down now, he's

emphasised his point, I've got the message. I'm off and away on my own terrible tangents. But he has a last salvo – an encapsulation or some such;

> "It takes your enemy and your friend, working together, to hurt you to the heart; the one to slander you and the other to get the news to you."

And that does it. That thought is enough – a best friend and an arch–enemy – Rebecca and Damien – working together.

Working out together…

I kick the Christmas Cupboard. And I know I shouldn't do that – its constructed of mid–price relatively solid Swedish flat–pack material. It cracks but so do my toes. I have to laugh. I should do at least. But I can't quite manage to.

Instead, I yelp.

Rebecca

It transpired that Robert's theory was based along the lines of a miscommunication through fear, how the risk of revealing our emotions ensures we often do not. I can still hear him now; in a weird kind of way his voice is still with me. His voice and so many images. I can see him getting up from the table and pacing. I can see his hands clasped behind his back and his head bent in a mock professorial manner and I can hear him.

"Then sometimes someone shows their hand. The brave or the needy. The hopeful or the reckless. They can't take the wait so they take the gamble. Knowing they're the one that will lose. They're the only one who can now lose. Because now the other knows, now the other has the surety, now they have the power. Now it's all on their terms. And so the temptation is to bite the tongue. And its fear that holds them back. And it's not a weak fear, it's a fear far greater, it's a fear of hopes dashed. Hopes crushed. It's an honourable fear. An understandable fear. And it's the worst kind of fear because it's a logical fear. It's the instinct for self–preservation battling the urge to reveal. It's not imagined. It's a true fear."

I can remember him pacing and earnestly spouting and I can remember being impressed by his unorthodox analysis of all and sundry and realising, generally just further realising that he was very insightful, hugely entertaining, much brighter than he let on, very difficult to predict and a borderline headcase. Realising all of that but mostly realising that I, that we, were very lucky.

Chapter 36

It's hours later. Possibly. Or days. Maybe merely a morass of minutes. I've been limping. Perhaps that's a clue. And I've been reminiscing. And now I'm revisiting. I've obviously dressed and travelled west. A long way west – to the Kings Road and the *Saatchi Gallery* to be precise (scene of Date Adventure 7). I don't know why I'm back here. Repeat to punish perhaps? Re–trawl to recall?

And I do recall. Everything. All the gory. They were showing work by Germans and I was immediately questioning whether mind–mashing mushrooms were legal in Frankfurt. One 'piece of art' looked to be a metal coat stand and hanging from it was one solitary item – a grubby purple towel. I had frowned and wondered was art appreciation a complex cognitive issue. Was worth earned or assumed? Was the cynic happier than the lemming? Were the Emperor's clothes deemed designer by default? These were the questions I asked Rebecca. We'd had a chat, a discussion, a two–way tease and she had explained. We'd finished up smiling.

That's what we always did.

I chuckle a little, more in than out and then I reach for her hand.

It's not there.

I wander on. Alone. Past a painted piece of French bread. Then four apple cores threaded together. I continue to browse as once before but know that I'm now uncoupled. My mind's eye reacting with every step but unable to project my previous partner. My memory thrusting long forgotten details – recalling the minutiae – our discovery that the photos were on the top floor (clever that – keep the best stuff up top to ensure a full traipse through). I take the stairs.

I discover they're celebrating an anniversary of the *Sunday Times* magazine and have blown up some of their most proud pictures. Jean Shrimpton is looking good in collage, Colonel Gaddafi is looking a bit Michael Jackson in gold drapery, Amy Winehouse is looking iconic as Amy Winehouse. And a seaside coastline pic is looking comparatively incongruous.

Hang on though – don't be hasty – see beyond. Read the small print – indulge the caption – it reads... *Beachy Head!* And apparently that was near Eastbourne! Which isn't that far!

Message received! Focus restored! I immediately shrug off my Cloak of Whimsical Reverie and fish for my phone. She'd popped her number in at the party. She'd insisted.

"Wenchy! Fancy a road trip?"

It was a phone call and an enquiry I never envisaged I'd make but she'd sprung to mind instantly.

Curious.

Very curious.

Somewhat curious?

I was a little surprised when Emma instantly agreed to my suggestion. Just like that, no hesitation. She said she loved a spontaneous invite and was glad that I'd called as I was "Quite an amusing Knob–end."

I hung up then and rang Sis.

I can remember that one espousal of Roberts' pretty much verbatim, his 'Love is a Gamble Theorem' as he said he'd shorten it "for the layman." I remember his sincere pacing, his slow deliberate explanation and then his sudden crescendo.

"That's how it works, that's how it always works. Admission ensures vulnerability... Surrender... Defeat… An abdication of any power… An abdication of any self–protection… Most often that's how it works… most often that's how it transpires… Nearly always... and so the words are withheld and the imaginings remain imagined. And life is safer but lesser than it potentially could be, lesser than it should be because the gamble is not taken. But not this time! This time I took the gamble! I said it. I admitted it. I shared it. I offered it. I said it and then you said it too! The gamble paid off! I was rewarded! We were rewarded! The imaginings are no longer imagined! I LOVE YOU REBECCA SUSAN MORLEY!"

With that he had ripped of his t shirt and shouted "Faster than Flatley!" His dancing always made me laugh. It always got me and it proved he wasn't borderline; he was a complete headcase. He was *my* complete headcase.

It seems impossible that we let it slide.

Chapter 37

I'm meeting Emma at 11. We're driving to the coast. Her text says she is looking forward to seeing me.

I'm thinking about that expression now: twisting it for truth – *looking forward* and *what two*? I'm also thinking about how sometimes things just work out. As if they're predetermined. *With the help of our friends* – Mark no doubt arranged for that photo to be on display in the gallery. Sis has lent me her car and filled it with petrol. She said a trip will do me good and it was perfect timing as she and Bruv–in–law were headed to Gibraltar for Christmas and wouldn't be needing their excessively cheery bright yellow Mini Cooper. They were going to leave it at Gatwick anyway so if I agreed to drive them to the airport then it was all mine. I agreed that it was perfect timing. (I thought it was best that Sis would be out of the country too. Though I didn't verbalise that relief.)

In fact, I spoke very little enroute to the airport; Bruv–in–law and I do not chat excessively. I sensed he would have been happier leaving Herbie in Long Stay. He sits in the back and says things like, "Fuck me! Watch what lane you're in!" and, "Concentrate you Muppet!"

Sis tells him to shush and reassuringly pats my knee.

As soon as the suitcases were out of the boot Bruv–in–law was on his way into Departures, he didn't thank nor tip the driver. Sis lingered and said, "Your driving was a little erratic Robert…are you o… We could always cancel if… I know I did tell you months ago that we'd be away at Christmas…but that was before…we booked it before…"

I assured her I was fully tickety–boo and that I had fine festive plans of my own. Then I told her to watch out for the aggressive

Barbary Apes. Although if she wanted a jolly yuletide grin then why not surreptitiously slip a couple of custard cream biscuits into Bruv–in–law's trouser pocket and watch him get monkey fumbled.

I kissed her cheek then, waved her away then got back in the car. I noticed Sis had left a packet of fruit pastilles on the dashboard. I couldn't have asked for a better sibling. I do know that.

Rebecca

Robert would do things I initially (and often) thought were slightly ridiculous things – like talk to strangers – shop assistants and the like. He'd hold up the coffee queue simply to chat beans with the barista (which in truth he'd have no interest in – at home he was always tea by choice). Then ask for a "most marvellous muffin" recommendation. He'd order us coffee in Starbucks and insist they jot our names as Thomas Jefferson Snodgrass and Olivia Louise Langdon. Ridiculous but it worked – he'd get people to smile – to buy into and go along with his imaginings. To believe in his fantasies.

He was always giving me little gifts too; leaving chocolates in my coat pocket or presenting me with Robert–made cards. I've a whole box that I used to look through occasionally (more often recently). One of my favourites is covered in hand–drawn steamboats and stained with tea and Monty saliva. It states that Robert will always strive to be worthy of my compliments. Headcase.

Chapter 38

FAST FORWARD whoooooosh!

"I'd like to see the stats for suicides on the way to Beachy Head."

Emma doesn't reply, Emma just grunts, Emma's doing Sudoku. The drive is proving interminable; we crawl through Royal Tunbridge Wells then we trawl through tunnels of trees along the A26. One's not as grand as it sounds and the other is downright gloomy. The traffic is horrendous and intermittently, though regularly, when she's not scanning rows, checking columns or applying the logic of elimination, Emma is landing playful caresses on my thigh. She has referred to our expedition as a "sexy spin to the seaside" and I haven't had the energy to try and correct her. Indeed, I'm becoming morbidly fascinated by her apparent enthusiasm for what lies ahead but each new squeeze still catches me off guard and causes me to tremblejump.

Emma seems to find my discomfort amusing. She finds lots of things amusing; we pass a road sign for Lower Dicker. Emma points and laughs. Exorbitantly. Then, ironically enough, there's one for Laughton. That gets me wondering – laughed on? Laugh ton? The ton of laugh? Next there's one for Upper Dicker just before the Boship roundabout near Polegate and I know I've lost the battle.

I grasp the steering wheel tighter. I try to remember the basics – manoeuvre–mirror–signal and keep your hands at ten past two. It helps. A little. In time we reach Eastbourne.

Sunshine Carnival Possible Delays. Bus Tours. Beachy Head Departures.

"Did the sign really say that?"

Emma doesn't know, she wasn't looking, she's started a new puzzle, what's my point? Never mind. I Grasp the steering wheel tighter. Grasp and grit.

Nearly there but too early to check in to the hotel, stop instead at the *Birling Gap Café*. Coaches outside. Three coaches. Come ye tourists one and all. Germans in the main. I buy tea for me, a latte for Emma and decide we should share one of the solid–looking rock cakes offered at £1.75.

We search for a seat then sit in a kind of booth – a table against a wall. There's a man opposite with two shaggy dogs and a pair of Wellington Boots. He looks at us and we look at him. There are gaps in his teeth. Emma strokes a head, a tail thumps, and we all relax. It actually *is* peaceful here. To our right is an olde photograph in a frame. It shows the cliff top outside and hordes of holidayers. It has a caption underneath.

> *'The Hollington Boys Club from Dulwich were among many groups that camped in a football pitch sized field behind the Birling Gap hotel, between 1947 and 1960. They had 40 tents with straw pallets on iron beds to sleep in, a mess tent and marquee where they ate bread and dripping and drank cocoa in the evenings.'*

I feel emotional.

The man with the dogs and the boots and the gaps in his teeth gets up to leave, he nods at us and we nod at him. Emma holds out her hand and the last of the cake is licked from her palm. We're alone now. And I wonder what's going through her mind. And I recognize this is unusual, atypical, *this has become unusual, atypical*, I'm considering the thoughts of others. She seems focused, I wonder why and so I ask. It turns out she's busy scouring the café's inhabitants.

"I'm trying to spot potential jumpers."

She knows the history after all.

I feel momentarily chastened; perhaps I've over–assumed her vacuity. I ask her how she'd know one if she spotted one.

"Well, for one thing – they wouldn't be sharing their cake."

Perhaps I've under–assumed her depth of humour too.

I don't analyse my assumptions for too long though – I'm otherwise distracted – I'm suddenly wondering why they're referred to as "victims".

FAST FORWARD wheeeeeee!

We've checked–in.

Rebecca would have liked this. That's my first impression. It honestly is. And it's an open and generous thought. Then there's a split second or two before it becomes bitter tinged. Before it becomes *Rebecca would have liked this.* She would have liked it because it is 'unusual' 'quaint' 'unique' 'arty' 'boutique' words like that. We would have both been pleased upon entry. Emma however, is not overly awed – perhaps Emma assumes a hotel is just a hotel. *Ha! She obviously has no idea.* Emma suggests we get out of here quick. How about as soon as she's changed and ready I get her drunk at the imaginatively titled '*Beachy Head'* pub and then I can bring her back here and shag her royally? She actually phrases it like that – makes it sound like a regal reward. She doesn't want to sit or read or stare at the sea.

"We're here to have fun, Knob–end."

I don't know why I chose this hotel but perhaps I do. *OF COURSE I DO.* It's a lighthouse that's really a hotel – it's not actually at sea but you can easily imagine. I feel it has resonance; it of course reminds me of *A Room for London* – all is not what it seems – there's an element of malignant deceit. More importantly, it's perched on the cliff edge.

Whilst Emma's in the shower I strip down and put my pyjamas on. They're sky blue. And new. And T–Rex patterned. I then put my socks, jeans, shirt and jumper back on over them. I never usually wear pyjamas. I bought them on a whim. They're alleged to glow–in–the–dark. Perhaps they'll provide illumination.

I imagine Emma may be a long time preparing so I take the opportunity to go for a walk. As I exit the hotel, I ponder the phrase 'checking–in' and then the phrase 'checking–out.'

Rebecca

Nowadays, I often wonder about fate and coincidence and opportunities that open or are offered and our choice regarding how we respond to them. For example, I wonder what would (or most definitely would not) have happened if no–one had come up with the idea of *A Room for London*. If no–one had then been impressed with the idea and commissioned its go ahead, If generous support had not then been given by groups with names such as *The Company of Angels*. I wonder how certain lives would be very different now if that piece of art hadn't been allowed to happen. If it hadn't been given prominence. If it hadn't been allowed to captivate and enchant. I was hooked instantly – from the moment I heard about it and all the more so when I discovered the boat's design was an homage to the *Roi des Belges*, the vessel sailed by Joseph Conrad up the River Congo; the setting for his most famous work *Heart of Darkness*.

(A title that I think about too. When I'm being most unkind to myself).

Chapter 39

FAST FORWARD whoah!!!

Emma says, "We're like a famous couple, you know like Bonnie and Clyde or something..."

People *are* looking at us. They have been since we entered the pub. I imagine it may be the attire. Emma said she had a treat for me and it seems it may have caught the eye of others too. The heels of her shoes are six inches high and painted gold. The shoes themselves are white patent and resplendent with a union jack on the left and stars and stripes on the right.

Emma says, "Or John and Jackie…"

It's possibly not just the shoes though. When we attempted to enter the pub there was a bit of an incident. I had to pull hard as the evening was gusty and the door jammed tight. When I threw it open the wind took advantage and a sudden whoosh of air ensured I was knocked backward and much of Emma's outfit was momentarily sent skyward. We quickly grabbed for each other, steadied ourselves then fought valiantly with the door in a shared fit of fluster. We eventually managed to wedge it back shut and it was only then that Emma was able to smooth her outfit. During those dramatic moments it had become apparent to me that Emma had a slogan on her underwear. I wondered if others had noticed too.

Now Emma says, "Or David and Victoria Beckham…"

Emma has sat down and crossed one leg over her knee. I can see rather a lot of her thigh. There's a notable space between the top of her stocking and the hem of her fur–trimmed dress. Perhaps that's deliberate – I can't claim to know an awful lot about fashion. I do know however that like the one at the party, this outfit has a name – "It's my Little Miss Red Riding Santa Outfit." Emma had informed me such when emerging from the hotel bathroom. "It's the little the treat I've been hinting about. A little thank you. It's very nice of you to take me away for the night."

"If my sister could see you now…"

"Haha, Knob–end! She'd probably laugh. But we'll keep it our little secret. Now get me to that pub!"

I notice the tops of her stockings are decorated with golden bells and mistletoe. Despite some effort my eyes are inexorably drawn. I say, "Did you know Mark Twain invented an adjustable garment strap?"

It's true. But Emma appears not to hear. Or care. Emma says, "Or Brad Pitt and Angelina Jolie..."

I've noticed Emma's cleavage now too. It was unavoidable. She's just leant forward to poke me in the chest and ask if *I'm* listening. And now she's speaking again.

Emma says, "Or William and Kate…"

I suggest one. Perhaps to prove that I am listening. I say, "Or Kimberley Clarke and Armitage Shanks?"

She ignores me. I like that. I envy it. It's more than ignoring, she just doesn't hear me. She only hears what she likes to hear. She can filter effectively. Not all that witters is told. I envy her greatly.

Emma says, "Or James Dean and Marilyn Monroe…"

"Were they ever a cou…"

Then I stop myself, engagement is futile. Instead I go to the bar where I enquire if they serve arsenic. No, it's not one of those Swedish ciders. No, don't worry, it's OK, it was kind of a joke. Guinness is fine.

The Beachy Head is the sort of establishment where an ordered cup of tea comes in a china pot with a separate jug of milk and a small bowl of sugar on a tray. Emma laughs shrilly when I place it in front of her. Then punches my arm and says, "Another G and T you Knob–end!"

I return to the bar and realise I am not being as nice as I could be. I'm being unfair and selfish. *Emma has done me no harm.* I take a moment to think about the positive and encouraging message that she had inadvertently displayed when we'd made our entrance. Red embroidery on Emma's white underwear stated 'Season to be Cheerful.' I order her a double Bombay Sapphire, Fever–Tree tonic and a selection of savoury snacks.

When I return, Emma smiles and tells me Cheese & Onion is her favourite and asks me how I knew. It's a little disconcerting. She's still wearing her Santa hat and the white fur of the cape draped around her shoulders makes her seem almost queenly. *Emma in Ermine.* I mirror her smile. I genuinely do. Curiously, the Royal theme then continues – Emma tells me how she fantasises about Prince Harry and I manage to relax a little more. She has a theory.

"I reckon a lot of happiness is linked to a healthy sex life, you just have to get to know and trust someone, find out what they like. Then do things you both enjoy."

"Not tantric."

"What's that?"

"Not something I'd recommend."

"Right, well anyway, back to the Prince – I imagine him – Harry – coming round to mine with that cheeky grin suggestively brandishing a large jar of marmalade. That's why he always looks happy I reckon – he definitely has a healthy sex life – you can tell. It's in the eyes – a shine. He has it and I think maybe you've lost it. Who do you fantasise about?"

" I.. I only ever… no–one…"

It's hard to have thoughts when you're filled with emotions. Rebecca and I preferred other breakfast spreads. And, apart from the one occasion, only on toast.

I return to the bar.

FAST FORWARD fuuuuuuuuu!

And now I find myself pondering upon the expression 'sex mad'. It's an unusual expression if you think about it. Sex deranged? Sex crazy? Sex obsessed? Sex mad – it's a strange one – we don't say 'love mad' and yet I was love mad, *we* were love mad. Rebecca and I were love mad. *Don't worry about him – e's a bit mad, Love.* It probably means keen – sex keen, not sex mad – madness is different to keenness. And I'm realising Emma is healthily keen. And undeniably skilled. On a purely nuts and jolts level she's top of the game. But this is solely sex. And nowadays I find that impossible to understand. It's somewhat intriguing and it presently feels rather nice but I sense I will only end up feeling sorrow.

We continue however and although my focus is somewhat erratic, I'm grateful for one small mercy – at least tonight Mark Twain hasn't decided to join us. And then in a curious moment, Emma and I make eye contact. For a second something locks. Connects. Ties. There's a shared fragment of stasis. A slither of peace. Understanding even. Then in another moment it's passed. Diminished. Gone. Soon after, Emma says, "You can cum now if you want."

Then shortly after that she falls asleep. Her final words before slumber were, "Hopefully I won't but sometimes I snore when I've been drinking."

Her words before that had been, "I can't believe you kept your pyjamas on, Knob–end."

I hadn't said much in reply.

After a time, Emma does begin to snore and I take that as my cue – I begin to dress fully once more. I check in my pockets. Yes, it's there – I have remembered the key-ring torch. It's a Lego man and he shines through his feet if you press him on his stomach. He is blue and red and yellow and beams in traditional jolly fashion. He was a gift. I named him Laurence of Lego.

I hope his light will suffice.

Rebecca

It was ironic really or unfortunate at least, Robert liked everyone but he didn't like George. (Well, George and Damien.) He never hit it off with George and I guess you could say he began to bring his work home with him. It was bad timing too as although I tried to be understanding my growing resentment about aspects of our own relationship meant I wasn't overly sympathetic. In truth my patience was limited (or worn) and I guess that truth tells its own story.

Yes, truth Rebecca! Come on, this is a 'truth' letter – so you better tell it!

OK, here goes – I guess the *sex thing* was an issue that needs admitting – and even acknowledging that is difficult (and incredibly frustrating) because initially it was perfect. It was passionate and natural and Robert was always eager to please. He was mortified the first few times by what he very charmingly referred to as his 'premature jubilation'. It was a tiny bit frustrating but mostly flattering really. An issue we would later refer to as "the quickness stage" and one which we soon rectified (Radio 4 became a much–favoured station). I'd never laughed so much during sex and that shipping forecast episode was indicative of our whole relationship – from the start it was fun, open, trusting and inventive. It was loving. But then time passed and things changed – or rather they didn't and (ironically) that became an issue. I had growing concerns that we were not progressing toward any tangible goals and that was creating a resentment. Meanwhile Robert had to deal with his Dad's death and then there was his new boss, George, who really seemed to irritate him and subsequently things really began to unravel. First there was his bizarre tantric phase and then I instigated the stubborn and ridiculous standoff. We were losing so much of our intimacy and not even realising. We were erecting our own barriers. We became inadvertent masochists.

Chapter 40

Beachy Head itself is not as you might imagine. It was certainly not as I imagined. I'd anticipated something wholly different. My afternoon walk had proved very educational. One thing I hadn't been expecting was the scale – it's huge. It's a vast winding edge of green that nature (*The Beast*) has savagely sliced. It's a wavy series of wedges created by the cruel swipes of a merciless elemental blade. It's the precise product of a soulless incisor – a lustful fury cruelly culling stone to unclothe its softened milky innards. My afternoon walk had stoked my poetic side – I hadn't anticipated that either. And realised I was probably rusty. No matter though – it evidenced that I had felt… *something*.

I'd walked the coastline all the way from the *Belle Tout Lighthouse* hotel to the *Birling Gap Café* and then to the *Beachy Head* public house that Emma had spotted on our way in. Now I was returning filled with raw air, adrenalin and a sharp sense of validation – I had definitely come to the right place. I was brimming, overflowing, ready to espouse, ready to share, ready to earnestly debate.

Emma was lain on the bed wrapped in a towel.

"Where the fuck have you been?"

She talks like that sometimes. It's less provocative than it sounds. She's almost smiling when she says it. She's not truly agitated. That's how I gauged the situation at least. And seeing as she'd asked where I'd been so I began to tell her where I'd been. And all the details I'd seen.

I told her of the tiny wooden crosses and the occasional bouquets that decorated the cliff. I told her of the white chalk mosaics – the chippings of cliffs gathered and arranged as hearts or flags or messages of love. *Memorial monuments*. I told her of the gamut and juxtaposition of emotions. The overflowing intermingled mismatch of squeamish – excited – awestruck – horrified – thrilled – inspired. I talked about natural beauty and the history of human suffering. I talked about the atmosphere near the edge. Words spilled – words like 'tragic' – 'noble' – 'romantic' – 'uplifting' – 'haunting.'

Words spewed in fact. Streamed out. Babbled even. I mentioned a heightened awareness. An *actual* awareness. I talked of abdicating autonomy to the elements – I spoke of the wind wobbling faces with a sardonic sense of merriment. I mentioned the brash buffetings and recalled the pervasive sense of sudden ending – the sheer drop always prominent on the periphery. I mentioned the fact that there were no dogs chasing sticks. I had laughed at that thought – what a way for a loyal mutt to go – just chasing sticks. Undone by a blinkered urgency to please. *A myopic self–destructive trust.*

I relayed that to my surprise there was no fencing – no barriers – nothing that physically stopped the deathly determined. Just little wooden signs stating 'Cliff Edge'. Ha! *Cliff Edge.* A good name for a hard–rock front man. *Cliff Edge and the Loose Bowelled Lemmings...*

Whoops, I was drifting again. I wasn't focused and I should be – this felt important. I'd like her to understand. I note then that Emma's eyes have taken on the look of the long since double glazed. I try to get back on track, I know this should be riveting. I tell her about the German teachers organizing their class photos – children allowed forward two at a time for a close–to–the–cliff–edge photo. One teacher either side of the couple being snapped, one teacher behind the couple being snapped. German efficiency at its finest – no risks, no chance of a wayward wander, a backward stagger or a dramatic dash. School Outing Rule Number One – the same number back on the coach as that which departed.

The eyes clear a little. Emma smiles and her voice is not unkind.

"Right, well, it sounds like you had a lot of fun, now how

about we do something I like? I've done my nails, my lashes and my makeup – now I just need to get dressed. I think you're gonna like what I'm wearing tonight."

Fair enough.

She has been patient.

And so we went to the pub.

As you know.

But now that's in the past.

And this is the present.

Emma sleeps.

The pub has long–since closed.

And the dark has fully descended.

Rebecca

This bit I'm finding hard to write. It's embarrassing me even though I'm the only person who will ever read it (I insisted Mary agreed to that even though she appeared disappointed). The tantric phase was infuriating and ridiculous but the standoff was worse in many ways. It was more damaging. It seems nonsensical now that I didn't take time to consider why I was punishing us both – to question why we were allowing such a division or to recognise that we were effectively self–harming. Very effectively. I guess it had kind of started as a tease but it soon became a battle of wills and principle. We discovered we could both be stubborn.

Chapter 41

I think I'm alone now. And that thought makes me smile and then it makes me sing. *'There doesn't seem to be anyone around…'* Then I stop singing because the lyrics aren't true – thankfully I am not alone. I know if I wait then he will come. Especially if I ensure I'm in a pertinent poignant position – ready to go as it were. And as long as I ask for his attention respectfully. I get down on my hands and knees. Then I lay flat. After a time, I take a breath and begin to crawl.

Grass is different at night. Dew–draped not pollen–riddled. It tickles your nostrils but it doesn't annoy. Its assault is tender. As my face grazes the ground so the blades react. They respond and yield, they interact and investigate. Gossamer–light proddings – wet tendrils in then out – slippery slithers of thin eager tongues – up the right – up the left – or bend unto the bridge.

Suddenly I've reached the edge. Fingers first then face. Now my head hangs over. The wind roars and a sparse remembered childhood trip to Southend is recalled – a soft voice – a mother's voice. "Take deep breaths, the sea air is good for you. Breathe in through your nose and out through your mouth."

Exhilaration.

Of a kind.

Once settled I fumble in pocket until I'm able to produce Laurence. My gifted Lego key ring still holds its label – an obvious oversight but no matter – being nice is never about the price. It states what it has always stated 'Reduced, £5.99'. I can feel its cheapened sticker rough against my palm. Undervalued yet proud. I never had the urge to peel it off.

I press the belly gently now and the feet immediately shine – a valiant effort but they're outdone by the night and there is no moon. I don't know which *part* of the edge I've reached but I'm sure that's okay – I'm sure it doesn't matter. I'm sure there's no strict etiquette; it can't be a case of one spot only. There are no wardens, no guides, no jobs-worths with megaphones *"Move along please, stick to the designated Drop Off."* No, it makes no difference – alight at Birling or Beachy or any ridge in betwixt.

I shuffle forward to allow my chest a taste of freedom; I stretch my arms out wide and I think of England. England during the war – the air defence artillery perched upon these cliff tops. I think of men desperate to protect and other men determined to destroy.

The dark has fully descended.

I loosen the two keys that dangle from Laurence's ring. A chunky brute and shiny Yale. Once precious metals with no value now. I hold them out as an offering. Flat in my palm. I'm offering all that was once offered to me. Nickel and brass.

The wind howls.

I flick my wrist and allow them to fall.

Rebecca

I told him I was fed up with him constantly complaining about George and not liking his employ and that consequently I had decided there'd be no sex until he had written a CV and applied for at least 3 new jobs. It was the first time we hadn't discussed things together – the first time I'd imposed something without giving him a say. It was frustration more than anything – I couldn't understand why he didn't just change things; I knew he could do much better career–wise. I was convinced that he could and that was part of it – I didn't want him working for low–pay in an admin job that it sounded like he could do standing on his head. Especially if he no longer enjoyed it!

But now I realise I could have helped more. I even refused to help him with his CV, I told him he'd have to at least make a start on it as I wasn't prepared to do everything for him. I can remember how he looked at me then, he didn't say anything but his expression said it all: *I would do anything for you. I would always help you…*

He would have too. I know that's true.

Chapter 42

Once the keys were gone, I lowered my arms. Let them dangle. And now my fingertips have come to rest – they've settled upon chalky white. Then they've scratched, scraped and dug in. I don't know how long I've clutched the cliff and waited but it's certainly a time. Experience tells me I now need to be still; I need to detach. I can do that. I am patient.

I try to be.

"Mark? I'm ready. Mark..?"

No answer.

"Mark? Mark, mate? Mark, mate, please… Mark… I need your help."

No answer.

"Mark? Come on man… Mark..? It's me… Mark, come on mate… Mark?"

> "They do say that when a man starts downhill everybody is ready to help him with a kick, and I suppose it is so."

That gives me quite a start. I nearly slip slide shudder completely over the edge. He wasn't usually so sudden. Or to the point. Or so loud. And I hadn't been asking for a kick – just advice, encouragement. He sounded cross today, impatient or some such.

"Hi, Mark, sorry, it's just that… I've been doing a lot of thinking…"

> "Man is a Reasoning Animal. Such is the claim. I think it is open to dispute."

Rather abrupt. I was starting to feel anxious; this wasn't like him, this wasn't soothing. I hoped I hadn't upset him again and realised I needed to explain.

"It's just being here, it's… I don't know… evocative… it seems like… I feel like I'm on the cusp… I think… I don't really know… I can't quite explain..."

"All of us contain Music and Truth, but most of us can't get it out."

Harsh and impatient. I felt my heart thumping. I was letting him down again, I wasn't matching up, I wasn't meeting him halfway. I was boring him.

"Mark, mate, I'm really sorry. I know I… I know I'm not… I know… I know it's… It's just I don't know if… if I'm 100 percent… ready…that's why I was hoping we could talk…"

"In my age, as in my youth, night brings me many a deep remorse. I realize that from the cradle up I have been like the rest of the race- never quite sane in the night."

That was better. In a way. He sounded more wistful than angry now, apologetic almost. He probably realized he was being tetchy; he probably regretted his insensitivity.

"That's alright Mark, it's okay, we're mates, it's cool. Yeah, the night time eh? Things seem different somehow don't they? What's your favourite time of day then? When's the best time to talk?"

Mark Twain didn't answer.

He was gone.

I waited for a long time, still face down and prone, halfway over with two fistfuls of chalky cliffside. But now there was only wind in my ears. I lay still and waited. I cleared my mind and waited. I considered the expression 'cliff–hanger' and waited. I lay and I waited.

After a time, I noticed a greyness – the beginning of dawn.

And then I felt my bladder nagging – *so much for the mind but ne'er forget the body*. I felt a flicker of déjà vu – a reminiscence of the museum. A Monte Cristo moment. A recall that could still make me smile. I loosened my fingers and scuttled back from the edge. Then I stood, unzipped and aimed my stream toward it.

Now, as dawn continued to rise indifferently, I turned away from the cliff and began walking in the direction of the café once more. I could see clearer now and I knew what I needed to do. Or had a clue that I knew what I wanted to do. I stopped and did three star–jumps. Just for fun. Then I headed toward the staircase.

Staircase was probably the wrong word it was more akin to a stairwell. *A stare–well*, Ha! That thought reminded me momentarily of Margot. I shook her off with a shudder. Refocused. I reminded myself it didn't need a name – suffice to say it was a series of cleverly constructed steps that led you down onto the beach. (I'd noticed them when Emma and I were sat with the man with the wellies.) It appeared they provided the only legitimate way down. I hurried – eager for the crunch of pebble. I was soon rewarded and immediately on my knees once more.

Thinking of Rebecca.

Wherever and whenever we found ourselves in such terrain we would search and we would not be denied. It was our thing, it was one of our things – part of our unique sub culture, our identity as a couple, our universe created. Whenever and wherever we found ourselves on a pebbled beach we would search for a stone with a hole. A whole hole. A stone with a hole through its centre. All the way through. Not a chip or a dent or a hollow but a whole hole. Because finding one was lucky. It meant something and it would be kept as treasure. It would have significance as memory and symbol. As a reminder. It was a ritual rummaging, a superstitious scrabbling. It was a shared extra layer, a regular re–affirmation. It was fun. And we would not leave the beach without one.

I find one immediately. *That's never happened before.*

It's the size of an egg but rounder. And the hole is huge, my whole pinkie can slip through unfettered. *The previous holes were never that big.* My index finger fits too. The hole should not be that big. *This one's been cleaved.* And it's not heart–shaped, it's not, not really. I know that. *I do.* I pause but then do put it in my pocket. Immediately feeling its ice against my thigh. I climb back up. It's a trudge now. I'm drained.

When I arrive back at the lighthouse Emma is resplendent on the bed. She is naked and still. I notice her mascara has run a little and her toes are red from their squeeze into those shoes. I pull the covers up over her. I pause then. I could lay a kiss on her cheek, tenderly. I could stroke her hair and softly whisper goodnight.

Damned if I do?

Now I undress for a second time. Or is it the third? I catch myself in the mirror – a joke in jimjams. I get on my hands and knees again. *For the fourth time?* I crawl and I squeeze and I wriggle and turn until finally I'm sufficiently wedged under. This time face up. My head won't fit so it stays outside but all my rest is trapped, safe, contained. Under the bed.

Emma snores above.

Rebecca

It seems hard to believe now because all I can really think about, all I really *want* to think about is the other stuff – the real stuff. What I know was unique and special and that which somehow we lost. It was just little things, things that others probably wouldn't understand but they were the things that connected us and entwined us – that made us *Us*.

I remember one day, Robert made me come to the bedroom window so he could show me evidence of and then explain all about 'Witches Knickers.' He pointed to the colourful plastic flapping on the roof of the 173 bus shelter outside and told me how it was customary for witches to leave their knickers behind after a night of broomstick and bedknobs japery. He explained that was how the Irish knowledgeably referred to what looked to the untrained eye to be mere carrier bags caught in tree branches or upon telegraph poles. He explained the truth of what he referred to as "exotic twig adornments" – flagrant flappings that he had seen liberally shed across the whole of County Leitrim. He then went on to make up a story about a randy leprechaun who happened to stumble upon a coven. In no time I was laughing and suddenly urgent to get Robert back into bed and to carelessly dispense of my own underwear.

Chapter 43

At some stage during the night Mark spoke to me again. He said,

> "You are a coward when you even seem to have backed down from a thing you openly set out to do."

He sounded angry.
Disappointed.
Frustrated.
Deflated.
Baffled.
Let down.

Again.

I shifted a little. Wedged myself tighter.

But somehow, we went from that natural fun enjoyment of each other to bizarre experimental tantra and then to a complete withholding. I wouldn't compromise – he asked me again to help him with the CV but I refused again. I was busy and I was annoyed with his assumption that I would. I was wrong to refuse. The no sex 'game' came to be something else altogether. Something symbolic and ultimately something demeaning. We were hurting ourselves. Destroying our relationship. Whilst not talking about the real issues or confronting the fact we were beginning to disconnect.

Chapter 44

On the drive back from Beachy Head, whilst Emma wore expensive looking headphones and stared yonder out the window, I'd given plenty of thoughts plenty of thought. I dropped her home to Hornchurch then immediately took to the bed upon my return to Dagenham. I then proceeded to pass a duvet dwelt, day–long duration blissfully ignoring calls from the office. (I was confident George was not ringing to enquire of my well–being, rather I assumed he was floundering on a payroll problem the likes of which even a hormone–riddled alcohol–addled adolescent mongoose could deftly decipher.)

Yet now all manner of unpredictable instances have occurred. I opened my eyes after a time and suddenly realised why George had been calling, it was December 23rd, it was the last day of work before yuletide. It would be an early finish; it would be cheap sausage rolls, microwaved pizza and a can or two of supermarket own–brand lager. And George obviously hadn't wanted me to miss out.

So I sat up, rose from the covers, rinsed my mouth, ran some fingers through my hair and headed off.

Surprisingly, George seemed surprised to see me. Taken aback as I complimented his tinsel. He self–consciously removed the single strand from around his neck and lowered the already low volume on his p.c. He had been listening to a song about Rudolf. He honestly had. Then he asked me to wait outside for a few minutes as he had to make an important phone call. After some time (which I spent nodding to passing colleagues and pondering Christmas jumper justification, then borrowing a black marker penand adding new letters and numerals so that George's door now stated Room 313 AKA Room 101) he beckoned me back in, sat me down and offered me a stollen bite.

After some more time, during which conversation was intermittent (though we did discuss Mary's Boy Child), he received a phone call. Then as soon as he put the receiver down, I was invited to follow him to the Board Room.

And now it's kind of a déjà vu but it's not a nice nostalgic one – it all seems slightly more sinister. And far too serious hence I'm having to fight down the giggles. It's a nice feeling, reminiscent of childhood – those gurgles that gather under the chin and try to prise your mouth open – *let me out let me out LET ME OUT!* And Almost Margot almost immediately asks me if I have a problem. That makes me guffaw with vigour. It's a knee–slapper. Almost Margot says she does not see anything amusing about this situation and states it would be a lot more useful to everyone if I simply answered her questions. And so I do.

"Oh yes Almost Margot, I have lots of problems, which one would you like?"

"I wondered if you had a problem that was causing you to laugh."

"Gosh no, my problems are certainly not mirth–worthy."

"I'm glad to hear that. This is not a trivial matter; we've arranged this meeting at very short notice. You weren't expected in. Luckily it works out, you may have noticed we have a guest with us from Head Office, it's a happy coincidence that Mr Rosman was visiting, he's an expert on disciplinary matters."

She's too much. She's said too much, there's too much to digest – *this is not a trivial matter* and *expert on disciplinary matters* – it's too much in one go. I don't know where to begin to giggle and so I don't begin to giggle. Instead, I invite the drifting to recommence. I close my eyes and evoke the Mississippi – it works straight away – there we are: Relaxed Robert, Cheery Huck and Kindly Jim all just lazily watching our corks bob in the hope of a fish supper. It's perfect. Everything makes sense.

For a moment.

"Mr Foxley!"

And perhaps it's Margot's sudden burst that has triggered it, for now I'm off the raft and I'm wearing a suit – I'm reminded of a Welsh Bride at a wedding in Tenby – a drunken reception and her revelation that she could expel wind on cue. This is a true story. *As far as I recall.* She was a friend of Rebecca's from university, a Jane perhaps or a Sarah, nice looking and friendly. I said to her "Go on then" and she replied "Front or back?" It *is* a true story, definitely, the recall is vivid – she produced raucously through her voluminous white dress and we all giggled. Chuckled in fact. Fell about. It was a happy moment. Truly joyful. I wish I had that bride's skill – I'd utilize it now.

Almost Margot is glaring. Unnecessarily in my opinion so I switch my attention to the new boy. He introduced himself earlier with a frown and a too–long too–firm handshake. His name is Daniel Rosman and he's obviously the artillery. You know the type, stubby fingers, shaved head, stretched suit, protuderous belly that would look ridiculous naked.

I tilt my head to one side in order to study him closely now. And then once satisfied I begin to growl. I feel it's appropriate as Pit Bull, albeit clichéd, is the image he obviously wishes to project. He doesn't growl back he just stares. I grow bored and stop growling. I wonder why these meetings always take such an age to begin. Protocol perhaps. And then I realise I like that word. *Protocol.* "Are you pro tocol?" "Oh yes! Very much so, Sir!"

I chuckle to myself. This gets a better reaction than the growl, Daniel curls his lip. But I shouldn't have thought that because now that makes me wonder, does a lip really curl and if so where does it go? I remember David Beckham curling a free kick into a Greek goal. I *see* him do it and I remember the emotion. But that's not the point, the point is he curled it *somewhere*, it didn't just curl and return.

I grow bored with Daniel, he's too generic. I switch focus. Almost Margot has a different brooch today. It's a white elephant wearing a Santa hat. It truly is. I'm surprised and wonder why would you? Rebecca once explained a white elephant is a valuable but burdensome possession of which its owner cannot dispose. I know this because that is how Rebecca referred to the scale size papier–mâché Penny Farthing bicycle I had constructed in the spare bedroom. I don't know why Almost

Margot has decided to wear that particular brooch but let's just say I already know that it's not going to aid my concentration. I suppose it's just her identity or something and should be accepted as such and I know I should stay shut up now but I shan't – it's all too tempting.

"Hey Margot! Congratulations on being unique. Just like everyone else."

It was churlish, I know that immediately. Unbecoming. Her reaction is difficult to describe but I focus and try, it's sort of a nose twitch, a lip quiver, and half a teeth–bare. All rolled into what appears a poorly practiced furrowed brow disdain. And now, immediately, I'm starting to feel a bit bad. I can sense a tense atmosphere developing. I'm sensitive to such things. I decide a joke is in order as there's far too much sadness in this room. And I believe someone once argued humour is our greatest weapon, I don't know for sure if Mark Twain can claim that one but someone of his ilk. Anyway, regardless of its truth or origin, it's surely worth a try.

"Ere, Mags." (I'm hoping she'll appreciate the familiarity.) Her frown suggests she doesn't but I plough on. "Ere Mags, did you know Davy Crockett had three ears?"

"Now look here Mr Foxley."

"You can call me Robert. Or. Bob. Bobby. Rob. Robbie. Whatever you feel comfortable with. Robster even."

"Now look here, *Mr Foxley,* I'm afraid this is a very serious meeting."

"Don't be afraid Magster, remember – the only fear is fear itself."

I'd seen that written on a T–Shirt. It sounded clever though I hadn't fully understood its meaning. Margot barely gives it an acknowledgement.

"Yes well, we are talking facts, not fears today, do you understand?"

"Yes of course, I'm sure Big Dan wouldn't waste his time on triviality."

"You may refer to me as Mr Rosman."

I'm losing the will but give it one last go.

"Okay… So anyway, Mr Daniel Dan Danny Boy Rosman and Ms Margot Magdalene Moriarty – did you know that Davy Crockett had three ears?"

"Robert, please…"

That last one was George, a gentle interjection that throws me slightly; it sounded strange, weird, almost compassionate or such like. That doesn't just throw me slightly that throws me completely and now even I've momentarily lost interest in the quip. I shut up properly this time and stare at George, he bows his head, but it's not an overtly smug manoeuvre.

Curious.

The meeting begins.

I don't take much in because now I'm wondering about Margot and Danno. Margot seems different today, smaller somehow and more girlish, I can't quite work out why. Not at first at least, but then I do, it's her hair, she has half the mane she used to have. That's it! That's what the 'Almost Margot' has been all about. On an unconscious level I'd known immediately – it's Margot but only almost, a big chunk of the original is missing, she's been heavily pruned. And she seems more alert today, more alive, more aware and I'm sure her hand just brushed big Dan's knee. I replay the incident in my mind, I back it up and slow it down, yes, there, just as she passes my personnel file – there's a tiny linger, a moment, one that only the trained eye would spot. *She fancies him!* And now all I can think about is a bulldog screwing a wasp.

And that makes me laugh because now I've tried to picture it. And it's obviously an inopportune moment to laugh as all three heads suddenly jerk up. I turn it into a smile but their faces don't relax.

I zone out again.

I think its George's turn to talk now, he's holding up the Late Book, passing it to Margot. And I can see his lips move, but there's nothing now, there's not even noise, not anymore, just silence. Ha! Finally! I've cracked it, I'm impenetrable. And I like that. It makes me laugh. Inwardly or outwardly I can't tell, but there they go again, there's a clue, three heads, three bobbins, three little jerks, one two three, heads up for Horatio, hahaha.

And all would possibly still be well, or as well as could be expected, but then I see the flower pot and I'm reminded of Alex Hurricane Higgins and I'm not 100 percent sure but I'm fairly sure *and who gives a sea shore*, but I think it was him who urinated in one during a live snooker match on the BBC and that's the trouble with triggers, if the idea is planted then it's hard to resist.

It might not have been him though. And that's what wavered me. I started to reflect if it might have been Steve Davis or Kevin Keegan or was it David Attenborough or Prince Charles? Maybe it was Desmond Tutu? He always seemed a bit of a laugh. Hahaha, but no, course it wasn't him, he played tennis table not snooker. Then I remember Mark. Mark Twain liked billiards. And I forget about urinating in a flower pot and I wonder what would he do. What would Mark Twain do if he was in my situation? And maybe just thinking about him broke some spell because suddenly there was noise again.

And it was her again. It was Margot Almost–Margot Margot.

"Have you been listening Mr Foxley? George has been telling us about your recent behaviour, he's concerned that your behaviour is passive aggressive and from what I've seen I would tend to agree."

Daniel Rosman nods too and it's all a lot for me to take in. Why is it first name for George and surname for me? And why hasn't Big Dan touched the plate of tree–shaped foil–covered biscuits on the coffee table – the ones placed directly in front of him and fully out of the reach of me? And what does 'passive aggressive' mean? I can never remember that one even though it does sound vaguely familiar.

I decide to ask.

"What does passive aggressive mean please Margot?"

"It refers to someone being deliberately obstructive but in a non–violent way."

"Oh. Thank you. And can you explain why Mr Rosman has yet to scoff all the biscuits?"

There's a momentary silence. A pause for effect perhaps. Or a taking stock. I wonder do they role play these situations. After a while we're off again.

"You've just displayed a good example of the behaviour your superior is concerned about Mr Foxley. And you've also provided many more examples in this book here. I assume you're not going to deny these are your entries in the Late Book? If you recall George introduced the system for recording unpunctual arrivals on October 17th of this year..."

I'm already slipping out again – it was her words again – or rather one word in particular, it was the word *unpunctual* that got me. I hadn't heard it before and I quite liked it, but not enough. I assumed it must be a real word, Almost Margot was the type to prepare. I wondered if she could have used others though – I wondered for example about dispunctual.

I could probably think of more but now Margot has started reading. And I realise she is Almost Margot no more, I've become re–accustomed to her, I've taken in her new persona, she is Margot. I now see her as she is now, I realise perception can change rapidly. People can change and often they do. And then we see them as they are now and not how they were then. A phrase comes to mind, a clever one – "perception is nine tenths of the flaw". I grin, Daniel is probably a legal beagle, he might like that one, but I'm not really in the mood for sharing.

And it's maybe not that clever.

Not clever at all.

Margot is still going.

"October 18th. Reason for late arrival – Murderous mayhem instigated by marauding Vikings on the District Line... October 21st Reason for late arrival – Freelancing at Feisty Ferret Freeing Festival in Farringdon… October 22nd Reason for late arrival – Befriended lost and lonesome Leprechaun at Leicester square – Crock of Gold retrieved but ructions with Ryanair over return baggage allowance… Shall I go on?"

I feign enthusiasm; she seems to be enjoying herself.

"Oh yes! Please do."

"November 4th Reason for late arrival – Diverted via Didchurch due to disaffected dentist drillings… November 10th Reason for late arrival – Ovulating ostrich orchestrated Oyster card outage… November 11th Reason for late arrival – Pirate-prepped prattling parrot provoked Piccadilly public address panic… November 14th Reason for…

At this point, and it happens simultaneously which again is curious, I yawn and George taps Margot's shoulder and gives a little shake of his head. Margot closes the book. She peers at me somewhat sternly and an expression immediately comes to mind – *little piggy eyes.* It's maybe a description not an expression but I'm off and running with it. I wonder what little piggy eyes look like, I've never studied a little pig but I imagine their eyes to be akin to their arses – red ringed and soulless.

It's not a pleasant thought so I try again to lift the spirits.

"Would you like to hear my joke now? Davy Crockett had three ears – did you know that?"

"No. I did not and I care not. I can see we're not getting very far here."

"Oh, I don't know, some of us might be. I note you have the keens for Head Office's finest."

I wink at her and then at Daniel (try to wink at least) and it seems to have an effect. Margot's mouth is open – I wonder is that a jaw drop – is that what the expression means? I notice three gold crowns. I think of kings visiting a new–born. And I think she blushed. I'm pretty sure she blushed but now she's recovered.

"George also mentioned your immaturity."

"He's too kind. Did he also tell you about his wife in just her…"

George definitely blushes. And that's both ironic and unnecessary because the thing is, I wasn't going to finish the sentence. I was just messing with him. I wasn't overly angry about that anymore, I'd moved on, embraced bigger and wider concerns.

Margot ignores my interjection and ploughs on, she has a path to follow, a purpose to pursue.

"We are sorry to say that we feel we have no option but to present you with an official written warning."

There it was again, jargon, gruesome gibberish – they were

making it sound like a gift.

"You are sorry?"

"Yes, yes we are."

"All of you?"

"Yes."

That cracks me up – *bunch of sorry individuals.* And I'm still laughing when they get up and leave. Margot thrusts a manila envelope into my hand, George bows his head and Big Dan pockets a handful of biscuits on the way out. *I swear to Twain I saw him do it.* I jump up and run after them.

"Oi wait! Wait! Wait you fret–faced fuckers!" (Recently my language has degenerated beyond all recognition. It's not admirable.) They stop and turn. Dan's nostrils flare. *Big piggy snout.*

"Apologies for the French folks, but you left too early, you forgot something, you forgot to listen to the FUCKING PUNCHLINE!" Swearing isn't particularly clever. Nor is shouting. But both sometimes gets a reaction so perhaps they have their place – everyone is looking at me now.

"Davy Crocket had three ears, a left ear, a right ear… and a wild front ear."

Margot and Dan hesitate. Share a look. Raise their noses then turn on their heels. George pauses and stares at me for a moment, a long moment. *Curious number three.* Then he turns and departs too. I suddenly feel tired. Exhausted. I sit cross–legged on the corridor floor. I notice then pick up a wastepaper bin. I place it over my head. Inside there are a few post–it notes, a half–chewed toffee and a number of Kleenex tissues (possibly menthol but there's a mix of odours). It's a good fit and I can cope with the weight on my shoulders. I worry again about the expletives – the girls on reception will have heard. They were innocents. Collateral damage.

"Under certain circumstances, profanity provides a relief denied even to prayer."

He's trying to make me feel better, he's providing justification, giving me an excuse. Mark Twain is the most benign man that ever lived – "known by everyone loved by all". Without him I'd be lost. And I'm painfully aware I've had enough of this. I hate sitting cross–legged. And it's not just because of the tantra – right now it reminds me of school and a frustrated infant during a wet playtime. Sit in the hall in a circle and sing *if you're happy and you know it clap your hands.*

"Why aren't you clapping Horatio?"

'I'm not happy."

"Don't you try and be funny with me!"

Don't try and be funny.

You shouldn't need to try, I know that. Maybe my joke wasn't that great, or that new, maybe my delivery was not up to scratch? I wonder if they got it? Maybe I should go in search of the happy couple and tell it again. Enunciate it clearly, *wild–front–ear...*

> "Explaining humor is a lot like dissecting a frog, you learn a lot in the process, but in the end you kill it."

Hahaha, yes! That interjection makes me laugh, timing is everything, the man's a genius!

"Yes Mark Twain! Explain this hilarious scenario! No Mark Twain don't! You'll ruin it! Hahaha..."

After a time, Liam passes. I recognise his brogues.

Rebecca

Not that it happened overnight. Robert was always entertaining and the tantric phase was amusing at first, well, initially anyway, the *first* time was funny, in that way that things always were with him, it was hard to not smile. He bought some daffodils and placed them around his bedroom, one in each of his dozen or so colourful mugs. He explained he was creating the right atmosphere. I mentioned we'd be struggling if we felt like stopping half way through for a cup of tea. He didn't laugh but told me I had to focus and take it seriously or it might not work. I was tempted to mention the irony of him asking me to be serious but sometimes he got intense about unusual things and so I bit my tongue and went along.

He invited me to sit cross legged and naked astride him, he then told me to send energy to my MVP (Most Veritable Pudenda) or 'Sacred Yoni.' So there we were, face to face and bits to bits and of course it was all rather nice. That was one thing, one constant, one clue, our bodies always responded – their recognition was never out of synch. That had always been one of the things, one of our things. But now suddenly there were new rules and no matter how powerful the temptation I wasn't allowed to touch his MIA (Most Important Appendage) or 'Wand of Light' as it must now be known. That gave me the giggles a bit too, the *first* time. I kept thinking of Daniel Radcliffe.

Chapter 45

"Did you know Mark Twain's first date with Olivia Louise Langdon took place at a reading by Charles Dickens in New York in January 1868?"

I researched all that sort of stuff after I had 'become obsessed' as Rebecca would tease. I'm sure she liked it really. I would hit her with a new MTDYK (Mark Twain Did You Know) on every Date Adventure. Pleasingly, I discovered there were many coincidentals between Mark and Olivia's relationship and our own, facts and fancies which I would espouse over Pinot Noir and the like. Happenstance such as 'Olivia Louise Langdon was younger than Samuel Langhorne Clemens.' (Rebecca Susan Morley is younger than Horatio Robert Foxley). And 'Olivia Louise Langdon was erudite, genteel and possessed of a keen sense of humour' (ditto ditto and ditto). And 'Olivia encouraged his literary career and was his ideal companion' (somewhat ditto re an indulgence of my poems and very much ditto re the other).

I wasn't making any of it up. I told her things like the things President William Howard Taft had said upon hearing of Mark's death on April 21, 1910 in Redding, Connecticut. (Officially of angina pectoris though it was just as easy to believe he had merely chosen to exit once Halley's comet was once more in the vicinity. Mark Twain – a man always in control of the things that mattered.)

President Taft had said: "Mark Twain gave pleasure – real intellectual enjoyment – to millions, and his works will continue to give such pleasure to millions yet to come... His humor was American, but he was nearly as much appreciated by Englishmen"

Nearly as much and more.

Rebecca

So anyway, like I said, it was fun the first time, frustrating but fun nonetheless, it was just weird not to be allowed to touch him, weird that he was so worried he "might expend" and all would be ruined. He explained there was no need for an ending, indeed it was essential that it didn't occur; a finale was not a viable option, not anymore. It wasn't about *that,* it was about sitting opposite each other and inhaling each other's breath and humming mantras and focusing on chakras and re–channeling our sexual vibrancy back and beyond and wherever (I forget the full details). But the main thing, the thing I won't forget, the one most important and essential thing, was that his resistance, his restraint, his non–ejaculation would give him power and energy and strength to deal with George. So he believed. Looking back, it was completely ridiculous and I probably shouldn't have indulged him at all.

Chapter 46

Mr Twain is a funny guy. He can make you laugh even when you don't feel you have the reason. Suddenly, out of the blue, just like that, all unexpected and un–summoned like he whispers to me.

> "Why is it that we rejoice at a birth and grieve at a funeral? It is because we are not the person involved."

Just like that. Out of the blue. *Out of the blue blue Christmas.* That's what I like about Mr Twain, you don't have to explain things to him, he just knows. The party had not been a success and now we were on the tube once more. The party had not been a success largely because of the illuminated snowman – he'd provided the inspiration. But now that didn't matter. Or at least it mattered less. I whispered back to Mr Twain.

"You're a funny guy."

I maybe should have gone home after the meeting and the wastepaper bin and the gloating brogues and perhaps I would have but after I'd sat for quite a while, the kindly milk monitor Sarah 2, had left her seat at Reception, helped me to my feet, brushed me down and asked if I was "coming to the shindig." I told her such had always been my dream. She told me to clean myself up and she'd see me there.

In no time I was holding a paper plate containing twiglets, a fondant fancy and three green olives on a stick. Sarah 2 was now nowhere to be seen but I realised that was OK, I'd just do as Sis would do – I would mingle. And it was shortly after I started doing that that I misinterpreted the request from Marie in

Marketing. In hindsight I should have known, she was never the most frivolous of funsters, but then again it was Christmas so perhaps I thought, maybe…

I didn't for a moment consider that I might have misheard.

Ironic really – I gave her the benefit of the doubt and yet I ended up with the clout. I thought she'd requested that I get on the chair and produce some risqué verse. And I thought I was doing OK, especially considering I'd had no warning that I'd be called upon to entertain. I'd looked over at the illuminated yuletide inflatable and the words had tumbled out.

I'm a miserable snowman
And I don't care who knows
And I'm always blinking freezing
And have a carrot for my nose

They dress me up in hat and scarf
Then leave me out the front
The local kids all laugh at me
Saying look at that silly...

And at that point she clouted me. Marie gave me a right–hander. She genuinely did. A rather forceful pre–emptive strike. And an uncalled for one. The last word was going to be 'Snowman' – that was the trick you see – 'look at that silly... *snowman'* Ho ho ho – you thought I was going to say... well you know... Anyway, her attack was uncalled for but that didn't stop everyone else from laughing.

At me.

Especially once I'd recoiled from Marie's assault and toppled off the chair.

So how about that for a fun night? How about that for a misheard causing mayhem? Apparently, so she claimed after, what she had actually said was "Take the stair if risk averse." (There were rumours someone had vomited in the lift.) I explained all this to Mr Twain on the District Line. And he did not laugh at me. Instead he pointed out.

“Laughter without a tinge of philosophy is but a sneeze of humor. Genuine humor is replete with wisdom.”

I thanked him and said I agreed.

And I realised I might sleep well after all.

Indeed I was already dropping off.

And that was fine.

Rest was probably a good idea.

I’d a busy day ahead.

Tomorrow was Christmas Eve.

“Goodnight Samuel Langhorne Clemens… Goodnight Thomas Jefferson Snodgrass… Goodnight Mark Twain...”

I asked him "Really?" And I asked him what was the point? I queried him increasingly. He informed me the point was energy – because he was not finishing his performance he was not diminishing his energy, rather he was effectively boiling it all up and then retaining it, he was controlling and corralling his sexual energy so it could be used as a coping mechanism, a strength provider for when things got tough, for when George was "Being a helmet." He was convinced that through our unique non–tactile connection and through our intimate breath sharing and as a result of our earnest chakra chasings, his stress hormones would lower and his serotonin "would shoot through the roof."

Which was an image I found rather distasteful.

But he insisted that we persevere and in next to no time 'non–tactile stimulation' suggested punishment instead of experiment, and my frustration and my resentment began to grow. I guess my patience wore out a bit too.

Chapter 47

I'm aware this is a special night. It's a night in which a star was once followed. The night before a saviour was born. It's a night of significance. I am not following a star. I am re–treading old ground. I am marching on familiar territory. I walk along the Archway Road and I'm filled with wonder – the Archway – the Arch way? The way of the Arch. And then I'm filled with chuckle because I realise it's perhaps appropriate, I am walking along the Archway to meet the Arch Enemy.

There is quite a breeze tonight, a chill, that's appropriate too. I cast a glance toward *The Woodman*, venue of the third Date Adventure – our first Pub Date Adventure and I'd been late. Rebecca had walked through the snow all the way from Muswell Hill and I had been a half hour late. Rebecca was sat at a table in the corner when I arrived; she was wearing a green knitted hat and reading a book. She did not look cross.

It had been Christmas then too, more or less. I'd had a quick drink after work with Christine, a festive toast and thanks for all your hard work kind of affair. I had enjoyed it, in a one eye on the clock kind of way. Christine had kissed me on the cheek and given me a Christmas card that contained a £50 note and a written note. The written note explained that the £50 note was probably more use to me than a Christmas jumper. It also thanked me and praised my performance. I had kissed Christine's cheek in return, praised her insight and considered my good fortune. And then I had dashed for the tube and cursed the weather induced service delays.

When I arrived, Rebecca was sat at a wooden table in a corner; she was wearing a striped woollen scarf that complimented the hat. She looked relaxed and poised. Beautiful. I'd taken a moment to drink her in, paused mid–approach just to admire and enjoy. Maybe she sensed my presence. She looked up and smiled, she did not frown or glance toward her clock. Instead, she put down her book and offered me her lips.

I apologised for being late, explained about the trains Rebecca said

"It's OK, you don't need to explain, I know you're not an arse."

And then we had kissed again. And then I had apologised again because she was Rebecca and she deserved everything to be perfect. And she had laughed again and she had told me to be quiet and that I was here now and all was well. And then she had elaborated, she had gone on to state that actually in truth I was a heroic figure, a well wrapped winter warrior trudging all the way from London's East to meet an eager Christmas Maiden. We then joked about maidens and maidenhood and chivalrous Knights and a saucy serf cavorting with a mulled wine enlivened kitchen colleen, and things had relaxed into the fun friendly flirty frivolity that I was already beginning to recognise as something greater than any man deserved.

I wrench my eyes from *The Woodman* and walk on. I'm further determined but I'm still thinking back – this is familiar territory – a memory–laden minefield. Recall now of another Sunday Funday – Date Adventure 12. Freud/Ellis/Orwell/Keats (I recorded them all. I bought a special notebook that was pocket–sized, purple coloured and moleskin.) I never told Rebecca about it but planned to surprise her one day in our future.

I know.

The Freud Museum wasn't my cup of tea, it was all settees and chairs and statues that appeared dismembered – shoulderless heads. There was also an old weaving machine and a quote from Goethe which Rebecca read out – "Just once he treads and a thousand strands all twine together." It sounded unsafe. The museum shop was calmer. They were selling a 'Freud and Couch Finger Puppet Set.' They honestly were. Keep moving – on and out and soon past the point where Ruth Ellis shot her philandering lover – the bullet holes still resplendent on the side of the *Magdala* pub. Rebecca explained all about the evening of Easter Sunday 1955 when revenge was taken and Ruth was deemed guilty and became the last woman ever executed in Blighty.

A philanderer murdered. It hadn't had such resonance at the time.

Next up, and opposite the Royal Free Hospital, was a coffee shop that was once a bookshop where George Orwell beavered. So proclaimed the plaque. We'd nodded respectfully and had been half-inclined to bow.

Then it was round to John Keats house where he wrote his love letters to the incongruously named Fanny Brawne.

They closed at five and it was one minute to and so we were turned away. I still managed a peek in the window though and I saw a young man with fingers steepled under his chin looking out mournfully toward the garden. He was sat on an ancient looking sofa where perhaps the great poet's backside once settled. A thought had quickly grinned me and I explained it to Rebecca – the serious youth was obviously a wannabe bard seeking some Johnnie Keats arse–osmosis type inspiration. He was simultaneously clenching his jaw and his buttocks and attempting to suck esoteric essence from the cushion covers. I declared if we'd have gotten in, I'd have given it a go too. At which point Rebecca said

"Yes Robert."

Then linked my arm and led me away. Adventure 12 was a fun date. They all were.

Once upon a long long time ago.

I walk on.

Past the RSPCA charity shop and that triggers a smile too, a reflex lip slip. I realise I am nostalgia–ising. I'd never been in a charity shop before I'd met Rebecca, I'd believed there was a stigma. I'd *known* there was a stigma – if you were seen entering one then you'd be mocked, ridiculed, verbally slaughtered. I'd seen it happen. But it turned out things were different in Muswell Hill and Highgate and Crouch End and Hampstead; here it was a middle class must–do. There were no furtive entries in these necks of the wood. We'd discussed it, we did things like that, we agreed there was an irony, we decided charity was a different beast dependent upon location. Or perhaps need. We realised people who could only afford to buy from charity shops were often the ones too proud to enter. We recognised the irony that in loftier areas you would be congratulated on a wondrous charity shop "find" whereas in the lower echelons of post code you would be cruelly taunted for wearing cast–offs.

I'd shrugged my shoulders that first time, what the heck? I knew no–one around here. I'd enter and be damned. Later, after I'd exited the RSPCA with a Paul Smith embroidered shirt easily as good as new and my wallet a mere £12 the lighter, I was cocksure no more. And I was also warmly amused because inside the shop there had been a 'Please place a tin of cat food in the bin' sign and people did, they actually did do it, they dropped a tin in the bin and loudly declared, "Hello, here's a donation for you!"

The bin was half filled with tins and I imagined the shop owners running an after–hours feline soup kitchen; I envisioned an earnest team driving around at night searching for hungry tile walkers. Maybe there was a rota. I'd smiled then and wrapped a clasp around Rebecca's waist, gently squeezed a thank you for opening up another new world. Then one day, not much later, in a different charity shop in Muswell Hill, I'd smiled again when Rebecca grabbed another man's todger.

There's a real wind now, it's more than a breeze. Harsh. I've begun to shiver.

I remember the incident clearly, the mind holds many things, it has its own inscrutable storage system – it stacks things up then chooses when and where to spew them out. It was a Sunday afternoon and it all was innocent enough. *On that occasion.* We had laughed it off. After the apologies and the explanations and my calm–the–situation jokes suggesting that Rebecca was often doing things like that – that she was a recovering Swinger and had watched far too many episodes of *Wife Swap*.

It had all started with me being very amusing. I'd donned an inappropriate Reiss shirt in the make–do–and–not–really–

adequate changing room (think cupboard with a curtain instead of a door). The shirt was cerise in colour with pearl buttons and a silky feel and when I emerged theatrically from behind the curtain and performed an Elizabethan bow Rebecca had vigorously shook her head and explained that it was probably from their women's wear range. I'd feigned disappointment then popped back behind the curtain and she'd continued browsing the donated china.

It was a few minutes later, when I was out and onto a perusal of the paperbacks, that I heard the commotion. I turned to discover a large lady in lavender angrily berating Rebecca. And a flushed, flustered, bald and bespectacled man peering from the side of the changing room curtain, protectively clutching a pair of bright yellow swimming shorts.

I didn't begrudge the chap – he'd gotten lucky was all. He was an innocent a–pawed. I didn't hate him for his good fortune, his was an inadvertent fondling, a gift of fate. Personally, I found the whole incident hilarious but Rebecca was in shock. I took her to a coffee shop so she could sit and recover. I bought her a fatty latte and added three sugars. Her face was red and she kept re–telling, continually confessing, she seemed to need to though she had no need to. It was probably therapeutic.

"I can't believe I did that! I thought it was *you.* I saw a pair of jeans on the floor and I thought what on earth is he trying on now? I was convinced it was you! And it was all spur of the moment – which isn't even like me. I just sidled over and secretly slipped my hand in behind the curtain. I couldn't see you but I never thought it wasn't you. I just assumed. I was playing a trick – I was going to poke you in the ribs or something, give you a fright. But then when my fingers just landed on it. Well – I was *sure* it was you – it never crossed my mind that it mightn't be. So I gave it a little pull. Oh God. I actually did that. I don't know what I was thinking – The poor man jumped a mile."

I consoled her; I explained how she had probably made his day, perhaps his month, maybe even his year. I reassured Rebecca by assuring her that when that man next made love to his wife (who had been understanding enough once she'd calmed and I'd offered her a Murray Mint) that it would add a little extra edge, an extra inch most likely, to their enjoyment. In his mind he would be reliving the moment a beautiful stranger had reached out to him and imagining how it might have developed. I theorised that in many ways Rebecca had done them both a great service. And I assured her that in time she too would be able to look back and laugh, for it was surely a tale where all were winners.

And sure enough she did; a month or so later (though it still caused her to blush) she was able to look back and smile and it strengthened us both, it added an extra layer, another fragment to our history, another thread in our tapestry. It provided us another shared secret, a further fun incident. When we visited future charity shops I would sternly take her arm and lead her away from the changing area. Or I would do things like wait until she was occupied a–browse and then I would slip behind the curtain and call out along the lines of

"Rebecca Tugwell to Cubicle Two please."

This was all before the Damien Damnation of course. Now the joke isn't funny anymore. Now I think of Rebecca reaching out toward *his* putrid pecker and it sickens me. Because in my mind I can see her do it and I can see that this time it is intentional. This time it is not an innocent mistake in a shop full of cheery tat but a conscious and despicable decision in an art hotel for two. And this time it is in no way amusing. It is the opposite. And I try desperately not to see it but I can see it – every day I can see it – every hour – again and again I can see it – and I cannot stop the seeing.

Rebecca's fingers are long and slender, her hands are soft and smooth, her nails are manicured, she has a delicate and sensuous touch. A magical touch. A touch that instantly delights. I knew that touch and it had been exclusively mine.

And then one day it wasn't.

It is properly cold now. Bitter.

"Perhaps we're doing it wrong?" I suggested hopefully one afternoon, after I'd been invited yet again to "come and sit and energise" and had known that any anticipation would be unrewarded. "I mean perhaps you haven't researched it fully?" I didn't want to spell it out or hurt his feelings but I missed the full intimacy, the complete joining. "Surely you could still put your co.. I mean your *wand of wonder* inside the *scared yoni* once in a while… I mean surely if we're careful… surely there's more to this tantra than…"

I was wasting my time. He seemed shocked at such suggestion, disappointed that I was doubting his knowledge, that I might be casting aspersion upon the legitimacy of his ten minute google rummage.

Chapter 48

I speed up my march, I have a rendezvous to make and timing is important. I march on. Past the *Highgate Curry House*, past the *Highgate Hill Murugan Temple* opposite the *Caipirinha Jazz Club*, then turn right, then turn left into Tile Kiln Lane. Then, before that final path I take a pause and look back. I look back across the street at a huge figure on a crucifix, an icon reaching out unto the traffic. I know of him and his environ, I've been past before and he struck a chord. I've memorised his details,

> CHURCH OF ENGLAND DIOCESE OF LONDON
> The Parish Church of Saint Augustine of Canterbury.
> Sunday 9.15am Morning Prayer
> 10.00am Parish Mass (Sung)

He is who he is and he's an impressive sight but that particular palace has less relevance tonight. I'm not concerned with his congregation; I'm more interested in the Catholics.

Tile Kiln Lane – a short cut – pleasant enough. I notice a purple door for number 4. And there are new builds – houses clad in wood – sustainable or some such – built by men with beards and integrity. I reach the end and I turn left. I've finally arrived: Hornsey Lane Bridge also known as Archway Bridge (or "Suicide Bridge" to locals less sensitively inclined).

I stand in the middle and wait.

And I think. *Of course I do. The thoughts keep coming, they are relentless, they are tireless, they keep on coming.* I remember it's referred to as a "fall" in the press, which is curious really. Or perhaps it's not, maybe that's the way the rest cope – "He *fell* from a bridge

– there was no jump involved". If we don't understand or we don't wish to confront then we'll happily re–classify?

Or perhaps it's purely a kindness.

I have other thoughts too, which side do you choose? How do you make that decision? I cross back and forth, looking down the views from the bridge vary but both are impressive – dizzying lights of the murky metropolis. A constant stream of headlights. Steady traffic even at this late hour on this much praised day. I peer for a while then return to the middle, sit down and wrap my arms around my knees. Other thoughts come, that other church, the Catholic one, St. Josephs, the one whose congregation I was interested in, the one where the corner stone was laid on 24 May 1888. I'd memorised his details too,

> Masses
>
> Saturday: 7pm
> Sunday: 8am, 10am, 12noon, 1.30pm (Polish), 7pm.
> Holydays: 6.30pm vigil, 9.30am, 7pm.
> Bank Holiday: 9.30am
> Sacrament of Reconciliation Saturday 10–11.00am, 6.15–6.45pm
> Weekdays: immediately after Mass (on request).

And of course,

> Midnight Mass on Christmas Eve.

I think now of *The Old Crown* opposite the church – a hostelry with ambiguous welcome – one sign stated 'Come in, we'll treat you like royalty' another warned 'Please respect your landlady's wishes and keep the noise down or otherwise you will be punished!' Rebecca and I sat outside that pub one sunny Sunday afternoon, we drank orange juice with lemonade and shared a bag of salt n vinegar. We smiled as we watched First Communion children enter St Josephs – a legion of young innocents in white. Cute. Maybe we imagined our own little angels someday but were too shy to verbalise. I don't remember that possibility distinctly and I'm aware how certain recall can twirl, but I do remember the ashtray exactly. *I do now*. It bore the face of Marilyn Monroe. It was impressively constructed – a movie poster melded onto metal; Marilyn was smiling as only she could and the poster proclaimed 'How to Marry a Millionaire.' Rebecca had admired the ashtray, she liked clever design. She had toyed with it in her hand for a while then sighed exaggeratedly and said

"Damien's the only rich man I know."

I'd raised a disapproving eyebrow and we had both smiled. It had seemed an innocent moment. A shared joke at his expense.

It is savagely cold now.

A few minutes pass; I spend them admiring the goose bumps on my thighs; I know the time is nigh and I'm dressed for a poignant occasion. It's just a matter of waiting now. I wonder are they truly goose *pimples* – are pimples and bumps the same? I wonder which is more accurate – are they more bumps or pimples and why goose and not turkey? Especially at this time of year. I wonder who decides but I have no–one to ask so it has to be internalised, a debate within. I wonder alone.

Things were not always this way.

My buttocks feel numb, ditto my fingers, it's to be expected I guess. I raise my left cheek and slip my left–hand underneath then I raise my right cheek and my right–hand slips under. I'm on Suicide Bridge sitting on my hands. It suggests a metaphor but I'm not of the mood to form one. I rock from side to side and a little warmth returns.

There's still time for a further recall – another arm–hooked stroll through Highgate and an observation of a gaggle of tourists resplendent in union jack jackets and *I love London* T Shirts. It had stirred me to mention the union jack flag being iconic, it had stirred me to muse how I supposed the Royals had helped make it so – what with all their pomp and circumstance and weddings and jubilees and what not. And I surmised the Olympics had probably helped too. And then I suddenly wondered about something else and so I asked Rebecca, because Rebecca knew many things.

"When did Britain start being called Great Britain?"

"When it was a bloody fucking up your arse Empire!"

"Oh..."

Rebecca could be quite political sometimes. She had opinions. She knew her own mind.

And she had chosen me.

But that was then and this is now.

I am frozen.

And I know it is time to focus, time to ensure my mind is set. It was a simple enough idea, simple hence genius. We'd worked on it together; myself and the great man from Missouri had planned it out after a tearful watching of *A Wonderful Life* on BBC 2. Rebecca knew Damien because Rebecca's mum knew Damien's mum. They'd been in the same maternity ward. They were also regular church attendees; indeed, they were very much the go–to do–gooders of the local parish – flower arranging connoisseurs who could iron a cassock in under four minutes. They more than did their bit. And both families always attended the Christmas Eve Midnight Mass at St Joseph's on Highgate Hill.

Rebecca had told me all about it, how she never ceased to be amazed by Damien's behaviour; apparently on these occasions he always insisted on staying behind to "Have a word with The Man." (He meant the priest, Father McBride.) And "having a word" meant passing the priest an envelope stuffed full of high value sterling notes. Apparently, he did this every single year, he couldn't just put his donation in the offertory basket like everyone else because he was a "flash git" (Rebecca's words not mine) and enjoyed being invited in for a quick celebratory sherry.

This annual "private audience" as he would fondly refer to it, seemed inordinately important to Damien. I remember wondering what the priest must have thought of him. Whatever the case I was sure Damien's routine wouldn't have changed hence Mr Twain and I were confident that if I hung around the Hornsey Lane Bridge at approximately 01.30 on Christmas morn, my self–satisfied nemesis would soon be short–cutting his way along. And so it proved.

Mark spotted him first.

> "Who is that smooth-faced, animated outrage yonder in the fine clothes?"

Here he was at last! Smart suit, shiny shoes and jaunty self–righteous waddle. I jumped to my feet, stepped into the light and greeted him effusively.

"Bonne Noel Mon Enemie!"

He jerked rather pleasingly; his right leg half–buckled and his arms shot up above his head. They truly did. I had to laugh.

It gave him time to recover.

"Oh Christ... you... what are you do..."

I had intercepted him with my own arms open. And now I broke into date–appropriate song.

"'Tis the season to be jolly – fa la la la la, la la la la – Crush devious skulls beneath a Waitrose trolley – fa la la la la, la la la la…"

He interrupted before I really got going.

"What are you wear..."

"Don we now our slay apparel – fa la la la la, la la la la…"

"You've been to a fancy dress."

His arms were down now and he was regaining his composure, slipping back into smug presumption. I immediately put him straight.

"The party's over."

"Right... well, I hope you enjoyed it...where did you get the outfit?"

"eBay."

It was true; the green velvet shorts with bells attached were part of an Ann Summers elf costume, as was the matching hat and dickie bow. The wings were a 'dark fairy' design, black feathered and rather tight across the shoulders – they'd only had a size 12.

"You look... special..."

He sounded insincere; I wasn't convinced he was appreciative of my effort, 'twas the season for flamboyant fibbage and he was a fine exponent. He was standing tall again now and I realised it was time to end our preliminaries.

"I want you to help me with something."

I've spoken clearly, carefully. I'm not smiling now. I've slowed my language down. I am enunciating. Dagenham provides its own education. It has the desired effect – Damien nervously looks over his shoulder.

"I should be heading back, I..."

I interrupt him this time.

"How was mass?"

"Mass was mass. Hymns, prayer..."

"Envelopes and sherry?"

"Fuck you."

Damien tries to step past me. I step in front of him.

"I need your help."

"I'm going home."

"I need a leg–up."

"I don't want no trouble..."

Damien seems agitated. Unsure of himself. Smug–free and wary. I make him an offer

"You can come with me."

He does another step to the right. I do one to the left. He knows why I'm here. I sing him some more.

"Follow me in merry measure – fa la la la la, la la la la…"

"Look, about Rebecca..."

"You can help me fly."

"It just... it just happened alright?"

"You discovered the value and then paid less."

"No. I wasn't… It was just…look, let's just have a chat…"

He wants to talk now but I don't – surely we both know there's no point? I stick to my agenda.

"I want you to see me soar."

He doesn't give up.

"It was one time, that's all, just one time! Fuck's sake, she cried after."

"Villainous acts always upset her."

"She was upset, guilty, ungrateful – it was a fucking disaster, a fucking expensive waste of time. She's a fucking nightmare."

Mark's been listening, he sounds incredulous. I can tell he disapproves of the tone and the repetitive coarse language. His comment is heavily laced with sarcasm.

> "What a talker he is. He could persuade a fish to come out and take a walk with him."

I want Damien to shut up too but he keeps going.

"You weren't even meant to find out. She shouldn't have told you. I didn't give a shit."

I have to shut him up. I grab his arm.

"I need a leg up."

He shrugs it off.

"I'm not helping you."

I grasp his lapel.

"It's the season of goodwill."

He pushes me back.

"You need help."

"Yes! I need a leg up."

"Seriously, you're not funny."

I disagree and sing him some more.

"See the blazing fool before us – fa la la la la, la la la la…"

"Fuck off."

"Give me a leg up!"

"Fuck off!"

He suddenly sidesteps me and is walking away. Fast.

"A curse upon your Fortnums!"

I give chase but he's started to speed up his walk – escalated his gait into a half–jog. I flip flop after him – choice of shoe had been a major quandary – what did an elf–styled yuletide Icarus wear upon his feet? Probably not a pair of blue Billabong thongs but my special occasions wardrobe was embarrassingly limited. He was escaping.

"Come back and help me! I need a leg up! Come back! Reindeer sucking philanderer!"

I tripped then and Damien took advantage. When I stood up again he had sped up and disappeared. I noticed my toes were bleeding, red atop blue. I started to fully shiver. It hadn't gone according to plan. Revellers in a passing car called out to me. Rude words. I limped back to the middle of the road, tentatively chose the right–hand side, gave it a long and appraising look, began a run up but then slowed halfway, realised I could never scale the bridge. Not on my own. Not really, not now, not without energy nor audience. Hopefully Mark would understand.

"Labrick!"

He made me jump. That was my first reaction and then that thought gave me a giggle – *he made me jump* – but I hadn't jumped. I could jump now though, I could jump for glee, it was like that every time I heard him. I wasn't quite sure what he was saying though.

"Labrick?"

"The term labrick was in constant use by all grown men except certain of the clergy in the state of Missouri when I was a boy. It had a very definite meaning and occupied in the matter of strength the middle ground between scoundrel and son of a bitch..."

"Labrick..."

"But...let me brush aside the ornamental and give you the plain and authentic definition

```
of the word. Labrick is substantially ass, a
little enlarged and emphasized”
```

“Yes! Damien the Labrick! Yes! Thank you! Merry Christmas Mr Clemens!”

Clemens like the name Clemetine is derived from the adjective ‘clement’. To be clement is to be lenient and compassionate. Mark is like that – he lifts you when you most need him and he’s not cross or angry if he knows you’ve genuinely, sincerely tried. His words had given me the strength I needed. I’d find my way home somehow. I kicked off the restricting flip flops, flapped my arms twice and broke into a cheery canter. As I ran an image of that kid and his flying snowman came to mind. It honestly did.

I flapped some more as I re–passed the *The Woodman.*

Then let out my banshee wail.

Rebecca

This is a frustrating task (in so many ways). I feel I want to write in the third person – Rebecca thought X but the reality was Y – that kind of thing. It's difficult to find 'truth' when all you have is memory. The more you dig the denser the doubt. Through an urge to be totally (and brutally) honest I'm concluding that memory can be clouded by many things. I'm sure, for instance that Robert wouldn't recall in the exact same details as I. It feels disloyal even writing this. "A truth letter". A true love letter? Is such a thing possible? And whose truth is it ever truly going to be?

Chapter 49

The realisation was hitting me (and that's the right expression) that I was a bit predicamented. Having cantered then walked then limped for numerous miles in what I'd hoped might be the right direction, I was now sat shivering in a shelter waiting for a night bus that in my heart I knew wasn't going to come, I hugged my knees and noted my ragged feet and then considered the date and wondered if I was bleeding just like Jesus. Wasn't there a theory that suffering was good for the soul? But then I remembered that was Easter not Christmas. Christmas is about the little one – new born and innocent. Yet to know anguish, sorrow or pain. It was hard to empathise so I stopped musing the irrelevant and refocused my efforts on willing a red double–decker.

"No buses tonight mate."

A celestial voice confirming my heartfelt fear?

"No buses tonight mate, wanna lift?"

I looked up. A chap in a black cab had pulled up. And for a moment my heart froze. But not in the bad way.

"Mark?"

"What? Where you headed mate? You look like you've had a rough one."

It was a black cab that was painted white and that's what threw me. That was the association. The driver's head was now leant toward the wound–down window and it was clear he wasn't Mark Twain – he was a man with no moustache. And he was staring hard at me now.

"Wow. I take it back. You look like you've had a *proper* rough one. Get in."

"I'm not sure I have the wherewithal..."

"Just get in mate – it's Christmas and I'm knocking off now anyway."

I did get in and explained I lived in Dagenham and I thought that quite rightly he'd tell me to get out again – it wasn't like I was just heading up the road. But he didn't, he said, "Nice one, we can have a decent chat on the way." And then he passed me back a pack of wet wipes and said "Use these to sort your feet out a bit and I'll pump the heat up for you." And then he did another thing – he produced a fleece blanket and passed that back through the gap too whilst saying "In the meantime wrap yourself up in this."

And that did it. I started crying then. I honestly did. And it was probably a bit embarrassing for both of us because we drove in silence for quite a while. Then, a further bit later when he'd obviously gauged it was safe to assume the backseat blubbering had fully abated, he pulled up to the kerb and parked the cab. This time he produced a flask of coffee. He genuinely did. Then he provided an explanation "It's no biggie – the wife always sends me out with one – she'll be disappointed if it doesn't come home empty. Oh, and she's packed some shortbread but I don't want to set you off again..." I smiled at that. It was hard not to. He was obviously a humourist. "You're okay" I assured him "I think I just had something in my eye." His turn to smile then "Yeah, that's exactly what I thought."

He drove me all the way home. And on the way he explained that a lot of people hired white Hackney Carriages for weddings and other events and that those jobs could be quite lucrative and a lot of fun. I asked him if he knew that Mark Twain was famous for wearing a white suit. I told him about the great man and said I imagined he would have liked to travel in a salubrious white cab. I realised then that I was very much enjoying it myself. We talked about other stuff too but I didn't go heavy – I spared him the Rebecca and Damien diatribe.

We shook hands through the Driver's window when we arrived outside my flat and I had stepped out of the cosy oasis. I asked for his details so that I could send him some money. He smiled and said "My name's Matt but that's all you're getting. I don't want your money. It's Christmas and no offence, but you don't look like a Rockefeller." I retorted with "Yeah perhaps, but maybe I'm an eccentric millionaire?" And he said "Yeah, and maybe I'm parked outside Trump Towers?" My turn to smile. And with that he passed me the last of the shortbread, offered a thumbs up and swung the cab round. I stood at the kerb and saluted him military style as he headed back up toward the A12.

And shortly after I watched the gleaming chariot pass through the lights at Selinas Lane and disappear into the sunrise, I had a thought – Matt was most likely short for Matthew. Mark and Matthew… Curious... Now, what if a Luke and a John turned up...? Perhaps with roast turkey and a sherry trifle...?

They didn't.

I spent the rest of Christmas Day recuperating, re–reading and re–evaluating. Then reappraising and finally realising. Yes, Mark Twain was my friend and yes, Mark Twain was doing his best to help, but understandably Mark Twain was getting fed–up and frustrated. Our relationship was too one–sided, he was doing all the work and I was just doing the waiting. I was not being pro–active. I was not going to him he was always coming to me. If I wanted a full and frank and unrushed and detailed audience with the marvellous man then surely the least *I* could do was to make the effort to arrive at *his* side? If I truly wanted the peace and calm and surety he offered then surely I needed to make the effort to track him down and hence prove I was worthy of more than his intermittent fleeting visits. I had to become the determined pilgrim willing to pursue a full enlightenment rather than remain the inert hopeful grateful for a few scraps.

I made a solemn vow of subservience whilst I watched the Queen's Speech.

Rebecca

I suppose there comes a time when you just want to shake someone and I guess that's the stage I'd reached. I no longer had that glorious rush of excitement when I was meeting Robert, not to the same extent at least. I was increasingly nervous about what mood he might be in or what outlandish tonic he might want to try. Looking back now with the benefit of Dear Ms Hindsight, Robert might have *truly* been desperate. Seriously struggling. Depressed even. It was often life's minutiae that he transfixed upon. All this 'think on truth time' means I can better appreciate how that could be harmful. I can try to at least – I need to make sense of all this. Maybe Robert was just desperately clutching for a solution and hoped tantric might provide it. It's laughable and yet it's not. It's tragic. All of this is tragic.

Chapter 50

Then I spent the rest of the dwindling yuletide day checking my facts and planning my quest. I found it liberating, I felt enthused and excited, I knew what I was doing was the right thing, it made perfect sense, I had to show my commitment to Mark Twain and at last I would. And by way of proving my new fully focused determination I realised I had to cut all irksome ties to other duty. I had to rid myself of any trivial distractions. With that in mind I began to compose a letter.

Dearest Mr Ainsworth,

My heart rose the first time I saw you – my heart rose and my bladder twitched.

Surely here was a man who'd know his P.A.Y.E. from his P.11 Deductions. And so it proved. (Eventually.)

But the road to self–worth realisation proved tough didn't it George? And it has taken much from us. I'm afraid I no longer adore you.

I hope this revelation doesn't prove too angst inducing and I'm sure that one day you will find a new assistant, perhaps one you will even grow to revere and cherish and beam upon in the manner in which you once beheld my visage. (Yes, I know you doted on me too.)

Remember George, that when you do, when you get that second chance, you must grasp it with both clammy paws. That bond is precious George, that devotion is the most generous of gift, that union a joy to be exalted and nurtured.

I no longer adore you George but I recognise and acknowledge you have had a major influence upon me. And so, after some heart retching soul scorching, I have come to this decision. You are a delicate bird and I am setting you free.

Fly George fly.

(Peck off.)

Oh, and I'm sorry about the salt in the coffee. That was churlish and unoriginal.

Yours extremely sincerely and with the very most fondest of regards,
Horatio Robert Foxley

P.S. In case there's any confusion upon reading the above – I'm resigning.

I folded it twice then chose one of the many dozen envelopes that littered the hall. I liberated two pages of red–framed printed gibberish from their brown paper captivity and inserted instead my exit note (written on the greaseproof paper that used to aid my efforts at treat creation for the dearly deserving). I then scribbled the office address over my own, resealed the envelope with a generous dab of Marmite and even added a poignant reminder on the back of the envelope that I was sure George would appreciate.

Never forget friends are like bras, close to the heart and always there for support.

Ideal.

I felt myself relax. Taking control of your life really did feel good. The day had passed quickly and without too much torment. *Doctor Who* and *Harry Potter* were both finished now and hence it was legitimate to go back to bed. I felt fine, confident even – the fact I knew what tomorrow signalled enhanced a suspicion that sleep might even arrive.

I kept nagging him and when Robert straight faced and adamantly informed me that we would not be embarking on "high congress" under any circumstance until he had reached full enlightenment (by that he meant learnt how to consistently cope with George), I very maturely responded by saying "Fine then, we shan't have any sex at all." Hence mutual punishment was effectively established. Or rather, firmly cemented. I stopped taking the pill, wore a onesie to bed and allowed a battle of wills to officially commence.

It was just as ridiculous as it sounds when I write it now. It was every bit as ridiculous as it sounds. It's so hard to believe it happened and yet I know I played my part in allowing it to develop. I fought against us rather than for us. I helped make matters worse. Suddenly it seemed we were working against each other. We should not have been nurturing resentment, creating divisions and backing ourselves into corners.

Chapter 51

Optimism can be overrated. Sleep has evaded me. And now I am sat on the kitchen floor staring at my iPhone. And have been for some considerable time. Hers was top of my list of 'Favourites'. *Of course it was.* And she hadn't been deleted. My thumb hovered, hesitated, twitched and poised. And prevaricated. And procrastinated. And lowered toward then jerked away. It did this most days. But today, this crisp St Stephen's morning, was obviously deigned to be different; I've just had an accident.

I suppose if you lose focus for even a moment then events can escape you. Or they can be triggered. I'd inadvertently grazed it and now it was ringing. And my heart was racing. And I was staring and panicked and horrified and unsure as to what I would do. What could I do? I couldn't hang up. She'd be doubly scornful of a missed call. I'd have to see it through, leave a message, perhaps pretend I'd dialled the wrong number. She was unlikely to answer, I'd just noticed the time, 04:13 am.

"Yes?"

"How's Damien?"

(I couldn't help it. It just came out, first sentence, not even a hello.)

"I have no idea."

"Really? Hasn't he been tickling your ivories?"

"Damien didn't join us for Christmas tea or play the piano this year. If that's what you're referring to."

"How do you tell the difference between a weasel and a stoat?"

(I couldn't help it. It just came out. I was obviously on a roll.)

Rebecca sighed. Heavily. I ignored the warning and ploughed on.

"A weasel is weasily wecognised, whereas a stoat is stoatally different."

"Yes Robert, very clever."

"He is venal and duplicitous."

"You've been using your thesaurus."

"I'm just interested in the truth."

"Then you know it was my fault as much as his..."

"No…"

"Yes. And it was partly your fault too..."

"Mine?" (I was taken aback. *Not rolling now Mr Foxley.*) "My fault? Oh yes, of course, curses upon me for being so naive and trusting."

"No, shame on you for being so unreliable, so frustrating... so FUCKING INFURIATING!"

Too much was happening too fast. I wasn't prepared. I wasn't ready to hear her voice. I wasn't capable of receiving her scolding.

"I'm... just... honest..."

"Honest? You actually believe that Robert? You're not honest... you're uncommitted... evasive..."

"I just try to..."

"You don't try! That's just it. When have you ever tried?"

"I try... I'm..."

"Deluded."

"Deluded?"

"Yes Robert. Deluded.

"You mean eccentric?"

"No. Deluded."

"Idiosyn... what's that word?"

"Deluded."

"Right... *deluded...* can we stop the word association now please?"

"We can stop the conversation altogether if you like."

"George said he liked seeing his wife in just her bra."

"*Oh, for fuck's sake.* Goodbye Robert. Get some sleep."

"Rebecca? Don't..."

Dead.

It hadn't gone as I'd hoped. No "Hi!" "Yay!" "Yo!" No feel-good factor. No Happy Christmas, no Bravo for Boxing Day, No glad tidings. Whatsoever.

Cursed thumb!

Realisations suddenly hit me; I realised my left buttock had cramped, I realised the kitchen floor tiles were incredibly cold, I realised a large grey mouse was staring at me and I realised I desperately needed the wise counsel of a trusted friend. *Deluded eh?* Well fine, we'd see what Mark Twain would have to say about that.

Rebecca

I don't know how it happened, not now. I don't know how we allowed it to happen, why we couldn't talk about it properly, why we didn't face it and resolve it, why we just let it slip then fester under the carpet. I don't know why we dug our heels in and chose martyrdom.

No, that's not true; I do know, I have a good inkling at least, on my side it was about resentment. Maybe (most definitely) it was all linked to the other issue, the big issue, our big issue, *my big issue,* my increasing frustration. Maybe all our interactions were becoming influenced by that major issue: COMMITMENT.

Chapter 52

I stood and stretched and rubbed the parts I could reach that were causing me pain. I limped a few circuits then laid myself out on the bed. I didn't sleep but that was scant matter. In fact it was a bonus as it gave me more time to recall and to remember. Mark Twain fell in love at first sight, which is remarkable enough when considered conventionally but Mark Twain fell in love at first sight when he saw a photograph. Mark was unconventional. Mark was on a steamship tour of Europe and the Holy Land and on his trip he met his future brother–in–law, Charles Langdon. And Charles showed Mark a pic of his Sis and Mark's heart melted. And later Mark and Olivia were married and for a time they lived at number 23 Tedworth Square, London, and that is where I would soon be heading. Because that is where love resided.

Unequivocally.

Hence that's where I will find Mark and ask all my questions and get all the answers. It made perfect sense. It was a go–brainer. It had crossed my mind then finally lodged, cemented. Of course! 23 Tedworth Square, the tube would take me there.

And it does.

And I discover South Kensington Station opens onto a wide pavement. I never knew that. There's so much I never knew. *So little I really realised.* I walk out, onto the vast panorama and immediately I see a placard. I decide to read it. It tells a story; it reveals a local secret.

THE SERPENTINE LAKE IN THE MIDDLE OF HYDE PARK IS ONE OF LONDON'S BEST-LOVED LANDMARKS, AN ARTIFICIAL LANDSCAPE FEATURE COMMISSIONED BY QUEEN CHARLOTTE, KEEN BOTANIST AND NURSE TO HER HUSBAND MAD KING GEORGE.

There's more but that's already too much. Sometimes reading is overrated. My decision was poor. *The Keen Queen – The Serpent – Mad George.* It's too much. Too shocking. A taunt before tea-time. I should move on. I have to. I shouldn't look around but I do. And of course, they respond. They've been there all the time. Watching. Waiting.

> I AM BENS COOKIES. I AM LAMBORGHINI LONDON. I AM CAFE MILAN. I AM GILDING THE LILLY. I AM QUALITY FLOWERS FROM HOLLAND. I AM CAFE CHINO. I AM KENSINGTON AND CHELSEA. I AM WC. I AM TOILET.

I can ignore them if I wish. I can. I know I can. I can ignore them and focus elsewhere. I can. I do. I can see a lady, a tall one with a hat, an iron lady. I am drawn toward her. Her name is Bela Bartok and she is a Hungarian composer, 1881–1945. She is a statue and she wears a tie. I stand in front of her and stare. She is taller than I. And I don't know why she is here and I suddenly realise something else, I don't know why I am here. I realise I am at the wrong station, I have not concentrated. I have wandered where I shouldn't. Bela is here but Mark Twain is not. I have erred.

Have I erred? I squint and wonder. Bela is a geezer? *Bela Bela well I never!* Maybe it's not pronounced Bella? Rebecca never mentioned this character. Consequently, I have no idea. I do know I have erred. *I do now.* I don't doubt I have erred. I've definitely erred. I've erred upon err. I need to get back on the train, I need to get back down, back down underground. I need to try again. Head East young man. One stop. One stop only.

I can do this.

And I do.

And I emerge on to a smaller pavement. And endure a new assault.

> I AM SLOANE SQUARE. I AM HUGO BOSS. I AM ROYAL COURT THEATRE. I AM TONI AND GUY. I AM STRUTTANDPARKER.COM. I AM THE BOTANIST. I AM CHELSEA BRASSERIE. I AM TIFFANY AND CO. I AM GIEVES AND HAWKES. I AM THE KINGS ROAD.

A rush of wonders. Mark's road? The King's road? No, not the king, better than the king, a king is not the thing, not always. March for the King, march to the King, march to Tedworth Square. Elvis king pelvis thing. No. Delete that. Focus. Breathe. Walk. Walk to Tedworth.

Pass the Saatchi Gallery. Remember the Saatchi Gallery? *Rebecca took you there, didn't she? Then you went back on your own. Then you went to Beachy Head. With another woman!* Forget the Saatchi Gallery. Forget forget forget. Focus. Pass by Bram Stoker, a neighbour of no consequence, not to me, his is not the blue plaque I seek. Look at the houses though, the opulence, the wealth, look at the refuse, the discarded boxes with designer detail. Don't look, too may triggers. Don't look at these boxes, the recycling left out – banished – boxes with names – 'Fortnum and Mason.' Don't look! Too late. Damien's gift at Christmas. A mother's delight. Damien delivering delight. *Damien taking his delight... quivering with delight… taking my delight...*

DON'T!

Head down and determine. Slow the mind. Tunnel the vision. Focus the feet. Find the man. Tedworth Square. Number 23.

> "The reports of my death have been grossly exaggerated."

That's what he said, right here, right there, in 1897, at the age of sixty-two.

> "The reports of my death have been grossly exaggerated."

Tell your readers that. That's what he said when the reporters came calling for confirmation. The papers had it wrong, they were wrong in their assuming, Mark Twain was well, perfectly well, alive and well and settled in 23. It was his cousin, James Ross Clemens, who had fallen ill. Mark was still alive.

> "The reports of my death have been grossly exaggerated."

That's what he told them when they came knocking, when they came knocking on number 23. He laughed and he told them straight. That's what he did. He told them straight. That's what he does.

I'm here now. There's a plaque outside which tells all and yet tells nothing.

Samuel L Clemens
"MARK TWAIN"
1835-1910
American Writer
lived here in
1896-7

It doesn't state 'legend' or 'genius' or 'sage' or 'confidante' but no matter, I am here and here he is. My journey has not been in vain, there is a blue circle and that's a good thing. A plaque is a signal and a proof. Like Bram's. Like all the others. But this plaque is his plaque so it is not like all the others. A plaque. A word that is also the cause of tooth decay. But no matter. No matter if it doesn't tell the whole story, no matter if it is not a monument, a cathedral, an obelisk, no matter if it is not enough, I am here.

Ha! Now I remember Rebecca. I remember Rebecca joking. I remember Rebecca telling me to keep writing my poems. I remember Rebecca joking that it was down to me to put Dagenham on the literary map. I remember Rebecca outside my flat joking and pointing up and saying "They'll put your blue plaque there... in the gap between the satellite dishes..."

I imagined it too. And it became a thing. We'd pause and look up each time we were about to cross the threshold. We'd pause and look up and she'd squeeze my hand. We'd do that each time before we reached out and pushed open the communal door that never locked properly and was a legitimate cause of security concern. The one she kindly never commented on.

But that was then.

And now I find myself performing a task. I have been asked to help and I am. I am helping a neighbour up the steps. I am doing a good deed at number 21. I am doing something Mark might have done. I am helping a neighbour. I'm being neighbourly in Mark's old neighbourhood. The neighbour is curious, interested, intelligent seeming. She stares at me as I help lift her buggy up the steps. I am thanked by a lady. The lady who looks after her. The steps are not pram friendly. Help is appreciated. I nod and smile and think I am charming and chivalrous, a young Mr Clemens. The baby stares at me. It seems to know something. Something I don't know. Something I should know? I'm thanked again and the buggy disappears inside before the child can tell me. I'm left alone on the doorstep of 21. I back off. I step back down and stare at the plaque next door awhile. Focussed and concentrated. Then I cross the road and sit on an ornate bench opposite number 23. I will watch from here. And I will wait.

I am fully prepared to wait.

I am used to waiting for Mark.

He will arrive when he is ready.

This time in the flesh.

I look across and study the house. It is big, bigger than I expected, bigger than is necessary. The trappings of success. *The trappings.* I don't like that thought – *the trappings* – be careful not to get caught in the trappings. Mark caught up in the trappings? Wealth divides and wealth warps but not Mark, surely not Mark? Never. *Maybe he became genteel?* But that's OK, genteel maybe but still gentle, always gentle, a gentleman. Young Samuel Clemens was Huckleberry Finn and when he grew he became Mark Twain and he was never trapped by the trappings, *never.* I'm convinced of it. I begin to count. 5 storeys, I count them again to be sure – one below and one, two, three, four above the pavement. Step up or step down. 5 storeys. 5 floors. 5 stories? Every storey tells a story? (5 is a lot.) 5 storeys, 5 levels, 5 floors, 5 boxes. Mark in a box. Everyone in a box. Boxes, big boxes, little boxes, compartments, boxes. Boxed up. Boxed in. Boxed. Trapped. Breathe. Relax. He will arrive when he is ready. I'm Looking forward to it. To the day. To the moment. To the time. *Looking forward to it.* I'm a forward looking individual. I'm a jargon junkie. I am nothing. Look forward/ look back. Look around, look back, pass the time. Think. Think about passing the time. "There you go Madam – the finest Swiss craftsmanship – when you are finished please pass it on."

Cuckoo.

Cuckoo.

In the meantime look around, take it all in. In the mean time? *In the time when a mean thing happened…* Think elsewhere. Free associate. Associate with the free. Those who would be free. Those who should be free. Like Mark did. Like Huck did. Let it flow. Like the Mississippi. Look around, take it all in. Look around, look back. LOOK DEEPER. Look back. Look better. Look back. Look behind.

Look behind.

Blimey…

Rebecca

Robert's life had been turned upside down all within a year. His Dad had died, his only sister had moved away, the peace of his workplace had been disrupted. And now his girlfriend was becoming impatient…

Wow. That bit is hard to admit.

I feel guilty about it now – maybe I hadn't been sympathetic enough, maybe I hadn't listened or helped enough. Maybe work really was as stressful as he made out. Maybe George really was as big an arse as Robert implied and I was failing to understand just how traumatic workplace stress can be.

I was lucky. I always loved my job and I just found it hard to understand why if he hated his so much, he didn't just do something about it, something practical. But I guess I was forgetting that Robert was Robert and practical was never his forte. My response was not admirable. It wasn't understanding. It was ridiculous. I should have taken control and helped him through it. I should have been the adult and helped put a grown–up plan in place. But that other issue was always nagging and I was increasingly cross – disgruntled even. I was too focused on what I'd like to happen in the future to appreciate what Robert needed there and then. I suppose I was only seeing a narrow picture too.

Chapter 53

Gosh…

A garden. A secret. I've been sat in front of a secret garden. No. It's not a secret. Not really, it's just fenced off. There are railings around this garden. A garden and a gate and a lock. And there it is! It's a sign! Surely it's a sign!

It is a sign. There's **BIG LETTERS** and smaller **BIG ONES.** And Capitals with an **ATTITUDE.**

TEDWORTH SQUARE

THE GARDEN IS PRIVATE AND FOR THE USE OF SUBSCRIBERS AND THEIR FAMILIES ONLY.

BUT A SUBSCRIBER OR ADULT MEMBER OF HIS FAMILY MAY TAKE IN NOT MORE THAN 2 GUESTS AT ANY ONE TIME. THE COMMITTEE MAY OCCASIONALLY GIVE SPECIAL PERMISSION FOR LARGER NUMBERS.
CHILDREN MUST BE ADEQUATELY CONTROLLED.
AND PRAMS, TRICYCLES ETC MUST KEEP TO THE PATH.

IT IS FORBIDDEN TO TAKE DOGS INTO THE GARDEN

IT IS FORBIDDEN TO WALK ON BEDS, PICK FLOWERS, INJURE SHRUBS, MOVE OR DAMAGE SEATS OR TOOLS, CLIMB THE FENCE, PLAY TENNIS, FOOTBALL, CRICKET ETC, OR USE HARD BALLS

THE GATE MUST BE LOCKED ON ENTERING AND LEAVING

KEYS MUST NOT BE LENT EXCEPT TO OTHER SUBSCRIBERS

BREACH OF THESE RULES MAY INVOLVE FORFEIT OF RIGHT TO USE THE GARDEN

The garden square is locked. The greens are out of bounds. To such as I? Hello and welcome? *Bugger off and sod you?* I'm confused. The words and the message. The said and the unsaid. THE FACTS and the suggestion. Exclusion inclusion. The lyrics. Forbidden. Four bidden? "Come 'ere you four!" Four forbidden. Four scruffy young tykes peering enviously through the railings. Huck and Tom and Oliver and Dodger. FORBIDDEN. *Get out! Go away!* No! Not ever! Not possible! These are not Mark's lyrics. He would not allow this. The sign and the fence must have been erected after Mark Twain left; he would not have allowed it. He just wouldn't.

In fact, I'm not quite sure why he was here at all; it seems a million miles from Huck's Mississippi. And now I'm thinking maybe Mark Twain became genteel? But if so that's OK, genteel maybe but still gentle, always gentle, a gentle man – in his youth he was Huck and Huck became Mark. Mark was Huck grown – I'm sure of it. I've had these thoughts before…

I turn my eyes away from the sign. Don't look back. Forget about it. Think elsewhere. Watch the house.

He will come when he is ready. The real Mark Twain. The true one.

Don't think about dubious things. *Don't ever doubt.*

Rebecca's parents live in a big house.

No doubt Damien does too.

Big Box – Big Box – Little Box – Cardboard.

It's dark now and this time my right buttock has cramped. The pain is welcome as elsewise there's nothing. I'm uncomfortably numb bar half a bum. Then I think of my mum. Perhaps simply because it rhymes. Bum – Mum. Mum – Bum. My bottom has dwindled recently, it's less insulated, its remainder offers scant protection. My bottom is much lessened – there's limited padding – all bone and no flesh. I don't remember much of my mum. I was too young. I do remember her saying "Sit down on your b.o.t. tom." I guess she was polite. Spell it rather than announce it. Be kind to all ears. The mum who never said bum. Protect the innocent. *Don't just leave him behind.* Time has passed. She has passed. Dad has passed. Mark has not come. Not yet.

"Hopes of my presence have been grossly exaggerated"?

No. DO NOT DOUBT.

Wait.

I don't feel well. It's the boxes. Too much thought upon boxes. Boxes. Boxed up. Boxing. Boxing matches. Boxing mismatch. Boxed up and forgotten. Boxed up and put away. Boxed into a corner. Boxed around the ear.

Why am I here?

Man on a mission.

Clown on a crusade.

Mark has not come. Why would he? That is his house no longer. That house is nothing. That house is just another box. Five storeys but just a box. Spirit cannot be contained. Not true spirit. Spirits roam free. Spirits wander. Free spirits do. They escape and inspire. Mark has been here all along. Of course he has. But no house could contain him – no box. Mark is here. But he is not *there*. Mark is in the garden! Of course he is! He must be! He's been behind me all along. He's been in the garden. He's not in a box he's in the garden. Scorning the rules, setting right the wrongs, challenging injustice and inviting all to enter.

Those railings look scalable.

Rebecca

Commitment. It's just a word, I realise that now too. It's just another ridiculous word. It explains nothing and everything and is nowhere near enough. I sound like Robert now. I realise I'm doing that thing now – the Robert and Rebecca thing – I'm dissecting a word; I'm analysing the minutiae of that word searching for its actual meaning. I'm doing the thing we encouraged each other to do. But not in the fun way that we used to do it. Not in the amusing tease–prone, light–hearted way. Not in the "Now let's just sit right down and discuss this shall we?" way we used to. Not in the carefree way we happily wondered about and juggled and ridiculed words that held no fear.

Commitment is a loaded word. It's one we give great store to, it's one we laden heavily and unfairly. It's one that carries a burden. Robert *was* committed. He was committed to us and he was committed to me and he was completely committed to our relationship. I know that. *I knew that.* But he wasn't convinced by convention and that was different. I know that now or at least I think I do. I don't know anything for sure and he's not here to ask so I can only surmise. I can only reflect and I can only wonder. I can only realise too late. Commitment does not just mean one thing, it doesn't. It truly bloody doesn't.

Chapter 54

I strip down to my Rebecca underpants. I do this because Huck was often naked on the raft and I am about to attempt a re–enactment. I keep my underpants on because I am sure nudity is not the whole point – I feel just as free without their removal. And another reason I keep my underpants on is because I like them – they are midnight–blue and slinky. Rebecca called them 'Modal'. They were a birthday present and enhanced my figure; they have the words 'Calvin Klein' written on their waistband. The underpants were an upgrade, a necessary sivilising perhaps. I don't remember the last time I removed them.

And as mentioned, there is no strict need now; the important thing is that I lie down on my back and concentrate. The important thing is that I lie down on my back and imagine the raft and the peaceful river. The important thing is that I lie down on my back and ignore the pain in my shoulder and the scrape on my knee and concentrate. The railings were scalable but slippery.

I need to block out the pain.

Then eventually open my eyes. Look up and wonder. *Wonder where all the stars are.* Tedworth Square is not the Mississippi, *what was I thinking?* No, this *is* right, it makes sense, they are out there, *they are.* The same stars that Huck saw and Mark saw are the same that I will see as long as I am patient and as long as I recall. And I do recall because of course I can recall. And because I can recall that passage, I will chant that passage, I know it by heart. I know it *in* heart. And if the stars aren't out then close your eyes. Close your eyes, recite and imagine.

'It's lovely to live on a raft. We had the sky, up there, all speckled with stars, and we used to lay on our backs and look up at them, and discuss about whether they was made, or only just happened – Jim he allowed they was made, but I allowed they happened; I judged it would take too long to *make* so many. Jim said the moon could a *laid* them; well, that looked kind of reasonable, so I didn't say nothing against it, because I've seen a frog lay most as many, so of course it could be done. We used to watch the stars that fell, too, and see them streak down. Jim allowed they'd got spoiled and was hove out of the nest.'

That passage was on page 179. It's one of my faves.

And it makes me think more about Huck and Jim, their friendship, their wisdom, their camaraderie. And then Mark whispers to me and I know unequivocally that I am in the right place.

> "The sky looks ever so deep when you lay down on your back in the moonshine."

And he's right – it does. It does and its perfect and things can be perfect. *But then other people can ruin the perfect things.* And suddenly I'm angry, my calm has gone and I screech out to the stars, to the moon and I suppose inadvertently to all the men, children and womenfolk of Tedworth.

"I HATE TOM SAWYER!"

And it's true. It's a thought and a feeling and a revelation that has been growing and gnawing. I hate Tom Sawyer! And it's not just because he turns up in an all–too–ridiculous and coincidental way and RUINS EVERYTHING that went before in the book. It's because in doing so Tom Sawyer also totally destroys the relationship between Jim and Huckleberry Finn. It's because Tom Sawyer ruins what they had. He lessens them both. And I'm infuriated because its suddenly all so clear.

"I HATE YOU TOM SAWYER!"

Tom Sawyer takes advantage of their perilous situation. He sees the potential in it for him and his eyes light up. He sees an opportunity. An opportunity to self–pleasure. And his brain which is book–infested with learning and privilege and unfair advantage starts whirring. And suddenly it's all clear to me.

IT'S ALL SO CLEAR TO ME NOW.

I was Huck and Rebecca was Jim and Tom Sawyer was Damien. And Tom Sawyer/Damien saw that we were in trouble and so he plotted and no doubt highly amused himself whilst doing so. He used his assets – his wealth and his connections, his lack of scruple, moral, sympathy or care. He enjoyed himself at our expense. And he lessened her and he ruined me and he destroyed Us.

AND I REALISE MARK WROTE THAT LAST SECTION OF THE BOOK AS A WARNING.

I realise that now. Suddenly. But I didn't before. I didn't listen before. Instead I just read it, three times, with increasing disappointment and disbelief. And then vowed never to read that section again. I disregarded it. I decided to enjoy the magnificence of the rest of the book and ignore the obvious warning. I went as far as to tear the offending pages out. I dismissed the unpalatable. The end was wrong so I would not consider it.

I didn't recognise its huge significance.

I was too much in love.

Too blinkered.

AND OF COURSE IT MADE SENSE THAT REBECCA WOULD GIVE ME THAT BOOK.

She was warning me. Or he was warning me – Mark was warning me. Rebecca had Mark Twain in her hands and she offered him to me and that was how it should be. She passed him on to me so that I would know. So that I would be forewarned. All that would unravel was being predicted and could be avoided if only I read and understood and *listened properly.* She put Mark into my hands just as Mark had intended her to do. Mark could then guide me and warn me, it was all there, it was all in the book. It was all foreshadowed.

But I had scorned the warning and ripped the pages free.

I HAD MISSED THE WHOLE POINT. I HAD DISMISSED THE MESSAGE.

No wonder Mark Twain had grown frustrated with me. That whole book was a parallel, I saw it clearly now, I saw it crystal. I was afforded 20/20 in the shadow of **23**. It was all a parallel – our dates were adventures like the Huck and Jim adventures, it was Rebecca and I against all that was evil, Rebecca and I against all that was wrong, Rebecca and I happy and floating along. Rebecca and I together, friends, companions and equals. It was Rebecca and I creating a better future. Ours were heart–led adventures, pure of heart adventures, innocent trust–filled adventures like those of Huck and Jim.

Tom Sawyer's adventures were different. They had evolved darkly from the days of being harmless and endearing. Tom Sawyer was not maturing into a fine man in the manner that Huckleberry Finn was. Tom was no longer making us smile as the loveable tyke conning others to pay him for the privilege of whitewashing a fence. Tom Sawyer's adventures had become like Damien's adventures – selfish, grandiose, underhand and indefensible. Adventures where nothing was learnt just personal amusement and pleasure taken. With no consideration of the cost to others. He had arrived in *Adventures of Huckleberry Finn* and almost sullied everything. But I had dismissed the message, ignored the warning and hence Damien had managed to go one better, successfully, gruesomely and irrevocably soiling the *Adventures of Rebecca and Robert.*

I could see it clearly now.

A true light bulb moment.

And now a light *is* shining in my eyes.

And it's not happiness. I know that. And it's not the moonshine.

"There he is, a filthy tramp!"

That sounds rather unfair. But I can smile. I have had a Mark Twain moment, a true revelation, he wrote *The Adventures of Huckleberry Finn* solely for me. I am drenched in his discharge and never prouder. He wrote for me because he foresaw where I would be. I am closer to Mark than ever. Hence the retorts are rushing within me. His words flow through me in a torrent. I'm receptive like never before, they're in my ear then out my mouth in the same beautiful moment.

"I am the rightful Duke of Bridgewater!"

"He's a nut. Or a pervert!"

"Bilgewater, I am the late Dauphin!"

"Look at him!"

"Yes, gentlemen, you see before you, in blue jeans and misery, the wanderin', exiled, trampled–on and sufferin' rightful King of France."

I've lied about the jeans, I know that, and one of the voices sounds feminine, but I have remained faithful to the great man's text, I'm not about to edit Mark's genius.

"He's trespassing... And he must be frozen..."

I jump up. In an in–for–a–penny–in–for–a–pound kind of way. I feel calm and confident. I am on stage and fearless. I throw my arms up and my head back and Mark Twain continues to feed me.

"Whoo–oop! I'm the original iron–jawed, brass–mounted, copper–bellied corpse–maker from the wilds of Arkansaw! – Look at me! I'm the man they call Sudden Death and General Desolation! Sired by a hurricane. Dam'd by an earthquake. Half–brother to the cholera, nearly related to the small–pox on the mother's side!"

"He's half–naked! Do something Giles!"

"Look at me! I take nineteen alligators and a bar'l of whiskey for breakfast when I'm in robust health, and a bushel of rattlesnakes and a dead body when I'm ailing! I split the everlasting rocks with my glance, and I quench the thunder when I speak! Whoo–oop! stand back and give me room according to my strength! Blood's my natural drink, and the wails of the dying is music to my ear! Cast your eye on me, gentlemen! – and lay low and hold your breath, for I'm bout to turn myself loose!"

Mark and I are speaking in unison – it's a perfect duet – he doesn't have to spoon–feed me tonight. I'd already memorised and performed this speech on Rebecca's birthday. In the bedroom.

"DO SOMETHING GILES!"

A brolley points in my direction. It looks expensive. I avoid its jab. Dance to the side. "Whoo–oop! I'm the bloodiest son of a wildcat that lives!"

"GILES! DO SOMETHING ELSE!"

I slap my palms on my thighs. Thrice. "Whoo–oop! bow your neck and spread, for the pet child of calamity's a–coming!"

I leap forward then – in the manner of a kangaroo. It's misinterpreted, I can tell. I don't mean to attack them – they're middle aged and sensibly dressed. There's no need for fear, it's just part of my performance. I'm no longer in Tedworth Square London, I'm in an 19th century Mississippi small town bar. I'm spoiling for a fight but not really, I'm a thespian, a crowd pleaser. I'm Prince of the Buffoons.

"GILES!"

I slip then; a pinecone or some such is my undoing – ouch–hop–whoops–and down. Almost immediately I feel the jab. *My performance is over.* I think of the Olympics now, I truly do. I think of fencing and then I think of medieval joustery and then swashbuckling sword fayre through the ages, *En garde!* I can't help but giggle, I'm in an incongruous predicament. I'm face down and the jab is now not a jab. It's a stake. I'm pinned down with a point between my buttocks. I laugh. I can't help it. What must I look like? My precious underpants are dew–sodden and my bottom cheeks divided by the tip of a Harrods golf umbrella.

Touché

Rebecca

I had a set of keys cut for him, it was something I'd considered for a while and I thought he'd understand the significance. I even found a nice keyring that I thought would amuse him. I guess it was a symbolic gesture which I hoped he might respond to. He said.

"Thanks. Wow, a Lego–man torch!"

Deliberately or otherwise he'd completely missed the significance.

"Yes Robert, I thought you'd like that. And a set of keys for you."

"Oh... Yes, in case you ever get locked out."

Robert was committed. (What a horrible expression, what a frighteningly ambiguous turn of phrase.) But he was. Robert was committed but he scorned convention. In some way he seemed to fear it. Or perhaps it's fairer to say he found convention unconvincing; he didn't readily accept the trajectory, the meet–engage–marry–procreate expectation. He wasn't convinced of its value. It didn't strike him as in any way original. But now, looking back, I don't think he doubted *us*. I don't think he ever questioned *us*. Maybe it wasn't commitment he was scared of, maybe it was just something else, a boredom that he associated with anything conventional perhaps? I don't know. I remember he wore a ridiculous pink t shirt once that praised not falling in line. I told him he hadn't struck me as a slogan type. Maybe it wasn't commitment as we typically frame it that he was afraid of, maybe he just feared a change? That we would change somehow.

I don't know because we avoided it, we avoided the

discussion, we avoided the potential discord, the potential hurt, the potential disconnect, the potential disappointment. He felt convention was just for couples who needed validation. But maybe I did need validation? Maybe I did need the reassurance, maybe I needed my friends and parents to recognise Robert was committed, that our relationship was serious, that it meant everything to both of us. That he could be reliable, that he was viable. Maybe I needed the façade that he feared. But we avoided discussing it, once we recognised there might be a dangerous disconnect – a potential conflict, we avoided it. We'd rather simmer and second-guess, which was ridiculous, masochistic and unworthy of what we had. But that's what we did.

And actually, *fuck him!* It doesn't have to be a façade. It doesn't have to suggest a falsehood. It wouldn't have had to… it could have… it wouldn't have meant that we had joined some generic throng… it wouldn't have changed us… we wouldn't be less true, less individual, less real. It wouldn't have hurt him.

It wouldn't.

Chapter 55

I've been incarcerated. And I like that word because it's a bit similar to embalmed. And actually, it's all been rather nice – I had my own cell and everything. In fact, it was more akin to a friendly B&B than the stuff–of–nightmares gang–controlled violence and intimidation environ that you sometimes see on subscription TV. I suppose I was in Chelsea after all.

It all began around midnight when I met a very polite chap called Officer Wiley. (I thought maybe he was joking when he told me that was his name but it turned out he was serious.) In fact, he was very polite and also very serious – a combination I always find hard to fathom. And then, as soon as I'd tried to fathom him, I'd thought 'fathom' and that meant that I was once more thinking of Mark. Because 'Mark Twain' means 'two fathoms' which is twelve feet or (3.6576 meters) and was the depth of safety for a riverboat and that's how Samuel Langhorne Clemens became Mark Twain. It's true – it was the cry of safety used on the Mississippi, he chose the cry of safety as his own name – it's OK here, you're safe. I'm with you. You can trust me –

"Mark Twain!"
"Mark Twain!"
"Mark Twain!"

Officer Wiley continued to be very polite and very serious and I continued to find it hard to fathom, perhaps because I associate serious with shocking. Or important. Whatever the case we had a conversation which I can recall verbatim. Here's how it went:

"Did you know you were trespassing sir?"

"No I didn't. Not morally at least. Did you know Mark Twain and Winston Churchill shared the same birthday?"

"Can I have your name please sir."

"Certainly, Robert, take it if you want it. Did you know that googling Mark Twain will bring up more than 67,500,000 hits?"

"Can I have your full name please sir."

"Horatio Robert Foxley. Did you know that Mark Twain was the sixth of seven children and only three of his siblings survived childhood?"

"Do you have a family sir?"

"I have a Sister. And did you know that Mark Twain, at the age of 62, lived for a few months, just over yonder at 23 Tedworth Square. Mark Twain was finishing a world lecture tour at the time and he was writing a book about his travels, at a rate of 1,800 words a day."

"And do you have her phone number sir?"

"Yes I do."

"May I have her phone number please sir."

"I'm afraid she's married."

"May I have her phone number in order to check a few facts please sir."

"Certainly. 07961 590208. She's on holiday in Gibraltar. And did you also know that during Mark Twain's reporter days in Nevada he was notorious for writing and publishing hoaxes?"

"Was he really. Have you given me the correct phone number sir?"

"No. I made it up. If you add the digits they total 47. That's the number of cats Mark Twain owned during his lifetime. And also his average score at Billiards."

"Can I have her real phone number please sir."

"I think I mentioned she's married. Bit of a cross chap in truth, but she seems to like him. Mark Twain was married too. His wife was called Olivia. Did you know two of Mark Twain's daughters, his only son and his wife all died while he was still alive."

"Would you like to come with me please sir."

"Did you know Mar..?

"Mind your head as you get into the car sir."

That was pretty much it, end of conversation, Wiley wasn't a great one for the chat. And yes, I know, an inaccuracy – I did indeed make up the stats re the cats and the billiards. I don't know why. Actually, I kind of do – Rebecca has a total of 47 freckles upon her body, I once spent a morning in bed counting them. Twice. (To ensure accuracy.) Officer Wiley might not have been interested to know that though. He seemed to prefer other stuff, the more mundane. He probably wouldn't be interested to know that Rebecca had grown concerned after my counting – that she had then pointed to my own chest and said I had a mole that she hadn't seen before and that it was important that I get it checked out by the Doctor as soon as possible. And that she would come with me if I liked and that we shouldn't worry until something was confirmed. Or that I had then looked down at it, realised it was a crumb of wholemeal toast, picked it up and popped it into Rebecca's mouth.

Office Wiley probably wouldn't have been interested to hear that; he wasn't much interested in Mark Twain either. I didn't give up on trying to educate the constabulary though, I tried again in the morning, I thought the new chap on the desk might be more amenable. I even tried to increase its relevance by offering a law–and–order related tale.

"Here's a MTDYK for you – although billiards was his game of choice, Mark Twain did attend the occasional bit of baseball and on May 18, 1875 he witnessed The Hartford Dark Blues lose 10–5 to the Boston Red Stockings. So what you might ask?"

He doesn't but I continue as if he has.

"Well, Mark Twain suffered a loss at that game too and it became public knowledge when he placed an ad several days later in The Hartford Courant."

REWARD

Two hundred and five dollars reward: at the great baseball match on tuesday, while I was engaged in hurrahing, a small boy walked off with an english-made brown silk umbrella belonging to me, and forgot to bring it back. I will pay $5 for the return of that umbrella in good condition to my home on farmington avenue. I do not want the boy (in an active state) but will pay two hundred dollars for his remains. Samuel L Clemens.

"He was a funny guy."

I had hoped he would like it, it always made me laugh and the umbrella link was there after all – I could probably have pressed charges against Giles.

I don't like the silence so I try another.

"Did you know the first edition of *Huckleberry Finn* came out in London and Montreal in December 1884? However, it was delayed in America as, in a late stage of preparation, it was discovered an alteration had been made by an unknown engraver which rendered an illustration on page 283 obscene. Apparently, if I'm not mistaken, and I'm too polite to probe Mark about it so please don't quote me, but apparently if I'm right Uncle Silas's todger was now prominently positioned on the *outside* of his breeches. And hence a place in literary history was garnered for a very minor character courtesy of a disgruntled print employee."

He didn't reply. He kept his eyes front and centre. Then gestured to his left.

"The door's over there. We don't want to see you again."

I assured him it was highly unlikely.

I knew where I was headed.

Rebecca

I think maybe Robert thought that it was perfect as it was and he was afraid to change it. Maybe he had a point. But equally maybe perfection can't last, maybe that's the flaw of perfection – the thing he couldn't understand. He didn't recognise that things have to evolve.

Whatever the case and whoever was right I don't know how we got from there to here. From the very first day to the sudden ending. I know the catalyst of course, the 'tipping point' if you must. I know what I did. I know what happened. But I don't know how it happened, how we let it. How we allowed the circumstance to rise. How we allowed the possibility. I don't know how or why I… how we…

Chapter 56

I'd never felt as close to Mark Twain as I had in the gardens of Tedworth Square, his presence had been immensely powerful once I'd found the right spot and fully opened my mind. I had done the right thing. It was logic. Pure and simple. Of course Mark's presence would be strongest in the vicinities of his previous dwellings? Of course it would! Hence here I was – a bettered man – no longer aimless and hopeful but pro–active and determined. Basically I was gambling on him haunting his old haunts, it makes sense if you think about it.

And I very much did.

And so here I was.

At Venue 2.

I've slipped down an alley (not literally, I'm not thinking literally, I'm trying not to think literally, I don't need to think literally, I didn't actually 'slip') off Fleet Street. And I've bought a pint of Taddy's lager in *Ye Olde Cheshire Cheese*, rebuilt 1667.

It's a pub.

And the smell is Dickensian or perhaps it's not but it is atmospheric because there is sawdust on the floor and Charles may have had a snifter here once or thrice and then again he may not. But I believe he did. And I believe that because Rebecca once brought me here and when she did she explained the pub's unique history and she talked of him most likely having a shwally or two in here and she also told of other previous patrons like Hogarth and she knew most of what there was to know when it came to such characters so of course I believed her. I very much believed her, why would I not believe her? I believed *in* her. I did in those days.

Those days that were the best of days, the early days when we were discovering things about each other and we were both impressed by what we'd found. She regaled with tales about writers and artists and paintings and literature and I teased her and quick–witted her and massaged her thighs and made her laugh. They were the good days, the great days, the days of learning and laughter, the days when she was yet to acquiesce to a deviant.

And today there are no free seats at the front bar and so I can't sit at the window like we did on that first *Cheshire Cheese* day and numerous subsequent visits and somehow, I knew that would happen. And for a moment I feel melancholy descend. And perhaps it's more than a moment, maybe I've been inert for some time because ye olde (quite young in truth) bartender has just tapped my elbow and asked if I'm okay.

His intervention does the trick – I remember I am on a mission and that I mustn't forget that and so instead of sitting where we always did, I take my pint of Taddy's and I descend into the bowels. I take the tricky staircase and full note of the numerous signs which all advise 'Mind Your Head.' I do. I bow my head and negotiate the tricky stairs until I finally find a booth deep in the depths. And when I do, I put down my pint and then, perhaps as its prominent in front of me, I pick up and peruse the menu. And a curious thing happens – I realise I am hungry. It's an odd thought, a forgotten one, an unfamiliar. And then I stand up and I bow my head again and I go all the way up to the bar again and this time I order soup of the day for £3.95. And the bartender seems to approve of this decision – his smile seems genuine, more than the standard professional expectation, kind even. He says "Good choice, sir. Soup always helps to sort you out." And then I am a given a device which he explains will buzz and flash blue lights when my order is ready. And I know for an absolute fact that neither Charles Dickens nor Mark Twain was ever given one of those.

You see, Rebecca didn't know then what I know now – Mark Twain drank here too, it says so on the internet. Not that he's ever mentioned it. Not to me. Not in person. But that's OK, he doesn't need to tell me everything. I don't know if he drank Taddy's or chose something else and I don't know where he chose to sit. I'm fully aware I don't know everything.

Some things I can only imagine.

And now I take my change again and I take careful note of the signs again and bow my head once more. And I return to my booth in the bowels. And after some time my device flashes and my device buzzes and some drunks look up and display a dull curiosity. And their lazy–eyed half interest does evoke a bit of a Hogarth moment but not enough to truly convince. And I stand up and I bow my head and I return to the bar and I collect my soup and then I bow my head again and I return to my booth in the depths again and I drink my soup and someone takes a photo. And I remember this pub is a tourist attraction.

After a while I have finished my soup and I have almost finished my Taddy's and now I need to urinate. And so, I stand up and I take note of the signs and bow my head and enter the toilet, and as I do, a German man chuckles and says, "Mind your head"

And I say, "Yar."

And then I do urinate. And then I wash my hands and I bow my head and I return to my booth in the bowels and I completely finish my pint. And then I lie down on the seat which in truth is a bench and I close my eyes and try to imagine I am amidst historical heroes. I imagine Mark Twain and Charles Dickens and I are having a beer and Hogarth is sketching us all on the back of a beer mat. It's a pleasant enough imagining. And I may have drifted off a little because the next thing I'm aware of is being shaken back to reality by an American lady asking if I'm okay and questioning if I really need all the seats at the table.

I open my eyes and solemnly inform her, "Actually I'm being held here to help regulate the service."

And then her confused gaze pours guilt into me as I know it is important to welcome visitors to London, especially compatriots of Mark and so I do the right thing – I get up from my prone position, I sit first, then stand. Then I put my head in my hands and try to wrench out the crick in my neck. Then I give up, tug my forelock and I leave. And I think she may have thanked me and advised me to have a good day.

But I'm equally able to believe she may not.

Rebecca

I miss Robert in so many ways. I miss our ridiculous conversations and his feigned outrage whenever I burst one of his bubbles. He wouldn't believe me when I told him doves were merely white pigeons, he said it was surely sacrilege to suggest such a thing and that I was inevitably headed for Hades.

Some of our teasing seems rather poignant now.

Anyway, enough reminiscing, how about a bit more truth Rebecca? Let's tackle the trickier stuff, the more shameful facts. I guess after a time I became more irritated by what I decided to assume was his state school attitude. I wondered had he somehow somewhere along the line been encouraged to lack ambition. His poetry was a good example, a paradox I suppose, he wrote beautifully but laughed when I told him he had talent. Was he not able to believe? Had he never been allowed to recognise his options? I'm sure he could have achieved so much more and I was convinced he still had the potential so why was he so happy to drift? It didn't matter to me at first of course and now I scold myself and wonder exactly when I began falling for the cliché of wanting a man with positive career prospects. Was I really so shallow under my proudly open–minded veneer? I mean at what age does practicality outweigh instinct as far as romance is concerned? Maybe I could have been more patient. Why didn't I at least question myself? Why was I suddenly less imbued by the unconventional and more concerned with a traditional path? I loved Robert, I loved the essence of him, so why did I start to allow the details to disappoint me?

And why on earth didn't we talk about it properly?

Chapter 57

And now I have bowed my head all the way back up the stairs, exited the Twain–less pub and moved on. Now I am stood opposite a horse with a pigeon on his head and a naked man upon his back. They are outside *Caffé Nero* on the corner of Dover Street. The man and the horse are streaked the greyish white of all such London landmarks and state the obvious as I stare.

I AM STATUE. I AM SHAT ON.

Green Park station used to be called Dover Street station; I know that because I know my history, I know London history, our history, *his* history – Mark's London history. I do now. Green Park station was called Dover Street station because it used to exit onto Dover Street. It doesn't anymore. To get to Dover Street you have to exit Green Park station, turn left and then turn left again.

Dover Street is the key. At least that is my hope.

When you exit Green Park station, turn left and then turn left again, then you immediately see the iron horse and the naked man and the flagrant pigeon and the countless streaks that he and his ilk have aimed.

And it suggests a welcome.

Of the somewhat foreboding kind.

And I shudder a little but I am not turning back.

Even if this doesn't feel right.

Even if I feel anxious. Even if my breath has become ragged and my legs heavy and my chest tight. Even if I do not know if

I can cope with another disappointment. But I must continue. I have no choice. I need to do this. I need to be here. I need to know. I need to find him.

And now I think I've found the place I'm searching for but it doesn't make sense. I'm staring through the window but I don't understand the words. This list is too confusing. This is not sustenance for the people.

> I AM FILLET OF LYME BAY TURBOT WITH KENTISH ARTICHOKES AND SAMPHIRE. I AM KINGAIRLOCH RED DEER WITH RAINBOW CHARD AND EAU DE VIE MORELLO CHERRIES. I AM HONEY–GLAZED LEG OF JIMMY BUTLER'S.

Leg of Jimmy Butler's... And it's not just Brown's lunch list – I don't understand much else. The whole street talks to me but it doesn't convey Mark's message. It's jumbled and it's wrong.

> I AM WOLF &BADGER. I AM PHILIP MOULD. I AM A RHINO SKULL – I AM £7,500. I AM TINA TSANG PSYCHOPOMP. I AM THE MAYFAIR CLUB. I AM THE FUTURE OF FRAGRANCE. I AM CLARENDON FINE ART.

Fine art…

Mark produced fine art, the finest, maybe that's the link? But no, no that's not what this seems to celebrate. I don't understand, art, fine art, *finite…* It's too hard to imagine. It hurts to imagine. Mark Twain stayed on this street. He sat in *Brown's Hotel*, he referred to it as 'the last civilised inn left in London.'

Maybe the menu has changed.

Mark visited the Bathhouse in this vicinity too and it is that fact that has led me here. It is the knowledge that he caused a stir wandering these very streets in his dressing gown that has drawn me here. If I close my eyes, I can picture him. Terylene flapping in the wind. An outrageous act at the time – headline news.

He was here then but he's not here now.

Why would he be here now? I feel ill and do not wish to entertain the word abandoned.

I wander away and think maybe that's OK – not all who wander are lost. So sayeth Tolkien saideth Rebecca.

I'm no longer so sure where I'm headed.

But find I'm in a field now. A big one. Close by. Maybe Mark would have wandered here? *Wandered only in a shroud?* He liked a bit of greenery. So I imagine. Americans tend to. The great outdoors. The front–ear spirit. I wonder would he recognize this place? Would he have strode through this very grass in his slippers? Would the same chilly cockney winds have whipped his ankles?

So many un-answereds.

And no peace in this place.

I AM ST JAMES'S PARK. I AM WAFFLES. I AM CREPES. I AM DECKCHAIRS. I AM UP TO 1 HOUR £1.50 . I AM UP TO 3 HOURS £4.00. I AM ALL DAY USAGE FOR £7.00. I AM SEASON TICKETS FOR STUDENTS, O.A.P'S, DISABLED & FAMILIES £40.00 EACH. I AM NON CONCESSION SEASON TICKET £100.00. I AM WWW.PARKDECKCHAIRS.CO.UK

I don't know when such seats were invented and these are hardly the originals in any case. And the newly unemployed must be careful with their cash. I will not purchase, sit and wait. I'm familiar with futility. I know it's not happening for us today. Not me. Not Mark. Not here. Not now. No.

I'm getting back on the tube.

I'm going to go home.

Tomorrow is a day.

Another.

But this one is not over, not yet. I've exited the tube and I am waiting for a train in a busy concourse throng and there are many things to see at Liverpool Street station and today I see a long–haired white dog on a lead. He brushes my foot as he is dragged past. As if to grab my attention.

"Alfie! ALFIE! No! NO ALFIE! NO!"

He is being dragged past in a panic–stricken manner, his owner is a young man wearing a trilby hat and red jeans. He appears very anxious, agitated even. I assume he does not want Alfie to lower his back legs and drop his arse to the floor as Alfie is very much doing.

I assume his owner recognises this signal.

But Alphie's gonna do what Alphie's gotta do and Alphie promptly does do. He does his doings. Three sausages appear in his wake, dark brown, plump and perfectly uniform. Not only similarly symmetrical but exactly equally spaced. I think of a doughnut production line. It's amusing. Alphie I salute you. And I think of you as a ph not an f type Alphie – you are an Alpha Alphie – you have style and a sense of occasion. You are a good dog. You have left a trail.

And I don't mean to be disrespectful (I'm aware Alphie's trail is not a savoury trail) but it's a trail nonetheless and the word trail reminds me that I need to continue to follow the trail. The trail of Samuel L Clemens aka Thomas Jefferson Snodgrass aka Mark Twain – the man who liked cats not dogs. Alphie's sausages are a sign. A clear message.

I need to get back on track.

As soon as possible.

Tomorrow.

At sun up.

When I'll feel less lessened.

Rebecca

Robert was unarguably a dreamer. But his dreams were fun and earnest in their own way. His dreams were always involving two. He always intended me to feel loved. I do know that. He'd make me feel special in ridiculous ways. I was never sure of the fashion value of the very modest nightgowns my mother inevitably bought for my birthday but Robert would insist I be polite and wear them. Then when I self–consciously did, he'd kiss my hand and bow and say things like "I adore well–to–do ladies in postmodern pyjamas!" He was sensitive, kind and funny – what else did I want? What else did I need?

Someone less quirky? Maybe, but it hadn't bothered me at first. Robert would proudly admit he was unconventional and liked the fact that Mark Twain seemed to be too. I definitely indulged him on that, it seemed harmless to suggest they were two of a similar outlook, after all I did admire them both. Of course, now I fervently wish I'd been reading something else that day.

Chapter 58

I do feel less lesser and hence I am able to think very clearly this morning – consequently I've decided I'm going to walk to the station via the industrial estate on Selinas Lane. It's not just 6 minutes quicker than an uphill traipse to Chadwell Heath High Street then a left turn, a long walk and another left turn before a cross at the crossing, but it's also quieter. At least that was the assumption. But it doesn't prove a good one. It doesn't prove a fair one. It's no good, they're all at it here too. They're worse today if anything. The clamour begins almost immediately.

> I AM CAPITAL HAIR & BEAUTY. I AM I D MORRIS BODYSHOP. I AM YOU BEND EM WE MEND EM. I AM SELINAS CAFE. I AM HALAL ENGLISH AND EASTERN FOOD TO EAT IN OR TAKE AWAY. I AM DOGS KEEP OUT.

And there are dozens of them and they all want to be noticed, they all want to introduce themselves. And it's not as if I can outrun them – the shoes I have chosen to wear are way too small – I've wedged my feet in somehow but every step's a pinch.

> I AM CHRIST DEFENCE MINISTRIES. I AM NUKAR MOTOR ENGINEERS. I AM HOO HING. I AM LAUNDRY FOR LONDON. I AM THE BEAVER CENTRE. I AM OPEN TO THE TRADE AND PUBLIC. I AM WARNING CCTV.

But now they're interrupted as I've suddenly had a jolter – a slip back – a deposit into the past. On January 22nd (Date Adventure 7) of the GED (Glorious Early Days) I stomped through 8 inches of snow on Selinas Lane to find and rescue Rebecca. I had told her not to come and that cruel inclemency had only temporarily defeated us. I had told her that the planned feast of chocolate sprinkled chicken–parcels and pickled onion honey bhajis could be postponed. I told her she could experience *Robert Does Culinary at His Palatial Abode* another day and that I didn't want her to catch a chill or suffer a shiver. She had scorned my warnings and secretly set–out anyway. Then had called from Chadwell Heath station to ask for the final leg directions. I was furious. And rarely more excited. I scolded her gaily then gave her the directions; told her Selinas Lane might be quickest. Then I planned my own surprise – I would meet her and greet her – I raced out of the door.

I'd like to say it was knee–high but in truth perhaps the snow was only up to the shin; whichever the case the road was pristine. *White and pure.* No traffic had even attempted it. I marched down the middle, leaving my imprint, crunching my path. I may have whistled. Then I saw her and I began to run. She was carrying a Waitrose bag – wine and truffles. There was no need – especially under these circumstances. But I discovered that was one of the things she always did. One of the things that made her what she was.

A gift.

She was burdened with a shoulder bag too; her stop–over accoutrements – clean knickers, a travel toothbrush and the ubiquitous novel. I learned all her ways. But that was later. Right now I just recognised she was laden and hence I was doubly determined. I waved with arms aloft and high – then broke into a sprint.

I fell face first.

Then was up and running again. A mouth full of snow and all a–wide with grin. I fell again and twice more before I reached her. Each time I rose I raised my arms in triumph. When I did arrive before her, I embraced and lifted her from her feet. She was laughing and clung tight. I decided a spin was in order but lost my footing halfway and this time we both fell. We floundered. Flailed.

I guess I had dragged her down.

When we righted ourselves she was crying. But they were the nice tears – happiness and fun and that other thing – the one we'd yet to state but knew nonetheless.

Miraculously the wine was intact.

Surely that was a sign?

Signs…

They're immediately back and relentless in their callings.

> I AM JIMMY'S HAND CAR WASH. I AM ABBEY CONCRETE. I AM BOOKER DAGENHAM. I AM AISHAH ISLAMIC CENTRE. I AM AMAZING GRACE CHRISTIAN SANCTUARY. I AM NO PARKING IN FRONT OF GATE. I AM DESIGNER DIPPING. I AM CHEAP HYDROPONICS. I AM ALL DAY BREAKFAST.

And this doesn't feel like the best route, not any more, not at all. There's no prize waiting to be claimed today, no beautiful midwinter maiden. This is the worst of all possible paths. Barren and anguished. And everywhere noise – yelps and chants and cries and shouts. In front, behind, left and right.

> I AM HOUSE OF PRAYER FOR ALL NATIONS. I AM WARNING HAZCHEM. I AM CARS BOUGHT FOR CASH. I AM RELIABLE AND EASY TO WORK WITH. I AM 15% OFF ALL TOOLS TODAY!

But soon *eventually* after an AGE and in no *inexorable* time at all, the end is in sight.

I exit.

> I AM SELINAS LANE

(which midway became)

I AM FRESHWATER ROAD

and I cross the road and turn right onto

I AM VALENCE AVENUE

(which almost immediately becomes)

I AM STATION ROAD

and pass by

I AM COFFEE TIME CAFÉ

and their sign now screams

I AM EVERYTHING £1.50 OR 2 ITEMS FOR £2

whereas before I'm sure it snarled

I AM EVERYTHING £1.

And that holds my attention for a nano – my payroll head does a quick calculation of the percentage increase – then I'm once more in mind of the discrepancy betwixt Georgie Boy's salary and mine and suddenly there's the Sherry Wife. And I have to stop momentarily to unclench my jaw.

I use both hands.

Then I continue my approach toward the station and I notice something else. I notice a woman staring into the beer garden of what was once the *Hind's Head* pub. After a time I realise I have stopped to stare just as she has. I am mimicking behaviour. The woman looks at me for a moment, I look back for another. We both look into the garden. I look back at her.

She speaks.

"He's in the long grass scratching himself. You don't usually see one like that."

She's right, I can see him too.

I don't answer her immediately. There's something about this woman, something admirable. She seems genuinely interested. It leads me to ponder the meaning of the phrase 'Foxy Lady.' I don't answer her immediately and when I do answer it sounds alien.

"No."

Well, perhaps not alien, more unexpected than anything. In truth I haven't been much of a conversationalist lately.

She retorts with a, "He probably feels safe in there, all that grass, camouflage."

I nod as if fascinated myself and again I pause before I reply. Then I hit her with, "There's probably half a dozen living in there."

"Yes!" She yelps this affirmative seemingly pleased as punch. She turns full face and smiles at me. I smile back. It feels natural enough.

Then I say, "Probably a family."

"Yes! Yes! I bet you're right!"

We smile again. Then I state, "I have a train to catch. Goodbye."

And she nods and smiles once more. And I nod and smile again too and I also attempt a pirouette. And I'm not even acting the goat. *Not totally.* I just do it. Then I walk away and I think perhaps we've shared a nice moment.

I feel strengthened.

And now I enter the station and approach the machine and put some credit on my Oyster.

I AM EMPTIED DAILY. I AM REMOTELY MONITORED. I AM ALARMED.

And then I scan it and I descend the stairs. And I think about the Foxy Lady woman as I wait on painted *3* on platform *3*. She was 60–ish, bespectacled and sporting a grey dress. She was medium build and was wearing white tights. She was no–one I knew and yet now I felt I knew her well. And I knew she was happy because I realised, she was easily pleased.

In truth, I don't particularly like foxes.

I AM PLATFORM. I AM DANGER. I AM RISK OF SERIOUS INJURY OR EVEN DEATH. I AM KEEP OFF THE TRACK.

I wait some more on platform *3* and whilst I do, I recall that the Foxy Lady's hair was silver and I remember her mentioning camouflage and safety. And then I suddenly recall that there was something else in the once–was–a–beer garden, there was a double mattress. An image I may have blocked. And now, immediately, without further ado, Rebecca is here again – slap bang and central. Courtesy of Lord Frontal Lobe or whomever it is that reigns over the jinks–filled cranium and decrees which scatter to squirt. Rebecca is here again; the random reward of relentless rushing roulette. Rebecca is here now; vivid and true.

But ha! It's OK, she's not on the bed with someone she oughtn't be – that trigger has mercifully failed to fire – no, this is a better one – an earlier on one – Rebecca is holding a plastic jug and she's smiling. *Ha! The mattress was not the trigger.* It's the fox in the foliage that has done it – Rebecca is smiling and I'm looking at the plastic jug and I'm at first dubious but then I'm grinning and then we both laugh and I take the jug from her and later on when it's dark we are both giggling and we are sneaking around her front garden and she is linking my arm as I carefully sprinkle the contents of the now half–filled jug around the edges of her lawn.

And after that there was no more problem with foxes. It was true what she'd read in a lady's magazine – to rid your garden of omnivorous invaders you had to mark your territory and only male urine would do. And it's a nice recall because it was a fun adventure. But then immediately after its recall it's a crushing assault, just one split moment after the fond flash comes the devastating scrotum snagging shock, the horror of the reality.

The pain of the present. The fact that that was then and now it's not.

And it can't be again.

And I know immediately that although I have successfully walked to the station and competently put some pay as you go credit on my Oyster card and without mishap scanned my Oyster card and smoothly descended the stairs to the painted *3* on platform *3* to await the 10:0*3* train to Liverpool Street, it has all been a waste of time. Mark Twain may not be waiting.

I look out onto the track.

I AM DISCARDED CHICKEN IN A BOX.

Fast food – poignant, precise and profoundly on–message.

I swallow hard then retrace my steps up the stairs. One barrier is open. I use it. I do not scan out. And I know that is self–harmful.

I exit the station.

I AM CASH FOR CLOTHES

Turn left and lo and be–hold! There's a man about to assault the phone booth with his crutch.

He roars "CHIPS!"

Then starts smashing his walking aid against the Perspex. A woman walking past flinches and gathers her children protectively, her two boys look more curious than terrified, they unashamedly stare. I admire that. It inspires me to walk closer and to stop mere centimeters from the arc of the swinging crutch. There is spittle at the edge of the man's mouth.

It simmers upon a stubbled chin.

I notice a liquor bottle in his coat pocket. I like the word liquor – it's American like Mark Twain. It causes a trigger – an old–remembered jape – one that Emma might appreciate.

"How did the barmaid hold her liquor?"

"By the ears."

But no, it's not enough – it's too easy, too crass, too old, too obvious – a joker is not a humourist. I must do better – spark like Mark. I focus on the liquor bottle – its contents sloshing as Crutch Wielder continues to hack and bark away.

"ANYONE IN THERE! Anyone in there? HEL–LO!"

There isn't anyone in there. That much is clear. The box is Perspex after all. This makes me more curious. Mostly now though I'm stuck on the line that I've inadvertently planted, 'Arc of the swinging crutch' it's morphing as such sentences increasingly seem to do 'Arc of the swinging crotch' 'Ache of the stinging crotch' 'Arch enemy and his minging crotch' 'Archangel bringing Scotch'.

"What ya focking want?"

He's turned to address me. His eyes are most parts red and he has three scabs upon his forehead. I count them

"Une deux trois."

"WHAT YA FOCKING WANT YA FOCK!"

"Oh hi, I just wondered if you were finished? I'm expecting a call."

He wanders off then, he just nods and wanders off toward the High Street, he looked at me for a moment and then he put his crutch back over his shoulder and then he nodded. Quite friendly. As if he recognised me. As if he knew me. And then he wandered off.

I'm not really expecting a call, I haven't been in a phone box for years and I don't know anyone who has. I guess they're relics, reminders of a bygone era. Things change, life moves on. Bygone eras... what used to be and now is not... bygone...

I'm gone.

Bye…

Rebecca

There's lots of other things I regret now of course. I wish I hadn't been so curt and unkind when Robert finally rang (in the middle of the bloody night). I shouldn't have been so angry with him, so frustrated. I should have realised he was close to, well, anyway. I don't know. I know I had no way to know. There's little point beating myself up about it now. So Mary insists at least. I wish I'd been less flippant about George too. I'd met him once when I came to meet Robert after work and yes, he did seem a bit of an idiot and that beard was definitely more akin to homeless than hipster, more suggestive of Real Ale appreciation than a penchant for a plant–based diet, but still. I always thought he was pretty harmless. Though he'd obviously gotten under Robert's skin and that was unusual.

The irony of the phone call was that I had desperately hoped he would ring. And I hadn't planned to be angry when he did.

Chapter 59

I felt emotional. It happened very easily. Suddenly. Immediately. I'd been taunted enroute, The Selinas Lane Sirens had been in full shriek…

> I AM COME BELIEVING. I AM GO BACK REJOICING.

Then, as soon as my corner was turned and the recognitions hit,

> I AM WHALEBONE LANE SOUTH. I AM BACK WHERE YOU STARTED. I AM BRIGHT YELLOW CAR. I AM NEWLY–DENTED. I AM SISTER'S PRIDE AND JOY. I AM ERRATICALLY PARKED. I AM UNLOCKED.

I immediately felt sick. All morning I had been going nowhere. Wasting time. I was no nearer to Mark. No closer to receiving his counsel. I slapped my face (twice, hard).

One the way up the stairs I had a brainwave. I would knock on a friendly neighbour's door. And I did.

"Ring doughnuts and Rosy Lee?"

"Wrong flat mate."

"Belgian buns and brandy?"

"Go away."

Our doors are heavy, thick, reinforced. They make an impressive noise when slammed. New neighbour was mistaken however – it's not the wrong flat. *It's just wrong.* Sharon has gone.

There'd be no tea for me.

Indoors once more I have another brainwave. Healthy body – healthy mind! Clichés, slogans and stereotypical stubble – stuff I so much enjoyed! *Used to at least.* I'd give it a go!

I search and select the appropriate attire, turn the TV on then begin running on the spot whilst simultaneously channel hopping, 4MUSIC, MAGIC, MTV, MASSIVE R&B, a plethora of options, more than, but little that pleases, every tune a different torment. It's all messages of love and joy and dance with glee.

No matter – I'm picking up the pace. Are you watching Mark Twain? I'm doing this for you! The tunes they are a–changing and the shoes they are a–chafing and I'm still a–jig–jag–jogging along… I pump my knees higher – entertain the endorphins! Bite the bullet by the horns!

I'd never listened to lyrics before, not really, not intently, lines that I have never noticed now screech and squawk and demand my attention. They rise above the images projected, they filter through the scantily clads and the flash cars and bright lights. They force their way to the surface, it's not the videos it's theirs words, and it's not the tunes it's their words, it's always the words. It's the words that carry the pain. The words that make the announcements.

It's all messages of love and joy and dance with glee.

Fortunately, there are many ad breaks, it seems to be a music channel must. I doubt it's done deliberately to alleviate my torture but I'm grateful nonetheless. This current ad has an Olympic champion attempting to direct my spending, it's all smiles and sincerity and a brand in the hand.

He's trying to sell me porridge.

And he's on his bike and now he's being referred to as a hero of the saddle. And it's that expression that has somehow got me here. Prone on the floor once more. It's that phrase that has stopped me in my tracks. I'm not grateful for the ad breaks anymore. That's all I needed – one thought – one expression –

one trigger. And a sudden jolting paralysis. *Hero of the saddle.* Heroes in the saddle? *I got back on the saddle?* In the saddle? *Isn't that a nice euphemism?* One that makes sense. A clever visual one. A worthy one. A delightfully visceral one. She's back in the saddle? She's riding again. I can see it. Saddle. Sidle. Sidled into the saddle? Onto the saddle. *His rotten scabrous saddle.* That's the clever little jockey–jokey phrase that has got me to where I am this very moment.

Frozen.

And now I'm imagining pistols at dawn, Damien and I and twelve paces. It's a misty morn and the bathers from the mixed pool have foregone their breaststroke in order to stand and stare. They have formed a line of spectate. It's a jagged and irregular one. A random arraying. They lack choreography – the short stand by the tall, the slim slipped between the not so. Their order disappoints but their wardrobe is rewarding. They are dressed for the occasion. Black costumes and trunks. Black lace veils for the women, bowler hats for the gents. No bikinis. Their mood is respectful. Respectful, sombre and expectant. An elderly gent in snug fitting speedos coughs. His breath wraps around him.

All else is hush.

I'm back on the Heath where it all began but now everything has changed. Life lived in circles. Tightening coils. And now I hear a horse crow and a cock snort and I'm aware that dawn is approaching to trigger Show Time.

Each dueller has a second, a friend to hold his weapon. Rebecca's dad is holding Damien's.

Mine is held by Emma.

She does wear a bikini, a tiny white one. And very high heels. She lifts her pink veil and says

"Good luck Knob–end. Don't fuck it up."

Then she rubs my pistol, smiles crookedly, lightly kisses my cheek and steps back.

Now Damien and I are standing back–to–back and Rebecca is emerging through the mist. She is wearing a full–length mourning dress and approaching with the starting flag – she's chosen a Grand Prix style beginning. She looks stunning. She is beautiful. *She is still so beautiful.* I will kill Damien. *Murder him.* Twelve steps, a sharp turn and one quick bang.

Rebecca comes closer and I recognise her flag, it's incongruous and yet appropriate, it's the last pair she revealed, her biggest pair, the pair she didn't risk until she knew it were safe, the ones she apologetically referred to as her "Grandma knickers."

When she drops them we'll begin.

Rebecca

Robert's smile got me every time, every time from that first time. It was just there, a flash, a reflex, wide and open, unveiled. It got me every time, it wasn't cocky or arrogant or practiced, it was just his smile, it was just honest, assured, it was just 'Hello, its me.' And I couldn't help but smile back and mine was genuine too, it sprung from within.

It's still there, that smile, it lingers like his voice.

Chapter 60

And it's a few hours later now and I'm lying face down on the bed as I have weeping blisters on both my heels. I think another may have just burst. I jumped a little when my phone rang. Winced when I reached to receive.

"Desperate Dueller's Recuperation Centre."

"Robert?"

"Sis."

"How are you? I've tried calling you loads. And you didn't reply to my text. How was Christmas?"

"I went hard then I went home."

"Oh... Oh good! You mean you've been exercising. That's good. Do you think it...helped?"

"Pain for gain."

"Well, I don't know, that's the expression. How are you otherwise? Have you been sleeping?"

"8 hours this week."

"It's Wednesday."

"Is it?"

"You. You know I'm finding it increasingly difficult to know when you're joking. You nearly had me then."

"*Had me.* That's an expression too isn't it? You had me... He had *her...*"

"Lots of things are just expressions Robert."

"Oh... Oh blast! There's someone at the door, sorry Sis, I'll call you back."

There was no–one at the door, I knew that.

But I still hobbled to it and checked.

And then I lay face down again, this time in the hall, and I wondered what had been the point of my daydream anyway? Chivalry had lost all its valour and Damien would never agree to my gauntlet. Then out of the corner of my eye I noticed the toe and heel destroying footwear I had so wisely favoured. They were just where they'd landed after I'd peeled them off, sworn and thrown. Just inside the front door on top of the pile of unopened mailings. There they sat – blood drenched, ripped–apart and resonant.

No–one would be wearing those plimsolls again.

Rebecca

The teasing was there from the start too; kind, clever, brilliantly funny but always gentle teasing. Robert was theatrically effusive with his compliments when I turned up on Adventure Date 4 hungover and wearing plimsolls. I'd been out with the girls celebrating Annabel's hen night, it had gotten messy and we'd all crashed at Pippa's. I hadn't woken till midday and then found one of my heels was broken – I was supposed to be meeting Robert in an hour and was panicked. Pippa had laughed and told me to calm down; she brought me a towel and told me to get in the shower. When I emerged, she handed me a pair of clean knickers and the plimsolls. She smiled apologetically and said "My aunt left them last summer, the shoes not the pants, mine are too big but these are a size 5 so they should fit." I must have looked crestfallen as she quickly added "If he's as nice as you say he is, and you told us how nice he was 76 times last night, then I'm sure he won't mind you wearing them." She was right. Robert was very taken with them and it was our best Adventure Date yet – a stroll through Regent's Park, fringe theatre at the Pleasance, drinks and a dance in the bar underneath. He decided I'd obviously worn them in order to be able to sway and said they complimented my red dress perfectly. He'd always insist after that they were his favourite pair of all my shoes.

Chapter 61

A pained start. An early start. A determined start. An important start. A fully enthused start. Yesterday's exertion has reinvigorated me. I am fit and refocused. I am leaving home once more. I am coming Mark Twain. I'm a–coming!

My feet are paying the flip–flop and plimsoll price but that only adds to the sense of pilgrimage. It's part of the accepted process – suffering before salvation. Limp wince repeat. Limp wince repeat. Limp wince repeat. It's okay, it aids focus, the muttered mantra filters out the noise en route to the station. Dampens it down. Limp wince repeat. Scan Oyster. Limp wince repeat. Descend stairs. Limp wince repeat. Halt at the number **3** on platform **3**. Board carriage **3**. Stand grit endure. Stand grit endure. Don't get a seat. Curse. Stand grit endure. Stand grit endure. Change at Stratford. Limp wince repeat. Board tube. Stand grit endure. Don't get a seat. Stand grit curse endure. Exit. Head for the escalators. Limp wince repeat.

Can you take a message? *Sometimes I can't.* Will you take a message? *Do I have a choice?* I have a message for you! *Oh no...* They start up as soon as I step on – brightly coloured rectangles that don't hold back.

The first informs me,

REAL MEN GET RAPED

The second states,

IDEAL HOME EXHIBITION

They're scrolling past me or I'm scrolling past them (it's a mute point). But what is a *mute point*? Soundless? Well, these are not – I'm on the escalator and they're scrolling past me as I ascend or perhaps I'm scrolling past them as I ascend – *scrolling scrolling scrolling rawslide.* But either way they are not mute they are back–chatting. And I don't know why that when I reached the top of the ascend I stepped off and then immediately on to the other escalator and began to descend again, but I do know they have seen me coming and so now they are more confident – more demanding – pro–active and eager – this time they are readied and clamouring. And I suddenly recall it's moot not mute – moot is unimportant or irrelevant – mute is silent. Rebecca had explained the difference. It makes no difference.

> I AM POSTER. I AM AD. I AM POSITIONED IN YOUR EYELINE. I AM ROCK OF AGES. I AM THRILLER LIVE. I AM SINGING IN THE RAIN. I AM WICKED. I AM WARHORSE. I AM SHREK. I AM WHAT THE BUTLER SAW. I AM LET IT BE. I AM LOSERVILLE. I AM DO YOUR COUNTRY PROUD – BIN YOUR GUM.

That's the loudest one. The least mute moot. That one shouts out. She's pretty and smiley and on roller skates and doing a sort of pirouette thing whilst very elegantly dropping her chewing gum into a wastepaper bin.

Rebecca liked skating. And it's nice to be reminded but it's also painful to be reminded. The thoughts collide – the happy recognition then the wrenching realisation. A split second of warmth then the icy crush. To make matters worse (infinitely worse) someone has defaced the poster – someone has biro–ed a phallus and scrotum aimed at the corner of the skater's mouth. And so of course now I'm reminded of Him. I imagine Him and

Rebecca and *Holiday on Ice*. I imagine the biro–ed bits to be His bits and... no, I can't allow myself to imagine. It's not Rebecca it's just a poster. It is just a poster. It is just a poster. It is just a poster. Fortunately, the escalator continues to descend; it's taking me down and away. It's carrying me beyond. I can leave them behind now. I don't have to look back. I can leave them behind.

I can try.

He got to see the knickers I was wearing that night too, for the first time. I never told him they were Pippa's. Some things are a little too weird. I never admitted to Pippa that he had seen them either. Even when she smirkingly enquired if they had brought me luck. She must have guessed when I blushed because she insisted that I should keep them as a memento. She didn't want the plimsolls back either so I decided to keep them at Robert's in case of any emergency – like the need to dash to the corner shop for milk. I was sure I'd never wear them in Muswell Hill.

Chapter 62

And I'm still descending – now with hands in front of eyes and thumbs wedged into ears. I stumble off at the bottom. Attempt a re–assemble of wits. Try to gather them about me. Succeed. Leave the escalators behind. Board the Piccadilly Line Eastbound (even though the map suggests it squiggles North). Wonder about that and then ponder again on moot and mute and the struggle not to give a toot.

I get off at Bounds Green – *alight here for bomb drop devastation.* I stand on the platform locked in a rigid probably not going to move anywhere any time soon type stance. But then, after a time, I discover there is another poster, this one is chanting at me –

> 'WHAT DOESN'T GO IN THE BIN CAUSES DELAYS ON THE TRACK – WHAT DOESN'T GO IN THE BIN CAUSES DELAYS ON THE TRACK – WHAT DOESN'T GO IN THE BIN CAUSES DELAYS ON THE TRACK – WHAT DOESN'T GO IN THE BIN CAUSES DELAYS ON THE TRACK – WHAT DOESN'T GO IN THE BIN CAUSES DELAYS ON THE TRACK – WHAT DOESN'T GO IN THE BIN CAUSES DELAYS ON THE TRACK.'

I realise Transport for London are obsessed with cleanliness. It's sort of OK though – the chant breaks the stasis – gets me going – gets me moving. I attempt a quick tap dance. But that re–breaks my blisters and in any case it was a poor effort – my hands are in my pockets and my heart's not really in it.

I get on the next train. Stand grit endure.

And I mustn't think of Rebecca, I mustn't. I have to stop because once freed those thoughts do not flee without great effort. I must focus on something else instead and today I am fortunate – the man sat opposite where I stand is offering distraction and hence I must grab it. His muttering is confident and his kagoul bright orange – I shall use it as an anchor. I turn on my attention – I twist it like a rusted tap. Then I aim its drip toward him. *Here – it's yours.*

I lean in and it transpires I have chosen wisely; he shows no surprise only enthusiasm. He addresses me like a welcomed peer.

"The future is all about the insects. Humans have stopped evolving, that's why we're doomed."

I have to admit it's a good opener.

"Doomed?"

I know I shouldn't encourage him. Actually, I don't *know* that at all. But I kind of recall that being the commonly espoused advice. I don't remember why. But whatever the etiquette he's here and he's now and that seems to be as good enough for him as it is for me. I *will* encourage him. I lean in further. I'm an inch from his lips – no, that's too close – his face is blurring. I ease back, six inches now, perfect. I note he has a large mole to the left of his nose. I've worked it out – my right is his left. Curious really. It quivers slightly as he speaks.

Adds gravitas.

"Yes! Doomed by our inability to evolve. Did you know some spiders castrate themselves during sex to escape the female who they know is likely to devour them afterward?"

I remember I like such questions – ones that start with *Did you know...*

"No, I didn't know."

"They play a bit of a trick on her actually – the phallus that comes off wedges itself and hence acts as a plug to stop any other spider men getting their prongs in."

"I certainly didn't know that."

"Yes, and not only that, it also still spews its good stuff even after the cut off period."

"Yikes."

"Indeed. So their ideal scenario is survival after the coupling and a sneaky impregnation to ensure their genes scutter on."

"Ingenious."

"Yes. The future is all about the insects."

"I can see how it might be."

"The self–castrators have to be very nippy mind you – generally the duration of copulation is very short and it's the females that initiate the break off."

That focuses me.

He goes on to rattle on about beetles, dungs and scarabs most likely, but I'm not listening anymore. I'm thinking about Damien's prong snapping off.

I hear the crack.

Rebecca

Although this a truth letter and I'm trying very hard to err on the side of giving all benefit of the doubt to the opposite viewpoint, I do feel the need to defend myself and my frustrations a little. Initially, I was more than happy to visit Robert and spend time in his flat in Dagenham even though after the first time I'd confessed the truth to Pippa – his bathroom was hellish and when the bigger lorries rumbled past during the night the whole building would shudder. Not only that but in the morning when I was leaving there was a homeless man asleep on the ground floor landing. Robert confessed the lock on the outer door had been broken "for years". He'd left a couple of pound coins next to the sleeping man. I guess Robert was like that – he often put my mind at ease by viewing things very differently. Soon I had few worries heading East.

But as time passed, increasingly there were incidents that genuinely shocked me. When I first knew Robert, he had a lovely neighbour across the landing, Sharon who would always smile when we passed on the stairs and say things like "Blimey, you're not visiting him again are yer?" Or "Aint you fed up with that clown yet?" They got on well really and there was a nice atmosphere in the block. Sharon was very organised and knew all the residents – she was the type who'd make sure the communal bins weren't overflowing and pop to the shop if the old lady on the ground floor had run out of cigarettes or needed a copy of the Radio Times. She did a lot of the little things that can make a big difference, I guess. One day I arrived to find her up in Robert's loft locating a stopcock in order to stem the flow from a leaking water tank. She was far more practical than he and hence made for a perfect neighbour.

One day she rang him up whilst we were still in bed – late on a Saturday morning. Robert answered then immediately dashed out from under the duvet and into his kitchen. I jumped out too and followed him wondering what the emergency was.

"That was Sharon on the phone – she told me to take a look out the window – one of our neighbours is having a dump in the B & Q car park."

A group of about 12 men had recently moved into one of the two–bedroom flats on the middle floor. There were always cigarette butts and patches of spittle on the stairs now and if any of the dozen were loitering when I arrived, they would brazenly leer. It wasn't pleasant but once I was inside Robert's flat and the door was closed all was well and I'd soon forget.

Minutes later there was a knock on the front door – it was Sharon, "Did you see him? Squatting there! Blatantly dropping a Richard! Dirty git!" She was obviously upset and Robert immediately put the kettle on. When it boiled, we all sat down and talked it through.

"You should have taken a photo."

"Of him curling one out?"

"Yeah."

"What for?"

"I dunno… we could've sent it to the local newspaper or something."

"Yes! Of course! You're right – they could have run a caption contest!"

Soon we were all laughing but the incident was indicative of a diminishing niceness. Gradually the flats had become rental properties rather than owner–occupied and when Sharon left after buying a house – "escaping" as she quite accurately put it – Robert was the only one of the originals I'd known left in the building. Infuriatingly, he still didn't seem to have any inclination to want to move.

Now that I think about it though and what happened, the guilt nags again – I realise Sharon flitting was simply one less reliable person around to look out for Robert. Maybe she could have talked to him after we... Talked some sense into him after I'd confessed. Sat him down with a cup of tea and provided some sympathy. Perhaps he would have talked to her. Opened up. Maybe she'd have fought my corner a bit and told him to talk to me. I know she would have at least offered him a dose of her practical realism and more importantly, she would have certainly kept an eye on him.

I guess Robert had suffered a lot of loss – we'd all abandoned him in various ways – his dad dying, his sister moving to Norwich, his old boss leaving, his next–door neighbour buying a house, and of course his *evil girlfriend* losing patience. And then doing worse. Much worse. I don't suppose any of it helped when it all became too much. He'd lost a lot of anchors. What was he left with? Who could he turn to?

Chapter 63

And now it's later and I'm aware I'm losing track and that's quite funny if you think about it because all the trains are on tracks. Actually, it's not really 'funny' but perhaps it's ironic or a smidgen mildly amusing. Harmless even. Until you then think *tracks of my tears*. In truth it's better not to think at all. Or to only think in small doses – or to try not to think in complete sentences – I am aware I am losing track of my journey. I have obviously gotten back on the system and journeyed on back or sideways for now the platform and the Bounds Green Bomb Scene are beyond me and instead at my feet there's a grooved floor and a tinny tannoy has foretold that I'm on a Hammersmith and City Line train to Hammersmith. The floor is fascinating – ploughed lines spattered with yellow and white paint. I look up, embrace the interior. The poles are yellow on this line, the cushions are green, yellow and pink – jagged squiggles on a dark grey background and none of it makes sense anymore.

My stomach mumbles but it's hard to decipher its message. *Listen to your gut – but what are you saying?* Change track. Tack. I have a seat now. There is a boy and a girl sat opposite and they have nice clothes and clean faces. I assume these are intelligent children who are likely keen on learning.

"Did you know Mark Twain took out a patent for a self–pasting scrapbook?"

They don't answer, they lean in toward each other and the boy says something and the girl giggles. Perhaps I was wrong and they are slow–learners.

I am undeterred.

"And did you know Mark Twain also invented a Memory

Builder Game?"

The boy says something else but that's not strictly true, it's more he makes a noise. I don't know why it's called a raspberry. I have never heard a raspberry make a noise.

I return the compliment.

Both children giggle. The boy kicks a leg toward me. An adult takes their hands and leads them to different seats, glancing at me as she guides, not unkind but not encouraging. From a distance the boy makes the sound again, the adult frowns her brow and shakes her head. She passes him a book. I imagine she is a good mother.

I realise the boy is lucky.

Then I hear a faint but familiar chuckle.

> "My mother had a good deal of trouble with me but I think she enjoyed it,"

It makes me realise something else, something more important, much more – I have spent the morn a–dawdle – yet again I have not come closer to Mark Twain. He's giving me a gentle reminder. He sounds patient but faint – I'm not surprised. I have become un–focused – rambling – I must do better. If I yearn it I must earn it.

Head home and start again?

Yes!

Return. Plot. Plan.

Succeed!

Rebecca

Robert's dad was kind and genial; he always hugged me and had that same open smile as his son. He frequently thanked me too. I think he was always a bit concerned about Robert – he'd say things like "He's a bit of a dreamer that one, I'm glad you're looking out for him." That was ironic too really, I often felt it was the other way around, Robert looked after me; his focus was always on making me happy. He'd get desperately concerned if I was ill or upset in any way. He was insistent that I let him nurse me even if I just had a mild head cold. He'd take my hand and say things like "It is my duty to protect and comfort and honour and esteem you above and before all others." And though we'd both be smiling I could see in his eyes that he meant every word. He was furious when I sliced my fingertip cutting aubergines and took myself off to hospital. He gave me a long lecture about how it was admirable to be independent but horrendous to go it alone.

That was Robert. That was what he was like.

Chapter 64

Returned. Re–evaluated. Refocused.

Restarting.

New dawn new day. Limp, wince, repeat. Limp, wince, repeat. Limp, wince, curse, repeat.

I'm sat uncomfortably (sit grit endure) and the train has just eased out of Ilford. I am happier now because I have a predetermined purpose – I am a man with a biscuit in his pocket and a mission on his mind. And although the window tells me it is raining heavily and the *Metro* mentions amber weather alerts and fears for New Year, I am determined to be undeterred. I am about to visit Dollis Hill. It will bring me closer to Mark Twain. It will bring me face to face with Mark Twain. I am convinced.

I have chosen somewhat unorthodoxly – my biscuit is not a Custard Cream nor is it a Bourbon. It is not a mottled Garibaldi nor a smashing orangey–bit–in–the–middle Jaffa. No: it is very much and every inch a *Go Ahead.* I have chosen unorthodoxly but rather well, I like the name, '*Go ahead!*' '*Yes, why not?*' And I like the colour of the packaging, green and red and white, those are happy colours, festive – it's a seasonally appropriate snack.

I study it carefully as the train rumbles – there are explanations and facts on its wrapper. I like that too.

I don't read as much as I used to and in many ways I miss the routine. And now I've discovered that if you raise the edge of the wrapper slightly then a quality guarantee is revealed and also a snippet titled 'Nutrition Information.'

I have never read such facts previously but today I decide I will.

Sugars 7.3g 8%
Fat 1.8g 3%
Saturates 0.8g 4%
Salt 0.1g 2%

There's loads more info too but I don't immediately continue as we have reached Stratford and many passengers are now disembarking which makes it hard for me to concentrate. They brush my knees as they file on out and for a moment I'm mesmerised by their exodus and the questions it poses – the where are they goings and the whys. Then, feeling slightly nauseous, I determine to look out of the window on the opposite side. And now I wonder about that giant squirly Olympic leftover – it doesn't look safe. Or inviting. It's twisted and gargantuan. A curled whirly. Red, foreboding, ominous and inexplicable. Garish metallic confusion complementing an unambiguous grey skyline.

I should look away, I have to look away, I fight to look away. I must exit the orbit of *The Orbit.* I need to look away from its snake–like tunnel built to encourage helter and skelter. It has no message for me. No savoury statement or kindly comment. Only suggestion. I determine to wrestle my eyes back inside.

I succeed.

I return my focus to the micro, back to the interior, back to the biscuit. I'm informed it is a 'twin pack' though really that's unnecessary as it is obvious once you handle the package. It goes on to reveal that each slice contains 74 calories and that that is 4% of an adult's guideline daily amount. I next discover they have their own website (this is a serious biscuit). It's www.123healthybalance.com which sounds like a mantra so I try it out. Just the once. One. Two. Four, three heads turn my way. Then away again when I grin. Soon we're at Liverpool Street station and it's time to disembark.

If you so decide. And today I do.

And as soon as I step through the ticket barrier, I encounter three Giant Pandas by the *'Sweet Chariot'* pick n mix stall. And I know immediately they are not correct. They are tall not fat. Eight foot skinny–malinks. Anatomy run riot. And also, they're not real; they're not really real I mean, they are humans in disguise. They are duplicitous.

Instantly I dislike them.

I hurry past, I don't return their two–paw wave. A small child sees them and begins to cry, the youth of England are not given enough credit. I salute the two–foot sage and up my pace. I head for the Metropolitan and Circle and Central Lines entrance and stop to pick up an underground map. I have to look up Dollis Hill, the index informs me it is Zone 3 and that's located on the map in grid B3. It truly is. My eyes head that way and discover it is on the Jubilee Line. I could have got on the Jubilee Line at Stratford. I have erred. I cannot get on the Jubilee Line at Liverpool Street. I will have to travel on the Circle or Metropolitan line to Baker Street and change thereafter.

And so I do.

And as soon as I step off the train at Baker Street, I realise that I am indeed back on track. Opposite me, just across the rails, is a poster loudly declaring,

GLENNFIDDICH – THE SPIRIT OF A PIONEER.

A pioneer. A man on a mission. The first to search. And that's not all. I now remember that Sherlock Holmes lives here. And I know he doesn't really but he does if that makes sense and it kind of does if legends are to be believed. And consequently, now here's another uncalled recall – Arthur Conan Doyle – he who was the Sherlock creator. It was a sat–up–in–bed situation – Rebecca reading aloud a bit about Baskervilles and telling me how his stories had proven longevity. I nodding my understanding then dipping my head under the covers and barking.

Giving a gentle nip or two.

I notice something else now. There's a tile on the platform wall that reads:

THE RED-HEADED LEAGUE - YOU CAN EARN £4 A WEEK COPYING OUT THE ENCYCLOPAEDIA - PROVIDED YOU HAVE RED HAIR.

HOLMES FINDS IT A 'THREE PIPE PROBLEM', 'OMINOUS RATHER THAN ECCENTRIC, AND TAKES WATSON AND THE 'YARD' TO THE CELLARS OF A LONDON BANK WHERE A SHIPMENT OF GOLD HAS ARRIVED FROM PARIS. THEY AWAIT DEVELOPMENTS.

I enjoy the surrealism, the incongruity. And the phrase 'three pipe problem', in my Photograph of Mark Twain standing outside Dollis Hill House he is clutching his own pipe. Mark and Sherlock, Holmes and Twain – men of the pipe. I wonder should I have a pipe and suddenly feel inadequate, I frantically feel about my person, I don't have one. *I knew that really.* I do find a stone in my pocket though, a pebble with a large hole in it. I remember Rebecca telling me about Virginia Woolf and her well–filled pockets. And then I relocate the *Go Ahead* biscuit. And that reminds me to focus.

Mark Twain once said about Dollis Hill that,

> "There is no suggestion of city here; it is country, pure and simple, and as still and reposeful as is the bottom of the sea."

It sounds perfect.

My train arrives and I board and that's it – goodbye Baker Street. I settle into my seat and return to my reading.

Nutrition Information: Protein 0.9g, Carbohydrate 13.3g of which sugars 7.3g. Fat 1.8g of which saturates 0.8g.

I get a bit bored at this stage but am determined to plough on.

Fibre 0.5g Sodium* <0.1g *equivalent as salt 0.1g
Calcium 60mgGelling Agent (Pectin). Strawberry
Concentrate. Emulsifier (Soya Lecithin).

It's excruciating but imperative that I finish.

Finished product contains 20% sultanas, 4% currants and the equivalent of 1.5% strawberry.

And that's that, I survived the whole text (though I can't recommend it) and here, right on cue, is Dollis Hill.

And as I step off the train I am promptly imbued with fondness – this is a nice station, one of the underground's overgrounds – it is open and breezy, houses on one side of the platform, trees on the other. I like it immediately; I feel close on impact. I take a deep breath and head for the exit.

And just beyond the ticket barrier I see a sign with an arrow which promises,

GLADSTONE PARK 440 YARDS.

Ah yes, I remember from my research, the park which houses the House which once was Mark's Happy Holiday House, was re–named to mark the politician's career. (It was controversial at the time.) I decide it works though – Gladstone – the glad stone? Glad's tone? I smile and I am glad – it's a sign – the stars do align. My path is crystal clear. Mark Twain is surely near.

I stride on, ignoring the elements that a lesser pilgrim might deem daunting.

In no torrential time at all, I come to a green painted bridge and I realise I have arrived at Grandma's cottage. Actually, I have not arrived at Grandma's cottage but at a place in the woods called *Dudding Hill Junction.* It is an olde–worlde signal box beside a narrow and picturesque tree–lined railway track. It's a white wooden hut that suggests timeless tranquillity and safety for all who travel on by.

Mark Twain once said,

> "Dollis Hill comes nearer to being a paradise than any other home I ever occupied."

And yes, I can fully imagine Mark here now. In fact, I know for a fact that I've been transported back to the turn of a century. My plan is working. And, as I stare in awesome wonder, I hear a steam train approach…

And then my anticipation is interrupted as a lady joins me on the bridge. One that looks a lot like Grace Jones on her Nightclubbing album cover – kind of Wow–but–perhaps–approach–with–caution. And with her she has a huge grey umbrella and a large muscular friend. And now I'm confused as I'm fairly sure they didn't breed such dogs in the year 1900 when Mark's wise head rested on a comfy Dollis pillow. And I'm somewhat distracted and so don't see the train pass beneath me but no matter as I'm fairly sure Casey Jones was not driving the train. For if he were surely he would have stuck his head out of the cabin window and waved or blown his whistle or pointed to the next clue or some such?

I realise this is a complex fairy tale, the metaphors are not clear and the signposts are smudged. I'm determined to persevere however and decide to test things out.

"Excuse me, just so we're clear, you're not on your way to Grandma's House?"

"Do what?"

"Nothing. I wonder do you know the way to Dollis Hill House?"

I half expect her to give me a bottle that has a label saying 'Drink Me' or to introduce me to Hansel and Gretel, but she doesn't, instead she says "Yes", she does know the way to Dollis Hill House. And then whilst her dog sniffs my ankles (he's far friendlier than Mr Rosman) the lady, who I now know for certain is Cinderella not Cruella, explains that I can follow the path up to the top of the hill. I thank her. And I don't ask if it's yellow bricked and nor do I enquire what she's up to after midnight. Instead, I break off the corner of one of my twin biscuits and drop it at the paws of her best friend, whose name perhaps is Buttons. Cinderella nods approvingly then asks

"Why aint you got a hood or an umbrella?"

And that embarrasses me a little as I had been unaware that I hadn't until she asked. Then I try and recall leaving the house and that seems once upon a faraway long long time ago. And so I mutter something about starting a new year resolution early then quickly scurry away.

Silly Pumpkin.

Rebecca

We would buy little gifts for each other, go out of our way to try and find something unique or unexpected. I once found a button badge in a second–hand bookshop that stated 'Cours camarade, le vieux monde est derrière toi'. It was honouring graffiti that had appeared during the civil unrest, strikes and riots that took hold of Paris in 1968. It translates as 'Run comrade, the old world is behind you.' I thought he'd like it (he did). I knew it would appeal to his bohemian take on life. I also felt it was reflective of us and all we were creating – our own unique world. I never thought, I wasn't suggesting anything other... I shudder now when I think, when I wonder. It's just another guilty cringe when I recall. All this, all that.

Write yourself a letter…

Chapter 65

I have now almost reached the summit and am faced with a ten–foot–high green panelled all–hindering wall. And a tremendous shock is starting to flood. It's a ten–foot–high green panelled all–hindering wall where someone has daubed the word 'STOP' in blue paint.

I do stop.

And a phrase arrives *Blue and green should never be seen.* I think it refers to fashion but I also fear it may be sinisterly apt – I'm beginning to get a very bad feeling about all this.

And I don't know how long I stand and stare but after a time I hear a friendly voice.

"Are you okay mate?"

Cinderella is back. Maybe she can confirm my fears. She certainly can, she is only too pleased to vent. She is not happy about the situation; she is resigned to it but she is not happy. She is not happy at all. She adjusts her umbrella so that it now shelters us both, asks Buttons to sit and then tells me of the succession of arsons and then the decision and then the demolition. She refers to the cost–cutting council as "Typical tight bastards." They have razed Mark Twain's Happy Holiday Home to the ground. She says it's a shame as "It used to be alright."

I cannot speak. I can only stare.

It's a grief gaze. Cinderella nods and says "Yeah…I know." Then she asks again if I'm okay and then when I manage to nod she nods too, turns and walks away. Buttons gives a bark and a nod too.

I'm alone again. Alone with my knowledge. My absolute

assumptions. Barbarous Philistines have destroyed Dollis Hill House and they have erected these stern green panels to conceal their GUILT, to block their BLIGHT, to cover their CRIME, to hide the godawful TRUTH.

And now I notice the ravens, *they may well be crows*, but either way I know they're guardians. Harbingers of doom, harbingers is the wrong word but it sounds right. Incorrect as the doom has already arisen, these are the carrion after the crime. Devilish death hawks perched atop the fence that hides the once was and the never will be again. They perch in pity and as reminder. A reminder that all is lost. Mark Twain lived there once but he's not here now.

I don't know how long I stare and gaze. It may have been some time. It may well have been open–mouthed. But when I do recover, I see that Cinderella and Buttons are mere specks in the distance.

I wander off now too, aimless, dazed, disappointed, bereft. I wander into the cruelly named *'Pleasure Garden'*, the irony makes me cackle. It's all that's left of all that was. And it's no consolation. It's nothing but flower beds, bushes and benches. The soul has departed. A man sleeps on one of the benches; his legs are crossed at the ankles, his arms across his chest, cardboard covers his face. He is a man in repose. The rain sheets hard upon him.

I wander out of the fern–filled falsehood.

It's a stagger in truth.

I straighten my back and march back to the callous wall. I do a full skirt of the garish green fence that hides the truth of the destruction of what was once so fine. I lay my hands upon it, slap my palms against its travesty. Then close my fingers and injure my fists. A few ravens flutter, a couple of crows look down, beaks stretched open in gleeful mockery. I aim a kick at the apathetic green panels that hide the destroyed Happy Home of Mark Twain. And then I aim another. Pain shoots – left foot then right. I'd consider a butt but my head already hurts. Hurts on the inside. *It's futile. It's all futile.*

There is nothing for me here. *Accept it Robert.* Turn away.

ACCEPT IT! I turn. I walk away. Limp wince attempt to accept. Limp wince shiver. I manage fifty yards before I notice a familiar structure in the distance. It's another kind of cathedral, another structure of hope. White metal to the fore this time – an incongruous semi–circle. Wembley Stadium and its New Age arch. For a moment I'm transfixed. I hadn't expected to see that.

And then suddenly, unexpectedly, wondrously, he's in front of me. I just looked down and there he was, right there in front of me, standing on his hind legs and showing me his chest. And it's more red than grey. Of course it is! Mark Twain was a red–head in his youth and so instantly I understand.

He seems to want me to follow him.

I'm convinced he does.

I step forward and he scampers away, he's leading me somewhere. I follow him, I mirror his scamp. He stops. Samuel L. stops. Aha! Robert stops. I clear my throat and I'm about to greet him.

But no, he's off again, he's on a mission too; T.J. Snodgrass has spotted a delicacy. He grabs it and begins to chew. He has turned his back on me and is nibbling contentedly. I am forgotten, of no interest, not anymore. I walk toward him anyway. I realise this may be masochistic and sure enough he confirms my fear – he gathers his prize, hops onto then over the duck pond fence and merrily claws his way up a tree. In moments he is out of sight. He has no time for me. He is not the rodent reincarnation of Mark Twain. He is merely a Northwest London squirrel chuffed to have foraged a blackened banana skin.

Rebecca

I can't believe that I slept with Damien. (Another ridiculous statement that Robert would tease me about if he were here to hear me.) I can hear his voice again now, kind and laced with twinkle. "If you know it happened then surely you have no option other than to believe?" Then we'd spend a time chatting and smiling about our ridiculous acceptance of illogical phrases.

It would be a bit of a re–hash now that I think about it. I agreed to watch *Match of the Day* with him once and I started to tally the number of times a commentator or pundit used the word "Unbelievable." It was a lot and I rather pompously pointed this out. I don't feel so smug today. Maybe we don't have the vocabulary to effectively describe certain things. Things that shock and surprise. Things that we never would have imagined.

Actually, I don't think we'd ever discuss and dissect that particular sentence – "I can't believe that I slept with Damien" – Robert made it clear he wasn't going to debate anything to do with that particular tale. But it's true – even though I've just written it down twice and I know with every ounce of torturous self–loathing that it's undeniably a fact, I still can't believe it.

Chapter 66

But perhaps Little Squirrel Not Twain did have a role to play for inadvertently or otherwise he has led me to the far side of the pond and to a wooden bench and that bench has a golden plaque and that plaque has an inscription. It reads,

> IN LOVING MEMORY OF DAVE BERRIE
> 02/05/31 - 29/05/09
> "REST AWHILE AND REMEMBER HAPPY TIMES."

And in truth that's a nice enough demand. I cannot sit on it and rest however as it is covered in fowl bowel evacuations. Instead, I stand in front of it, take a moment to hope Dave Berrie had a cheery life and then I turn to study the pond and the hideous horizon beyond it; the horrible horizon that hosts those gruesome green panels now seen from this new perspective. It's still as harsh. STILL AS BRUTAL. Dollis Hill House is gone, Mark's paradise has been destroyed. I stagger back and inadvertently I do sit. I land heavily on Mr Berrie's sodden seat. His message flashes but I cannot comply

Sorry Dave, but it's too painful to remember the happy times.

Instead and immediately, I'm flicked–back to school and that wet playtime.

If you're unhappy and you know it why recall...

I stagger back to my feet, take a few steps toward the water, look toward the mallards and the drakes. Look in hope rather than expectation. They know I have nothing for them and they'll offer me nothing in return. They turn and swim away from me and then they stop and duck, the ducks duck, they genuinely do. They duck or dive or rather they do that thing that's in between, that thing that's not exactly either. They dip their heads down and they raise their arses high. Synchronised mooning. I approve of their point, accept their taunt, take their banter on board. Then I hear a splash and I see a slight ripple and for a moment I think it might be an otter.

But it's probably just a rat.

In fact, I'm sure it is. One hundred percent. Suddenly I'm convinced – *it was definitely a rat!* A rat with a wet pelt. A sly mover. Stealthy. *A determined vermin. A predator!* No! Fight it! *Rats and wet pelts.* Don't let it roll, DONT LET IT LINK, don't let it form. *Damien hunting. Chasing. Stalking. Succeeding.* No! No!

Fight it!

And don't be distracted – think – nothing comes to he who doubts. Concentrate. Look for the links. I'm a pioneer and a pilgrim. And I know I know my facts – I increasingly speak them aloud – I'm doing it now – "Did you know Mark's Twain's Mississippi hosted 306 species of birds, 145 species of amphibians and reptiles and 260 species of fish?"

Fish?

"MARK!"

I stare into the water and scream his name. But there's no answer. Nor the slightest of ripple. No flash of fin. No glimpse of gill. Of course there's no answer. There's only me here. One man and a demolished dream house. What once was and was once all is all gone. Why would the spirit remain? Why would an apparition choose here to swim or wander? I've been chasing wild gooses.

Furiously I fumble for my biscuit. I rip the remaining full–formed treat from its wrapper and prepare to launch. I will fling it toward Wembley and that arch. *That ridiculous arch.* Where are the Twin Towers? *What did you do to the Twin Towers!* Mark Twain would have seen the towers – he would have stood at the porch and puffed at his pipe and gazed at those towers. Solid towers – twins – pillars of strength and dignity. Pillars of nobility – that's what he would have seen – two stood tall – a perfect pairing – honourable equals – Huck and Jim – *Robert and Rebecca*…

Ha! Dollis Hill House demolished and the Twin Towers demolished. Both torn asunder. Interfered with. Altered. Sullied. Destroyed. All that was good, gone.

I launch my biscuit with a furious cry.

"GARDYLOOOO!"

It doesn't even reach the tennis courts. Not nearly. It's pointless and ineffective and futile and ridiculous.

So I sit back down and eat the remains of the other one.

And as I munch I muse. I remember that the original Wembley stadium opened for an FA Cup Final in April 1923 with a capacity of 127,00 but an estimated 300,000 gained entry and a white police horse called Billy had to try and corral the hordes and Bolton beat West Ham two nil but it wasn't really fair as many of the 300,000 supporters were lining the pitch as the stands were full and those pitch liners effectively narrowed the pitch and that was harsh on West Ham because they liked to play with wingers.

Why do I know that?

Because everyone in Dagenham knows that?

No matter. The point was it was all irrelevant – Mark would have known nothing of it as he stayed in Dollis Hill House in the summer of 1900 when all of that would have been history yet to be made. Mark would not have seen those majestic erections.

But hang on, he might well have seen this duck pond...

Yes! Indeed, why not? It might have been here, under the benevolent gaze of the bronze Water Nymph that he first thought of the utterance that has brought me and my snack here today. It might have been stood right by this spot that Mark Twain first declared what he'd repeated to me last night. That he'd…

> "Never seen any place that was so satisfactorily situated, with its noble trees and stretch of country, and everything that went to make life delightful, and all within a biscuit's throw of the metropolis of the world."

Yes! Relief floods – she would have been here! The Lady in the Lake – the Pretty in the Pond. I don't know why I didn't notice her more before. I do now. Just as I imagine Mark Twain would have noticed her. I admire her intently from the pond edge – she's naked and her pose suggests she might be washing her hair or equally she might be tearing it out. And I know which I think it is. Especially as she's aged now and she has not moved from her spot and she has seen things that no nymph should have to see. She is ideally situated to have seen it all. Stood knee high in murky waters she would have watched as his house burnt not once but thrice. With fingers dug deep unto her scalp she would then have witnessed the house cruelly demolished. In follicle–clenching anguish she would then have watched the brutal green fencing being erected around where once it stood – callously attempting to block all access. To erase all memory.

And with a tear in her eye, she would have seen the soul–strong warriors with blue paint cans arrive to daub 'STOP' and 'SAVE OUR HOUSE' upon that harsh fencing. And she would have wept at that poignancy because they were right – it was *our* house. It was the house of Mark and the house of Me and the house of the Water Nymph and the house of All Who Knew – the house of All Who Have Insight, the house of all...

And it's not beyond the realms of possibility for me to get off Dave's bench and to step over the fence and to wade out to her. And to embrace her cold bronze torso and to hold her tight and to tell her that I understand her loss, that I share it. And then I could tell her that it's okay. I could clasp her to my bosom and whisper in her ear that it will be alright, that the pain will pass. But equally I know I can't tell her that because I am not a *liar.*

And also, I had not anticipated the logistical difficulties – I had not anticipated that I would sink into the mud – become embroiled in dirty detritus – find myself ensnared in dubious debris – the duck's turds and the rat's droppings. Or that I would lose a shoe and have to retreat.

And now I'm forced to face facts – I'm one–shoed and she's out of reach. I stare intently at the statue that is nude yet proud. And brazen yet beautiful. And exposed yet defiant. And tragic yet inspirational. And I probably watch her for too long because in no time she has made me wonder – she has made me consider – she has made me think that her figure is somewhat akin to that of she–who–must–not–be–now–thought–of.

Too late. She has made me recall Rebecca washing her hair in the bath and how on occasion I would be sharing the bath with her and that sometimes she would wash my hair too. And if we were going out that night then she would use a hair dryer and sometimes a thing shaped like a crocodile's mouth that was electric and heated in order to straighten crimple inclined locks. And if she were using it and I would wander in and perchance happened to be flamboyantly nude and distractingly playful then she would snap it toward my dingledoodie as a dire warning.

And it was fun.

It was one of our things.

But now I wince. I wince now. *That's my thing now.* I'm a wincer. I wince wholly and horribly. I wince wretchedly. I wince because now all I can see is Rebecca straightening herself for Damien. And I am helpless.

I have no more biscuits to throw.

Rebecca

I can't believe that I acquiesced, that I let him seduce me so easily. Hmm, there's that "unbelievable" tag again. I 'find it hard to believe' – maybe that's a more accurate vernacular. But it doesn't sound as horrifying. I can't believe I allowed him to convince me. I can't believe I was so foolish. I definitely knew how much it would hurt Robert. Of course I did. I can't deny that fact.

I knew that Robert probably hated Damien, I could tell. The ostentatious flaunting of his wealth, the confidence he gained from it, the fact my parents fawned over him, the fact their preference was overt. But none of that mattered to me – at least I didn't think so, not initially. Robert was different, he wasn't affluent or conventionally successful but he was kind and honest and patient – the sort of man who'd allow his kids to bury him in sand on the beach. I'd imagined that too and I know that's ridiculous but I could always picture it – a happy family at the seaside – only his head visible and the tide coming in. Two kids, maybe three, clapping their hands and squealing with laughter as he feigned panic and begged to be dug out.

Perhaps I had an over–active imagination too.

Chapter 67

I'm weary but unbroken. Indeed, I have a new resolve. It's a new dawn, it's a new day, there's a new year looming and my spirits are a–zooming. I slept little but I slept well. I slept in the right place. I slept where Mark Twain once slept. I slept under the stars like Huck and Jim. I laid my head where Mark laid his.

I actually slept under some planks of wood rather than atop a peaceful raft and I was wrapped in a roll of tarpaulin rather than the crisp sheets of the honoured guest bed. But I could see the stars. A few at least, more than in Chelsea. And I could fully sense his presence. I knew I was being watched and that I was winning approval. The climb up and over the cruelly erected green fence was a chore (much more than in Tedworth) but I made it. And I welcomed the pain of splinter and bruise. I understood clearly. I knew how it worked now – suffering has to come before reward. And increased challenge begets greater reward. I was proving my commitment hence I was getting closer. Much closer. I was facing every challenge. Passing every test.

And just in case I was wavering or beginning to doubt, Mark granted me further encouragement, he provided me with an early–hours reminder. A brief whisper, short but clear.

`"One must travel to learn."`

Yes! Of course, just like you did Mr Clemens; travel, seek, find the answers, make it happen, earn the insight. And immediately I was up and newly determined, I was up and focussed, buoyed with the knowledge I knew what I had to do.

And that's why today, after I'd climbed back over and waved

a cheery good morning to the naked nymph, and after I'd jogged–limped–winced three one–shoed laps of the destroyed house's boarded perimeter chanting "Labricks!" and "Unberufen!" to chase the chill from my bones, I headed here, to the London Borough of Brent. I've arrived at Kensal Rise. And as I walk out of the station, almost immediately I look up and I see a sign.

CONTROLLED ZONE MON - FRI 8.30 AM - 6.30 PM

Controlled zone... a zone controlled... Zone in or zone out? A zone of contention. And unusually, today there is a further message to this sign, a far clearer message, a salient reminder. Underneath the times, clear and cursive, someone has added an addition – someone tall or with access to a step ladder. They have added a more relevant and easier to understand warning. In very neat handwriting the graffiti states

'You're no longer in Kansas.'

I nod. Sincerely.

And head toward the dead.

The Kensal Green Cemetery. *London's foremost necropolis.* Why not? I'm in the environ. *Perhaps that's why I'm in the environ?* Perhaps I'm meant to detour. I've been here before.

With Rebecca.

But now I'm on my own. And it is not a Sunday afternoon and we are not having a 'Sunday Funday Date Adventure' and we are not doing something arty or interesting together. I'm on my own. And I'm not on a tour but I can remember the time when we were. We had met at the chapel in the centre of the cemetery for a 2pm start. And we had descended down into the catacombs with thirty or so other £7–a–pop payers and we had been amazed.

I remember it clearly. There was space for 4000 coffins and many of those spaces were filled and the coffins and their contents were all just there – just lain there – just as they had been when lowered by the impressive piece of engineering known as the catafalque. Now they were decomposing and gothic and crumbling and it was all a bit of an eerie.

But not particularly poignant.

Or painful.

Not then.

And I remember being informed that coffins are always carried feet first and so there was a swivel device on the catafalque and I remember Isambard Kingdom Brunel is also buried here but not in the catacombs. He was buried in a more familiar six feet under the earth manner. And thinking about it I suppose six foot would be one fathom – would be half a Samuel L. Clemens. *Arthur Twain.*

And I discovered that day that Rebecca knew lots about the dead residents already – she was always knowledge–laden. *Forever surprising me.* The tour had continued above ground and we were led to the graves of the best–known burieds. She could reel them off as easily as our man with the clipboard – Harold Pinter, Wilkie Collins, Charles Blondin – one after another, more after score, more until it all became too much – the dawdlings of the group and the nippings of the cold.

So then we hung back a bit at the back and we stood opposite each other and unbuttoned our coats, then we stepped closer and Rebecca placed her hands upon my ribcage and I placed my hands upon her ribcage and we rubbed each other up and down vigorously and stamped our feet earnestly and soon we were warm and sooner still we were laughing.

And when we had re–buttoned our coats and had re–joined the group, we had very much gotten the giggles. And we had become very childish and borderline puerile and we were now doing things like whispering our own alternative additional commentary.

'Fanny Fitzwilliam (1801–1854), actress, singer and theatre manager, scandalised london with her X rated exotic stage show 'Fanny Fitzwilliam and William Fitzfanny...'"

Hee–hee ho–ho. A happy day.

And that was then. But now, right now and today, at this precise moment, the only famed buried that jumps to the mind, the only famous departed and deposited in Kensal Green that bounces around inside my head, the only famed name of the dead that screeches loud within me is that of Anthony Trollope.

And I know why.

It's because my thoughts have slipped again and he's inside them again, inside them again and inside her again.

And I can't stop my thoughts and I can't stop him. And so now the only one who jumps to mind, the only peaceful–rester who resonates, the only dearly departed that demands my undivided, the only one that I can think of, the one and only one is the one called Trollope. TROLLOP. TROLLOP!

And that saddens me COMPLETELY. Because I know it's not true. It was never true. It couldn't be true. *I don't want it to be true.* And I don't want to label. I don't want to diminish. I don't want dirty doubts or tarnished thoughts. Or the overwhelming crush of continued confusion. I don't want any of it. I don't want the wonderings or the imaginings. . I don't want the thoughts or the words. The knowledge is enough.

Too much.

Rebecca told me that many were convinced this was a place where ghosts resided.

They were right.

Rebecca

When Monty had to be put down, I think Robert was almost as upset as I but he seemed to instinctively know what to do. He drove my car back from the vets and took us straight to Hampstead Heath. We just sat on a bench for hours – sat with his arm around me and my head on his shoulder – and he just let me cry.

Then, exactly 6 months later he turned up with a puppy. That was perfect too, any earlier and I definitely wouldn't have been ready. He'd put the puppy in a cat box and covered it in 101 Dalmatians wrapping paper and attached a tiny little card to its collar that read 'I know I'm not Monty but I promise to do my best.' I've no idea where he'd managed to find it but the puppy was an almost exact miniature of the dog he'd helped me bury under the cherry blossom tree. I burst into tears as soon as I saw it. Robert was mortified until I assured him they were the good tears. The smile tears.

Chapter 68

Ha! *One must travel to learn!* Travel more. Don't detour. Travel further. *Travel away from here.* Not far though. College Road NW10 to be precise. This is why I'm really in the environ.

And now I'm perusing the Kensal Rise Pop Up Library.

Though in all honesty there's not much to peruse. A few stacks of books. An orange Calor gas canister. Some plastic sheeting. Some plastic chairs. *Make do and make do.* The set up suggests things to me. It suggests pride and it suggests determination, but above all, way above all, it suggests tragedy.

Make do and make do. *Because it's impossible to mend.*

There's a sign that reads,

CHILDREN NEED TO READ.
SAVE OUR LIBRARY.

It's not a sin, it's a sign. But it's a sin nonetheless. An unequivocal. A sin has undoubtedly occurred here.

And now I walk to the front door of the original library, the permanent bricks and mortar, the original bricks and mortar, the real library not the pop–up–in–protest library. And I stand on the steps and I touch the handle of the door which is painted black and firmly locked. And where there's another huge sign attached, one that covers almost the whole of the black painted double–doored entrance, a sign that again states,

SAVE OUR LIBRARY

And then I turn away and I touch instead the windowsill, because the door might be new but the brickwork looks old and so there may be more chance that Mark Twain leant against the sill than pushed upon the door. And then I press my forehead against the wall and I wait.

And after a time a kindly looking lady (think Felicity Kendall morphed with Oprah Winfrey) taps me on the shoulder and when I turn my head I discover she has a leopard skin scarf and a pink beret. *Gorgeous and ornamental? Garish and ornamental?* Either way I instantly recognise it's another positive sign. And she immediately tells me that she is a friend of Kensal Rise library and I instantly like her. *Because I am too.* Or I would be if I thought it possible to be friends with a library. And if I could believe I could be a friend of any library I would be a friend of Kensal Rise library because it is unequivocally the most important library in London – it was opened by Mark Twain. But I'm unsure if you can or cannot befriend a library, it sounds a bit ridiculous and so I don't know what to believe and in any case I have enough to think about without entertaining another concern, but I think I might know what she means, I think she means she *believes* she's a friend of the library.

And that's OK, that's good enough for me.

And she has digestive biscuits and nice yellow triangular patterned shoes as well as the flask of tea. And she invites me to sit down in the pop–up library on one of the plastic chairs and she tells me things. She tells me about Rusty the library cat who still hangs around and that's good because it means I can tell her something too, I can tell her that Mark Twain loved cats. And she asks would I like to meet Rusty and I say yes as I know that's what Mark would like me to say. And also, it's probably the polite thing to say. And she points toward a blue plastic box, it is a box of books and on top of it, mostly inside of it, sleeps a ginger cat. Called Rusty. I stroke him and he feels warm, I feel his breathing, his ribcage rises and falls under my palm. I like him. And I feel I should tell him about Mark Twain, so I whisper a few MTDYK's into his ear, but Rusty doesn't even awaken. He appears blissfully unconcerned.

And some time later she (the friend of the library) has told me many things, she has told me all about the campaign to save the library and she has told me that the council have closed the library (I had kind of gathered that, that's what I meant when I referred to the sin, but it's a relief to have it confirmed, it's good to know I'm not just imagining things). And by now I have told her things too, I have told her that I know Mark Twain opened this library and that I even know the date and I have proved this by stating that he opened this library (which is now closed) in September 1900. And I have further proved my subject knowledge by telling her that Mark Twain had actually educated himself in public libraries.

And she has laughed and congratulated me on my knowledge and she has suggested it was perhaps because the Kensal Rise Library Committee knew that Mark Twain had educated himself in public libraries that may have been the reason why they invited him to come over and open their Public Reading Room in September 1900.

And she shares other knowledge which is of more interest even though what she is telling me is not something I didn't already know. She tells me there is a brass plaque in the library commemorating the opening and that there is a beautiful black and white photo on the wall that shows Mark Twain and eight members of the Library Committee, dressed very dashingly in evening dress with waistcoats and watch–chains. She elaborates and tells me how Twain sits in the front row, a fine figure with longish wavy hair, walrus moustache and bushy eyebrows. At this point I produce my cigarette case

"Is this the man you speak of?"

I ask her.

"Yes!" she exclaims after studying the image of Mark on the front. My picture is the one of him looking equally dapper, white–suited and a–lean against a tree. (I am a non–smoker but that doesn't matter, my bid was the winner and eBay delivered without question or quibble.) My cigarette case contains no tobacco products, my case contains one item only, it contains a business card. One I still look at every day. One that takes me back. Back and beyond. I look at it now, the details that impressed.

REBECCA SUSAN MORLEY
CURATOR: CONTEMPORARY BRITISH ART
TATE BRITAIN
MILLBANK LONDON

And I flip it over as I always do, then study the handwritten message scribed solely for me.

You seem somewhat peculiar sir, but my mind is like our galleries - open to all x

I used to read her message and smile. It was kind, a reminder of how all should be. She was ready to listen and to learn, happy to accept without suspicion. Now when I read her message I frown at its ambiguity.

She was open to all…

Rebecca

I don't know how it all slipped away, how we let it escape us. I suppose little things became big things and the ridiculous became important. I allowed irritations to rise and dissatisfaction to follow. I remember being cross with him after he'd come as my Plus–one to a works do – a drinks party at the National Gallery. Every time I introduced him to a colleague as "my partner" Robert would say "Howdy!" I remember crying after, when we got home, crying and shouting – "Well, what the hell else should I say? You're not my fiancé and boyfriend sounds like we're still teenagers!" I cringe now but at the time the hurt felt genuine. And I didn't leave it at that either – I told him if he sold his flat in Dagenham and I sold mine in Muswell Hill we could buy a small one together in Hampstead and then when he didn't immediately whoop for joy, I screamed at him that one day he might wake up and find that he wasn't free he was just alone.

Chapter 69

"How many people in Britain do you think would recognise Mark Twain? You know, if asked on a quiz show or something."

It's an important question and it brings me back to real–time. I kind of guess the answer before the friend of the library provides the answer. It's a *hugely* important question and I do guess the answer. I guess the answer and it brings great melancholy upon me. I guess before she confirms. Our estimates match exactly.

"Probably not too many. Not as many as should. Most are even unaware of his white suit insistence."

My crest is fully fallen now and perhaps I'm wearing my melancholy on my sleeve, for Friend of the Library reaches for Rusty, picks him up and places him in my arms. Then she smiles and tells me that Mark Twain was presented with an inscribed silver watch when he opened the Reading Room and in return, he gave them a signed photo and five of his own books. She tells me all of this information is listed on their website www.savekensalriselibrary.org and I imagine that's maybe why she knows it; I suspect her interest in Mark is mostly Kensal Rise related and I guess in a way that's OK.

I knew the info too of course but I still appreciate what she has tried to do so I don't tell her I already knew. I don't tell her *of course I knew that! Why do you think I'm here? I'm here because he was here and here he might still be!* I could tell her other things, I could give her a lecture that lasted hours, I could inform her that in 1873 on the 13th of October at 8 O'clock Mark Twain had delivered his first public address in England. And that it had cost the fortunates crammed to discomfort within the Hanover

Square rooms 5 shillings for entry to the stalls or 3 shillings for an unreserved seat. Only 15 pence to witness the great man deliver a 'lecture of a humorous character' on a subject he'd titled 'Our Fellow Savages of the Sandwich Islands.'

He did the comedy straight from the start too, I could tell her how he wandered on stage in the manner of an embarrassed manager delivering bad news and stated that Mark Twain would not be appearing. Then, when the crowd began angrily muttering about refunds, he did the classic "Only joking! It's me!" thing and he was off and away on a sea of chuckles.

15 pence...

And I could explain to her how he had explained to me that after an outstanding ovation he came back on stage and declared,

> "I am very grateful. I do not wish to appear pathetic, but it is something magnificent for a stranger to come to the metropolis of the world and be received so handsomely as I have been. I simply thank you."

I could tell her that I realise now that it was on that night that Mark Twain had decided the people of London were worthy of his time and deserving of his help. That each time he reminded me of that night and that declaration he was actually reminding me that he had always loved London. That he had always had time for Londoners. That he was prepared to step in when they needed support. I could tell her all that and much more beside but I don't. Instead I stroke Rusty's ginger fur and I hear Mark say,

> "When a man loves cats, I am his friend and comrade, without further introduction."

And I'm a little startled – his voice is loud, strong, enthusiastic. Booming. I was aware he'd been rationing his words, testing my commitment, but there'd been that whisper last night and now this. I'm hugely relieved, he's still with me, *of course he's still with me*, we're closer than ever. I feel a warmth spread and I'm aware it's not only due to the soft thuds of Rusty's heart or the contents of the library friend's hip flask or the puffy jacket she's placed around my shoulders.

Indeed, for a time I'd completely forgotten her but perhaps she's been somewhere and returned because now she's handing me a pair of running shoes and explaining that they were in the car and that her husband never uses them. And she gestures for me to try them on and very carefully without dropping Rusty I do. And when I do we agree it's nice to have two. They fit well enough and I wiggle my toes. Whilst Rusty breathes deep in my arms.

And now I'm aware I feel warm and aware I feel calm and hopefully I can smile because she's still there, the friend of the library is still sat next to me, staring intently, maybe noticing my change.

It's disconcerting in truth so I decide to chat.

"Did you know Samuel Johnson had a cat called Hodge? And more importantly than that he drank in the same pub as Mark Twain and Mark Twain also liked cats and perhaps, they discussed cats in *Ye Olde Cheshire Cheese*. Except they of course didn't as Samuel Johnson died in 1784 and Mark Twain didn't first visit London till 1872 but you know, they might well have if they could have, if you know what I mean? You can imagine it."

I can certainly imagine it and so I do, I imagine the two.

"Hello Sam."

"Hello Sam."

"Pint of Taddy's Sam?"

"Yes please Sam."

"Cheers Sam."

"Cheers Sam."

"Fine cat Sam."

"Yes Sam. Thanks Sam."

I know Samuel Johnson had a cat called Hodge because Rebecca showed me the statue of Samuel Johnson's cat called Hodge – there's honestly a statue –it's in the courtyard outside Dr. Johnson's house – number 17 Gough Square. Rebecca showed me it when she led me on one of our 'Literary Tours.' One of our early Date Adventures, on one of our mandatory 'Sunday Fundays'. There's honestly a statue of his cat and the statue's plaque states 'Hodge, a fine cat indeed.'

The friend of the library smiles and she says

"Yes, it's nice to imagine things isn't it?"

And I'm not sure what she means. Then she says

"When a man is tired of London, he is tired of life."

And I don't really wish to consider that one. And so instead I try to hand Rusty back and I half do hand him back, I hold him out but then I notice the noise, it's a kind of Rrrrrrrrrrrrrrr and its coming from his insides. The friend of the library smiles again

"He obviously likes you; he's purring."

Purring... pur–ring... pouring... is it coming from his heart?

I fully hand him over and we say goodbye and she looks at me and I look at her. And she presses a five–pound note into my hand and I've no idea why. It's an awkward moment and so I walk away. But before I walk away, I take a look through the windows of the library and I get little glimpses of what it was like inside. I press my forehead and squash my facial features and I get little glimpses. And the glimpses are worth getting. The inside of the library looks peaceful and inviting. I can see a stained coffee mug on a shelf and I can see an open book on a table. And it's obvious it all just ended suddenly. Just like that. A sudden end.

It all just suddenly ended.

Mark's library... Mark was in there, his plaque on the wall, his photo resplendent...

I was right to come here, of course he would still hover here, there's no more appropriate place. Mark hovers where help is sought and education is needed.

But I've arrived too late.

I sense that before I see that it's the only that one book on a table, I sense that before I notice all the shelves are empty, I sense that before I see the newspaper cutting that someone has sellotaped to the corner of the window.

> On Monday, between two and three in the morning, when most honest people are asleep, Brent council sent in their people to remove thousands of books in cardboard boxes from Kensal Rise library... worse, perhaps, the council heavies – flanked by two big security officers and a dozen policemen – took tables and murals painted specifically for the library... and unscrewed the brass plaque put up in 1900 to record its opening by Mark Twain – an act of vandalism that Michael Frayn has likened to the worst days of the Soviet Union, trying to make the library an un library.

Honest people asleep… sent in their people…council heavies…two big security officers… a dozen policemen… vandalism… unscrewed...

No! No! No! No!

I stagger a little as I walk now, stumble. Air–cushioned soles grip and keep me aloft. The friend of the library calls out to me "Take care my friend, look after yourself... Happy New Year..."

Happy New Year…

Rebecca

He must have really hated Damien. If I'd asked Robert he wouldn't have denied it. He would have been wary of such a conversation though because he wasn't stupid, but he wouldn't have denied it. He knew Damien was (through that annoying quirk of a similarly fated birth) a fixture in my life, he knew that Damien had known me for a long time before Robert and I met. He would have been wary of such conversation but he wouldn't have lied, he'd have admitted his distaste. Even if that was a can of worms answer, even if that led to reflection, comparison and questions on why. He would have been wary of the question but he would have answered it because one thing Robert was was honest, in his own way he was completely honest. He was always honest when he knew it mattered, if he valued something then it had to be truthful, that was when the teasing would stop, when the joking ended.

That's why I felt I owed him the truth too. To lie to him would have diminished him. To not tell him would have been a further betrayal. That's what I thought but now...

Chapter 70

I guess I switched off then. Auto piloted or some such. Freestyled? Tailspinned? Few phrases make sense when you consider them. I hadn't switched off my phone. That became apparent.

Ring ring.

"United Biscuits."

"Oh. Who? I was hoping to speak to Robert. Sorry, wrong num.."

"Mr Foxley is busy obliging the dough machine."

"Oh, it is you, Knob–end!"

"This is a recorded message. We are now taking orders for the second coming."

"Can you just shut up for a minute, there's something I've gotta tell you."

"Born–again crisp bakes are expected to prove popular."

"Look you're dumped OK? I just thought I should ring cos of your sister an that, I don't want to fall out with her. I'm just doing the right thing, right? I'm telling you to your face. On the phone."

"Our custard is our bond."

"Robert! No offence right, no offence and you're a pretty good shag an all that, but you sleep under the fucking bed! I woke up and I needed a pee and I stood on your head. Nearly gave me a heart attack! And when I screamed you just opened your eyes and said "Seats are available on the upper deck." I mean, no offence like, you seem nice enough and you're kind of funny, sometimes, when you're not all zoned out. But I think you're just too weird for me. And that's saying something. Believe me, that's truly saying something... Anyway, will you be OK?"

"Thank you for calling, we value all customer feedback."

"Robert!"

"Perhaps you could lick us on Facebook?"

"Fuck you! *Knob–end!"*

Beep beep beep.

"Cheerio."

Rebecca

It was one of things I admired in Robert – he always claimed to relish the truth, he always dug and scratched at the veneer, sought to expose the essence. That was probably why he wrote his poems, it was definitely one of the reasons I found him attractive, he would never passively settle for assumption. He had to be convinced before conviction. I admired that and I felt I owed him the truth in return. Even if it would hurt him. Even if he would most certainly not relish this one particular nugget. Even if this revelation would hurt. Even if it might damage us irrevocably.

I had to tell him for another reason too, I couldn't bear Damien having that over him, I couldn't bear the thought of him gloating and smirking and one day boasting of his victory. To have heard it from Damien would have been doubly devastating for Robert. I couldn't risk that happening and I wasn't prepared to spend the rest of my life begging the codpiece not to reveal, I could never have trusted *him*. Not ever. I couldn't let us become one of those couples with lies and fear hanging over us. I had to tell Robert, I had to.

Chapter 71

And now I take a look at my surroundings and they reveal I am sitting on a wooden bench outside the *'Coin Operated Laundrette'* on Whalebone Lane South. I must have made it back to 'my manor.' It's the one opposite McDonald's and near to *Kimling* which sell the finest Honey Chilli Prawns in all of existence – the best of the East in an East London niche. If you ever visit Dagenham you truly must.

But right now, I'm mostly focused on the *Coin Operated Laundrette.* I'm mildly wondering if there is a 'credit card operated' one in Highgate or a 'Scan mobile and 5G Ping it n Wing it Pirate operated' one in Crouch End. But mostly my thoughts are not overly profound. Although now as I stare some more, I'm half–smiling, I'm realising that's one of the things I like about Dagenham, one of the things that make it special

"No airs and graces 'ere mate, if it's a coin operated laundrette we're gonna call it a coin operated laundrette. It's not a lack of imagination it's a lack of bullshit."

I'm aware I need a different focus. I look up and providence provides. There are a flock of birds silvering. That's the way I choose to describe it. They fly together and then turn and when they turn (and they all turn in unison) the sun catches their underbellies and for a moment there is a silver light. A flash. It's quite beautiful. And it seems pointless, that's what most appeals, they appear to be doing it for fun. They're not getting anywhere. They just fly a bit, swoop a bit then turn and repeat. And each time there's that glimmer, that flash, that light. They're flying above the Methodist Church. But it's not spiritual, not overtly. It's just nice. It's just something else.

After a while they fly off. Properly fly off. Off towards Goodmayes by the look of their trajectory.

Leaving me alone once more.

A plane now trails white tail where my friends once flew.

It's probably Ryanair.

I switch attention to the church, which is interesting too, now that I take the time to consider. I wonder about its dome shape – is it just another odd-shaped box? Or a mildly curious cage? The best thing about it though is the serrated metal to ward off climbers. Vicious and jagged. I imagine it is to stop undesirables from getting onto the roof – from villains getting too close to heaven.

But I don't really know.

Not for sure.

Now I muse a bit about the fact I've returned home again – the wounded animal that heads for its lair? The poisoned mouse who seeks out his nest? Mostly though I think of Mark Twain. I think of his many posthumous enemies and all they have done to him, how they have messed with his menu, destroyed his house, fenced his garden, closed his library, pilfered his plaque, how they've been effectively erasing everything. And soon he'll be here no longer, there'll be no trace of him at all, no trail for me to follow…

Few clues left to consider...

Unless I just need to consider harder? Consider better. I think back and focus hard. I remember Wembley and make a connection – white horse/white suit. I remember Alphie and make another – white dog/white suit. Hmm. I look down and notice a solo bird pecking at the pavement, it's all white too, I know that's unusual. The word 'peace' comes to mind. I know that's incongruous. I shall talk to this bird.

"Pigeon can't be Twain. Coo coo..."

He ignores me – doesn't bat a beak – he just pecks on with an air of disdain that's really quite admirable. I have another recall then; Mark's friend and constipation–curer Mr Tesla liked pigeons – he actually fell in love with one. (I'd researched the details on all of Mark's friends.) And that pigeon was a white one too. And here's another fact that is curious but true nonetheless – Mr Tesla was obsessed with the number *3* too. He genuinely was. *I never understood that before.* He was obsessed with the number *3*, hopelessly in love with a white pigeon and died alone in Room *3327* of the New Yorker Hotel. One report described him as sad, confused and destitute.

And now my phone rings again. Ring ring. Its battery life is impressive. Ring ring it continues. I don't recognise the number, perhaps it's hi…

It's not. It's Sis. Calling from Gibraltar. And it's her concerned voice.

"Robert! Happy New Year! Well, New Year's Eve strictly speaking but I thought you might be out tonight. And also I was wondering are you okay? I've just spoken to Emma..."

"Ah, yes… dearest Emma. I don't think she likes cookies."

"Sorry?"

"Sorry. Yes. That's what I am. Sorry. I am sorry. I'm very very sorry..."

"Don't be silly. Look it's OK, I know Emma can be a bit of a handful... I just thought, you know, with Rebecca, well, off the scene as it were..."

"Off the scene..."

"Robert? Emma said she was worried."

"Please settle in your seats for the final scene..."

"She never normally worries. She worried me. Now you're worrying me. Robert?"

"I'm sorry."

"You don't have to apologise, just talk to me Robert, how are you, really I mean."

"Happy as Larry me – Woo Hoo for my Froo Froo! I've been watching whole arrays of smalls spin and tumble."

"Where are you?"

"Launderette. Well, outside now. There was an altercation."

"You've got a washing machine. Is it broken?"

"No."

"Robert... I'm worried... what do you mean altercation?

Robert..?"

"Sis... please... just... just realise... just accept... whatever happens... it doesn't matter... it's okay... it's... after... I don't want you to bla... "

"What can I do Robert? What's wrong? I can book a flight home this afternoon."

"Nothing. It's fine – enjoy Auld Lang Syne with the Macaques. Mark's looking out for me..."

"What? Who?"

"Should auld acquaintance be forgot and never brought to mind?"

"Robert? Do you mean Mark Twain…"

"Yes. Did you know his father died when he was just 11?"

"No I didn't."

"Yes. And did you know Mark Twain encouraged his young brother to work on riverboats like him too? Then he dreamt his brother would die and then a month later his brother's riverboat exploded? And he did die."

"No. I didn't know that either. But Robert..."

"Yes. And did you know Mark Twain's only son, Langdon, died at the age of two from diphtheria?"

"No."

"Yes. And did you know Mark Twain's daughter Susy died from meningitis aged 24?"

"No. But Robert..."

"Yes. And did you know Jean, his youngest daughter, drowned in the bathtub after suffering an epileptic seizure?"

"No."

"Yes. Or that in 1866 Mark Twain placed a pistol to his head and considered ending it all?"

"Robert. Stop. Please. Listen, you need to talk to me properly, how are you rea…"

"Sorry Sis gotta go, I think the pavement pecker needs change for the dryer."

And I hang up. And I guess this time I properly switch off.

[The altercation was over a knitted hat and scarf combo I thought I recognized.]

Rebecca

I didn't expect him to just walk away. Roberts's unique way of dealing with a problem perhaps, he could be so infuriating. If we could have talked about it then maybe...

But no, this is supposed to be truth – what did I really expect? Deep down I must have known. Damien of all people…

Chapter 72

Of course, there are some things about my Borough that I'm not always overly–keen on. I never claimed it was *all* the nice type of special. I told Rebecca it was just who I was. It was me. But it's not perfect. I do know that. Take this character for example – he's not an ideal ambassador for the neighbourhood – and in truth not completely atypical. He's also easily recognisable and tagged now that I have an extended vocabulary (thanks Margot). He's undoubtedly a 'Massive Aggressive.' And when we first met, I was very soon aware that his Dagenham stare was better honed than my Dagenham stare. (He seemed to ardently mean the menace.) We had a brief conversation in the laundrette and we have another one now that he has stepped out. It goes like this:

> He: I thought I told you to fuck off.
> Me: Yes, you did. And yet here I am.
> He: I'm gonna kick your ass!

And he actually said it like that, he went all American, he said "Ass" when he should have said "Arse" and I knew it would be pedantic to point it out because language was becoming more global and there hadn't really been a miscommunication but you know how I am and so I did point it out. *We were in Dagenham not Dallas after all.* And then remarkably, he repeated himself. And this time he enunciated much better and he emphasised the word am. He stepped forward and said "I *am* gonna kick your ass." And a part of me was so fascinated that he had said it with such a sinister delight – as if it would be a marvellous achievement –

the fulfilment of a long–held ambition or some such – that consequently I felt I was left with no option but to smile widely in reply, and say "Oooooooh."

And that was the end of the preliminaries. I guess he was more a man of action than repartee. And perhaps he was fondly familiar with the gift–giving traditions of Yule because in the next moment he was bestowing generously upon me – first a push, then a fist, then a kick, then another which facilitated my staggered introduction to the pavement.

And now he's happily a–stamping an a–kicking on me. (I've gone a bit American too.) *Yee–ha!* And I'm still a bit smiley as I realise he's performing irony in motion – despite his earnest promises none of his kicks reach my "arse" or my "ass" or anywhere near – they're all landing on my head, groin and torso. And now, curled up tight I'm deciding to sing and then I am singing and what I'm singing is "We wish you a Merry Christmas... We wish you a Merry Christmas... We wish you a Merry Christmas..." And when he doesn't join in I briefly wonder if he even knows the words.

Instead of belting out the chorus he delivers a few more kicks. And I stop singing then because I'm getting a bit emotional – I'm suddenly realising how much I miss my Dad. And maybe he senses my distress because he stops mid–hoof and he looks down at me and we share a moment. And it's all very poignant. And then I cackle up at him and ask "Penny for the Guy?" I honestly do. And that probably confuses him again and he definitely gets angry again and immediately there's fireworks again. He directs a couple of hearty boots again – he's definitely re–enthused again. But he's wasting his time because by now I'm proper chuckling and I can't stop and eventually he shakes his head and he's the one who stops. He stops his left foot right foot stamp it all about routine and begins to walk away from me. And as he does so he states "Fucking nutter." And now, out of the corner of a swelling eye, I spot his friend who has been watching our little tete–a–tete give him a congratulatory clap on the back. And that makes me chuckle all the louder. And I feel the urge to shout out after them and so I do shout out after them. I shout

"Hey! Excuse me sirs, would you like to add a gratuity?" And this seems to anger Massive Aggressive anew for he pauses now and he turns his head and he clears his throat and then he aims a large glob of spittle at me. And it soars majestically through the air and it lands directly in my ear. It honestly does. And the phlegm feels dense, diseased and wretched. And of course, by then I'm giggling uncontrollably.

I guess Dagenham had it plus points – one at least – the Honey Chilli Prawns from *Kimling* – they were truly divine. Two portions of those, a shared egg–fried rice, a quality box set and we were all set for a Saturday night. Maybe we weren't all that different. Maybe we were though. It always felt like we were. Even that prawns discovery seemed precious – ridiculous really but it did – it was our "secret unearthing of splendour" that few knew about. The best takeaway dish I'd ever tasted.

We never ate from McDonalds even though that was literally a weak–armed stone's throw away. Indeed, I used to worry about their customers being able to look up and see through the unfrosted glass of the bathroom window when I was in the shower. I felt the same when the bus pulled up outside too. When the 173 changed from a single to a double–decker I started closing even the top section of the window to ensure everything was immediately steamed up. Robert used to laugh and say I was mean to deny the gawpers. It always felt you were very close to others when you were in the borough of Barking and Dagenham.

I always felt I was very close to Robert. Closer than I'd ever been to anyone.

Chapter 73

I lie awhile after the barbarous brethren depart and my laughter eventually subsides. I notice the white pigeon is back. Then wonder if perhaps it has never departed. It pecks nonchalantly and appears unperturbed by all that has just passed. Accepting I suppose. I realise then that we're on the same level now and can finally see eye to eye. I try another "coo coo" but it doesn't sound convincing even to me. I feel the urge to spit now too. I need to rid my mouth of blood and stop my ridiculous gurgling.

After I spit I study the puddle – its ruby with a hint of enamel. Curiously, that amuses me too and in an instant I'm linking gurgles to giggles and about to relapse into fits but then Mark Twain speaks to me once more. He's using my dry ear and perhaps is referencing the 'fucking nutter' accusation. Providing solace and reassurance in the manner only a genuinely great man can.

> "No one is sane, straight along, year in and year out, and we all know it. Our insanities are of varying sorts and express themselves in varying forms - fortunately harmless forms as a rule."

His words are a tonic and I think I can now muster the effort the stand. He truly is a marvel.

Rebecca

I admired Robert's attitude at first, it seemed brave somehow, logical even. If he was happy getting up each morning and fully enjoyed the company of his boss who had become a good friend and together they got the job done with the minimal of hassle and lots of fun then why wouldn't you wish to preserve that? Why rush to the 'next level' if it held no promise of improvement. Christine was lovely; I could understand why they got on; I didn't resent his lack of ambition. Not at first at least. I suppose his attitude toward our relationship was the same, he saw no need to take it somewhere further, somewhere else, as far as he was concerned it was perfect so why tinker with it? Why risk the alteration? He had no urge to consider a new job and saw no need to move the relationship on. *Whatever that even means.*

I think about this stuff all the time now. I try and get inside his head and find the answers but I know it's pointless. I guess he would argue that a relationship should be allowed a natural evolution rather than forcing it in an assumed, expected or pre–conceived direction. Which sounds pseudo–reasonable when I write it down but is it really feasible to live like that? Is it possible not to squirm when the clichéd questions increasingly get thrown your way? 'How old are you? Have you met anyone serious? Are you married? 'Do you have kids?' 'Isn't it about time you thought about it?' Sometimes I want to scream and sometimes I feel like laughing – *have you met anyone serious…*

Chapter 74

After a time, I guess I switched on again. And I assume I must have decided to go underground once more. Mark's intervention had been a timely reminder – I wouldn't find the answers or indeed the great man himself in the London Borough of Barking and Dagenham. He had never physically visited these particular pavements. I needed to be nearer to where his toes *had* landed.

But now I've had a confusion. A confusion and a bit of an embarrassment but mostly a confusion. I'll tell you what happened – I got in the lift at Russell Square – a curious tube station that has no escalator – ideal you would think. But not so – the doors of the lift opened – I walked in – and I then I walked straight out the other side. I had erred – I had foolishly followed the crowd – I had stepped in and joined the flow of exiteers – the ones just descended – and in no time I was back on the platform. And confused.

This happened three times. I foolishly and repeatedly went with the flow.

And each time had to backtrack and try again. During my confusions I thought intermittently about words – two words in particular – 'lift' and 'elevator' – I called them 'UK' and 'USA' and wondered which I preferred. I then thought about 'lifted' and then I thought about 'elevated' and then I thought about what Rebecca had done for me. And that led me on to the phrase 'myself but better' and that rather cruelly led on to *Yes, but what did you do for her?*

And at that point I lay down on my back outside the Lift/Elevator entrance/exit and clasped my hands together over my chest. And then immediately, beautifully and perfectly sublimely, Mark restarted his whisperings

> "Death, the refuge, the solace, the best and kindliest and most prized friend and benefactor of the erring, the forsaken, the old and weary and broken of heart."

"Yes. The weary and the broken of heart…"

I knew what he was saying.

> "To die oneself is a thing that must be easy, and light of consequence; but to lose a part of one's self-well, we know how deep that pang goes, we who have suffered that disaster, received that wound which cannot heal."

To lose a part of one's self… to lose half… It was kind of him to talk like this, I knew that. But that was Mark – he was generous of nature and prepared to share his insight; I realised yet again how fortunate I was – Mark Twain – known by everyone – loved by all – and choosing to talk to me. Allowing me of all men an audience.

Then the doors opened and the embarrassment happened and it interrupted what was proving a pleasant enough tangent flow. I had moved on from pain and returned to boxes – I guess it was my pose as much as Mark's prose but I had been considering the life cycle – from the cradle – through the boxes – to the pine overcoat – the ultimate box – the final box – the funeral box – the resting box – the mum–in–a–box dad–in–a–box – *the Bob–in–a–box.*

Then the doors had opened and people started stepping over me. And that caused me to half–open my eyes. And a skirt that can only be described as a tie–dye purply–orange, sequined and voluminous effort, brushed my cheek and then it snagged upon my earring which wasn't actually strictly speaking *my* earring, but a gold hooped one last worn by Rebecca and recently found under the bed and instantly pushed painfully through my reluctant lobe.

It's hard to pierce your own ear.

The snag was unexpected and the pain sharp and it meant that I looked up with sudden focus and consequently I saw a sight that I didn't mean to (and then quickly closed my eyes again). But the skirt was still snagged and now it tugged as its owner forward momentum–ed and I involuntarily yelped and reached up to unclasp it and unintentionally caught hold of a bangled ankle. And then there was a scream and I heard someone say

"He's grabbed the hippy bird!"

And I heard someone else laugh.

And now we join me as I manage to unsnag and unclasp and roll to the side. And now my hands are over my ears and my knees are to my chest and new words are offering themselves for dissection and prime among them are 'undignified' and 'humiliated.'

And now Mark Twain is back in my and he's reminding me that,

> "Man is the only animal that blushes. Or needs to."

And I know now, with absolute certainty, that I will take the stairs even though the sign states there are 175 steps and it is only advisable in an emergency.

Rebecca

Robert used to love quoting Mark Twain to me, each Adventure Date he seemed to have memorised a new one and was always gleeful when an opportunity arose. He'd try to set them up, start a conversation merely to deliver his hero's punchline. I didn't mind really; it was fun and inventive and of course I admired Twain too. One day he accused me of 'devastating the larder' (I used to enjoy his playful use of old–fashioned terminology too; he probably *had* read too much Enid Blyton during his formative years). He stormed into the bedroom carrying a tray of tea and toast and saying he had looked upon the kitchen wine rack with a mix of shock and awe. He then demanded to know just how much wine had been devoured this last week. I told him not to be rude and that I had no idea and I reminded him the girls had been round and he knew how it was when that happened. It was the right thing to say for now his eyes shone and his smile burst and he theatrically sucked on an imagined pipe before solemnly delivering his latest learned one–liner. "If you tell the truth, you don't have to remember anything." And I rolled my eyes and said "Another Twain?" and he replied "Yes ma'am" and he told me not to worry however as he would replenish my stocks and I told him to get into bed and then pinched him when he did and remonstrated that we didn't drink *that* many bottles. Then we smiled and we snuggled and that's just what it was like. And If only that was true, if only once I'd told the truth we didn't have to remember. If only after spilling the truth we could have just forgotten it and moved on, better and stronger for the sharing.

If only.

Chapter 75

I did take the stairs and then I may have walked for hours. And by crook or via nook I have arrived at Tower Hill. And now I am stood and staring at the Tower of London. And I am recalling that we had visited there, sometime in the distant past, sometime when Rebecca's cousin Chloe was visiting from Canada. Not that long ago perhaps. We toured the tower then drank in the *Dickens Inn* at St Katherine's Dock. Chloe got a little tipsy and told Rebecca I was "cute" and "charming". It seems a long time ago. It all seems ancient. Like the Tower.

And now I am also recalling that the Tower houses torture devices to extract confessions. And I ponder again why people confess. Is it selfless or self*ish? What of he that thou confesseth to? What doth thou thinketh he feeleth!* I think of the irony that most confessions have to be forced and yet the freely offered are the ones with most impact. And I guess I am also trying, most valiantly trying, not to think of Dick Bastardly Demonic Dark Knight *Damien* but that's fiendishly difficult as I am having a third vivid recollection; bloody executions took place at the Tower.

Death to the traitorous.

And I spend a while thinking about justice. And I'm obviously not the only one.

> "All crimes should be punished with humiliations-life-long public exposure in ridiculous and grotesque situations - and never in any other way."

His whisper is more mournful than his words suggest – I know what he means – it's not a laughing matter – certain crimes should be punished without end but too often it's the instigator who retains the smile. The victim remains the victim. The laughing stock. *The laughing stock?* Yes – dropped into the laughing stock – a soup infused with ridiculous dreams and romantic follies. Wallow, flail then drown in putrid juices created by trouser–less charmers emptying their filthy spittoons.

There is no justice only outcome. There's victor or victim – nothing in between.

I'm sure I'm somewhat confused but equally I know Mark knows what I mean.

> "Isn't human nature the most consummate sham and lie that was ever invented? Isn't man a creature to be ashamed of in pretty much all its aspects? Is he really fit for anything but to be stood up on the street corner as a convenience for dogs?"

I agree. But it doesn't help. I picture Damien as a convenience for the likes of Plop Plop Alphie and Dearly Departed Monty – I picture piddle–splashed fashion shoes – fiery streams sprayed upon his buckles and tassels – but I know he's not suffering enough. Not nearly.

So I sigh. Heavily. And then I head off again.

Rebecca

Robert was funny, that's one of the things that I miss the most. He was often hilarious and even when he wasn't I could tell he was trying to be. That's probably why I always forgave him, even when his antics teetered on the edge of acceptable.

I think he usually knew. He would realise when he had gotten carried away and it would nag at him after. Robert was a little subdued after that Christmas at my parents, he didn't let on but I'm sure it had affected him. The next morning, he told me he might spend the next one with his sister; I squeezed his hand and told him that sounded nice. Then I insisted we get up and drive to Highgate Woods and smile at the *really* posh people.

Mostly though, Robert was genuinely very funny – his observational talents could be quite joyous. He once likened Damien to a "70 quid lobster sandwich." I knew exactly what he meant. That thought still makes me smile.

Chapter 76

Refocus.
Remind.
Remember.
Remember.
I do remember.
I vaguely remember.
Remember.
Remember.
I do remember.
Of course I remember.

That's why I am here.
Greenwich Park.
Gren–itch? Groin–itch?

'*The Honest Sausage*.' It's actually called that. I'm not making it up. You couldn't make it up. *The Honest Sausage*. It's written on the side of the uptown burger van. (I prefer the word 'uptown' to 'upmarket' – it's the fault of the song – I sometimes sang it to Rebecca.)

The Honest Sausage. It's a food truck joyously declaring 'Free Range – Free Spirit.' *The Honest Sausage*. I'm not hungry. I'm certainly not now. I walk past the stall because I know I am not hungry. And I know such a place is not healthy. It's not healthy for me. I will only think about it. That's what I do. I know that. *Too late*. I do it now. I'm thinking about it now. An honest sausage. The sausage of truth. The sausage, the whole sausage and nothing but the sausage. The sausage of judgement. All of life dictated by the sausage. A sausage led existence. A life ruined by the sausage. By one errant sausage. One sausage.

My sausage was honest.

His sausage was not.

Walk on. Quicken the step. The National Maritime Museum.

I AM A SHIP IN A BOTTLE. I AM A SHIP IN A BOTTLE ON A PLINTH.

It's huge and it's noisy and it's not as clever as you might imagine. There's a trick, a knack, a malarkey that allows it to happen. I know that.

You can't just bottle it up.

Can't hope to.

Ha! Hope.

Hope.

What a load... hope... Actually, I do have hope. *I hope Damien's dishonest sausage will shrivel and fry.* I hope Damien's dishonest sausage will shrivel and fry, fall from the pan and be mauled then munched by a no–nonsense dog like Buttons.

Then shat out of its arse in a fury.

Walk on. Walk on better now. "*Good Boy Buttons!*" Smile a bit. Almost. Walk on.

Many times (hundreds of times) after that ridiculous early Boxing Day morning phone call I thought I should ring Robert back but I knew he wouldn't answer. (Or so I convinced myself.) I fervently hoped he might call me back too. Then I realised that actually it was probably best if he didn't ring me again either – what could I tell him that he would want to hear? Things had changed. Life had intervened. I couldn't undo what had been done. The bubble had been burst – it couldn't be recreated. Our bubble… Our unique little bubble. Such a fragile one as it turned out – a delicate gossamer blister protecting our preciously crafted world.

Chapter 77

'The Royal Observatory Greenwich is the home of Greenwich Mean Time and the Prime Meridien of the world'. I know that because I've just read it on a leaflet. A tourist–friendly lady (crinkle–ready mouth, blue spectacles and a cardigan) passed it to me and now she spares me a beam and says

"We only started charging recently."

She doesn't mean into battle. She means to get in the gate and into the courtyard and to stand in a line to stand on the line. I think that's what she means at least, I don't think she is suggesting anything else. She smiles as if to wait for an answer, that's how small talk works, one starts and another joins in. It's a dance of sorts.

"I have money. But no inclination."

Her beam of welcome falters a little. She says, "I was just saying"

She says 'I was just saying' – she actually says that.

"You were just saying you were just saying?"

I cackle. In better days she might have laughed too. I used to make people laugh. Maybe my delivery's off. She doesn't laugh. Not even close. So be it. It's a no duck's water off my skin back nose off. It's not important when I remind myself why I'm here. And yes, you can probably guess, Mark Twain is connected to this place too. What the leaflet didn't say but should have said is something I learned long ago – it is here that you can straddle two hemispheres at the same time and stand upon the official centre of time – or, more succinctly – east is east and west is west – *and here's the relevant bit* – but the twain meets at The Royal Observatory in Greenwich. And of course, my interest is in meeting the Twain.

Ha! But if you think that's somewhat tenuous, perverse or twisted then let me reveal more – Did you know that Mark Twain lived for a time in Greenwich Village? And yes, I know Greenwich village is in New York, USA but it's still Greenwich and if you liked Greenwich there then why mightn't you decide to visit Greenwich here? And there's more – did you also know that in 1954 there were proposals to demolish the house that Mark Twain had lived in in Greenwich and that such plan was criticised by the Kremlin? Which of course beggars another question – did you know that Mark Twain was HUGELY popular in Russia? (In fact, I'm sure Mark Twain would've/could've sorted out the Cold War in no time – known by everyone – loved by all.) There's East and there's West and there's Divide – but the Twain meets harmoniously in Greenwich. It makes sense. If you think about it. Think about it hard. The connection is there and so Mark may well be here.

Though now I've just suddenly realised there's another reason I'm here too – it's because of Rebecca. And the promise she made – "One day I'll show you Horatio."

She showed me alright.

She didn't mean that though. She meant something nicer, more innocent – we'd been discussing names. She asked about the Robert thing – the middle name preference thing. I asked her if she had grown up in Dagenham would she have happily called herself Horatio? We talked then about self–preservation, about practicalities, niceties and necessities. We talked about terrain and territory, rules unwritten and fallacies that had to be adhered to. Then we laughed. We always laughed eventually, we dissected things down until the core was reached, tickled and tormented. There was always fun if you were determined to find it.

"Maybe you could have shortened it, called yourself 'Ho'?"

"Hmm, yes or made it sound scientific? Highbrow. I could have said I'm named after a famous mathematician – the one who discovered the Ho Ratio."

"Yes, that might have worked, I wonder how you would work out the Ho Ratio?"

"Be quite tricky I'd imagine, might be fun trying though..."

Things like that. Not overly funny but fun nonetheless. Light–hearted, frivolous. Not funny at all now. I don't like *Ho* jokes. Not anymore. I remember them though. I remember us. Light–hearted. We were light–hearted. That's what we were. We were light of heart.

But that was then.

And she never did show me Horatio. So I'll just have to show myself.

But not yet. Not quite yet. I haven't finished here yet. I'm looking down out and over. Views of London – the O2, Saint Paul's, great monoliths covered in mist. Eerie looking icons. Shifts and reveals. Changing landscapes. The good, the great and the gone. No Olympics, not any more, nothing down there now, no more equestrian, no clip clop hooray. No Nick Skelton with a gold, no Royal with a silver. No more celebrations, no more heroes.

No proud kiss from a mum…

Walk on. Ready now. Find the entrance. Step inside. Turn outside to inside. Take a breath.

It's huge.

The Painted Hall of Greenwich Hospital...

"19 years in the painting. So they say."

So *they* said. So said one of them – one of the two in the matching T's. I overheard them.

There are mirrors on trolleys, there truly are. You stare into the trolley and you see the roof above. The roof that took 19 years to paint, so they say, so they said, so said one of the two in the matching T's. They're staring into trolleys too.

I stare some more then walk on.

An antechamber or some such now. And there it is – Nelson's table. Nelson's table in the '*Nelson Room.*' His body placed there. His body placed there prior to his lying in state in the hall which took 19 years to paint. His body placed on that table in January 1806.

Suddenly I hear, "Horatio?" and I jump. I literally do, my leg does a judder thing, then a hop. I jump and then I spin, I spin around. My breath is held and I am expectant.

But it's not She.

And neither is it He.

(It's just one of the two in the matching T's.)

And they're not talking to me.

I'm still spooked though; I'm spooked and piqued and freaked. I fumble for my phone – I need to know. Recent numbers. Redial.

"Sis."

"Robert! I'm so glad you rang back. I was worried you know. Things are worrying here too – it's getting a bit tetchy – he wants me to practise a duet, can you believe that? Karaoke on New Year's Eve. In Gibraltar. I sometimes wonder how he ever got me up the aisle. More importantly though are you sure you're alright? There's a flight tonight at six, I've checked. I can come home – we can spend New Year together."

"Sis."

"Yes?"

"Sis. Why am I called Horatio?"

"Mum."

"Mum?"

"Mum. That's what Dad told me."

"Dad?"

"Yes. Dad."

"Dad is dead."

"Yes..."

"He never told…"

"Did you ever ask him?"

"No…"

I didn't either. It never crossed my mind to. My mind was crossed to the idea. He never mentioned it and neither did I. He didn't tell me it was mum's idea...

"Why didn't he tell me?"

"He knew you didn't like it."

"Horatio?"

"Yes. Robert? Are you ok?"

"*Mum*… Mum chose it... I didn't like it…"

"It doesn't matter Robert."

"Horatio Robert…"

"It's just a name."

"Horatio Robert Foxley… It's just a name…"

"Robert? Robert, where are you?"

"A 200 year and then some table…"

"Sorry?"

"It's still here."

It was. I was seeing it. I was seeing it and more. I was seeing Horatio lain in his casket for all to gawp at. Form a queue. Form a line. Horatio laid there on that very table. Horatio laid out. *This is what Rebecca wanted me to see?* This is what she wanted to prove to me? Horatio could be laid out? Horatio could be left laid out with everyone gawping.

Horatio laid out flat.

"What is? Robert? What is still there Robert?"

"Mum chose it..."

"Yes. Mum chose the name, her great great grandfather sailed under Horatio Nelson or something."

"Sailed under him..."

"Yes. And loved him apparently. All his men did. Listen Robert, are you okay? Have you been sleeping? Are you eating enou"

"Lord. Lord Admiral! Lord ADMIRE–ABLE. A good lord. GOOD LORD! GOOD LORD MADAM! WHAT ARE YOU DOING? WHAT WERE YOU THINKING!"

"Robert? Robert..."

"I don't... I don't remember much about mu..."

"I know but she lov"

"She named me..."

"Yes. Yes, she did... Robert? Robert...?"

My mum named me Horatio and Rebecca wanted me to be here. She wanted me to see.

The two in the matching T's appear to be staring at me. I read their message. Their matching T shirts say 'Honeymoon Honeys.' And there's the same picture on each – their two faces inside an unbroken heart.

Two hearts…
I turn away.
Picking up pace.

Rebecca

Damien is a codpiece. But I am to blame. If we agree it was all down to one instance, one incident, then I am to blame. It was my choice, I had options.

Chapter 78

Running now.

Phone dropping and bouncing but it can't keep up.

Running.

Fleeing.

Running.

No more walking. Running for cover.

RUNNING.

Running until.

The Greenwich Foot Tunnel.

NO

CYCLING BUSKING ANIMAL FOULING LITTERING LOITERING SKATEBOARDING SKATING SPITTING

DOGS TO BE KEPT ON LEADS

KEEP LEFT

The lift does not make sense. It brings me down. Down to Floor –1. The floor minus one? It's not right. One minus floor? One minus floor equals tunnel. It opens. I run. Run again. Run to the Isle of Dogs. The isle of dogs? The aisle of dogs? Isle – aisle – I'll show you…

RUN!

Slow down. Walk. Pant. Pant like a dog. Sniff. Sniff like a dog. Smells of old London. Damp puddles. *Damp puddles?* What? Victorian tiles. Drippings. Ominous drops? Keep out Old Mr

Thames. Don't look up. *Don't let him in!* Imagine. Don't!

Distraction now. Entertainment. *Of a kind.* Conflict. The Gentry versus The Oiks: Hooded youths on wheels fast approaching and now faced with an immovable obstacle – A leather–gloved palm held out with confidence and an unerring expectation of obeyance.

"STOP! NO CYCLING! WALK! IT'S DANGEROUS!"

A palm that's met with a slap – a sly five. A ride–by incident.

"Fuck off slag!"

Laughter then. Raucous. Echoing. *Different rules below ground.* Laughter. Laughter echoing.

RUN!

Rebecca

It seems so surreal now – the two men were so different – but then again maybe that's a ridiculous statement too – Robert was one of a kind and I liked that, he was eccentric but often hugely insightful. He ripped the complete end section out of *Huckleberry Finn.* He read it twice in that first week after I'd given it to him then on a third read he pulled out a chunk. I was shocked when he showed me and quite offended but then the more I considered it the more I felt perhaps it was quite courageous. I was always too fearful to even underline or write a comment in a margin; it wasn't right, we should have a reverence for books. My initial reaction was incredulity then I felt an urge to be cross, to scold him, to be angry even but then a moment later I wondered if he was right. If something wasn't perfect why shouldn't you strive to improve it? He still insisted it was the best book he had ever read and it was obvious he idolised Mark Twain. To me it seemed a shame – it seemed that it was now a tatty kind of half–tome; 70 or so pages shorn but as far as Robert was concerned the book much bettered for it, he continued to always carry it with him and pore over it.

Chapter 79

Out the tunnel. Run. Up the street. Run. Take a turn or two. Run. Take another. Run slower. Stop. Too tired to run. Too weary. Look up. Another sign. A beacon. A beacon beckoning

> I AM MUDCHUTE. I AM ACTUALLY CALLED MUDCHUTE. I AM THE DLR. I AM DRY, WARM AND SOMEWHAT FAMILIAR.

It's an enticing call.

Rebecca

Maybe I should have worried more about that intensity. But Robert was Robert and it kind of went with the territory. He was the same about us and that was incredibly flattering and regularly exciting. When he believed in someone he was very much all or nothing.

Chapter 80

I must have had a power nap. I boarded and sat and the DLR slid off. I only awoke when receiving a poke. "Final stop mate. You can't sleep here. Gotta empty the train." Then I did the escalator thing again then. Quite successfully. I guess I was still drowsy. I was up and out and onto the streets again with very little to boast in the manner of major incident. And now It transpires I'm outside Bank Station. And it's quiet now. And it's dark. And it's sleeting. And I'm just about to realise I'm in the heart of the City of London. Home of the money makers and the industry shakers. *Territory of the Damiens…*

Run!

I do. For as long and as far as I can. And my stamina has surprised me. And my shoes have sustained me. And now I catch my breath (another curious expression) by virtue of leaning against a lamppost. And I look down at my trainers and think back to the cat – to Rusty and the friend of the library. I think of kindness and strangers. And as if on cue, there's a friendly face at my side now too.

"Fucky weather, fucky weather…"

I nod. And though I'm not really in the mood I attempt a smile; her language is crude but she's correct: it is undeniably inclement. She smiles now too and I can sense I've brightened her day. She thrusts a flower into my hand,

"Fucky weather! Happy New Year!"

"Yes! Fucky weather! Thank you very much."

I fake another wide smile, give a theatrical sniff to my new bouquet, wave and walk away.

She follows me.

"Fucky weather!"

She has her hand out and her face has changed. I speed up.

"Fucky weather!"

My heart begins to thump.

"Fucky weather!"

I begin to jog. It hurts. My shoes have sustained me but they haven't healed my wounds. I don't look back but I know she's there, I can hear her scream.

"FUCKY WEATHER! Bad luck! You will have bad luck! FUCKY WEATHER! Bad luck for you!"

I sprint the last yards toward another tube entrance. The upside is a minefield – scurry back below. And there's another lady by the barriers. She sports a clean ironed uniform and a welcoming smile – it's an unusual combo. I thrust the foliage into her hand.

"Oh. Lucky heather... you haven't been giving money to… sorry, I mean, thank you..."

Another penny slowly drops, I can visualize it; it's like Emma's but my penny is slower – it spins through translucent treacle and comes to a sticky end.

I blush.

Head down.

Head underground.

Rummage for my Oyster card first

> I AM ENTER. I AM ENTER. I AM SEEK ASSISTANCE. I AM ENTER. I AM ENTER. I AM NEAR EXPIRY.

Ignore the ticket barrier. Deflect the tunes. Fruitless search. No card. No clue. Panic! No option. Hurdle the barrier. Hurry down. Ignore the shouts. Board a train. Pick up a discarded *Evening Standard.* Attempt to relax. Fail.

> I AM THE SMALL ADS. I AM SEEKING HIGHER WISDOM? I AM APPLY TO JOIN A SECRET OCCULT ORDER. I AM BECOME AN ADULT

MOVIE STAR. I AM SAY GOODBYE TO TOENAIL FUNGUS.

Everyone wants an ear, wants *my* ear, not every*one* every*thing* wants an ear, wants *my* ear and *they* cannot be ignored. The words are graduated now, intermittent, I don't hear them all. There's too many now …....faith.......... Aunty .... violent….. doctor...... birthday…. Distant…........ pact............ recovery .... clinic........ X .... knew............. Y...... ...... she ....pulled… pissed… when… pushed... wise....... .novice......... ..crush… please…… chew…….. cheese……..salad ....savage....... ...free...too.... …don't do …. yes.........because....... Z … why … I …....no …… knot ……mine…

And I want an ear too – I want Mark's ear. I want Mark in my ear. I want him and not the others. But it's not working like that – not anymore. I have displeased him and he is punishing me. I was too late to his house and too late to his library, I didn't rip rails from his garden nor tear strips from his menu. I have proved of no use.

"Alight here."

"Pardon?"

No answer. Was that a meant–to–be–heard? A clue? An instruction? For me? A message? For me? Alight here? *Guy Fawkes?* A hero? *A failure.* Thwarted and tortured. No, this is not the Tower. I've been to the Tower. This is not Westminster either – there's no gunpowder plot – not today – not tonight – that was then and this is now. *Where worse plans are hatched.*

Exit anyway? Yes! Alight here? Yes! At Embankment? Yes! Why? Why not!

A bridge again…

Oh.

Up and over and

Oh...

Rebecca

I try to stay angry with Robert sometimes, there are some who say it will help but I know in my heart it won't. It can't because it would be unfair. Honesty and truth Rebecca, remember? Everyone liked Robert, the vast majority did at least, there were always some who found him a bit too eccentric, a bit too much, but I was hooked from the start. Robert was infuriating but very old–fashioned in some ways, endearingly so, he was always very protective of our bubble. Childlike almost, naïve but in an appealing way. More sensitive than many would have imagined and maybe that made him more vulnerable.

Robert said that what we had was nice and nice was enough, more than enough. "Nice" was a big word for him, it meant a lot. He said it was the second–best four–letter word and went in tandem with the other, the top one, 'love'. Loving someone meant being nice to them. I didn't necessarily not understand; he'd explain it in his ridiculous clowning manner but I knew he was earnest, more sincere than his antics might suggest. I understood what he was saying too, I partly got it at least, we were lucky so why push it, why change anything.

But…

Chapter 81

Oh…

Fickle feet! Now I'm stood underneath it. *IT!* The mid metropolis murky monstrosity. The nautically themed nightmare facilitator. I most probably ran from Embankment station and turned right and climbed the stairs up onto Hungerford Bridge and then followed our familiar route. But this time alone and without the seeing and the pausing and the hand clasp and the kiss.

And now I'm here.

Below.

At the bottom.

Where the clitter of skateboards clatter. *Can a clitter clatter?* Does it matter? They're all attempting things – jumps and spins – innocent things. And there's soundtrack to their ambition – the clitter clatter of tiny feat – I acknowledge their tune but my eyes aren't drawn.

My gaze is locked skyward.

Fixated.

It's lit up now that night has fallen. Bright red. Scarlet. Very appropriate.

The Room for London. The boat above. £300 for a room with no crew. Indeed, you are the crew – that's the genius. It's just you and your chosen. You and a you and a view and no crew. It's not accessible to all.

And perhaps it was meant to inspire not destroy but I've become suspicious of artful intent.

I look up but I can't see in. The insiders have the power. They make the decisions. They can forget about those on the outside.

Block them out. Darkened windows to keep the sordid safe. I can't see inside the boat so I attach my gaze to the spinners that top it. There are three of them. *Three.* Three individual steel circles. Each with its own spinning innards. They're a little incongruous but then so is it all. You can't spend a night in a boat perched on top of one of the buildings of The National Theatre on London's Southbank. It's absurd. You can't but you can.

There's some who can.

And it's curious that you can feel nautically nauseous on dry land. And I might, at this very moment, vomit or weep or even worse except suddenly there's an interruption in the periphery. A flash of white. And now my body that was resigning itself to a crumbling and was threatening both mess and predicament steadies a little. There's been an interjection. And it might not be…

But I have to follow in case it is. And I do, I dash up the steps and onto Waterloo Bridge. But he's moved faster than I would have imagined and he is gone. Just like that – one flash – one flicker of white – then gone.

This bridge is less familiar. No immediate haunt to taunt. All history is personal. Each battle unique. But now I realise I am even closer to the *Room for London.* I have a new perspective. There are neon lights underneath that are visible from this angle; they flash a message 'Power to the People'. That's art too. Harmless art. Benign. It doesn't threaten nor remind. But above it perches the boat and its three circled spinners and its impenetrable portholes that reveal no deep inner secret to the unwitting outsider.

I lean against the bridge rail and stare again. Fixate once more. I can't help myself. I shouldn't be here but now that I am I am. And the visuals are suddenly upon me. The lights have come on. All is illuminated. Clarity cruelly provided. I can see clearly now. I can see all that happened. Rebecca is wearing a red dress. Scarlet. *I'm aware there's a theme.* She is bent at the waist with her face to the window. Her hair is messed and her breasts are freed. *Unique sailing points.* Damien is standing behind her. Tuxedo and grin. Teeth possessed of impeccable veneer. They can see me. They've been waiting. Rebecca smiles and waves. She is beautiful. Damien sticks his thumb up and leers. The boat shudders. Shimmies out of focus. The nausea builds again, rapidly this time, an icy invader rushing from toes through ankle then onto shin loins and gut until triumphantly crystallising around the four chambers of the heart and sending out slithers of coil to contract mercilessly around the throat.

I fall to my knees.

I can't breathe.

Then I hear it. Suddenly all else is silent and I hear it.

The softness. A sound felt as much as heard. A gentle seeper. A calmer. A soother. And I know without any doubt now. It was who I wished it might if only be. The softness is his. The softness is him. And immediately it's clear that he understands and he knows and he can make sense of it all even when it makes no sense at all. Rebecca with Damien. In a boat that is truly a hotel. But still mostly a boat. High above water. Impossible to fathom.

Suddenly all else is silent and I hear it.

> "Of all the creatures that were made, man is the most detestable. Of the entire brood he is the only one-the solitary one-that possesses malice. That is the basest of all instincts, passions, vices-the most hateful. He is the only creature that has pain for sport, knowing it to be pain."

Yes! Yes! Yes!

Weren't that the truth.

He's referring to Damien!

And that gentle whisper. Those four soothing sentences. That brief mutter of wisdom and insight immediately unblocks my bronchial. It helps to melt my ice and unbuckle my kneecaps. And after a time, I can vomit. Then later I am able to sit and begin to take stock.

Mark Twain has spoken to me once more.

I am **NOT** alone.

I look around. No man well suited. No ivory jacket and matching strides. Still I answer him. I call out regardless. I use a word I know he used often himself. A word that's more than just a word. A word that's an expression. An exclamation. A roar. I tilt my head back and open wide my throat.

"UNBERUFEN!"

It translates as 'Let the devil stay unsummoned!' It's a hopeful expression. Positive. Defiant. It's one of Mark's favourites. And though he doesn't answer I know that he can hear. And that helps too. His partial appearance was a message – a further reassurance. I am here for you Robert. I truly am. I'm here. Close. Don't despair. Keep searching. Come find me. And now, after a few deep breaths, I can turn my eyes toward the *Room for London* once more. And now, when I open them, it's back as it was, back as it should be: imposing but private. There are no figures a–fuck at the window; no flaunting taunting fornicators. All I see now is an art hotel disguised as a boat perched on top of a building. And all I feel is the spin.

Rebecca

Anyway, back to the brutal aspects of the truth (great idea this, Mary!) Part of me was a tiny bit pleased when Christine left and George started and he and Robert didn't hit it off. But that was wrong, unkind, it wasn't a solution. I knew Robert well enough to know that of course he was never going to react in a 'normal' manner to a tricky workplace environment. I'd have been contacting employment agencies in the first week if it was truly as bad as Robert implied. But that would be the logical and proactive reaction and I should have known that wouldn't be the Robert way.

I sometimes wonder was that the trigger? George? Could it be that simple? *Of course it wasn't, be honest Rebecca!* (Writing to myself and scolding myself now – these psychotherapists sure know how to pile on the pain.) Of course it wasn't just George, more likely all the symptoms were there and the new work situation just furthered the disease.

Robert didn't seem to do stress until George and maybe my pressurising. Suddenly he was having to cope with the loss of his father, an increasingly irritated girlfriend and an overwhelmingly irritating boss, ha! Poor Robert facing the perfect storm. All blissful drifting henceforth cancelled.

And then of course, there was that bloody boat. I was a little bit obsessed looking back, desperately hopeful of spending a night there. I can still recall how it was described on their official website :

'There can be few places to stay a night in London quite as unusual, poetic and life–enhancing as *A Room for London* Living Architecture's 'boat' perched, as if by retreating floodwaters, on the very edge of the Queen Elizabeth hall at the Southbank Centre... The one–bedroom installation is intended to offer guests a place of refuge and reflection amidst the flow of traffic at this iconic location in the capital.'

Refuge and reflection...

I think about art and its interpretations too, how rare for two to ever experience abstraction in the same way. How precious it is when such osmosis occurs. The most exclusive hotel room in London, the most imaginative and sublime and yet I wish it had never been envisaged.

Today I find little refuge from reflection. I find myself in sleepless pursuit of the pointless, comparing a seaworthy boat with a pretence, true beauty with the only imagined, one man with...

A codpiece.

Whenever possible I try to focus on the good memories and there are so many – I was thinking about our Edinburgh trip yesterday. We went up for the fringe and literary festival and walked a lap of Arthur's Seat each morning. During that daily yomp we decided we had to tell each other fascinating facts and stories (not Mark Twain related – I'd made him promise they had to be about Scotland). I explained to Robert that over 75% of the city's buildings were listed and that the world's only knighted penguin lived at the local Zoo. He told me that the Royal Mile wasn't actually a mile long and that in ye olde medieval no–indoor–toilet–times, you had to shout "Gardyloo!" as a warning to passers–by before throwing your plops and slops from the window. We weren't always highbrow but we were almost always in synch and most often smiling. We always enjoyed each other. Always. But then somehow...

In truth *(in my defence?)* I had no intention of doing anything other than meet Damien for a drink. I genuinely thought it would just be the usual – the every–once–in–a–while–meet–up to stop mum fretting; a dutiful task to prove I wasn't being unfriendly toward her best friend's pride and joy. I assumed it would just be the usual predictable routine – a couple of glasses of something he'd pompously recommend, a lengthy update on his latest big deal, overt innuendo once he was tipsy, my insistence we were both better off just being friends, a deflection of any interrogation re my love life then finally a black cab home. (One which he'd noisily insist on giving me the money for.) I only agreed to it out of duty and because he sounded so eager – he insisted he had news that he had to share.

Codpiece.

He wouldn't tell me what it was at first, he insisted we drink champagne but wouldn't tell me what we were celebrating. Then he said we should take a walk along the Southbank and I told him that I should really be getting back but he insisted, he said he had something to show me. Something I'd like.

So we walked from Embankment across the Hungerford Bridge and I didn't feel comfortable walking with Damien along that Bridge because I knew the Hungerford Bridge was Robert's favourite bridge, and we had strolled across it many times in the better times. Days when our hands automatically slipped together and we laughed at the same things and there was no agenda, no elephant lurking. I liked the bridge too of course and I liked it more after Robert pointed out the man with the six–string guitar and the pontoon where skateboards went to die. I liked that, I always liked that, Robert noticed the details. I guess that's not a bad way to describe him – Robert was a details man and the big picture often escaped him. (Or he chose to ignore it or he granted it no value.) Robert was a man who noticed the minutiae – the largely unseen details and he'd noticed that the man sat with the paper cup hoping to collect coins had a six–string guitar; a *literal* six string guitar – the strings were actual pieces of string, thin strips of rope glued on to the neck. The man held it proudly but didn't strum and that was the best bit – Robert said he loved the nobility of the irony – "the flaunting of the bullshit." Robert would always drop coins and a smile as we passed.

Then further on he would insist we stop to lean over and look down at the broken skateboards on the ledge underneath the bridge. He'd invite me to ponder about who had owned them and how sub-cultures evolved, and he'd get me to wonder were these the discarded tools of those who entertained the tourists in the colourfully graffiti'd tunnel underneath the Royal Festival Hall. And he'd tell me interesting curiosities like the fact that area was known by the skaters as 'The Undercroft'. Then he'd encourage me to wonder if when a wheel was broken or a board was cracked and withered was there a ceremonious dropping to the pontoon? Was there a sombre march of skater boys and girls? Was there bowed heads and remembrance? Was the ritual casual or intense? Then when we looked up after our wondering he would always kiss me and I would wonder about our own sub-culture, our own unique story.

We never rushed across that bridge.

Robert and I would always stop in the middle of the bridge too. We'd stand close and look across at the view – St Pauls, Waterloo Bridge, the OXO Tower, the National Theatre, the *Room for London.* Then Robert would perhaps point out the crowds or "swarms of wanderers – all with a moment in mind" as he once described the throng. Robert would urge me to imagine all those people and their stories and the motives for their traipsings. To think about all their individual adventures that intermingled and reigned right here and right now. Then to consider all those that had done so long in the past and all the ones that would unfold in the future. I would laugh then and call him a "bloody poet" and tease him that maybe there was a bit of Dickens interlaced with all his Twainery. And he'd pretend to be outraged but we'd both be amused and we wouldn't really then think about the city so much, rather we would be reminded of something we both knew but never needed to articulate.

But somehow things changed and now, suddenly there I was walking across that bridge with Damien and he was not noticing the glued strings and he was not stopping to point out or count up the dead skateboards. Suddenly here I was walking with my arms determinedly folded because I had no intention of taking Damien's hand even though I'd twice felt its hopeful brush against my hip.

I had no intention of anything.

Even though if I'm as brutally honest as Mary has suggested, of course I always knew there was the possibility. The offer was always on the table. That was the trouble with Damien he seemed to buy into our mother's nonsense; he appeared to relish and encourage it – all those jokes about us being destined for each other "The cutest two from Ward Number 2." He enjoyed all that "wouldn't it be nice if only you two would get together" teasing, that excruciating chat made him beam whilst I would cringe. He'd play along; he'd say things like "Oh I'm sure she'll come around in time won't you Rebecca?" "She'll realise one day, won't you Rebecca?" "Don't worry mums; never give up on the fairytale – I'm sure you'll get to arrange our big day one day soon." Hohoho.

Codpiece.

Such commentary appeared increasingly loaded as time passed and Damien became more successful, it did from my mum's side at least and increasingly my dad had begun to go along. He'd traditionally bristled at any male interest – had given the steely eye to every boyfriend, had frightened the life out of Russell in Year 10, but now I guess Damien was offering him a benchmark, a parental ideal. Steady, reliable, successful, secure, uncomplicated. He had begun to indulgently nod when Damien bemoaned my reticence, smiled benignly when Damien vowed he would continue to try and win my heart and then my hand.

I didn't put them straight because how could I? Not in the passionate way I wished to. You can't discuss certain suspicions with your parents. There are some things you just can't explain to them. You can't tell your mother that you suspect her best friend's son doesn't really cherish the prospect of happy ever after with the girl from the cot next door. You can't tell her that you suspect he just has an ego that rivals his wallet, and that it irks him that such knowledge doesn't adequately excite or impress her daughter. You can't tell her you suspect he fawns purely in an attempt to facilitate some need, some validation. You can't tell your dad that maybe Mr Boy–Done–Well just wants to claim another success, that perhaps Mr Charm and Influence just wants to seduce his daughter to claim her scalp. Just wants her in his bed to prove his progress. Just wants her body to bolster his pride. To prove he's one of life's winners.

You can't discuss those things with your parents, just as you can't argue the curiosities of romance with your parents; you can't convince them that one choice is better when the other seems to hold all the aces. You can't explain that emotion should trump pragmatism. You can't defend a choice that seems defenceless. You can't compete against comparison.

Damien is different to Robert. I know that sounds obvious, trite, shallow and glib but it's the one mantra that repeats when I try and make sense of it all. Damien does not have much of an imagination, at least not an unfettered one, not one he allows to wildly ramble. Damien's focus is more mainstream. Damien *has* a focus. Damien has focused. He has focused on career and the trappings of career. His picture has always been big, he has never doubted the value of affluence. He has never questioned the pursuit of wealth. He is well aware of what money can buy.

Suddenly there we were, we were no longer on the bridge, my arms were no longer folded and my mouth was suddenly agape. Damien had finally managed to surprise me.

Damien had taken me somewhere I didn't think possible. He had steered me through a cleverly disguised doorway and into a very small lift, then had placed his hands over my eyes and ensured we stepped out together. I was genuinely shocked when he removed his paws and shouted "Surprise!"

Damien had succeeded where Robert had failed. He had been able to pull strings rather than curse bad fortune. He had achieved where Robert could not. He had taken me to a place that Robert had failed to. I guess he had proved something.

It felt wrong. I knew I shouldn't. I was where I desperately longed to be but with someone I had never dreamt of being in such a place with. But the boat was beautiful and I was already half tipsy and then Damien produced more champagne and said

"Welcome to a Room for London. It's ours for the night." And I asked "But how…?" And he just winked (adequately) and made a money–suggesting gesture rubbing together his thumb, middle and forefinger. Then he eagerly filled me a glass and we looked out over London from a new vantage and it looked just as magical as I had imagined it would. We were presented with our own private view; we had a unique perspective in the midst of millions. Just the two of us.

It was truly stunning.

And I certainly wasn't expecting him to kiss me… not really… and then he did... and perhaps I was just curious… and feeling neglected… vulnerable… and perhaps I was a little drunk... and impressed… excited even… and there's no excuse… not really…

There just isn't…

There SO bloody isn't!

And I guess that's it, the end, I've told it all and taken ownership just like I was advised. I've written a long honest letter. To myself. I've relived all of the story –

Robert, Rebecca and the Cleverest Codpiece.

And I'm still struggling to make sense of it.

So, I might as well sign off.

Yours...

faithfully?

Oh Robert...

Chapter 82

Turn away now. Jog. Run. Sprint. Stride. Walk. Limp. Worry. Wander. Wonder.

Head Underground again?

Warmth.

Refuge.

Safety.

Comfort?

LADIES AND GENTLEMEN PLEASE KEEP YOUR OBSSESSIONS SAFE

Holborn station, central line platform, eastbound, next train 1 min. Mark Twain travelled on the first ever Central Line train, it's true. The crowds would not have been like this then though – bodies are everywhere, squished and squashed. There's noise and merriment. Celebration, And there's a poster opposite asking me about drones and where do I stand. And I know I hate all who drone and I also know I think it apt to name a destructive weapon a drone and I think of course of George and his cretinous ramblings and I know I'm off kilter and I know I've taken the debate elsewhere. Where do I stand? *I was hoping to stand on the platform minding my own business* but you didn't let me. None of you will let me. And now there's a bulbous lady standing next to me. I notice her adornment – she's wearing a badge – I recognise the logo – the iconic London underground symbol – and there's a message – her badge reads 'Baby On Bread.' And that does it.

I shut down.

I shut out.

I shut off.

DO NOT LEAVE YOUR LONGINGS UNNATTENDED

And then. just when you're absolutely not expecting…

Suddenly he was right there in front of me.

For the first time.

Actually there.

In the flesh.

Solid.

Not in my ear but here.

Three–dimensional.

Here he was.

Finally.

And immediately he was taunting me. I'd let him down. And so he had come to mock me. I'd failed him. I'd had my chances and hadn't taken them. And so he had come to shame me. I'd disappointed him. And so he had come to provide me with a public humiliation. He'd come to provide a how dare you let me down dressing down. He'd come to deliver a tirade against my wasting of his time. And he was in no mood for preamble. Mark Twain made a wristy gesture and said,

"Wanker! I knew you wouldn't do it!"

And in this very public performance he didn't talk like you might suspect. He certainly didn't talk as I expected. He didn't speak with the same intonation that he had employed in our private chats – when he was only in my ear and not standing face to face. He didn't have that soft southern drawl – it wasn't like in the song – there was no black velvet if you please. There was no black velvet at all: it was white serge, that's how I recognised him, that's how I instantly knew. His white suit, his ubiquitous white suit, his unmistakeable dontcareadamn suit. It was Mark Twain, it was Samuel L. Clemens, it was Thomas Jefferson Snodgrass , it was *Him!* It was the man himself. My confidante and my confessor. My hero and my inspiration. My advisor. Living and breathing. Flesh and blood. In my face not just inside my head. Here he was. The legend I had let down. The legend whose patience had run out. The legend I had angered. The legend now turned avenger. Verbal abuser.

THEY MAY BE REMOVED WITHOUT NOTICE

The legend making a wristy gesture and declaring,

"Wanker! I knew you wouldn't do it!"

His verbal assault was instantaneous. And brutal. And unforgiving. And fully deserved. And it was harshest as it was localised. He made sure it was colloquial. He ensured there'd be no confusion. He spoke loud enough to be heard over the rumble of the approaching train. To emphasise his fury, he talked to me in the language of London. To press home his point, he used the symbolism and words of our age.

He made a wristy gesture and said,

"Wanker! I knew you wouldn't do it!"

And so I did.

I

stepped

off

the

platform.

I'm closing my eyes now.

THE END

About the author:

H. B. O'Neill was born in London where he continues to live. He is a prize-winning short story writer and has collaborated on creative projects with musicians, visual and multi-media artists. He is currently working on a TV sitcom and completing a second novel featuring some of the characters introduced in *According To Mark*.

Acknowledgements

Who to praise and how to phrase my gratitude?

In time-honoured style, I was assuming I'd simply produce a list of worthies to name and acclaim. However, recently my friend Dieuwke confessed she reads the acknowledgments in books avidly and revealed that some were "works of art." And so then I felt under pressure to attempt something a little different from the usual gratitude spew.

I considered at length, then decided perhaps I should recall and reveal some of the thoughtful comment, sage advice and motivational scepticism my supporters have provided to help spur me along the way.

Lord Hirsty:

> *"Thought you said you were gonna write a book. How's that going?"*
> *"Not bad. I've written 60 pages."*
> *"Right… What font size?"*

Mr Tuohy:

> *"What's it about?"*
> *"A bloke who thinks Mark Twain is talking to him."*
> *"Mark Twain? You've got no chance of getting that published! You should change it to David Beckham. At least everyone knows who David Beckham is."*

I've learned in life that the greatest friendships are able to navigate the precarious cusp of helpful humour and sarcastic abuse sublimely.

I've also discovered the creative path can prove a tricky travail but (if you're lucky) you meet some fine people along the way. I want to thank Ian for his belief and Chris for his faith. Indeed, I'd like to humbly thank all the people who have helped me along my journey – all those who have shown a genuine interest in my writing – the encouragers and believers who wished me well and truly wanted me to succeed. The power of such conviction and generosity can never be understated.

I also wish to thank my hugely talented (and very patient) IT consultant and website developer, Luke.

Hmm. And now I fear this *is* in danger of becoming merely a traditional list of mentions. I'll stop soon, but three others fully deserving of praise are Lena, Lisa and Habib from Pen to Print. They work tirelessly and selflessly to encourage and promote creative writing in my native borough of Barking and Dagenham and have always enthusiastically encouraged my career. They're great people who do an important job. Hats off to the Arts Council too, for recognising the value in such endeavour and providing the funds for them to operate.

Right, enough already? Okay, but to conclude, I'd like to urge the people who have been and always will be important to me to recognise how very much they have mattered. Suffice to state, I know I've been extremely lucky (and not always deserving). Thank you.

Oh, and if anyone has just finished reading this book and is the type who does then bother to read the acknowledgments and hence is currently reading this at this very moment, an appreciative "Cheers" to you too.

More books from Fahrenheit Press

The Beloved Children

Three young women; Chrysanthemum, Rose & Orage are thrown together performing as The Three Graces on the stage of Fankes' Theatre during the closing days of the Second World War.

It's there they come under the spell of wardrobe mistresses Dolores and Janna – a chance encounter that will guide and change all of their fates forever.

Set in the dying days of vaudeville theatre and laced with mysticism, fortune tellers, ghosts, and evocative descriptions of the closing days of the War – The Beloved Children will literally make you laugh out loud and perhaps even shed the odd tear.

The Beloved Children is wise, funny, heart–breaking, joyous, poignant, and entirely entirely enthralling.

Tina Jackson has conjured characters that you will fall unapologetically in love with and placed them in a world that you won't want to leave.

This book genuinely weaves a spell around the reader and once you make friends with Janna, Dolores, and The Three Graces you'll never want to be without them in your life again.

"This gloriously offbeat tale has shades of Angela Carter, with its beguiling characters weaving a magical spell."

– Kitty Marlow, The Mail On Sunday

Pure by Jo Perry

Caught in a pincer movement between the sudden death of Evelyn (her favourite aunt) and the Corona virus, Ascher Lieb finds herself unexpectedly locked down in her aunt's retirement community with only Evelyn's grief–stricken dog Freddie for company.

As the world tumbles down into a pandemic shaped rabbit–hole Ascher is wracked with guilt that her aunt was buried without the Jewish burial rights of purification.

In order to atone for this dereliction of familial duty, Ascher – in her own words 'a profane, unobservant, atheist Jew, frequent liar and grieving loser' –volunteers to become the newest member of Valley Haverim Chevra Kadisha, a Jewish burial society on–call twenty–four–seven during lockdown and performing Mitzvot at no cost to the bereaved.

What follows is a journey through the insanity of lockdown in Los Angeles as Ascher attempts to bring peace to a troubled soul, and perhaps in the end redemption for herself.

This novel is everything.

In the hands of a lesser–writer a novel set in the time of covid could lead to a cliché ridden trope–fest, but instead with the skill and grace we've come to expect from Jo Perry she has delivered a book that is wise and beautiful and uplifting.

In our opinion with *Pure*, Jo Perry has surpassed even her own high–bar and written the finest novel of her career to date – but don't take our word for it – here's what some of her fellow writers say…

"Faultlessly imagined and beautifully written, this is one of the best novels I've read all year." –Timothy Hallinan, author of the acclaimed Simeon Grist series

"Pure is an immersive, twisting and turning metaphysical murder mystery set in the L.A. of 2020 with its Covid lockdowns, conspiracy theories and ethnic hatreds. Highly recommended." –Seth Lynch, author of the 3rd Republic mysteries.

"Perry's mysteries never fail to mesmerize...With Pure *she's outdone herself..." –Jeffrey Siger, author of the celebrated Chief Inspector Andreas Kaldis novels*

Black Moss by David Nolan

In April 1990, as rioters took over Strangeways prison in Manchester, someone killed a little boy at Black Moss.

And no one cared.

No one except Danny Johnston, an inexperienced radio reporter trying to make a name for himself.

More than a quarter of a century later, Danny returns to his home city to revisit the murder that's always haunted him.

If Danny can find out what really happened to the boy, maybe he can cure the emptiness he's felt inside since he too was a child.

But finding out the truth might just be the worst idea Danny Johnston has ever had.

"As one would expect from a writer with the skill and experience of David Nolan, this haunting book deals with very difficult issues in an incredibly sympathetic manner while at the same time throwing a light onto one of the most complicated and shaming areas of our society – the failure to protect those who are the most vulnerable."

The Perception of Dolls by Anthony Croix

"It's almost as if history is trying to erase the whole affair." – Anthony Croix

The triple murder and failed suicide that took place at 37 Fantoccini Street in 2001, raised little media interest at the time. In a week heavy with global news, a 'domestic tragedy' warranted few column inches. The case was open and shut, the inquest was brief and the 'Doll Murders' – little more than a footnote in the ledgers of Britain's true crime enthusiasts – were largely forgotten.

Nevertheless, investigations were made, police files generated, testimonies recorded, and conclusions reached. The reports are there, a matter of public record, for those with a mind to look.

The details of what took place in Fantoccini Street in the years that followed are less accessible. The people involved in the field trips to number 37 are often unwilling, or unable, to talk about what they witnessed. The hours of audio recordings, video tapes, written accounts, photographs, drawings, and even online postings are elusive, almost furtive.

In fact, were it not for a chance encounter between the late Anthony Croix and an obsessive collector of Gothic dolls, the Fantoccini Street Reports might well have been lost forever.

Cash Rules Everything Around Me by Rob Gittins

Morrissey Jarrett is fresh out of prison and back on the streets of his hometown Cardiff.

During his enforced absence the city has been re–developed to within an inch of its life and a disoriented Morrissey falls back into old habits as he scams, schemes, and steals whatever he needs to survive.

Morrissey has big dreams though. Dreams of making one last huge score, dreams of leaving his life of crime behind, dreams of reuniting with the love of his life and dreams of walking off into the sunset with her. Happy. Ever. After.

All he needs is a plan.

Luckily, the circles Morrissey frequents provide ample opportunities for ill–gotten gains and soon the perfect job literally falls into his hands.

And so, along with a hastily assembled crew of misfits, Morrissey embarks on planning the perfect heist. With all their eyes fixed steadily on a payday that could change their stars forever – all they have to do is keep their heads down, play it cool, and follow the plan to the letter.

What could possibly go wrong?

Printed in Great Britain
by Amazon

47156107R00233